# THUNDER ROAD

## TAMARA THORNE

GLASS APPLE
PRESS

# COWBOYS AND ALIENS

There's a little wild west amusement park in California's high desert. Old Madelyn Ghost Town attracts tourists every weekend. There are all sorts of rides and attractions peppered among the historic buildings. Here, you can take a ride through the Haunted Mine, have an old-fashioned chicken dinner, or watch a Wild West show... And if you camp out, you just might see a UFO or two.

Between the modern town of Madelyn and the historic park, lies the compound of The Prophet's Apostles. They think the lights in the sky have been sent by God to warn of the coming apocalypse. They want to convince and convert everyone they can -- and they'll do so by any means necessary.

As a young serial killer stalks Madelyn, leaving blood-soaked horrors in his wake, the earthquakes begin. A monstrous freak storm pounds the arid desert, and the military harasses an astrophysicist and her assistant as they study the night sky ... Sheep are mutilated. People are flayed. And Prophet James Robert Sinclair realizes that God is truly speaking to him.

The Savior is returning. The Four Horsemen are about to ride. And the Apostles are taking no prisoners.

**THUNDER ROAD**

"Somewhere east of Edwards Air Force Base, south of Fort Irwin, folks have seen the signs in the sky, stirring weird beliefs and strange desires. That's only the beginning, because the forces that converge over the desert have designs of their own—and desires that transcend human flesh. Tamara Thorne has captured the flavor and terror of such alien intrusions, but she forces us to take another forbidden step beyond the edge of obsession, with profound consequences the reader cannot forget, or survive with innocence intact."

—Jacques Vallee, author of *Passport to Magonia*

"Tamara Thorne knows it's no fun being scared unless you're having fun being scared. She'll take you on a weird and harrowing trip down **Thunder Road** that's a helluva fun ride."

—Aaron Hughes, *FantasticReviews.com*

**BRIMSTONE**

"Tamara Thorne is the Mistress of Malignant Mansions, the Go-to Gal of the Grand Guignol; and her latest, **BRIMSTONE**, solidifies her place in the pantheon of modern Gothic storytellers. With a kaleidoscopic cast of characters, a rich sense of place, and ever mounting suspense, **BRIMSTONE** brims with chills and thrills. Highly entertaining and highly recommended!" - **Jay Bonansinga, the *New York Times* bestselling author of THE WALKING DEAD: RETURN TO WOODBURY, SELF STORAGE, and FROZEN**

Tamara Thorne's **BRIMSTONE** is deliciously scary. Thorne's finely-etched 11-year-old heroine, Holly Tremayne, sees ghosts, but it never really bothered her until she moves to Brimstone, Arizona. She meets a fascinating, colorful cast of characters, each one harboring a dark secret from their past. Earthquakes, nightmares, aberrations and ghosts keep the reader constantly on-edge. **BRIMSTONE** is like a hair-raising, fun trip through a house of horrors. But it's not just one house, it's a whole city. **- Kevin O'Brien, the *New York Times* bestselling author of They Won't Be Hurt and The Betrayed Wife**

"**BRIMSTONE** includes great characters, especially Holly. This little eleven-year-old girl is so endearing with her past and her heart-breaking relationship with her mother. The history and the Native American folklore with supernatural elements made this book one of my favorites of the year. I highly recommend this book; you will definitely not be disappointed." **-Book Review Crew**

**THE SORORITY**

"Thorne's take on Green Man mythology crossed with skewed Arthurian legend and evil cheerleader B-movies finds its niche—and hits its stride—with dead-on portrayals of witchy, bitchy sorority brats —some of which turn out to be immortal sorceresses, members of Fata Morgana, a secret coven within the Gamma Eta Pi sorority of Greenbriar University, home of the Forest Knight."

—Bill Gagliani, *Cemetery Dance,*

"Too many of today's horror writers are so concerned with being stylish that they forget to have fun. Tamara Thorne never forgets, and as a result **The Sorority** is a whole lot of fun to read ... **The Sorority** makes for highly entertaining reading from start to finish."

—Aaron Hughes, *FantasticReviews.com,*
on The Sorority

**THE FORGOTTEN**

"Tamara Thorne is at the top of her game with some of her best writing to date."

—*Horror World* "Tamara Thorne has an uncanny knack for combining the outrageous with the shuddery, making for wonderful, scary romps and fun reading."

—*Chelsea Quinn Yarbro*

**CANDLE BAY**

"Think Mario Puzo meets Anne Rice ... Balance is what Thorne does best ... **CANDLE BAY** is a love story. A mob story. A family drama. A wise combination of creepy, thrilling, titillating, and good old vampire fun ..." **-Michael Schutz, Darkness Dwells Radio**

"This is not an Anne Rice knock-off. Thorne has added her unique touch to the much repeated vampire tale with gratifying results, which makes *Candle Bay* a treat."

—*Horror World*

**HAUNTED**

"A wonderful, terrifying book ... a worthy successor to *The Shining* and *Ghost Story*."

—*Nancy Holder*

"Don't read it if you have something else to do ... it just might have to wait."

—*After Hours*

"Combines eerie eroticism with page-turning terror."

—*Pasadena Weekly*

**BAD THINGS**

"One of the most entertaining horror novels that I have ever read ... with characters to die for, *Bad Things* comes highly recommended."

## PRAISE FOR THORNE & CROSS

### MOTHER

"A great combination of strong characters that remind me of my V.C. Andrews characters, wonderful creepy twists, and a plot that will recall Mommie Dearest in an original take that shocks and delights at the same time. This is a full blown psychological thriller worth the investment of time and money." **- Andrew Neiderman, Author of The Devil's Advocate and the V.C. Andrews novels**

"Thorne and Cross bring the goods with **THE CLIFFHOUSE HAUNTING**, a clockwork mechanism of gothic chills designed to grab the reader by the scruff and never let go until the terrifying conclusion. Atmospheric, sexy, brooding, and brutal, the book manages to be simultaneously romantic and hardboiled. Highly recommended!" **- Jay Bonansinga, the New York Times bestselling author of *The Walking Dead: Invasion***

"In **THE GHOSTS OF RAVENCREST**, Tamara Thorne and Alistair Cross have created a world that is dark, opulent, and smoldering with the promise of scares and seduction. You'll be able to feel the slide of the satin sheets, taste the fizz of champagne, and hear the footsteps on the stairs." **-Sylvia Shults, paranormal expert and author of *Fractured Spirits* and *Hunting Demons***

# THUNDER ROAD

## TAMARA THORNE

GLASS APPLE
PRESS

Thunder Road

**Cover Design by Mike Rivera**

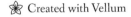 Created with Vellum

*For Jacques Vallee,*
*Keeper of the rare trinity*
*of science, wit, and wonder*

# ACKNOWLEDGMENTS

Thanks to John and Kay for guidance along the winding road

To Quinn and Q for reminding me to stop and smell the Joshua trees

To Damien, traveling companion

To Jacques Vallee for continued inspiration

To Paul Najarian, M.D., and Dana Issacson for good advice

To my ghost-loving pals for stocking the road with phantom hitchhikers

# PROLOGUE

## APRIL

The last things Madge Marquay saw were the balls light darting across the night sky.

*How long ago? Hours? Days? A week or more?* She couldn't be sure in this unending darkness. All she knew was that after working late at Madland, she had strolled out to the amusement park's apparently deserted parking lot and paused by her car to breathe in the crisp desert air. Then she glanced up at the midnight sky, at the brilliant dusting of stars.

She had heard about the lights from friends and neighbors, but it was the first time she'd actually seen them. The orbs were amazing, simultaneously magnificent and frightening, as they cavorted above the stark silhouettes of the Madelyn Mountains, flashing in and out of existence at whim. Suddenly she understood why no one who had seen them believed they were aircraft from the military bases, weather balloons, or ball lightning.

Madge had been easy prey for her attacker as she stood, mesmerized, staring at the sky, wishing Hank were here with her. Suddenly someone had grabbed her from behind and clamped a chloroformed rag over her nose and mouth.

And then, nothing. Now she wondered if the strange lights would be the last things she would ever see.

She could hear the tourists, but she couldn't make them hear her. Madge Marquay, bound, gagged, and blindfolded, lay somewhere below the Haunted Mine Ride in a cold rocky room that reeked of death, in a darkness so thick that it seemed to clog her lungs. Far above, one of the little mine trains rumbled by, and she moaned around her gag, trying to free a scream that could no more escape her lips than she could the mining pit.

Tears ran down her cheeks as utter silence resumed. Hank had to be looking for her, had to be worried, but would he ever think to walk the old passages in their own property, to climb down the ancient iron ladders to find her here in a pit dug and abandoned 130 years ago? She'd be a fool if she believed he would. Hank, their friends, and the police would search the canyons and mountains, they would look behind rocks and in brush-clogged drainage ditches, just as they had when Kyla Powers vanished a month ago.

But they never found her, or Joe Huxley, for that matter. But Madge thought she knew where they were. Down here with her. Despite the chill, she could smell death all around her. It was not an odor that numbed her sense of smell, but one that grew stronger, breeding sick panic in her gut.

She lay there, slowly being hypnotized by the dark, by her thirst and hunger, barely aware of the searing pain in her arm where her captor had peeled away her flesh. Her mind drifted, escaping to the past, to the time nearly fifteen years ago when she and Hank had leased the old Moonstone Silver Mine from the County Parks Department and turned it into the biggest and best attraction in Old Madelyn.

They rigged music to play in different parts of the ride, using the *Grand Canyon* Suite for the tame vistas, "Night on Bald Mountain" for the runaway train sections, and "In the Hall of the Mountain King" for the huge central showcase, a room containing treasure boxes filled with gold-painted rocks that were guarded by

Disneyesque dwarfs and presided over by an imposing golden- haired king on his throne. It wasn't perfect, or even terribly original, but it was the product of their labor and they loved it. It was their dream.

Shoring up the dirty old mine, making it safe, then running the wiring and track for the passenger cars had been Hank's job, while Madge did art and design in her spare hours. As a history teacher, she loved digging into the books of Irish mining lore and turning the tales into figures and images to delight and frighten visitors. The stories had become so vivid to her that, in her mind's eye, she could see the dwarfs sneaking up on an unwary human miner, their pickaxes ready to strike.

Another train rumbled overhead, bringing reality with it. She moaned around the filthy rag between her teeth, felt the tears coursing down her cheeks and wished to God she could suck them into her mouth. She was so thirsty. So very thirsty.

# PART ONE
# TALES OF THE NEW WEST

Perhaps they have always been here. On earth. With us.
—Jacques Vallee, *Dimensions*

... Make straight in the desert a highway for our God.
—Isaiah 40:3

I will be disappointed if they [UFOs] turn out to be nothing more than advanced spacecraft.
—Jacques Vallee, *Confrontations*

# ONE

# TOM ABERNATHY
## TUESDAY

Sheep, thought Tom Abernathy, damned stupid sheep. He hopped down into the runoff ditch to avoid getting caught in the mass of wool coming up behind him, thinking that these days he spent a good portion of his time avoiding one sort of flock or another.

Soon they were everywhere, Christly dirty, dust-kicking sheep, before and behind him, chewing and bahing, stinking and shitting, filling Thunder Road and trampling the orange and yellow wild-flowers for twenty yards to the north. Marie, whom he had yet to glimpse, wasn't so bad (quite the opposite, as a matter of fact), though she usually smelled of lanolin and dip, which Tom supposed was a fitting perfume for a lady sheepherder. Truth be told, for two years now that aroma, combined with the soft, sweet scent of Marie's skin and hair, had intoxicated him.

He wasn't unique: A lot of the men in town were smitten by Marie. While Abernathy kept his yearnings to himself, Phil, the morning counterman at Ray's Truck Stop Cafe, down in New Madelyn, was so in love with her that she could have smelled like owl shit and swamp water and he wouldn't have cared a bit. Phil's courtship consisted simply of serenading her with "I Get a Kick Out of Ewe" whenever she came in for coffee; not particularly original, but not bad for the likes of New Madelyn, and Marie didn't seem to mind. Men working at Madland, which was what you called Old Madelyn Historic Park if you were employed there, were a bit more creatively uncouth in their comments, which included such songs as "Marie Had a Little Ram" and questions along the lines of "Ewe want me, Marie? I want ewe." Franklin Hank Flinn, the Owner of the octopus —Flinn called it the octopussy because he liked to be dirty—once asked Marie about the longevity of ram erections, and that was the only time anyone could ever remember seeing the sheepherder lose her temper. For such a tiny woman, she had astoundingly strong hands, and Frank Hank swore that with one quick grab and twist, she'd almost removed the source of his happiness forever.

Tom sneezed, sucking in dust, coating his teeth with the stuff. "Goddamned sheep," he grunted, pulling a faded red bandanna from his back pocket. He flipped it, folded it crosswise, and tied it over his nose and mouth *bandido*-style. He loved doing that as much now, at the ripe old age of forty-two, as he had when he was just a little stick of a kid. For good measure, he tilted the brim of his brown beaver felt Stetson down a little.

"Hey, cowboy!" Marie's voice, clear as birdsong, rose above the bahing of the sheep.

Aiming for nonchalance, he halted and glanced up. "How you doin', Marie?" Squinting, he pushed the hat brim a little lower against the bright spring sun.

"Doing good." She swung off Rex, her raven black gelding, and let one rein fall. Dorsey, one of her border collies, made to grab it, but she stopped him with a meaningful glance. Tail down, he quickly rejoined his partner, Wild Bill. "Get back to work, you two," Marie told the dogs as she joined Tom in the trench. "Come," she told the horse, and he obediently moved two steps closer to the dry canal and waited to follow wherever she might go.

*She sure has a way with animals,* Tom thought, catching her scent. "Bright out today."

"That's why they call it the desert."

"You're a smart-ass woman, you know that?" He wondered how she kept the dust off her teeth.

"I know it, cowboy."

Marie Lopez had light olive skin and big chocolate eyes, and if she had favored bright skirts and cheap jewelry rather than Levi's and chambray shirts, and if she let her wavy dark hair flow loose instead of keeping it tied back under a straw cowboy hat, she would have made a great gypsy.

He ran his tongue over his teeth to clean off any remaining dust, then pulled the kerchief down around his neck. "So why don'tcha give up these stinkin' sheep and read fortunes at Madland?" he asked for maybe the thousandth time.

"Because I like to make an *honest* living," she replied for maybe the five hundredth time. She had about another five hundred answers, all different, all colorful and pleasantly obscene, and that's why he asked her the same question so often.

"You sayin' Carlo ain't honest?" Disappointment at being handed the stock answer made him feel feisty.

She cocked her head and drilled him with her eyes, but he didn't do anything except let a calculated smile crack his long, leathery face.

She grunted. "When I look at you like that, you're supposed to tuck your tail. between your legs and run like hell, Abernathy."

"I am?" The smile widened.

"You're okay," she said, dead serious. "You don't spook."

He nodded, determined to start something. "Carlo don't spook either, but you write him off because of his dishonest profession."

"Quit trying to yank my chain, cowboy. Carlo's a shrink in gypsy's clothing. He doesn't do anything but make people feel good."

That was true. The Madland fortune teller and Marie were a lot alike: smart, hard to figure, and moody as hell, which was probably why he liked them. Carlo Pelegrine, like the shepherdess, spent a lot of time fending off the opposite sex. The only woman who seemed unaffected by Carlo's moody good looks was Marie, and Tom occasionally worried that their similarities would pull them together, cutting him out of the race before he even got around to getting into it. And most likely, he thought, his teasing them only worsened the odds.

"Tom?"

"Yep?"

"Why aren't you riding today?"

He shrugged. "Belle's getting new shoes right now." The pure truth was, he could have taken one of the other horses, but he'd been in need of the kind of peace and quiet that anything made of flesh and blood, except his favorite mare, would disrupt. He needed to be alone to think: Things were on the wind. He smiled grimly. Things besides sheep.

"You were walking along so slow, Tom," she persisted. "What were you thinking about?"

He kicked a dried-up horse potato with the toe of his boot and drawled, "Oh, about that time you nearly twisted Franklin Hank's wiener off."

Her delighted laughter do-re-mi'd down the scale. Everything about Marie was musical. "I love it when you talk dirty, cowboy."

"You sure didn't love it when Franklin Hank talked dirty."

"There's a difference. He's a dirty old man."

"He's not much older than me."

"Oh, don't play stupid, Abernathy. There's ten-year-olds who are dirty old men. They're born, not made. Frank Flinn's a dirty old man, and no natural woman can abide him. He's dirty even when he's clean. Even his eyes are dirty. And that slimy old voice. Flinn could ask a woman to go to church with him and end up slapped."

They walked along awhile longer, jumping rapidly from subject to subject because Marie was taking the flock a couple miles north to graze in Rattlesnake Canyon and they wouldn't get to chat again for a week or so.

With all the weirdos acting up lately, Tom wished she wouldn't go out on the range by herself, but he knew better than to say so.

Instead, he told her about the ribbons two of his horses won last week in the barrel races in Victorville, and then they shot a little shit about the new expanded stunt show that had been drawing the tourists to Madland on the weekends. By the time the ditch ran out, they'd also covered self-proclaimed prophet James Robert Sinclair, who insisted that the apocalypse was now, the latest UFO sightings, most of them by Janet Wister's Space Friends club, and Franklin Hank's aborted attempt to seduce Frannie Holder, Tom's horse trainer. (Rumor had it, she'd stuck her riding crop where the sun didn't shine, but he doubted it since Frank Hank would like that sort of thing.)

"Well, here's where I head for the hills." Marie swung herself up into Rex's saddle. "Time to get the flock out of here," she added, smirking. She whistled and, when the dogs came running, she raised her arm and pointed toward the hills. "Dorsey, Bill, turn!"

The collies barked once, in unison, then took off, beginning to shift the direction of the flock.

"Amazing," Tom said. "I bet you could train crows if you had a mind to."

"Thanks, but I can't take the credit. The boys are smart." She smiled gently, watching them work. "Guess I'll see you in a week or so, Tom."

He shivered despite the warm spring sunshine. *Devil just walked on my grave.* "You be careful up there, Marie. Don't let any snakes in your bedroll."

"Don't worry. I'm leaving Franklin Hank down here with you." She turned the horse, ready to follow the flock.

"Marie?"

"Yeah?"

"Those sheep you lost last month ... You really think a mountain lion got them?"

"I haven't found a better explanation." She paused. "Why?"

"Watch out, okay?"

"Aren't you an old worrywart today? Sure, I'll watch out for the kitty. But I'll be fine. The boys sleep right beside me and the rifle's on my pack, see?"

"The Space Friends think space aliens carved 'em up, so you better watch out for little blue men, too."

"Little blue men are better than no men at all." She gave him an indecipherable look. "See you later, cowboy."

"See you, Marie."

He stood there in the middle of Thunder Road, watching until she and her sheep were nothing more than specks against the jagged red hills. He shivered, despite the warmth, the hairs prickling up on the back of his neck again. "You be careful, girl," he whispered, and started walking again.

His worrying worried him as much as anything. Tom took great pride and satisfaction in his tranquil nature, as well as in the fact that his laconic cowboy act wasn't much of an act at all: It had become a way of life. "You'll never amount to anything, son, if you don't get out there and compete," his dad had often told him. His father, who had graduated at the head of his class from Harvard, had gone on to become one of the most respected cardiologists in the country. For a man like that, to be stuck with a son who dropped out of college, had no interest in medicine or, worse yet, football, who wanted nothing more than to own a horse and be a cowboy, had to have been the ultimate trial.

He smiled to himself. His dad, though incapable of understanding him, had always accepted him, more or less, and could actually respect him now. He'd begun referring to Tom as a breeder of champion quarter horses ten years before that held a lick of truth. Possibly his father's stories planted the idea in Tom's head, or possibly not, but either way, it was a good excuse to surround himself with horses instead of being content with just one. However it had happened, now Tom had a dozen prizewinners (the horses being far more competitive than Tom himself) and they brought in sizable amounts of money, allowing him to pay their trainer, Ms. Frannie Holder (also far more competitive than he) very well to keep them in top form. With Frannie doing the dirty work, Tom was free to spend much of his time at Madland, where he lassoed and did some fancy shooting in the stunt show, taught city kids about the burros and farm animals in the petting zoo, or simply sat around shooting the bull with Carlo or the stunt show people or anyone who happened to be handy.

He indulged in other pleasures as well. During spring and fall, the main tourist seasons, he often rode down to the campground to tell a few ghost stories around the campfire. And just about every week, he had company over to his big open- beamed ranch house with built-in and central everything. People loved to visit, but whether they came for the company, the air-conditioning, or his ranch manager's skill with a char-broiler—Davy Styles could barbecue a vulture and make it taste good—Tom didn't really know or care.

But his favorite thing to do was to ride into the Madelyn Moun-tains with nothing but his bedroll, guitar, and cooking supplies. Sometimes he'd go into Spirit Canyon, at the east end of Thunder Road, where the hills were so chock- full of mineral deposits that at sunset they glowed with copper greens and ferrous reds and purples. Other times he traveled due north, taking the trail that Marie was on now, over the hills and down into Rattlesnake Canyon, a starkly beautiful, eerily isolated area full of Joshua trees and mesquite. Wherever he landed, he'd build a campfire, then pick bad guitar and croon out of earshot of everything but the coyotes. After that, he'd lie back and count the stars, all by his lonesome.

*Marie's alone out there.* The goose bumps stood up once more, and as he glanced north, he hoped she was right in thinking that a mountain lion had been responsible for the attacks. He wasn't so sure.

For one thing, the kills he'd heard about sounded too neat; carni-vores made a mess. If an animal died of natural causes and nothing got at the body but insects and birds, you sometimes got that neat-ness. There was nothing like dry air and a hill full of ants to cause the clipped and missing organs and incision-like inroads in the flesh that had the UFO nuts hollering Interstellar Surgeons! and Jim-Bob Sinclair and his flock of faithful crying Satan! just as loud.

And then there were the disappearances. In the last three months, as many locals had vanished without a trace. While it was true that Joe Huxley occasionally took off unannounced for a few weeks or even a month when the prospecting bug bit him, this time he'd been gone since February. His Jeep was still in his carport and there was no sign of him at his claims in the Madelyns or Spirit Canyon.

Then, late in March, Kyla Powers closed up her leather shop one night and disappeared into thin air. Maybe she'd gone to visit her mother, like Cassie Halloway thought, but Kyla wasn't the sort to shut her business down and leave during tourist season. The latest disappearance, just last week, was the most suspect of all, because Madge Marquay was a full-time teacher at the high school, and Madelyn's socialite. Her calendar was always filled and she never missed an appointment or a day of work. Until last week. Poor old Hank Marquay was beside himself, and Police Chief Moss Baskerville and his sole officer, Al Gonzales, were poking around in earnest now, with the unwanted help of Madge's friends. Yesterday a small flock of blue-haired Miss Marples had shown up on Tom's doorstep armed with notepads and pencils, hoping that he might supply some clues.

Flocks of old ladies, flocks of sheep, of UFO nuts, religious fanatics, and even tourists who wanted to see UFOs instead of Wild West shows were all conspiring, it seemed, to upset his peaceful, happy existence.

A plume of dust rose to the east, where Thunder Road narrowed into a twisted rut of a one-lane trail as it entered Spirit Canyon. A second or two later, a vehicle emerged, moving toward him at high speed.

Curious, he paused at the intersection of Thunder Road and Old Madelyn Highway. A moment later, he saw that it was a military jeep, an open CJ-5, and as it slowed to turn south on Old Madelyn, the three uniforms gave him a good once over. The two in front were grunts in cammies; in the rear sat a glowering beetle-browed officer dressed to show off his lettuce. Air Force, most likely.

Military types were nothing new to Madelyn: You had Edwards Air Force Base to the west, China Lake and the defunct Fort Irwin due north, and Twenty- Nine Palms to the southeast, among others, and if it wasn't convoys tooling down Interstate 15, it was jets booming overhead. And every now and then you got soldiers in jeeps sniffing around the hills and canyons behind Madelyn. Tom wondered if they were there for the UFOs, the mutilations, or just to instill a little more paranoia in the locals.

He dismissed the uniforms when he noticed something out of place. It lay on the ground across rutted Old Madelyn Highway, not far from Fort Madelyn, the park's newly restored Union outpost. "What the hell?" he asked aloud, squinting at the mound. It was probably just a big white garbage bag tossed by some thoughtless tourist, but he thought it looked a little like an animal. He crossed the road in five long-legged strides.

"Sweet Jesus." It really was an animal, a white goat, and it lay with its limbs broken and twisted, its head flattened and mushy-looking in the lengthening afternoon shadows cast by the fort walls. "Damn," he whispered as he kneeled and saw the silver choke chain around its neck. It was one of Cassie Halloway's pets. "Damn. Why the hell did I have to be the one to find this?"

Standing again, he saw an unnatural number of stones and rocks scattered around the corpse. One sharp chunk of quartzite was half-buried in the animal's belly. Sadly he shook his head, sick to his stomach. That a human being could do something so cruel to an animal was beyond his comprehension. This was worse than the mutilations: This poor creature had suffered horribly.

Purposefully he trudged back to Old Madelyn Highway, turned south, and walked the hundred yards or so to Cassie Halloway's place. As he approached the driveway, he saw something that tied his gut into an even tighter knot: The numerals "666" had been painted in red across the side of her aluminum mailbox. Gingerly he touched the paint. Dry. It had to have been there awhile, but he hadn't noticed it on the way up. Checking, he saw that the numbers were only painted on the north side of the box. No one coming up from town would notice it.

Wondering how long the numbers had been there, he walked down the dirt driveway to Cassie's neat yellow bungalow. As he ascended the steps onto the shady front porch, he could hear Popeye cartoons playing inside. He knocked. "Cassie? It's Tom."

He heard feet running, then the front door flew open. Giggling, little Eve Halloway grabbed one of his fingers and pulled him inside. "Mama, Tom's here!" she squealed, tugging him down onto the couch in front of the television.

"Be right there, Tom," Cassie called from somewhere deeper in the house.

"Mama's in the bathroom," Eve told him.

"My Lord," Tom said quickly, "that Popeye's one strong fella, isn't he? Wish I could tie a bull's horns in knots like that."

A wispy, deceptively frail-looking child, Eve stared at him with those astoundingly huge dark gray eyes of hers. The six-year-old bore little resemblance to her redheaded mama, and since Cassie wouldn't reveal the father's identity, some of the more rabid Space Friends were convinced that a space alien was her other parent, what with those big eyes and all. Tom, however, was 98 percent sure that police chief Moss Baskerville, who not only had steel-colored eyes, but quite a bit of blond left on his big graying head, was her daddy. Especially since that's what Eve called him. Moss and Cassie had been keeping company for a decade, and you could find him here just about as often as at his little house in New Madelyn, but for some reason, you weren't supposed to mention it.

"Mama got a new tattoo," Eve announced, plunking down beside him.

"Did she now?"

Eve nodded soberly. "Uh-huh. Know what it is?"

"Let's see." Tom removed his hat and scratched his head. "A big old elephant?"

"Huh-uh."

"Oh, well then, I guess it's a can of spinach."

Hands on her hips, Eve suppressed a giggle. "No, silly. It's sixes."

"Sixes?" he asked, a fresh set of goose bumps rising.

"Hey, Tom!" Cassie entered, dressed in jeans and a sleeveless T-shirt that showed off her pictures. She patted the pink towel turbaned around her hair.

"Sorry to keep you waiting. We were putting the finishing touches on the backgrounds for the new play today, and I had a little run-in with a can of paint."

She was proud of the Langtry Theater. It not only paid for the Halloways' modest needs, but in transforming the shabby building at the northern edge of Madland into a saloon-style vaudeville playhouse five years ago, she had transformed herself from itinerant go-go dancer to respectable businesswoman. "I was starting to think I'd never get that stuff out of my hair."

"Mama's hair was purple!" Eve giggled.

"How did you—" began Tom.

"Walked under a ladder. Guess that old superstition has some merit after all." She grinned. "So, Tom, did Evie tell you I got a new tattoo?"

"She said it's a battleship," Tom said somberly.

"Did not! He's fibbing, Mama!"

Tom stood up. "There's no foolin' that girl."

All of Cassie's tattoos were basically the same. The first dated back to the late sixties and was, true to the times, a set of three psychedelic paisleys above her left breast, sort of like the ones Goldie Hawn had on the old "Laugh-In" show. Cass didn't actually start collecting them until she came to Madland nearly twenty years ago and met Gus Gilliam, retired biker turned tattoo artist. Gus had a copy of the Metropolitan Museum of Art book, a real talent with the needles, and he soon convinced Cassie to let him balance out the psychedelic paisleys with a new trio on her right breast. He did them Grandma Moses-style, with tiny American primitive pictures of the seasons within the teardrop shapes. Cassie was hooked. He went on to do a set of Renoirs, Brueghels, and Remingtons before he died.

Fortunately, Gus Junior had inherited his father's gift and his interest, and he took up where his dad left off. Cassie's back, torso, upper arms, and thighs were now a living tribute to the masters. Gus Junior had been on an impressionist kick lately, and Tom wasn't much for them. He favored the Remingtons.

Cassie turned her left arm to expose the inner flesh just above the wrist. "Aren't they gorgeous?"

"They sure are." These were done in a new style and were the first art to appear south of Cassie's elbow.

"They're art nouveau, Aubrey Beardsley," Cassie told him. "Gus outdid himself, don't you think?"

"The colors remind me of Carlo's little Tiffany lamp." She nodded, pleased. "Same era."

"Look at the detail on that dragonfly wing," he marveled.

"See the little fairy dancing on the flower? Isn't she lovely?"

"She sure is." He hesitated. "Cassie ..."

"What's on your mind, Tom?" Cassie lowered her arm.

"Need to talk to you about something," he said reluctantly.

"There's coffee on in the kitchen."

"Sounds good."

As they settled at the dinette table, Eve skipped in. "What're you doing?"

"Honey," began Cassie, "why don't you go outside and—"

She silenced as Tom shook his head no. Watching him, she said, "Go watch some more cartoons while Tom and I talk."

"I want to talk too."

"No, Eve."

"But I want—"

"Okay," Tom interrupted. "We're gonna be swapping some recipes. You got some recipes on you?"

"Yuck!" Evie disappeared back into the other room and the TV's volume increased slightly.

Suddenly there was a cracking noise and everything gave a little jerk.

"Earthquake," Eve trilled over the television's chatter. The house creaked and settled in agreement.

Looking at each other, Tom and Cassie waited for another, but it didn't come.

"Been a lot of those little shakers lately," Cassie said.

"Yeah. Hope it means the land's keeping itself settled, not working up to a big one."

"Damned scientists can't make up their minds. So, Tom, what do you want to talk about?"

"Well, I was just thinking about something Eve said," Tom began. "She called your paisleys 'sixes.'"

"Always has, ever since she learned her numbers. From a distance, they do kind of look like sixes, don't they?"

Tom nodded. "And they're in sets of three."

"Sure. Keeps 'em symmetrical."

"Cassie, somebody painted three sixes on your mailbox."

"What?"

"You know. Six-six-six, like the devil sign. In red. When I saw 'em, they put me in mind of that satanic cult that was around here a couple years back. Six-six-six. They carved the numbers in that gravestone on Boot Hill, then killed a bunch of black chickens—"

"And now somebody's painted some sixes on my mailbox." Cassie sounded unconcerned. "I'm a safe target, so far out of town. You think the cult's back?"

Tom shrugged. "I don't know, but I think maybe it's not random vandalism."

"Shoot, Tom, of course it's random."

"I'd agree with you if Eve hadn't said that about the sixes. Or if ..." He trailed off, not wanting to tell her the rest.

"Spit it out, Tom."

He stared at her a long moment. "Cass, something else happened. One of your goats is dead."

"That can't be, Tom. They were both here this morning before I took Evie to school." She stood and opened the back door and stepped out onto the stoop. "There's Daisy. Iris? Iris?"

"I found her across the road, by the fort."

Cassie turned to him, her face blanched white. "A car hit her?"

"No. It was done on purpose. Cassie, by the looks of things, I expect she was stoned to death. Moss needs to go take a look."

Cassie sat down slowly. "Lord, I loved that rotten old goat."

"I know."

"So did Evie."

"I don't think you should let Evie go out by herself until Moss figures out what's going on."

"You think the goat and the mailbox are connected?"

"I believe I do," he admitted, wishing he hadn't been the one to find these things, wishing to be gone from here.

Tears threatened to overflow her eyes and she wiped them roughly away. "Those damned satanists. Somebody oughta stone *them*."

"What about the Apostles?" Tom asked.

"Sure, they can do the stoning."

"No, no. I mean they've been getting awful crazy lately with all their apocalypse talk."

"You think they might have done it?"

"Maybe. You ever hear Sinclair's radio show?"

"No." She stared at him. "Tom Abernathy, I'm surprised you'd listen to such garbage."

"I must confess, I listened once or twice way back when they started the station, just out of curiosity. I thought they were sort of amusing." He paused, considering. "I thought the Apostles were harmless, you know, like Janet Wister and her UFO-worshiping friends. But the other night, I caught the program again. Sinclair was ranting and raving about floods and earthquakes and how the Four Horsemen are gonna ride right down Thunder Road and herald the end of the world."

"Sinclair and his group are full of hot air," Cassie said dully.

"Yeah, they are, but it's self-righteous hot air, plus they've got themselves a time frame. They may be up to something."

Raising her eyebrows, Cassie said, "Let me guess. The end of the world will come with the eclipse on Sunday, right?"

"Right you are. Sinclair claims he's been charged with some holy mission to destroy sinners for God. He says the Apostles are the chosen ones."

"Most religions claim that privilege."

Tom nodded. "True, but not like the Apostles, at least to hear Sinclair tell it. Calls himself a prophet. Seems to believe it. When he broadcasts those sermons, you can hear the converts in the background hallelujahing everything he says. They're real riled up. They're zealots, and zealots worry me."

"Well, they have been annoying the tourists," Cassie allowed. "Moss's had to run 'em out of Madland every weekend lately."

"I was thinking about that," Tom said.

"But still, they're a regular Christian religion."

"I don't know, Cass. When Sinclair talks, they're always 'the Prophet's Apostles,' never 'Christians.'"

"Their crucifix is pretty weird, I'll give you that. That big old lit-up cross on top of their church puts me in mind of Las Vegas."

Tom nodded. "You ever notice how they have it rigged?"

"Yeah. It disappears on Sunday morning and shows up again late at night."

"Must use it to gussy up their services. Pretty strange, if you ask me."

"Still, they worship God, not the devil, and I just can't see them killing a poor defenseless animal."

"Maybe," Tom said. "Christians used to sacrifice them all the time and, well, hell, they're still doing ritual cannibalism."

"What?"

"Communion. Christ's body and blood. Thursday night, after the barbecue, maybe we'll give it a listen, see what everyone else thinks. You're coming, aren'tcha?"

"I don't know if I'm gonna feel like socializing, Tom. Moss'll be there if he can, though." She shook her head. "Wish he'd get around to hiring a new man, what with all that's been going on."

"Cass, you can't miss Thursday night." Over the years, dropping in at Tom's on Thursday evenings had become a habit set in stone. "I don't think you should be out here all by your lonesome, anyhow. Especially with this six-six-six business."

"I'll think about it, but don't play daddy, Tom. It's unbecoming."

"How come it's okay for you women to tell us men to be careful, but we get our heads taken off if we say it to you?"

"Changing times." She grinned. "We gotta be as chauvinistic and obstinate as you boys were and make sure you all *know* we don't need you."

"Why, that's just silly."

"Yeah, I know, but it's the way things work. Bunch of fanatics on one side, bunch on the other, have to fight it out. Finally they find a middle ground." She smiled. "As for us women, as soon as we know we've convinced you we can take care of ourselves, why, then I guess we can all tell each other to be careful."

"Women don't make sense," Tom said, shaking his head.

"Men don't either." Cassie gave him a wink. "That's one of the things I like about them."

"You got a point." Tom reached behind him and snagged the phone receiver from the wall. "We need to let Moss know what's going on."

"Fine, but don't you put any of that stuff about paisleys looking like sixes in his mind. If you do, that man'll be breathing down my neck every minute."

"I thought you liked him breathing down your neck," he chided gently.

"Don't start, Tom."

"Yes, ma'am." He left a message for Baskerville, then took his leave, carefully refraining from telling Cassie to be careful. Instead, he put his Stetson back on and said, "Hope we see you Thursday."

"Tom?"

Hand on the doorknob, he turned and raised his eyebrows.

"What do you think happened to Madge Marquay?" she asked, a tentative tone in her voice.

Once more, those damned goose bumps did a little dance. He stared solemnly at Cass. "Nothing, I hope. Maybe she and Hank had a spat and she took off, and maybe Hank is too embarrassed to say so." He knew that she knew he was spouting bullshit. "What does Moss think?"

She shook her head, her customary bravado gone. "He thinks it's bad. Real bad."

"What about Kyla and Joe?"

"Joe, well, he doesn't know about him, but he's afraid whatever got Madge got Kyla. He's out of leads. None of her friends or relatives have heard from her." Cassie paused. "He's worried, Tom."

"I don't envy him his job." He turned the knob and pushed the door open, anxious to be on his way. "I'm sorry, Cass, I've got a four o'clock show."

"You get going, Tom," she said softly, a little too much under-standing in her eyes. "We'll see you later."

Outside, he glanced at his watch, then began walking briskly down the road toward the Madland entrance. Because of the goat, he'd have to ride one of the horses in the stunt riders' corral instead of stopping by the ranch to fetch Belle, who knew his every move. He felt a surge of annoyance, followed by one of guilt. "Abernathy," he muttered as he crossed the road and walked up the wide rock-lined path to the park's entrance, "it's your own damn fault. You don't want to get involved, you shouldn't be so damned curious."

# TWO

## JUSTIN MARTIN

Starting into the medicine cabinet mirror, Justin Martin carefully placed his forefingers on each side of the single corpulent pimple sprouting in the cleft of his square chin. Slowly he began to squeeze—

"Justin?" His mother's cloying voice filtered through the closed bathroom door. "Justin? Are you in the bathroom, dear?"

*Who the hell do you think is in here?* Annoyed, he stabbed his fingers into the blemish. It held. Wincing, he pressed harder, and suddenly yellow pus spewed all over the mirror, leaving only a small red mark on his otherwise perfect chin. He grinned, a wide flash of white framed in dimples.

"Justin? Are you in there?"

"Yeah. I'll be out in a minute."

"Honey, are you sick?"

*Sick of you.* "No," he muttered, thinking that the speckles of pus on the mirror bore an uncanny resemblance to the constellation Orion.

"You've been in there a long time. Do you need some Pepto-Bismol, honey?"

"No!" he spat, then added more gently, "I'm fine."

She cleared her throat but didn't speak. Her foot tapped, once, twice. *She thinks I'm beating off.* Amused, he put his hands to his face and pinched the flesh out on each cheek, then pulled in and out, shaking his head at the same time. The resultant liquidy noise was just the sound she expected, and almost instantly he heard her retreating footsteps, exactly as *he* expected.

Grinning again, he pulled his comb out of his back pocket and ran it through his thick dark hair. The first time he'd driven to Supercuts in Barstow and got a real haircut, his mother had nearly had a coronary. She thought she owned his hair, thought only she could cut it. She'd given him a load of shit about wasting his money, but it hadn't taken him long to charm her into forgetting about it. Keeping parents under control was a pain in the ass, and sometimes he found it very difficult to keep the smile plastered on his face and the cajoling words pouring from his lips. Sometimes he wanted to pull a Lizzie Borden.

Someday, he might, especially if the Voice suggested it. *The Voice.* It came, sometimes, with the lights in the sky and he had heard it more often in the last year. For several months now, it had been a clear and vital force in his life. It guided and respected him. It gave him what he needed.

He returned the comb to his pocket, took his little bottle of Oxy-10 from the cabinet, and massaged the medicine into his face. The blemishes rarely got out of control, but it was a constant, annoying battle, another pain in the ass, but he supposed it was a small price to pay for the hormones that had, with the advice of the Voice, plus a little weight training and running, turned him from a loose-boned kid into a broad-shouldered jock early last summer. Pseudo-jock, he corrected, using a hand mirror to check the back of his head. He had no use for the imbeciles who devoted their lives to chasing balls and tackling each other. *Bunch of closet queens.*

By the time he began his senior year last September, he'd saved enough from his job at the Haunted Mine Ride in Madland to replace his glasses with contact lenses that changed his watery blue eyes—his only flaw—to rich periwinkle. The black '78 Mustang coupe his parents gave him for his birthday last November completed his physical change. Now, at seventeen and months away from graduation, he was no longer an ugly duckling. He'd become a swan.

Of course, during the last year, he'd had to perform a little surgery on his personality to go with his new look. He read books on sports so that the moronic jocks would accept him, and he read books on dating so that he'd say the right thing to get laid. He also learned to keep his brains hidden and never to talk about his real hobbies.

And it had worked, better than he ever dreamed. People were stupid, easily fooled, and their memories were as long as Coach Butz's dick. Christie Fox, the bitchy little cheerleader who used to make fun of him, told him last week that he looked like Christian Slater. Of course, she was still going with Rick Spelman, the captain of the football team, but that was just another challenge to be met. Meanwhile, Justin pretty much scored with whomever he wanted whenever he wanted. The girls who threw themselves at him bored him, though he never showed it. After all, he now had a reputation as a great lay to live up to: The sexual technique books he so carefully studied had paid off almost too well. Now he wanted to use those techniques—and others—only on Christie, the last holdout worth having. But she told him she loved Spelman and said she wanted to be faithful. *Stupid bitch.*

"Jussstinnn!" His mother's voice echoed from the kitchen. "Dinnnner!"

*God.* His parents ate dinner every day between three and four o'clock and went to bed by eight, the stupid fucks. He took one more look in the mirror, then left the bathroom. Stepping into his room, he grabbed his wallet and keys, and slipped on his Levi's jacket. Everything else he'd need tonight was already locked in the trunk of his car. Now he just had to get past good old Mom and Dad.

Which was easy. Dad was sitting at the kitchen table, his face buried in the *Daily Press,* and Mom, wearing a pair of Garfield oven mitts, was just setting a big glass pan full of lasagna on the table. His parents were fifties throwbacks. Ward and June. Barney and Betty. Jim and Amanda Martin, all-American dweebs.

"Justin?" His mother crossed her arms, which made the Garfields look like they were humping her elbows. "Where do you think you're going?"

"Gee, Mom. It looks really good," Justin said, glancing at the casserole. She used cottage cheese and cheddar instead of ricotta and Parmesan because that's what the old man liked, and Justin knew it tasted like Chef Boy-ar-dee had barfed in the pan. He smiled winningly. "I thought I told you—I have to work. Some schools are out for Easter vacation already and Madland's doing quite a bit of business."

"I can't imagine Hank wanting to work with Madge missing," said good old Mom.

"I guess it helps get his mind off things." Seeing that sympathy for Old Man Marquay would work best on his mother, Justin forced his eyes to glisten and poured compassion into his voice. "I think maybe he needs some company, too."

The paper rattled down from his father's face. "Justin, what could he possibly want you to do on a weeknight?" He sounded suspicious. The old bastard had always been harder to convince than Mom.

Without missing a beat, Justin replied, "Mr. Marquay wants to get the mine ride all fixed up before the Strawberry Festival. You know, paint the cars, make sure the dummies are all working right."

His father stared at him a moment. "You know, if you worked for me in the garage, you could earn just as much money—maybe more—and not have to keep such odd hours."

"Jim," Mom scolded gently. "Justin is doing the Christian thing. We should be proud of him." She turned to Justin. "Why, he's even joined a church, dear. I would think you'd be pleased."

"That's no church. It's a damn circus sideshow," Dad grunted, and went back to the sports section.

"Justin, you ought to have something to eat before you go," his mother said as he made for the door.

"Sorry, Mom. I'm supposed to be at work in five minutes. I don't want to be late."

She opened her mouth.to mother him again, but dear old Dad said, "Can't argue with the boy about that." He pushed the spatula into the lasagna and lifted a big drippy blob onto his plate. It was red and yellow, like the viscera and fat of a chicken.

Justin hid his disgust. "I'll pick up something in Madland later."

"Well, I'll leave you a plate in the oven." She paused. "Maybe you should take some to poor Mr. Marquay. You wait just one minute and I'll make up a plate."

It wasn't worth arguing about, so he waited while she got a small casserole dish out of the cupboard and spooned some of the glop into it. After covering it with tin foil, she pushed it into his hands.

"See you later." Carrying the disgusting dish well away from his body, he headed out the door.

"Honey?" she called.

*What now, you old douche bag?* "Yes, Mom?"

"You did your homework, didn't you?"

"Of course," he said. That question never failed to insult him. He could do a page of trig in five minutes, a thousand-word book report in twenty, without even reading the book, and still get an A. Madelyn High was made for morons. Even the teachers were morons, unable to see past his dazzle of bullshit to realize he didn't know the material. The biggest moron of them all had been Old Lady Marquay, with her moles and warts, some of them with hairs growing out of them— she didn't even have the decency to shave them off—and her ability to make English even more boring than it was already. At least she wouldn't be turning her warty stare and her Julia fucking Child voice his way anymore.

"Give Mr. Marquay our best," Mom called as he pulled his Mustang out of the driveway. He gave her the dimples and waved.

He looked forward to tonight's big event as he made a left on

Cactus Street. Tonight at midnight, he and Christie Fox's boyfriend, Spelman the Jock, had a date to play chicken out on Thunder Road. Setting it up had been as easy as Justin had expected. Spelman himself had thrown down the gauntlet, encouraged by a few simple remarks concerning his girlfriend's sexual talents.

Before tonight, though, he had lots of things to do, like picking up the pair of boots he'd had his eye on at the Thieves' Market down in Victorville, and stopping in the bookstore in the mall to see if they had any new books ... about his hobby. Then he'd come back to town and stop in at the café to see if he couldn't talk Christie Fox into having a soda with him after she got off work.

Cruising Madelyn's tacky little suburbs, he checked to see who was home and who wasn't. Every house looked lower-middle-class, even the few that were owned by people with money. The desert had that effect on everything. Houses, cars, people, they all looked dead and dry and wrinkled.

Before he left town, he had one errand to take care of—he had to check the snare and see if he'd caught anything. He pulled onto Old Madelyn Highway and turned north. "Highway," he thought, was a fucking fancy name for a rutted dirt road. Everybody in this hick outpost thought they were such big fancy shits, but they weren't. They were nothing and they didn't even know it. They were as ugly and stupid as their town. The only exceptions, possibly, were Jim-Bob Sinclair and a few of his flunkies.

He'd been going to the church because the Voice in the sky had told him he should. He balked at first, but it kept returning, invading his brain, telling him it was a means to an end; a part of the greater plan. Justin was never one to trust people, but the Voice was something else and it had always been right before. He did as it asked, and in the last few weeks, he'd managed to impress Sinclair with his own hardworking honesty and concern.

Of course, if he could fool a scam artist like Sinclair, that meant two things: He was a better scammer than Sinclair, and the evangelist wasn't as smart as he seemed. That was a bit of a disappointment, but dealing with the man still held some excitement: Sinclair couldn't have gotten to where he was if he weren't very, very good, so the excitement lay in the possibility that Sinclair was scamming him. Perhaps more interesting than Sinclair himself were his "Elder Apostles"—a churchy name for "lieutenants." Round, angelic-faced Hannibal Caine, who spoke in a soft, sweet voice, had more going on than met the eye. A hell of a lot more.

Caine was still suspicious of Justin, though perhaps it was only jealousy. The other, Eldo Blandings, rarely said a word, had a ridiculous gray toupee, long, sour face, and seemed to see everything with his equally long, pale blue eyes. Justin found him fascinating and wondered what he and Caine wanted besides the obvious: power. Anyone but the sheep wanted power: That was a fact of life.

A mile up the road, he passed the gates for El Dorado, Tom Abernathy's ranch. His was the only place that looked really good, but that old Roy Rogers reject had money dripping from his dick, and other than Sinclair, was the only one who could afford to build a halfway decent house.

"Fucking desert." As he approached Madland he slowed for a dark green minivan as it pulled out of the parking lot. It was full of kids. One of them waved at him and he smiled and waved back as the van passed. *Fucking tourists.* Justin punched the radio on and hit scan. "This is Charlie Ray, with ten easy hits in a row." "Yeah, right," Justin grumbled, and changed the station. Twangy country shit came on, which gave way to a radio shrink, then some beaner rattling off Spanish a mile a minute. The next station it landed on was Sinclair's Jesus station. After that, a Whitney Houston song was ending, then Charlie Ray, Victorville's answer to Howard Stem, announced three in a row by Michael Bolton. "Shit!" He scanned across the dial again. They didn't play shit out here, and when Sinclair's thundering voice blared again, Justin locked on the station. "The time of reckoning is upon us, my friends!" Sinclair intoned. "And it is up to the Prophet's Apostles, those who have been blessed and enlightened, to deliver the

Word to the ignorant masses, that they, too, may be saved in these final dark days!"

"Jackasses," Justin Martin said, and chuckled. Sinclair's compound was loaded with followers, and on Sundays people came from all over to go to his church. Sunday mornings the dirt roads were packed with human sheep headed for the church in the compound.

Originally he hadn't bought Sinclair's religious crap, and he still didn't, not a speck of it, but he certainly admired the man's game and wondered how he was tied to the Voice. Jim-Bob's voice had power and charisma, and the fact that the afternoon show wasn't live, but merely a tape, didn't lessen the effect.

"Listen to me now!" Sinclair roared, as if he'd caught Justin's thoughts. "There is no redemption for sinners! Only the righteous, only the faithful, shall be saved! Join us right here, on this station, tonight and every night at nine, to learn about how you, too, can be saved before the Four Horsemen ride again! Until tomorrow, I am your faithful servant, James Robert Sinclair, humbly saying farewell."

"You're a shameless son of a bitch!" Justin muttered appreciatively. As he approached the end of Old Madelyn and slowed in preparation to turn right onto Thunder Road, he felt around for a cassette, any cassette. His fingers closed around one on the floor next to his seat and he slid it into the player, instantly silencing old Jim-Bob.

*"And I'll buy you a stairway to heaven—"*

"Shit." Not in the mood for moldy oldies, he ejected the tape, slapped off the radio, and concentrated on his surroundings. He glanced at tacky Fort Madelyn as he made his turn, then stomped the brakes, staring at the white mound that lay in the fort's shadows. "What the fuck?"

He checked the mirrors and the crossroads, east and west, saw no one, then pulled the Mustang onto the narrow shoulder and parked. He trotted over to the mound.

"All *right!*" he breathed as he stood over the dead goat. He glanced at the sky, half expecting to see the lights hovering overhead, hoping to hear the Voice. But the sky was clear. Only mildly disappointed, he turned his attention back to the goat. He sure as hell couldn't have caught anything this big in his snare. Quickly he returned to the car, opened the trunk, and spread out a blue plastic tarp on the ground. Then he returned to the goat and dragged the heavy corpse across the ground to the car. He rolled the body onto the tarp and tediously wrapped it up so that he wouldn't get blood, dirt, or the animal stink on his clothing.

The corpse was surprisingly heavy and Justin was sweating as he dumped the carcass in his trunk, but it was worth it. After taking one last joyous look at the animal, he placed the casserole in the trunk, making sure it wouldn't spill by nestling it between the goat's belly and rear quarters. Then he slammed the trunk, climbed in the Mustang, made a U-turn, and headed back down Old Madelyn. Pushing the Led Zep tape into the player, he grinned, glad he didn't need to check his rabbit snare. If he'd caught something, it could wait: This was a thousand times better.

# THREE

# JAMES ROBERT SINCLAIR

James Robert Sinclair took one last look at his manila folders filled with securities and investment papers, at the pile of bank books, and last, but best, the banded stacks of bills—twenties, fifties, and hundreds—that added into the hundreds of thousands. Pushing the heavy door to the safe closed, he twisted the dial. This was merely petty cash; much more substantial amounts were kept in church accounts—and even more impressive ones in accounts in Zurich and the Caymans. Those were his private accounts. Sinclair smiled. In just under a decade, the Church of the Prophet's Apostles had, indeed, turned some miraculous profits for church and for the Prophet.

He pressed a button on a hidden console in his desk and the oak wall paneling slid smoothly over the safe, hiding it from all but his most trusted faithful. Only his two elders, Hannibal Caine, who was his designated successor if anything happened to him prior to the "Apocalypse," and Eldo Blandings, were aware of the safe. In another safe, this one rather obviously "hidden" beneath a portrait on the wall, he kept less important property, but this safe was insurance, the one any would-be thieves were supposed to find. In this one, he kept enough to satisfy—and catch—any thief: fifty thousand in invisibly marked bills, plus gemstones and jewelry donated by his converts. There were even two of the gold ingots turned over to him by a wealthy widow, a convert who, like many, had hoped to receive his physical favors.

James Robert Sinclair knew exactly what he was: a handsome boy grown into a handsomer man, one who'd charmed his way through school on charisma and mediocre grades.

Absently he stroked his neatly manicured beard. He hadn't started out with the intention of founding his own church—entering the ministry was his parents' dream, not his. His first love had been magic, and by junior high he was an adequate magician. In high school he captured the interest of a professional magician and came under his tutelage, and in college he became a regular at the Magic Castle.

Using the money he earned with his act, he moved out of his parents' home, though he had remained in divinity school for another year because it didn't occur to him to quit. It was a thing drummed into him since early childhood — his father and grandfather were both ministers—so he didn't question them when they told him that pulling a rabbit out of a hat was a fine hobby, but he couldn't make a living at it. But one day he realized he was making a very good living with his magic, and so began his revolt.

He had tried for the two years of college to be what his family wished, but he didn't *believe*—he never had. He couldn't fathom the term "faith"—he needed proof, always, which was his big failing where religion was concerned. Faith seemed silly, religion and its miracles no more than a magic, not so different from his own brand. And so he had dropped out in his junior year. Disdain for those who believed had turned to pure contempt, and very nearly, hatred. He had even begun to hate himself for his own hypocrisy.

He'd turned to magic full-time until that, too, turned empty. Despite that, it had given him the understanding that had eventually brought him back to religious magic. In religion there was true power;

that was, if you were a real leader, not chief follower, but someone truly in command. He had always had a gift with women, but when he established himself as a "prophet" and began the church, his attractiveness progressed geometrically. Perhaps because of the power he held, perhaps, too, because they now perceived him as forbidden fruit.

In the first years of the ministry, when he was in his twenties, he had partaken freely of the gifts his feminine followers bestowed, but sometime during the fourth year, he developed an odd aversion to sexual relations with members of his flock. He knew himself well—knew his own selfishness, his own ego—and almost convinced himself that the aversion was akin to his earlier aversion to believers: He told himself he saw these women as mindless sheep, unworthy of him because of their very willingness to believe, to have faith in a man who was a charlatan.

He believed it for a while and he prided himself on his superiority, on his selfishness and pragmatism. But finally he had to admit to himself that even though this may have been true in the beginning, he had slowly come to accept the true reason—and at first it appalled him: He felt sorry for these grasping, needy people. They needed someone to tell them what to do, and in effect, they had created him just as people created every god. He had played the role of the wise father until he had become the role.

These days he saw the conviction as an asset rather than a weakness to be fought. If absolute power corrupted absolutely, then this one thing kept his ego from going over the edge or allowing him to make the mistakes so many other evangelists had made by letting their lusts get in the way.

Fortunately, he felt no similar qualms over taking their money; he knew he earned it. He gave the Apostles so much, he gave them what they needed: acceptance and structure, something to believe in. Their moneys were his due, for sometimes the people and their needs drained him beyond feeling. He weathered those times by telling himself that soon he would be free of his flock.

Sinclair tilted back in his chair and put his feet on his desk. He twined his fingers behind his head, absentmindedly twiddling the rubber band that held his wavy chestnut hair in a discreet ponytail that he always kept hidden beneath his shirt collar. Again he smiled to himself: He didn't know why he kept his hair long or why he hid it —another of his quirks, he supposed. Perhaps, at thirty- four, he already felt very old, and he kept it long as a reminder of his youth. In his days as a magician he'd worn it loose to complement his white spandex bodysuits: The hair drew women to him as much as his hypnotic brown eyes or his sculpted body.

The long hair, the eyes, the muscles rippling beneath the spandex, and his rich baritone had given him power over women and over audiences—but no true power. Back then, he'd tasted success, but when he decided to combine his religious background with his own physicality and his knowledge of magic, when he'd changed his name to James Robert Sinclair and become Prophet and founder of the Apostles, he had gained almost as much power as God Himself. He chuckled. That was, if there *were* a God.

# FOUR

# ALEXANDRA MANDERLEY

"This may be our last chance for a good meal for weeks." Eric Watson pressed the brakes and the red Ford Bronco halted at the bottom of the deserted Madelyn off-ramp. A green highway sign announced that Old Madelyn Road was to their right, but Eric's attention was directed to the left, where a huge neon sign slowly twirled above Ray's Truck Stop Cafe. The café itself stood amid a complex of buildings in the center of a huge parking lot. Eric glanced at Alexandra Manderley, hope and hunger in his grass-green eyes.

"*Good* meal?" Alex asked, then smiled at her youthful assistant. A graduate student, Eric had a long, gawky body, unruly auburn hair, freckled cheeks, and a shy boyishness in his manner that effectively hid the sharp, skeptical intellect that had made her choose him as her assistant. "Sure," Alex said. "Let's eat."

"Great." His grin creased deep dimples into his cheeks, making him look about ten years old instead of twenty-three with master's degrees in physics and aeronautics. On this trip he hoped to gather the last of his material for his doctorate. It wouldn't be long before Eric would be needing his own assistant at APRA—the Aerial Phenomena Research Agency—and she didn't look forward to losing him. In fact, the thought made her cringe. *At least you're losing him to something good.*

Her last assistant, Jack Matthews, had just received his master's degree when she lost him on a trip to the White Sands area of New Mexico four years ago. It was an excursion much like this one, to check out reports of UFOs in the area. The fifth night they saw them, followed by a clutch of military helicopters. During the melee, Jack disappeared, along with his video camera. Totally, completely disappeared. She didn't believe he'd been abducted, at least not by aliens, and she'd never quite given up looking for him, even though her initial suspect—the U.S. government —did its best first to placate her, then when that didn't work, to discredit her research. It was a long time ago now. *Poor Jack.* She looked at Eric Watson out of the corner of her eye and swore that she wouldn't let anything happen to him.

They pulled into the parking lot, joining two dozen big rigs and a handful of cars and pickup trucks. "I could eat a horse," Eric declared as he slipped the Bronco into a tight slot in front of the café. It had a seedy art deco look; the low- slung structure sported rounded edges, walls of faded yellow stucco, and dark- tinted windows that were lined up like those on an old-fashioned passenger train. Above the chrome and glass doors, the eternally winking neon waitress held a tray emblazoned with the words RAY'S over her head and leaned against a vertical post that flashed TRUCK STOP CAFÉ in dancing yellow and red bulbs. None of the bulbs were burned out, and that, Alex thought, was a good omen.

"This'll be great," Eric declared. "Truckers always know the best places to eat."

Alex glanced at the windowless building next door—its sign, complete with a tilted martini glass, read Ray's Tavern —and wondered if Eric was right or if the truckers preferred the bar.

"I can smell the onions from here," he added as he pushed open one of the heavy glass doors and held it for her.

"Thanks." Alex stepped across the threshold onto the worn but spotless black and white checkerboard floor, her stomach growling as she caught the pleasant odors of burgers and fries unsullied by rancid grease. Western music twanged softly on the jukebox. A few families occupied the booths with old-fashioned speckled gray Formica tables and overstuffed orange vinyl seats that lined the outer walls of the L-shaped cafe. The age-beaten maple tables and chairs scattered through the center of the room were empty. Men, mostly burly, several wearing cowboy hats, sat at the counter hunched over their food, talking, smoking, occasionally laughing. One overweight man, the back of his neck beet red, his shirt sweat-stained, glanced around at the newcomers, then glanced again, his little piggy eyes roaming the length of Alex's body. She drew herself to full height and put on her sternest I'm-a-scientist face, but that only made him look harder and elbow the man next to him in the ribs. This one stared approvingly from under a dirty baseball cap, then whistled. Other heads began to turn. "Ain't Red there a little young for you?" he called.

Just as Alex started to tell Eric they were leaving, *now*, a deep voice commanded, "Behave yourself, Roscoe!" A man who could have been James Earl Jones's younger brother was giving the trucker a schoolteacher's glare from behind the cook's window. His arms were crossed over his white apron and his spatula stuck up like a ruler.

"Sorry, Ray," mumbled the whistler. He stole one more glance at Alex, and his neighbor started to laugh but was cut short by the cook's stern "All of you, mind your manners." They shut up.

Ray nodded apologetically at Alex and Eric. "Waitress will be right with you folks." He disappeared and a moment later, a pert little blonde, no older than seventeen, bounced up to them. "I'm sorry," she chirped. "I broke a nail and I was Super-Gluing it." She smoothed her pink and white uniform.

"That's okay," Eric Watson said quickly. "Christie," he added, reading the name embroidered on her breast pocket. Alex smiled to herself: It was good to see that Eric thought about something besides science.

The girl, unaware, directed a brilliant smile at them both. "Anyway, welcome to Ray's. Table, counter, or booth?"

"A booth, please," Alex said quickly.

Brow furrowing, she glanced around, then the dimpled smile reappeared and she pointed at the booths lining the short far wall. "How about over there?"

"Thanks. That will be fine," Alex said. Three of the booths were empty, but a stiff-shouldered man in an air force officer's uniform sat in the fourth, glowering intently at a cup of coffee. A black leather notebook lay ignored at his elbow. She wasn't surprised to see him: Where UFOs made appearances, so did the military.

"Right this way." Grabbing menus, Christie led them across the room to the booth right next to the military type's.

Alex stood at the edge of the table, about to ask to be seated a booth away for privacy's sake, but the air force man glanced up at that moment and, catching her eye, glowered darkly at her from beneath thick salt-and-pepper brows. It was a look meant to scare her off, but it only served as a challenge. She slid into the seat, keeping her eyes on him until Eric blocked her view.

"Coffee?" the waitress asked.

"Please," Alex said, opening her menu. Eric nodded, and the girl hurried toward the kitchen.

"Dr. Manderley?"

"Eric, I thought we agreed that you'd call me Alex when we're not at the institute."

The young man blushed. "I know. It just seems ... sacrilegious or something."

She laughed. "You've got to get over that. You've nearly got your doctorate, after all." As she spoke she saw the air force man—a colonel, she noted, named Dole—bend closer, eavesdropping. She hoped he hadn't caught her name: She was, she knew, just a wee bit of an annoyance to them. A small challenge, she amended, smiling smugly to herself.

# FIVE

# JUSTIN MARTIN

As usual, Madelyn was Monday-night-dead. All the gas stations were open, and the vacancy sign at the Satellite Motel flashed brightly, but only one car was in the lot. Though a fair number of big trucks and an occasional car flew by on the interstate, there was virtually no movement here on the business loop. A Coors sign flashed in the window of the Cactus Flower, a bar where people went to two-step on the weekend, but its lot was nearly empty as well. Justin was pleased that there was no sign of the old fat sheriff, because Baskerville gave him a real pain in the ass.

A moment later, he turned in to the huge lot holding Ray's Truck Stop complex and pulled in next to a new red Bronco in front of the café where Christie Fox was working tonight. He killed the engine, took a bottle of Obsession from his glove box and splashed a little on, then checked his hair in the mirror a final time. Perfect.

Justin pushed open the glass and chrome diner door. The heavenly scent of burgers and fries assailed him—the food here was incredible despite the fact that the place looked like a greasy spoon.

Justin sat down in a booth in Christie's section and admired his new boots, shiny black with western heels. Then, bored, he took in the booths holding harried-looking travelers with their whiny brats. Ray Vine was standing behind the counter bullshitting with some locals and truckers. Nothing new there. Then he turned his attention to the pair sitting in the next booth.

The male had his back to Justin and he couldn't see much except for the carrot red hair and limber, long-fingered hands that kept forming boxes in the air as he spoke. He had an enthusiastic but mildly adenoidal voice that made Justin instantly dislike him.

The woman was another matter altogether. She was older, maybe thirty or even more; she possessed one of those ageless faces that wouldn't betray her for years to come. The man said something to her and her laughter sounded like smoke. The most intriguing thing about her, however, was her genetics.

Her shoulder-length black hair was very wavy, very glossy, and her skin tone was an unusual dusky toffee color. He could barely see the faint sprinkling of freckles across the nose and cheeks. Her large dark eyes had the slightest tilt, and her lips were full and dark. He wondered what she looked like naked.

She looked up at that moment. Without missing a beat, he caught her eye and gave her a varsity grin. She smiled back. She was probably used to being stared at.

"I'll be with you in just a second, sir ... Oh, hi, Justin," Christie called breathlessly as she flew by laden with dishes for one of the traveling families.

"No problem," he said, pulling his new paperback from his pocket. *Murderous Minds,* fresh off the press, featured an entire chapter on the Peeler Murders, and he opened to it now, quickly reading through the text for the second time. The text contained nothing new, but that was fine: Flipping a few more pages to the photo insets, he studied the photo that had made him buy the book. It was a shot he had seen in another book, but it had been too small to do more than just give him the intriguing impression that he knew one of the people in the picture.

The photo here was larger and slightly enhanced. It showed a sheet-draped body halfway down an alley, and several people standing closer to the camera. The caption read: *"Police talk to witnesses Charles Pilgrim, 17, and Victor Pilgrim, 15, who discovered the partially skinned body of Sally Cantori, 19, in this Brooklyn alley. The youths were on their way to school when they found the body. Cantori was the Peeler's third and final victim."*

Justin studied the grainy photo. The Peeler murders fascinated him because so little was known about the killer. Justin wanted to know how the Peeler did his work so exquisitely, why he did it, and how he got away with the crimes. He intended to find out all those things and more, and he had hoped one day to get the answers from the Peeler himself. Now he was virtually certain he would succeed. The Voice had told him so, and now the photo was proof.

There was no mistaking the aquiline nose, the thin face, the regal Roman jut of the cheekbones and jaw, or the dark-browed eyes.

Even the names were the same, one Anglicized, one Italianate. Pilgrim. Pelegrine. Who would have thought that a serial killer would be reading fortunes in a little dump like Madelyn?

*I know who you are, Carlo Pelegrine. You're the Peeler.*

"What are you smiling about, Justin?"

He closed the book and looked up into Christie Fox's twinkling baby blues. "About seeing you."

She snorted and set a glass of water down in front of him. "You think you're pretty smooth, don't you?"

He shrugged disarmingly.

"What are you reading?" Christie snatched up the book. *"Murderous Minds?* Gross!"

Hiding his anger, he took the book from her and put it away. "I'm interested in all sorts of things."

The exotic woman at the next table signaled Christie. "Just a minute, ma'am," she called. "Justin, I can't talk right now. What can I get you?"

"Double cheeseburger, rare, chili fries, and a chocolate malt. I'm in a hurry right now," he added apologetically, "but I wanted to ask you if you want to go for a soda after you get off work. You mentioned you needed help with your algebra, so I thought we could go over it then."

She looked doubtful. "I don't get off until eleven."

"I'll come back and pick you up. And I'll make sure you ace your homework."

"I have to get home by twelve or my folks'll kill me."

He gave her a sheepish grin. "Mine'll kill me if I'm later than eleven-thirty, so you'll be home in plenty of time."

"Well, okay, but it's just a friends thing. Dutch treat."

"If you insist."

He watched her as she moved to the next table and assured the odd couple their order was coming right up, then wiggled her ass for him all the way to the kitchen to deliver his order. He'd made progress: Last time he tried this, she wouldn't even go dutch treat. Her loyalty to Spelman was starting to slip—or at least her grades in algebra. *Good thing, too, bitch.*

Christie said something to Ray Vine and he stared at the couple at the next table, then smiled and walked over to them. "My waitress tells me you folks are here to check out our UFOs."

The woman smiled and put out her hand. "Alex Manderley."

"Ray Vine."

"This is my assistant, Eric Watson," she added, and Justin detected a slight British accent.

"Well, you two don't look like uniforms."

"No, we're with a private institute," Alex Manderley said. "Do you get a lot of military types around here?"

"Now and then," Ray replied softly. "Unfriendly sons of bitches, excuse my French." He gave a little half smile, obviously aware of the colonel in the next booth. "Bad tippers."

"They're the bane of my existence." The woman chuckled.

Vine stepped back as Christie set their plates before them. "One of my waitresses is really into the UFOs."

Manderley glanced warily at Christie.

"Not me," the girl said before leaving. "He means Janet."

"She even has a little club she organized—the Space Friends."

"I'd like to interview her eventually," Manderley said. "But for now, we're trying to keep a low profile."

Vine nodded. "I understand. My lips are sealed. Some of those Space Friends are a little eccentric. Most folks around here call them the Hole in the Head Gang. Not in front of Janet, though."

"I'm looking forward to meeting them," Manderley said as Christie put Justin's burger platter in front of him.

"I'll see you at eleven," he said quickly, wanting her to stop blocking his view and making noise.

Nodding, she moved on.

"By the way," Manderley was saying to Ray Vine, "how difficult is it to find Spirit Canyon in the dark? We have a map, but you never know about dirt roads."

"Is that where you're setting up?"

Manderley nodded and Ray rubbed his chin. "Well, if you've never been there, it's a little tricky. There are some sheer drops that about take your breath away, but if you hug the mountain, you'll be just fine."

*Damn!* Justin couldn't have these UFO morons anywhere near Thunder Road tonight. They'd ruin his plans.

He ate silently, and by the time he finished, he had a plan. He paid his check, timing it so that Manderley and her nerd were right behind him. Walking to the door, Justin turned and waved at Christie, bringing himself face-to-face with Alex Manderley.

"After you." He held the door for her and the redheaded weenie. "I couldn't help overhearing your conversation with Mr. Vine," he said, once they were outside.

"Are you interested in UFOs?" Eric Watson asked.

"I'm interested in everything."

"Have you witnessed one?" Watson persisted.

*Shut the fuck up, asshole.* "No, not me." He smiled self-deprecatingly. "You mentioned camping in Spirit Canyon?"

"Yes," Manderley said slowly.

"It really is pretty treacherous if you aren't familiar with it, but I'd be glad to lead you up the road."

Manderley smiled. "You're serious? You wouldn't mind?"

"My pleasure."

"I'll pay you, of course."

Anger bubbled, hidden just beneath the surface. "No, I won't take your money," he said firmly.

# SIX

## MADGE MARQUAY

For the thousandth time, she tried to loosen the ropes binding her hands; for the thousandth time, she failed. She lay back, exhausted, trying to think, but her arm blazed with fiery pain, and she knew that death was close.

Perhaps not close enough.

Though her hands and feet were numb from the ropes, the pain lancing her left forearm was exquisite, worse now because it was hot and swollen with infection. As best she could guess, her captor had visited last night, or perhaps the night before. She knew it was night-time only because the mine ride wasn't running.

When he came down he tied her to something, perhaps an old shoring timber from the days when this place was a real silver mine, so that she couldn't move while he cut her.

After he cut, he pulled the flesh free, leaving an agonizing rectangle of pain burning on her forearm. Her fear and pain were so great that she had wanted to die, but she'd only fainted. When she awoke, she found that he'd released her from the timber, though not from her bindings.

She wondered if he'd come back tonight, if he'd come back at all.

She wanted to kill him. Barring that, she wanted to kill herself rather than endure more pain, endure the sound of his slow, steady breathing.

The thought of his return brought back raw terror, and with that came a rush of adrenaline. Suddenly it occurred to her that perhaps she could rub the ropes against the timber—or better, against one of the jagged rocks that composed the walls. She began inching along, stopping when her head bumped against something soft. The rank, sweet smell of death rose around her in a cloud.

She shuddered at its strength, at the horrible sweet smell of rotting meat in a trash can in the summertime, of the dead opossum her father had found under the house when she was little, but somehow different, a hundred times worse. Retching behind her sour gag, she wiggled backward, suddenly glad of the darkness.

She waited a moment, telling herself over and over that it was an animal carcass she smelled, telling herself it didn't matter. Finally she set off in another direction.

*Keep going keep going keep going.* After seconds, minutes, hours, who knew how long, she came to a wall and moved her body along it until she found a sharp outcropping. Rolling over, she put her bound hands to the rock's edge and began rubbing the thick ropes against it.

SEVEN

# JUSTIN MARTIN

H e led them far enough into the canyon to hide their view of Thunder Road. Alex Manderley thanked him, saying this would do nicely for tonight.

"For tonight?" he asked innocently as evening wind caught at his hair and blew it into his eyes.

"It's fine," she said, smiling. "Thank you very much."

*Cunt,* Justin thought, the sweet smile never leaving his face. "I'll see you folks later," he said like a true desert nerd.

Driving off, he slid a cassette he'd bought in Victorville into the player, and Jim Morrison's moody voice sang softly to him. He drove slowly until he'd put two hairpin curves between the researchers and himself, then rolled down the windows, stepped on the gas, and turned up the music.

The rear of the Mustang slid out from under itself at every curve, and dust clogged his open mouth as he laughed with exhilaration at the good sound of the dead goat bouncing back and forth in the trunk.

It took him just over a minute to clear the canyon. As he rounded the turn that led onto Thunder Road, he turned off his headlights and, as the road straightened, slowed to a crawl, watching for the three Joshua trees to the south that marked the location of his rabbit snare. After a moment, he spotted them and pulled onto the hard-packed earth, parking his Mustang behind them. He turned off the engine and checked his watch. Nine-thirty. Plenty of time, he told himself, climbing from the car. Squinting against the dusty wind, he trudged twenty feet across the desert to the snare.

"All right!" Pushing his hair out of his eyes, he grinned at the big ugly jackrabbit he'd trapped. The creature struggled to escape as he approached, then went catatonic when it realized it couldn't.

He seized the ears and twisted its neck with confidence born of long practice on neighborhood pets, then carried the limp body back to the car. Opening the trunk, and seeing the tarp-covered mound of the goat corpse, he marveled at his good luck. He withdrew a duffel bag, then sat cross-legged on the ground and emptied its contents in front of him. Ignoring the sand that blew into his eyes, he removed his jacket and pulled a plastic rain slicker over his head. Holding a penlight in his mouth, he carefully reread the section on skinning game in his mother's *The Joy of Cooking* before applying a filleting knife—the best he could come up with on short notice—to the animal.

The rabbit would be a little gift to the Peeler, a first hint that he had an admirer.

It took twenty minutes to get the hide off, and he was barely in control of his temper by the time he finished. The job was sloppy, the nicks and slices in the flesh nothing to be proud of, and he knew he needed more practice. *Oh well.* It would have to do. Now that he was almost sure that the Peeler was right here in Madland, he didn't want to wait any longer.

He carefully placed the body in a white plastic garbage bag, then removed the blood-spattered rain slicker before he washed up with water from a gallon jug. After rinsing the slicker clean with the remaining water, he tossed the rabbit skin into the desert, wiped down the tools, and replaced them in the duffel. He put everything back in the trunk. The entire job had taken one half hour.

With an hour to kill before his date with Christie, and two before the race with Rick Spelman, he decided to drive down to Madland, dump the goat in the mine, and take Mom's casserole and a little sympathy to his boss, Old Man Marquay. It never hurt to kiss a little boss-ass. Besides, she casserole had been riding around in the car for hours and it just might make Marquay sick enough to keep him in bed for a few days and put Justin in charge of the Haunted Mine.

# EIGHT

# TOM ABERNATHY

"We've got ourselves a pair of ghosts up on Thunder Road." Tom Abernathy lowered his voice and slowly looked around the campfire, studying each camper in turn. There were two dozen, give or take, including eight children. Not a bad turnout, but nothing compared to next week, when most schools closed for Easter vacation.

"Thunder Road?" one of the kids asked.

"Runs east to west right up there above Fort Madelyn," Tom explained. "They called it Thunder Road because the twenty-mule teams carrying silver from the mines to the stamp mills in Madelyn made such a noise that it sounded like rolling thunder down in town.

"The soldiers from the fort marched on it, too, and sometimes folks in town say they can still hear 'em late at night." He paused, letting the flames flicker their spooky shadows across his face. "If you listen close, you might hear them tonight. But the soldiers and the mule teams, those are things you only *hear*. The ghosts I'm going to tell you about tonight, why, sometimes you can even *see* them.

"In the daytime you can see Olive Mesa right over there," he said, pointing to the northwest. "It was named by Ephram Carmichael for his daughter, Olive, who was only sixteen when she died.

"Ephram and Olive lived out that way in the eighteen sixties. Now, Ephram, he was foreman of the Moonstone Mine—that's now the Haunted Mine Ride in the park—and he loved his job, but he loved his pretty daughter more than anything. She was the apple of his eye.

"Then came the tragedy." Tom waited a beat, enjoying the kids' wide eyes. Then he shook his head and said sadly, "It was a terrible thing. A horrible accident." At that, some of the adults moved closer together.

"It was early May, and the Strawberry Festival was coming up, just like it is now. Olive wanted to go to the dance with a young man named Caleb Gardner, who had a reputation for being a little wild. He wasn't really a bad boy, you understand, but Caleb's favorite thing to do was to race against his friends out on Thunder Road, just like some of the kids now do, only now they use cars instead of horses.

"The sheriff had run him in a couple times for scaring other people on the road, making their horses bolt and so forth, so naturally, Ephram wasn't too crazy about Olive going to the dance with the fella, and he told her so.

"Well, Olive was heartbroken, so Ephram, he finally had a talk with Caleb, and told him he could escort Olive to the dance as long as he hitched his horse to a carriage and they traveled in a sedate fashion. The boy promised, and off they went.

"They got there just fine and Ephram, who'd come with a widow lady from town, he was glad to see his little girl so happy. Well, he'd planned on taking Olive home himself, but she begged him to let young Caleb Gardner see her home. Since Caleb had proven himself a gentlemen and Ephram really wanted to see that widow lady home, he said yes."

Tom paused dramatically. "That was the last time anybody ever saw Olive or her beau alive.

"To this day, nobody knows exactly what happened, whether

Caleb simply had the one-horse wagon going too fast or if there was a race." Tom let his voice drop a fraction deeper. "Maybe a mountain lion spooked the horse. Or there could've been some ruffians hiding out on Dead Man's Hill. But most people figure Caleb couldn't resist a race, though whoever he was racing never admitted to it."

"What happened?" whispered a youthful voice.

"Well, a while later, Ephram came riding home and his heart about stopped beating when he found the wreck. The wagon had crashed and overturned. First he saw only Caleb Gardner, half under the wagon, his neck broke. Snapped like a twig. And for a few minutes Ephram thought maybe Olive was okay and walking home, because there was no sign of her.

"Then he found her, and Lord, it was an awful sight!"

"What?" breathed one of the kids. "What'd he see?"

Tom hesitated, looking hard at the kid. "Well, it was so awful that I don't know that I should say—"

"You gotta!" screeched one.

"Please!" begged several others.

"Well, okay. It was a freak thing that happened to Olive. She got thrown quite a ways from the road and landed in a little gully. Thing was, there was this rusty old saw laying there, blade up." Another pause. "When she landed, she got her head cut clean off."

"Really?" they asked.

"Really. And her daddy about went crazy. In the morning they found him wandering around in the desert, carrying her poor head tucked underneath his arm. She had the purtiest blond curls," he added wistfully.

Clearing his throat, Tom put his hands on his knees and leaned forward. "Every now and then, about this time of year, people hear and sometimes even see a runaway horse pulling a wagon with a young man in it. Folks hereabout believe it's the ghost of young Caleb Gardner. All I know is, it's a spooky sound if you're up there by yourself."

"You heard it?"

Tom raised his eyebrows and drawled, "Many times." Then he added, "But that ghost is nothing compared to the other haunt. Lots of people have seen a girl hitchhiking up on Thunder Road. Why, I even know one man who picked her up in his truck. She was a pretty thing, standing out there all alone, dressed in a long, old-fashioned pink dress. My friend figured she worked at Madelyn Park and was dressed in a costume, so he pulled over, and sweet as you please, she asked him to take her home. He asked where that would be, and she pointed toward Olive Mesa.

"The only thing out there nowadays is that church compound, and he thought she meant she lived there, but when he pulled up, she said, 'No. Up there,' and she pointed up the old trail to Olive Mesa. My friend had his eyes on the road and he told her he couldn't take his truck up that trail. But she didn't answer, so he turned to look at her, and she wasn't there." He paused. "She'd just vanished into thin air."

Tom scratched his chin and added nonchalantly, "Wasn't the first time Olive hitched a ride home. Won't be the last."

"Is all that really true?" one of the adults asked.

"Why, sure it is," he answered, smiling to show it was really a wagonload of manure. It amazed him how seriously some people took a windy. In a way, Tom envied them their naïveté, because if he really believed he might meet up with Olive's ghost on Thunder Road, why, life would be even more interesting.

"Time to head for the bunkhouse." Tom stood up and stretched. It was quarter of eleven now, so his half-baked plan to go into Rattlesnake Canyon to visit Marie was out—it would be at least midnight before he'd arrive, and she didn't take kindly to having her sleep interrupted. Still, he felt like taking a ride, and thought maybe he'd go around the back way through Spirit Canyon, then down Thunder Road and home. He smiled to himself: Maybe Olive would be looking to hitch a ride.

"Mister, um ..."

"Tom, ma'am," he said, turning toward the short woman who had tapped his arm. "What can I do for you?" A thinner, equally short woman with a baby on her arm stood with her, and their husbands waited behind them, clearly interested and trying to look bored.

"Well, we were just wondering ..."

"Yes, ma'am?"

"About the UFOs."

"I see," Tom said slowly. At the word "UFO," several more people moved closer. Although he didn't especially mind the UFO business, it drove him a little nuts because it just didn't go with cowboys and horses any more than whisky went with a dish of ice cream. "What about them?"

"Have you seen any?"

"Oh, well, I couldn't really say," he began. "I've seen some lights in the sky, but I'm more of a mind to think they're the spirit lights the local Indians used to tell stories about."

"What are spirit lights?" the thin woman asked.

"I'll tell you about them Friday night, ma'am. Right now I have to hit the trail."

He tipped his Stetson and walked toward his horse, leaving them wanting more. It occurred to him as he petted Belle's silver muzzle that he'd have to come up with a story about "spirit lights," but that didn't worry him. Truth was, he probably wouldn't know what spirit lights were until he sat down to tell the tale.

Belle whinnied softly, then snorted as he got into the saddle, his tan duster flapping in the wind. He held her still, realizing that most of his audience had followed along. He looked down at them and spoke in his most serious tone. "When horses snort at night, it means they're seeing a ghost." A couple of the kids looked around themselves, scared spitless, and Tom realized he'd spread it on too thick tonight. "Don't worry, son," he said to a five-year-old who looked on the verge of tears. "It's a well-known fact that a little singing makes ghosts happy. Then they go away and won't bother you the rest of the night. A few verses of 'Home on the Range' will do the trick."

"Are you sure?" the boy asked.

"I guarantee it."

The boy looked happier. "Will you sing?"

Tom preferred dying to singing in public. "Young fella, I've got a voice that'd scare the hair off a coyote." The boy giggled. "And I'll bet that cowboy there"— he pointed at a young father who'd been wearing a guitar and looking hopeful all evening—"would be just the fella to lead you folks in a song or two. Night, all."

He rode out of the campground, smiling at the sound of a guitar's twang, followed by a bunch of voices singing about the antelope and deer playing on the range. He knew he shouldn't saw off whoppers about ghosts when little bitty kids were listening, but it took a heck of a lot of willpower to control himself. A little more than he possessed.

Exiting the campground, he pointed Belle toward the far end of the tall but narrow Spirit Canyon east of the main range of the Made-lyns, where Marie was spending the night. Invigorated by the wind, he let the animal have her head and Belle took off at a trot, only slowing when they closed in on the skinny dirt road into the canyon.

There wasn't enough moonlight to see up here, but Belle knew the road. She loved their midnight rides as much as he did, and wanted to go faster. He had to keep holding her back.

They took the two winding miles at a fairly leisurely pace. The night was clear and dark except for the glittering stars and the crescent moon overhead. Not a UFO in the sky, Tom was glad to see.

When he'd told the campers he'd seen some lights, that had been the truth. In fact, he'd seen them several times, just like most everybody else around here. They were funny things, zipping back and forth way up in the night, flying like nothing natural, except maybe fireflies, but they didn't get him very excited. Some folks claimed to have seen actual UFOs, big saucery things, not just distant lights, and he took them pretty much at their word, though as a certified spinner of tall tales himself, he knew how easy it was to believe your own stories, and how much better they got each time they were told. So, although he didn't disbelieve, he had decided to withhold judgment until he saw the things with his own eyes.

Suddenly Belle's ears went back and her muscles tensed. She hesitated, sniffing the air.

"What's wrong, girl?" he whispered, thinking she smelled a coyote. An instant later, she relaxed a little, then Tom heard human sounds. "Campers, Belle. Just campers."

He was possessive of the place, even though he had no call to be, and he disliked sharing his canyon with strangers, but there wasn't much he could do about it.

"Come on, Belle," he said, pushing his heels into her sides. "Let's go say howdy." The horse started moving again, sedately, and her ears were slightly forward now, signaling that she didn't like strangers up here any more than he did.

Around the next bend, he spotted a dusty red Bronco, a big tent, and a bunch of equipment set up in a large turnout. A woman holding an electric lantern came out from behind the Bronco and stared at him.

"Howdy, ma'am," he drawled. He found that a good drawl generally kept folks from spooking. "Nice night for a ride."

"Dr. Manderley?" came a young man's voice from inside the tent. An instant later, he stepped out, his hair glinting red in the rays of the woman's lantern. Tom had yet to get a look at her.

"Are you the sheriff?" she asked, trying to sound sure of herself and almost succeeding. Without that faint foreign accent, it wouldn't have worked at all.

Tom laughed gently. "Why? Are you gunslingers on the run?"

The woman relaxed. "Would you care for a cup of coffee?"

"Don't mind if I do." Tom swung down from Belle and tethered her to the Bronco's bumper. "Tom Abernathy," he said, holding out his hand. "I own the El Dorado Ranch down off of Old Madelyn Highway."

"Alex Manderley." Her handshake was nice and firm. "And this is Eric Watson. We're here hoping to capture some of your UFOs on film."

"Hi," Watson said. "Dr. Manderley is one of the most respected researchers in our field." The poor kid, already on the defensive about their work, had a handshake that needed work.

"Nice to meet you, Mr. Watson," Tom said kindly. "You've come to the right place for a UFO show, though it appears a bit slow tonight."

"I'm relieved to hear it," Alex said, setting the lantern on a card table next to the tent, and motioned Tom to take a seat. She sat opposite him. "We hear rumors about a location, but you never know what you're going to find. Thanks, Eric," she added as the young man carried a pot of coffee from the Coleman stove and proceeded to pour. "Pull up a chair," she added when he looked unsure whether he should stay or not.

"Lots of places have UFOs," Tom said. "How'd you come to choose Madelyn?" By the flicker of lamplight he noticed that Alex Manderley was a breathtakingly beautiful woman. No wonder Watson was such a nervous young pup.

"Madelyn is one of the country's hot spots," Alex explained. "There've been sightings for many years—a number of Project Blue Book's investigations were in this region, and in the last two years, the rate of appearance here is one of the highest in the country." She smiled. "But the most important reason we chose this place is because the military is trying to keep it a secret."

"From what I've heard," Tom drawled, "they try to keep everything a secret."

Alex laughed, a pleasant throaty sound. "That's true, Mr. Abernathy—"

"Tom."

"Tom. I'm Alex. Anyway, that's very true. But they try harder to keep us out of some places than others. Like Madelyn."

"What do you mean, 'keep you out'? It's a free country, last I heard."

"They withhold information and go to amazing lengths to debunk the sightings. They're very subtle in a blundering sort of way, if you get my drift."

Tom laughed. "I do indeed."

"You wouldn't know a Colonel Dole, by any chance?" she asked.

"Big slab of a man, looks a little like Richard Nixon in his Watergate days?"

"Yes! That's him. Do you know anything about him?"

"He was eavesdropping on us in the café," Eric Watson explained.

"Colonel Dole, huh?" Tom scratched his chin. "I've seen him and his flunkies driving around up here now and again. Might've been him I saw today on Thunder Road. Ray Vine says he spends a lot of time in his diner, and that he never tips the waitresses."

"We met Mr. Vine." Alex grinned. "He made some pointed remarks about the military right in front of the colonel."

"Ray doesn't much cotton to rudeness, not even in uniform. Gets his back up," Tom explained. "Way up."

# NINE

# JUSTIN MARTIN

At eleven-forty Justin had returned to Thunder Road and parked near the entrance to Spirit Canyon. Pissed because he hadn't even got a good-night kiss from Christie —she thanked him for fixing her homework and slipped out of the car before he could make a move—he spent the next quarter hour sitting back with his fingers laced behind his head while he fantasized about the things he would do to the little blonde cheerleader when he finally got the chance. He'd thought about the things he'd make her do to him, too.

Now it was one minute until midnight, and he looked to the sky, hoping to see the lights, hear the Voice, but no one was there. He revved the engine, enjoying its smooth powerful purr. He'd already queued up the Doors cassette to "Roadhouse Blues" and now he fed it to the player and drummed his fingers in time with the driving beat.

"Put your eyes on the road, your hands upon the wheel," he whispered in time with the music. He pulled silently onto the road, lights out, the black Mustang a ghost in the dark, windy night.

*The witching hour.* He revved the engine and counted to thirty, then, choreographing his movements to Jim Morrison's voice, he eased out the clutch and pressed the accelerator, hitting eighty miles per in just under ten seconds. Spelman's GTO would be doing the same, or close, at the other end of the four- mile straightaway, with a short head start. Assuming the jock didn't run into any unplanned traffic as he passed the Old Madelyn intersection, Justin figured they'd meet up at Dead Man's Hill, the huge pile of boulders just this side of Old Madelyn Highway.

Blowing dust and sand hit the windshield as he accelerated, but it didn't matter—he would have been driving blind in the darkness anyway. Fortunately, he knew the road by heart. In the distance, Spelman's headlights were two tiny points of light.

They grew bigger and brighter by the second—Spelman had his brights on to blind Justin. "Asshole," he whispered, "you're dead." His fingers hovered over the car's lamp switch, ready to startle the guy off the road at the last second.

But with less than a hundred feet separating them, the jock's car wavered, telling Justin that Spelman had seen the Mustang despite the blowing dust storm, the darkness. Justin continued steadily forward, now flicking his brights off and on to further fuck with Spelman's pea-sized jock brain.

The cars moved closer and closer, and time drew out into delicious slow motion as Justin drove. *Five. Four. Three. Two.*

*One.* Spelman chickened and yanked his wheel hard left.

"Yes!" Justin whispered as the GTO flew off the road and smashed into Dead Man's Hill. Metal rent and screeched as it crushed against the boulders.

Justin applied his brakes, then backed up to survey the damage. Pleased that the sandstorm would cover his tracks, he pulled on a pair of leather driving gloves and took a half-full bottle of Cutty Sark out from under the passenger seat.

He carried it to the wreck.

Rick Spelman's body and the steering wheel had merged bloodily into one unit, but El Jocko was still breathing. "Hey, Rick, man, I'm sorry you lost," Justin said, removing the cap from the whisky. "Here, drink this, it'll help."

The jock stared at him, trying to focus. Blood bubbled from between his lips.

As he held the bottle to Spelman's lips, forcing him to drink, he noticed a couple empty beer cans on the backseat. "Rick, you've done my job for me," he said, as the boy coughed out blood and liquor. Justin let the bottle fall on the seat. "Well, Rick, I gotta go. I have a date with your girlfriend. I'm gonna screw her brains out."

Spelman stared at him blearily, then mouthed the words "Fuck you."

"Same to you, bud." Justin pulled a cigarette lighter from his pocket, grabbed the liquor bottle again, and poured some on the backseat, out of Spelman's reach. He dropped the bottle back in Spelman's lap, then held the lighter over the alcohol-soaked upholstery and flicked. Flames licked the cloth once, twice, then took. "Ta ta for now," Justin said with a grin.

He hurried back to his own car as Rick Spelman screamed and sobbed for help. *Needle-dicked baby, that's what you are, Spelman.*

Before he turned down Old Madelyn Road, he flicked his headlights on. He drove sedately, then, as he turned, it occurred to him that it was possible someone could have heard the crash, specifically that old whore Cassie Halloway, who lived nearby. And if her boyfriend, the chief of police, heard it, too, that could be a problem. Turning off his headlights, he slowed to a crawl as he approached the dimly lit house. He stared hard, searching for Baskerville's cruiser. His luck held—it wasn't in sight. After idling in the middle of the road a moment, he pressed the accelerator and peeled out.

# TEN

# TOM ABERNATHY

"So why'd you think I was the sheriff? he asked Alex Manderley over his second cup of coffee.

It was too dark to see if she blushed, but she sounded embarrassed. "I don't know. I looked up and saw you on that beautiful white horse—"

"Belle's a silver-gray," he interrupted.

She smiled. "Silver-gray. You looked like Gary Cooper riding into town to shoot the bad guys."

"Ma'am, you do know how to turn a man's head."

She laughed. "It wasn't intentional, was it, Eric?"

The young man smiled. "Alex always says what she thinks."

A distant crashing sound, metallic, reverberated against the canyon walls.

"Do you have any idea what that was?" Watson asked.

"Probably an accident down on the interstate."

"That far away?" Alex asked.

"Well, I hope so," Tom said slowly. "Sounds like that can get amplified and distorted by the canyon walls." But even as he spoke, he realized the hairs were prickling up on the back of his neck and his thoughts turned to Marie. *She's nowhere near any cars, you fool.* He stood up.

He walked over to the edge of the encampment, but hills blocked the view in every direction. "You folks picked a funny spot for sky-watching. You're not going to see anything that's not directly overhead."

"A local boy guided us here and we thought we'd wait until morning to move."

"Good idea." Tom walked back to the researchers. "Thanks for the coffee. I'd best be getting on home now." He shook their hands again. "Look me up at Madland or the ranch if you need anything." Feeling an urgent need to get moving, he climbed into the saddle and gave them a salute. "See you, folks.

"Okay, Belle, let's go see what's going on." He urged the mare forward and she moved more quickly than wise in the dark hills. She was a smart horse, damned impatient, and too curious for her own good, but that's why he liked her so well.

# ELEVEN

# MOSS BASKERVILLE

"You ever notice how David Letterman always tells people they smell nice?" Cassie asked.

Moss Baskerville stretched his arms across the sofa top, then dropped the left over Cassie's shoulders and pulled her closer. "That's a little weird, if you ask me."

Cassie poked him in the ribs, then snuggled closer. "I think it's nice."

"That's because you have the hots for him."

Cassie shot him a smirk, then turned her attention to the TV.

Baskerville had had a hard time relaxing tonight, but he started getting it right because Cassie, as unruffled as ever, had refused to let him spend the entire evening worrying about the goat or the graffiti on her mailbox. Then, about fifteen minutes ago, he'd heard squealing tires in the distance and something that sounded like a crash. He'd wanted to have a look, but Cass had taken his chin and stared into his eyes and sternly reminded him that he'd left his best man, Al Gonzales, in charge tonight.

His only man. Since Jay Kettleman left two months ago, he hadn't bothered to hire a replacement because he and Al seemed to be enough. But when he heard those squealing tires, it had occurred to him that things might not stay so quiet. A third man was needed to keep an eye on the outskirts of town: to occasionally stake out Thunder Road and discourage the teenagers from racing.

And then there were those damned Apostles. They were getting pretty rabid lately and they'd be too much for a lone cop if they decided to invade Madland and harass the tourists en masse. Usually there were only a few and easy to run off if they got obnoxious, but he thought things could get ugly as the eclipse— the Apostles' chosen day of apocalypse —approached.

Baskerville's ulcer, long dormant, took a little twist as his thoughts leapt to his other problem: missing people.

Joe Huxley, he wasn't sure about. Nobody was missing him, and he'd taken off before, though he'd always made sure to arrange for someone to take over his night watchman job in the park before this. *That's another reason you need another man; we're pulling double duty cruising the town and the park.*

He was virtually certain that Kyla Powers had met with foul play, but until a few days ago, with the disappearance of Madge Marquay, he'd been pretty sure that whatever had happened to her hadn't happened in his jurisdiction.

Cassie snuggled closer, tucking her hand around his elbow, and Baskerville pushed his worries aside—he was here to get some rest, after all. He'd been working too hard, and he knew he needed a night off, but it was hard to make himself do it.

On-screen, Letterman was torturing a new guest, a chef who was laboring in vain to get the host to bread a piece of fish. Instead, Dave was flicking it through the air and humming the tune to *Jaws*. "So, Cass, what is it you see in that scrawny little smart aleck?"

"Well, now, Moss," she drawled, "a man who notices how people smell makes use of all his senses, and that means he's probably pretty damn good in the sack. Besides, he's funny," she added as the fish went flying toward the band. "He thinks of unusual things to do with everyday objects." She gave him a coy smile. "He'd know how to make a lady feel appreciated."

Baskerville knew a hint when he heard one, and bent his massive head to nuzzle Cassie's neck. "Mmmm. You smell like sweet petunias on a hot summer night," he murmured, then kissed the soft white hollow at her shoulder blade. "And I've got a few tricks of my own." She moaned softly as he worked his way up to her ear and sucked the lobe into his mouth, wriggling his tongue over it the way he knew she liked.

She turned slightly toward him, running her hand up his chest, undoing a button on his tan uniform shirt and slipping her fingers inside to comb them into the thick chest hair. "You smell pretty good," she said softly, "for a cop."

"What's that supposed to mean, 'for a cop'?" His hand trailed down to cup one of her breasts.

She chuckled softly and undid two more buttons. "Like a man. Warm. Musky." She put her mouth to his flesh, gave it a little lick. "Salty. Tasty." She kneaded one nipple, gently, then moved her hand down to his belt buckle. "Wanna fool around?"

He kissed her, tasting her lips, yielding, slightly open. "What about Dave?" "Let him get his own girl."

Her arms went up to circle his neck and he scooped her into his arms, then rose. Though she was tall, she didn't weigh much over a hundred pounds, and there was something about carrying her to the bedroom that always excited him. As he stepped around the couch, he saw a brief flash of headlights through the north living room window as a car turned onto old Madelyn Highway. It was moving slowly. He waited.

"What's wrong, Moss?"

"Maybe your graffiti artists are back." The car was crawling down the road. "Better check." He lowered her to her feet.

"Moss," she protested, "it's nothing."

"Honey, it's my job. You just remember where we left off." He went to the front window, stood to the side, and peered out. "Turn off the light, will you, Cass?"

"Sure," she said, her tone indicating boredom. "Nobody's going to pull anything with you here, you know."

"I parked in back, remember? They don't know I'm here."

"For surveillance purposes," she said, sounding long-suffering now. "I thought it was because you were spending the night."

"Of course I am."

With nothing but the television's glow illuminating the room, he could just make out the car. It was crawling along the road, still a little north. Suddenly it stopped moving and its lights went out. An older car, he thought, with round headlights—or, nowadays, it could be a brand-new one.

"Cass," he said, moving across the room to the kitchen, "I'm going to go out the back way and sneak a look. Whoever it is, is just sitting there in the dark."

"Be careful," she called softly as he headed out the door.

Gun drawn, he walked to the south side of the house, past his cruiser and Cassie's little vegetable garden. As he moved toward the front, the car suddenly revved, burned rubber, and tore down Old Madelyn, lights still out.

Baskerville ran to the front, squinting, but saw nothing but dust and one flash of brake lights as the vehicle neared a pothole. *Only a local would know about that.*

As he turned on his heel to get his cruiser and take chase, the front door opened. Cassie stepped onto the porch. "You won't catch him," she said, reading his mind.

"Cass, I have to try." He joined her as she came down the steps, and together they walked out to the mailbox. Nothing new marred it.

"Another minute and we wouldn't have heard that car anyway," Cassie said, taking his arm and leading him back toward the house. "It's probably just a dumb kid having some fun."

"Yeah, maybe," Moss said. "Maybe. You keep this place locked up tight when I'm not here?"

"I always do." She kissed him lightly on the lips. "Now, come on, we have some fooling around to do."

Baskerville cast one more look out the road, then put his arm around her narrow waist. "If you didn't smell so good, I'd be after him like I oughta be."

"Good thing for me I smell so good," she replied as they went back into the house.

# TWELVE
## CARLO PELEGRINE

Peeling an orange was, perhaps, the greatest guilt pleasure in Carlo Pelegrine's life. At the end of each day, he turned the OPEN sign on his shop door to CLOSED, shot the lock, and pulled the old-fashioned fringed blinds down on the windows. He then selected an orange from the citrus that he kept in a twig and moss basket in the center of his display of crystals and incense burners.

Today he chose a thin-skinned juicing orange, and as he moved through the green velvet draperies into the privacy of his card-reading room, he held it to his nose and inhaled the sweet tang of its bouquet. Smiling to himself, he passed the small round reading table with its purple linen tablecloth and straight-backed chairs, and seated himself at a small rolltop desk in the shadows at the back of the room.

He unlocked the desk, pushed the cantilevered cover smoothly up, and pulled the brass chain on the green case-glass desk lamp, revealing cubbyholes filled with silk-wrapped tarot decks, and shelves lined with well-thumbed books on card reading and palmistry and every other sort of divining. In the drawers were candles and oils, burners, charcoal, and incense; everything the well-prepared fortune-teller could possibly need.

Setting the orange on a beige linen napkin he took from a small, deep drawer, he then extracted a whetstone and a paring knife. He sat back, letting the chair rotate so that he faced the room. With a contented sigh, he drew the knife across the whetstone, then turned it and brought it back. Eyes closed, he continued the actions, finding calm in the repetition, music in the *swish-swish* sound of blade against stone.

Finally he opened his eyes, sat up, and turned back to the desk. He used the edge of the linen napkin to polish the blade, then tested it against his thumb: perfect. Any true pressure would break his flesh.

He picked up the orange in one long-fingered hand and turned it back and forth in the lamplight, admiring the pebbly texture, treasuring each tiny imperfection in its skin.

Finally he put the blade to the orange and, as always, felt a shiver of anticipation, one that centered in his groin and spread throughout his body in pleasurable electric tendrils.

Beginning at the stem, he began to cut at an oblique angle, taking the zest, the color, but leaving the fleshy white covering beneath it intact. His concentration never wavered, nor did his knife, and he steadily cut around and around until the delicate, thin skin, all in one piece, lay in a fragrant mound upon the napkin.

He set the orange down, the knife, too, and lifted the skin in both hands, bringing it to his nose and breathing in its nectar. He placed it on the napkin again, took the orange and the knife, and repeated the process, this time removing the white underskin, until only the pulpy orange fruit was left.

Holding the orange in his right hand, he cut carefully between the segments, separating them without piercing the delicate membranes. Finally he set the knife aside and let the orange drop from his fingers into his other, cupped, hand. The smell of oranges permeated the room and he breathed it luxuriously as he opened his hand.

The fruit flowered on his palm; perfect, untouched, sweet citrus.

He took one segment, held it under his nose, then placed it in his mouth.

Carefully, not breaking the membrane, he felt the segment with his tongue, tasted it, and finally tested the tension, feeling the juice move beneath the thin membrane, so delicate, so lovely. So perfect.

He bit into the fruit, letting its flavor wash over his tongue, savoring the flesh, chewing slowly. After the first segment, he quickened his pace only slightly.

It was the biggest pleasure he allowed himself, this small thing. He had denied himself women for twenty years, his unrequited cravings obsessing him, before he discovered this outlet, this relief from sensual pain. Peeling an orange had become his way of making love, though he never allowed himself release.

When he was eighteen, he had promised God he would remain celibate for the rest of his life, as penance for his sins.

He still wondered why he and his brother had taken a shortcut through the alley off Thirteenth Avenue to get to school. Perhaps it was only curiosity. Tall redbrick apartment buildings loomed ahead as he stood at the mouth of the alley, his heart beating quickly, and challenged Vic to a race to the other end.

Carlo let Victor sprint ahead, never expecting him to stop and stare at the trash cans. Vic, pale, turned to stare at his brother, and as he approached he saw the bloodless hand sticking up from between two bins.

Carlo stared at it, then grabbed Victor and told him they were going to be late for school. But Vic insisted they had to tell the police, and Carlo acquiesced, knowing it was the right thing to do.

He was never charged with any crime, was never even under suspicion, but fear nibbled away at him. He managed to finish high school, and then he struck out on his own, telling his parents and friends he was going to travel for a year before entering college.

He had to get away, because he couldn't look them in the eye anymore. After six months, he faked his own death and changed his name. Also, so close to temptation, he found his religion again and made his promises to God.

In the first years, his obsessions were difficult, nearly impossible, to control. He traveled constantly, taking odd jobs, making enough money to get by, and managing to pick up the odds and ends of an education. It wasn't until he arrived at Madelyn eight years ago that he found any peace.

Carlo slowly chewed another piece of orange. It had been twenty years since that last crime, and intellectually at least, he knew he was safe. Aside from one bad newspaper photo of himself and Vic in the alley, he'd never had any notoriety. The photo, though it had been reprinted once or twice in true crime books, was of too poor a quality to be a problem.

He had come to Madelyn by accident. Feeling the old urge to move on, he had left a good job in Cincinnati. He'd been there two years—the longest he'd ever remained in one place—and had a good, respectable job as a chef in an Italian restaurant. There, he'd established himself, fittingly, as Carlo Pelegrine, a slightly corrupt spelling of the Italian version of his name, and had been reasonably happy until a platonic friendship with a woman threatened to turn into something more. The woman, vibrant and passionate, was the manager of the restaurant, and though he was mildly attracted to her, it was nothing he couldn't control. She, however, pursued him. He tried telling her he was gay, but she didn't believe it, and things got very tense over the next few months.

And so he left, traveling all the way to California, Carlo felt the old nervousness, and on some level he was sure she would chase him and find out his real secret. He ate another slice of orange and shook his head, smiling bitterly to himself: He never could handle stress. When he was a little boy, his mother would tell him not to worry so much. But even then, he knew he was a monster.

His motorcycle—a Harley meant for one was all he'd ever owned —ran out of gas in the Mojave Desert, twenty miles east of Madelyn. It was his own fault for not checking the gauge and he felt foolish as he trudged slowly along, pushing the bike, his clothes plastered to his body beneath the horrible August sun.

When a fancy, double-wheeled pickup truck hauling a horse trailer pulled up beside him, Carlo had no intention of accepting a ride: He was too wary, too nervous. But the man, who introduced himself as Tom Abernathy, had such an unconcerned attitude that Carlo decided accepting a ride to the gas station at Madelyn would be all right.

Tom Abernathy was a talker, and during that short drive, he managed to fascinate Carlo with tales of Old Madelyn. He didn't ask any questions, except if he was planning on staying in California for a while—the motorcycle had Ohio plates—and as they pulled into Ray's Unocal, Tom asked him a second question. He wanted to know if he was looking for work.

Carlo was amazed to hear himself say yes.

After he filled his gas tank, they went over to Ray's Cafe, where Carlo insisted on paying for their pie and coffee; he didn't want Tom Abernathy to think he was a shiftless drifter. Tom told him there was work on his ranch, and Carlo apologized and said he couldn't ride a horse. Tom only laughed and responded that he couldn't ride a motorcycle. Then he announced that he was the general manager of Old Madelyn Historic Park, and that he could also use a gypsy fortune-teller, and that he thought Carlo would make a fine one.

Carlo had been interested in metaphysics for years and he knew something about the occult—in a scholarly way—but he still remembered the shock he felt at that statement, coming from that down-to-earth cowboy. But Abernathy quickly explained that Old Madelyn had recently been sold to New Madelyn because the state couldn't afford to run it. Tom Abernathy owned most of the park, and what he wanted most was to make it into a real western town. He was sinking money into the restoration, but he told Carlo that without the right tenants for some of the businesses, Old Madelyn wouldn't get off the ground.

Carlo asked him why he'd ask a near-perfect stranger to man one of his businesses, and Tom looked him in the eye and said he trusted his instincts. He generally knew a bad horse or a bad man the first time he laid eyes on one. Then he added that Carlo had sort of a sad, mysterious air about him that lent itself to telling fortunes.

Carlo wanted to tell him his instincts were off where he was concerned, but he didn't dare. Tom could see how taken aback by it all he was, and he finally told Carlo, "Let's just say I believe in fate. Fate or God or whatever made you run out of gas on the first day in a month I had to be out that way. You're looking for work, and I need a fortune-teller."

Carlo had kept trying to argue with him, wanting to be certain that Abernathy wanted him—but Abernathy never took the bait. He merely reiterated his stand that maybe it was something meant to be, and finally capped it by telling Carlo to stop worrying: Maybe he owed him a favor from some other time or place. All he knew was that it felt right, and didn't Carlo agree?

Carlo agreed, because it felt right to him, too. Then, when Ray Vine walked up in his cook's whites, Carlo felt a moment of fear. The man had the bearing of a general, or a professor emeritus, maybe both, and a straight-on way of looking at you that had the intensity of a glare. Then Tom asked Ray if he didn't think Carlo would make a heck of a fortune-teller. Ray's stare nearly turned him inside out, and just when he didn't think he could bear the scrutiny any longer, the chef said he'd make a fine one, then welcomed him to Madelyn.

And so he had stayed. For the first few weeks he had accepted Tom Abernathy's hospitality. He was uncomfortable doing so, but he didn't know what might happen next or where his next dollar might come from. As it turned out, Tom kept him busy, putting him in charge of the building's renovation, suggesting he turn the upstairs into his own apartment, as some of the other tenants and owners had. Tom was an extremely generous landlord and insisted that, upstairs and down, Carlo furnish the place with high-quality furniture. Carlo, ever guilty, one night broached the fact that he didn't know how he could ever make enough money to pay Tom back for furnishing the apartment, and Tom merely said it went with the job, and that if the fortune-telling business was a success, Carlo would be able to afford to buy the place eventually.

Carlo, always a loner, was amazed that he found himself spending evenings with Tom and, often, his many friends, one of whom was Moss Baskerville, the chief of police. He was even more surprised that they were becoming his friends too. In this dry desert town, everyone was a little eccentric in his or her own way, and they accepted his own eccentricities without question. He began to feel at home.

THIRTEEN

# MOSS BASKERVILLE

After, they lay stretched out on the bed, the blankets pulled up, the ceiling fan turning lazily above them. Outside, the wind had picked up, whistling down the canyons, scuttling around the eaves of the house, blowing sand and dust. Moss Baskerville silently blessed Cassie for insisting he stay instead of chasing down the idiot drag racer. Now she slowly extricated herself from the crook of his arm and sat up, glancing at the fan. "You mind if I turn it off now?"

"No. Go ahead." He watched the paisley tattoos ripple across her upper arm as she reached up and pulled the fan chain, then the one belonging to the light. In the darkness she snuggled next to him, her head on his shoulder, her arm resting lightly across his broad chest. She made a contented sound that he loved, then asked, "Did you hear that?"

"Hear what?" he asked, almost asleep.

She didn't answer for a moment, then said, "It was probably just Eve getting a drink of water."

Wakefulness returning, Moss tried to listen to the familiar sounds of the house, but the howling wind masked them. Finally there was a lull, and above it, he heard something. He reached up and pulled the light chain. He and Cassie looked at one another.

"Horse," she said.

"Maybe Joe Huxley's finally dragged his sorry ass home." Baskerville climbed from the bed and began pulling on his pants.

"What're you doing?" Cass asked.

"I want a word with that stupid old cuss. See what he's been up to."

Cassie sat up, shaking her head resignedly. "What if it's not Joe?"

"Then I want to know who it is." He slipped his shoes onto his bare feet. "I'll just be a minute," he added, opening the bedroom door. He turned to smile at her. "Keep my place warm."

"You know it, sugar-butt."

He rolled his eyes, said, "I wish you wouldn't call me that," and let himself out of the bedroom, leaving the sound of Cassie's soft laughter behind.

He couldn't hear anything over the wind, but as soon as he lifted the curtain and peered out, he saw the silhouette of a horse and rider coming up the driveway. They were pale ghosts in the night, and though the man was slightly hunched against the wind, Baskerville recognized the light-colored duster and dark Stetson immediately.

"Cassie," he called, flipping on the porch light. "It's Tom Abernathy."

"Tom?" He could hear her moving around in the bedroom. "What in the world is he doing out this time of night?"

"Don't know." Baskerville opened the door as Abernathy swung down off Belle and led her up under the porch overhang by the steps, out of the wind.

Abernathy stepped onto the porch, pulling his bandana down from his face, then tilting his hat brim back. His normally expressionless face had a grim set to it. "Moss, glad you're awake."

"What's up?" Baskerville asked as Cassie came up beside him.

"Tom, come inside." She tugged Baskerville's arm and they stepped back.

"Thanks." Abernathy stepped inside, removed his hat, and ran his fingers through his brown hair.

The rancher's cheeks were flushed and his blue eyes were bright, but otherwise, he looked perfectly calm, grimness and all. Baskerville thought that the earth could open up and swallow the whole town, and Abernathy would still behave as if it were nothing but a crack in the sidewalk. He was a tough man to ruffle.

"What's wrong, Tom?" Baskerville asked.

"There's been an accident up on Thunder Road."

Baskerville and Cassie exchanged glances.

"It's a bad one," Tom said. "Fatal."

"Who?" Baskerville took his brown leather jacket from the coatrack.

"Don't know. Car and driver both burned. There's not much left. Maybe some kind of muscle car. GTO maybe, couldn't see much."

Baskerville slipped the jacket on and pulled his keys from the pocket. "Any idea how long ago it happened?"

"Not long."

"Cass, I'll be back later. You lock this place up tight, you hear?"

She nodded. "Moss, I'm sorry I stopped you from—"

He squeezed her hand. "No regrets, Cass—my choice."

He turned to Tom. "We heard tires squealing and maybe a crash, a while ago. It was hard to tell over the wind."

"A car came down Old Madelyn a little while ago," Cassie added. "It was creeping along, then took off like a bat out of hell."

"Damned teenagers drag-racing again," Baskerville grunted. "Goddamned teenagers."

"Maybe playing chicken." Tom put his hat back on.

"Maybe," Moss allowed. "No way to tell with the sandstorm, not until we locate the driver of the other vehicle. You want to come along?"

Tom looked slightly uncomfortable. "No, I'd better get Belle out of the storm. She needs a rubdown and I'm dead-dog-tired."

Baskerville nodded at the expected reply. Tom Abernathy wasn't one to get involved. "Just where's the wreck?"

"Dead Man's Hill."

"Fitting." In the old days, it had served as a hole-up for bank robbers and other miscreants.

"Some damn dumb teenagers," Cassie said softly.

"Yeah." Baskerville liked his job except for informing folks of deaths—and the worst was telling parents a child had died.

"Tom," he said as the cowboy put his hand on the doorknob. "You didn't see any suspicious characters or vehicles tonight?"

"No." He looked thoughtful. "I came around through Spirit Canyon from the far side—I was down at the campground earlier. Met a pair of scientist-types camped out up there, just arrived. They can't see the road from where they're at, so I doubt if they can help you much." His voice trailed off thoughtfully.

"Scientists?" Baskerville asked.

"Taking pictures of our UFOs."

Baskerville rolled his eyes. "Of course. What else would they be doing? Bunch of lunatics."

"They seemed normal enough," Tom said.

Moss nodded. Tom was right; they wouldn't be much help. People like that didn't live much in the real world. "I'll look in on them in the morning."

Tom opened the door and Moss quickly gave Cassie another quick kiss. "Remember, lock—"

"The doors," Cassie finished, with a soft smile. "You be careful out there. I'll be keeping your spot warm."

"I'm counting on it," he told her, and went out the door.

# FOURTEEN
## CARLO PELEGRINE

He finished his orange and sat back, lacing his fingers behind his head. Exactly one month after his arrival in Madelyn, Carlo moved into his new apartment, and one week later, as the fall tourist season began, he opened his shop. In the weeks prior, he'd spent a good deal of his time studying palm reading and tarot cards. Previously he'd primarily perused books on reincarnation, spiritualism, witchcraft, and the other philosophies, without delving into parlor games.

When he began his business, he felt guilty about letting others think he was psychic, but that soon faded. This was an occupation that allowed him to do good. He never prophesied, but made positive suggestions and saw to it that those people who came to him always left feeling more hopeful than when they arrived. He tried to inspire when he read the tarot, and he believed that the cards worked in the manner Carl Jung subscribed to: They were a tool to reach the subconscious mind. If one wanted to read negatives into them, so be it. He always read positives, except when he read for himself: Then he would allow negatives if they seemed powerful enough.

Reading palms was something else. Though he tried to inspire, touching another human, even on the hand, was something Carlo had avoided since ... since leaving home. Now, holding others' hands in his, he felt a secret temptation as a continuing test of will.

Within two years of becoming Madland's fortune-teller, he truly knew he was part of a family. Though he was still quiet, never telling anyone much about himself, no one minded. They accepted him, no questions asked. Once, he went so far as to tell Tom that he had a dark past, but Tom never pushed to find out more. He also told this much to Father Mike Corey, who was his friend, not his priest, and told him of his penance and promises to God, leaving out the nature of his sins. The young cleric had seemed impressed but mystified, and invited Carlo to attend his church, but he never did because, during his last confession, nearly a decade ago, he realized beyond doubt that he no longer believed in God.

Eight years had passed since Tom Abernathy rescued him from the highway, and Carlo Pelegrine's days of running and praying had ended. At last, he had found his home.

The sound of a car moving slowly down Main Street interrupted his reverie. This was a rare occurrence. Only vehicles making deliveries and those who lived here were allowed to drive on the streets of Old Madelyn, and then only when the park was closed. Most of the residents kept their cars in a small carport-style lot cordoned off from the visitors' parking, and Carlo kept his Harley in a small outbuilding behind his shop, which was adjacent to the park's rear access road.

He relaxed, realizing that the vehicle was probably a police cruiser. Night watchman Joe Huxley had taken his rounds on foot, but since he'd been missing, Moss or his officer merely cruised the area.

Suddenly the engine revved, and Carlo immediately padded into the darkened store. Lifting the door shade, he barely made out the silhouette of an automobile, its lights off, idling in the swirling dust on the lampless street. Abruptly it sped off.

Flipping on the porch light, he opened the door. Something thudded against his leg. For an instant he didn't recognize what dangled from the knob, then he realized it was some sort of animal. It hung by its neck from a piece of twine tied to the doorknob, and there was something very wrong with it.

Quickly he untied the loose knot around the knob and took the thing inside, holding it well away from his body. He turned off the porch light, then carried it into the small utility room at the very back of the store where no one would notice his lights burning.

It was a jackrabbit and it had been skinned.

Carlo's hand began to shake, and he forced himself to examine the poor creature. The flesh was cut and marked, patches of gray-brown fur still in evidence. It was shoddy, amateurish work.

He put the animal in a black garbage bag, wrapped it tightly, and went out the back door to carry it down the access road to the area where the trash bins were concealed. Around him, the wind howled and blew grit into his eyes, but he didn't turn back because he was afraid that if he kept it, he might stare at it the rest of the night. He reached the bin and dropped it in, covered it with food wrappers and a wad of junk mail.

Back in his shop, he locked the doors, then went upstairs to bed. Intellectually he knew this incident had nothing to do with him and that he should report it to Chief Moss Baskerville. Most likely it was related to the vandalism at Cassie's that Tom had mentioned this afternoon.

Still, that night he dreamed of beautiful women, of their soft, smooth skin. It was a dream that hadn't plagued him in eight years.

# PART TWO

# SIGNS AND PORTENTS

And I saw a star fall from heaven ...
  —Revelation 9:1

This is an age-old and worldwide myth that has shaped our belief
structures, our scientific expectations, and our view of ourselves.
  —Jacques Vallee, *Dimensions*

... What are these which are arrayed in white robes? and whence
came they?
  —Revelation 7:13

Could it be that someone, or something, is playing a fantastic trick
on us?
  —Jacques Vallee, *Dimensions*

# FIFTEEN
# MADGE MARQUAY
## WEDNESDAY

Sometime during the long, long night, hours ago now, she thought, something heavy had been pushed into the mine shaft from above. Madge felt the wind of it pass her as she worked on her ropes, and then caught the stink, the overwhelming, sickening putrid stink, as it fell on the thing—*the corpse, Madge, you know that*—that she had run into earlier. There was an awful, squishing sound and she knew the first body must have broken open because she had nearly passed out from the smell.

Madge didn't want to know what the thing was that her captor had thrown down, all she wanted was to break the ropes around her wrists. She had no idea how many hours she'd been working, only that it was a long time, and her thirst had become a physical pain. Several times she fell into a sleep that was more like unconsciousness, and each time she'd come out of it, she'd again set doggedly to work at the ropes.

She continued rubbing the bindings back and forth over the sharp rock outcropping and suddenly gasped as they loosened slightly. Elated, she went to work with renewed vigor, yanking down with all her might. Abruptly the rope snapped. She fell backwards and lay there a long moment, unable to believe she was free. Laughter bubbled up around the gag and she reached up and pulled the filthy cloth from her mouth, barely noticing the pain in her infected arm. Next she pulled the blindfold off her eyes, but as she suspected, it made no difference: Down here in the depths below the mine ride, the old shafts were as dark as tombs.

She went to work on her feet, tugging and working the tight knots. Her arm sang with pain now, and she paused to carefully examine it with her hand, appalled that the tight, hot flesh was twice the circumference of that of her good arm. Still, she told herself, she would be out of here soon. If there was no ladder to climb, she knew that morning would come and the ride would open. When it did, she'd scream for help. Her arm would be fine. *She* would be fine.

Finally she was free. She rose, feet numb and tingling, her ankles wobbling, knees threatening to give. Holding to the rock wall for balance, she walked in place, gently stamping her feet until the blood began to circulate and the numbness receded. "Oh Lord," she whispered, "thank You." She coughed and spat, and her saliva was like a wad of cotton, but nothing would stop her now. *Nothing!* She bent and found a piece of rope and hung it over the sharp outcropping to serve as a marker.

Determinedly she began feeling the walls, hoping to find a ladder of some sort. The pit was small, vaguely circular, and after only a few feet, her toes pressed into the rotting body, stirring up another putrid flurry. Holding her breath, cautiously feeling the corpse's width with her toes, she gingerly stepped over it, her mind screaming at her that the dead thing was going to reach up and grab her ankle or knee. *That's nothing but childish fantasy, you fool!* One foot came down on the other side of the corpse, then she brought the other one quickly across before allowing herself to lean her hot face against the cool rock wall. After a moment, she took another step, then two, more confident now. Her right foot caught on something and she tripped, falling hard on her knees and hands. The pain in her left arm made her dizzy. Blindly she felt for the wall, and her hand closed on something. At first she thought it was a thick stick or an old hunk of shoring timber, then realized it was an animal's leg. With a gasp, she pulled away.

Another moment and she was back on her feet, beginning to move along the wall again, slowly and carefully, shuffling her feet through the dust. She guessed she'd traveled three quarters of the way around the room now. Hope of finding a ladder fading, she inched along, hugging the wall until she found the outcropping with the piece of rope. She was stuck down here until Hank opened up for the day. Unless her captor returned. Refusing to entertain the thought, she eased herself into a sitting position to wait for morning.

SIXTEEN

# JUSTIN MARTIN

"Justin, honey, wake up."

*Fuck you.* Justin turned over and pulled his pillow over his head, but his mother kept calling him in that irritating June Cleaver voice, and rapping on the door like a sick woodpecker.

"Justin? Are you awake?"

At that he pulled the pillow from his eyes and grabbed the alarm clock, squinting at it in the gray dim morning light. Five-fucking-thirty. The alarm wouldn't go off for another hour and a half.

"Juss-tinn!" She tried his doorknob and the sound brought him bolt upright, furious. *How dare you, you dried-up old cunt!* "Justin? Honey? Your door's locked. Are you all right in there?"

*Jesus fucking Christ!* "I'm fine," he called in an almost civilized voice. "What do you want?" *You fucking prune!*

"There's a phone call for you. It's Mr. Marquay."

"Got it," he called, reaching for the extension by his bed. He waited until her footsteps receded, then picked up the receiver. "Got it, Mom," he said sweetly, then waited until she hung up. "Mr. Marquay?" he asked. "Is something wrong?"

Marquay's voice was rougher and sadder than usual. Justin knew he was really missing his cuntsickle wife, but something else was bugging him now. "Justin, I'm sorry to call so early, but I needed to catch you before you left for school."

"That's okay, Mr. Marquay. What do you need?"

"I woke up sick as a dog this morning, son."

"I'm sorry. What do you need me to do?"

"Well, I don't think I'm going to get out of bed any time soon, except to run to the bathroom." Marquay cleared his throat, and nearly retched in the process. "I've been up with the trots all night long. I guess I've got the stomach flu."

*Chef Boy-ar-dee had a heat stroke and puked in your stomach, Hank old boy. Like it?* "I'm sorry, Mr. Marquay," Justin said solemnly.

"Can you work this afternoon?"

"Sure. Do you want me to open the ride as soon as I get off school? I can be there by two."

"Justin, you're a godsend. If I get to feeling better, I'll be around. If not, I know I can trust you to run the place."

"You sure can, sir. Is there anything else?"

"Yes. Would you stop by on your way to school and put a sign out saying the ride will open at two?"

"No problem, Mr. Marquay."

Justin hung up and lay back in bed, stretching the sleep from his muscles. Finally he sat up and rubbed his eyes. Today was going to be a *very* good day. Assuming Spelman and his wreck had been found by now, he'd spend the morning consoling poor, bereaved Christie Fox. If not, he'd be self-effacing and charming when she thanked him for acing her homework. He couldn't lose. And today was a half day at school. He'd be off at eleven-thirty, which would give him lots of time alone in the mine before he had to open the ride.

# SEVENTEEN

# FATHER MICHAEL COREY

At dawn, Father Michael Corey entered his small church on the southwestern edge of Old Madelyn. Head bowed, he walked down the center aisle saying his prayers.

As always, he loved the atmosphere of the small mission-style Catholic church. Much of it was still made of the original adobe bricks from the mid eighteen hundreds, and the parts that had crumbled due to age or earthquakes had been lovingly restored by the parishioners over the last few years.

He walked slowly, giving thanks, drinking in the atmosphere of the place. It was a chapel haunted by the past, but haunted in a wonderful way. Always cool, even on the most scorching August day, the little church had an atmosphere charged with serenity. The thick walls held the remnants of the prayers and good wishes of a century of worshipers, and Michael felt privileged to be caretaker of this place. It was a parish no one had wanted, and he'd built it from nothing but a derelict building to a small but thriving part of the Madelyns, Old and New. Even vacationers came to the church, and he hoped they found more than just novelty within the walls. He thought they did, because he doubted that anyone could be untouched by the serene atmosphere of the place.

Three small stained-glass windows cast beautiful muted colors on the polished oak floor as he approached the altar steps. Still keeping his eyes on the ground, his hands clasped, he crossed to the center of the chancel and knelt as he finished his prayer. As he crossed himself, he looked up at his greatest joy: a hand-carved life-size Mexican crucifix.

The sorrowful, exquisite face of Jesus was coated with dried blood. Michael stood, gasping, then staggered back a step, seeing the damage done to the entire chancel. The cross hung slightly forward, as if someone had tried to pull it from the wall, and the blood had run from the head down the tortured body to the toes, and then dripped to the floor before it had dried.

In blood, the number of the Beast, 666, was written on the wall above the wooden cross.

Shocked, he stared around the chapel. In the right corner near the chancel, the pricket was overturned and the votive candles lay in waxy puddles and broken glass from their holders. He was suddenly glad the parish couldn't afford carpet, or there might be nothing left.

The statue of Mary nearby had been doused with blood, then shattered. Michael crossed himself again, sick at heart, and to his stomach. The parishioners would be arriving soon.

Quickly he ran back up the aisle and out of the church. He pulled the doors closed and locked them, something he had done only once before, after a group of cultists had left a dead chicken on the altar. It was horrible, but not like this.

Michael crossed the breezeway to his small house, went in, and called the police department. Moss Baskerville was there already, and he promised to be right out. Relieved, Father Corey went outside to send his few parishioners home.

# EIGHTEEN

# HANNIBAL CAINE

"Maybe we should discuss the plans with James Robert," Eldo Blandings said as he buttered an English muffin. "After all ..."

Hannibal Caine motioned their server to leave the room and waited while she pulled the door to the compound's private dining room closed behind her. As soon as she was gone, he looked across the table into Eldo's long, sour face and zealous eyes, and wondered, not for the first time, if it had been wise to take this man into his confidence, if only marginally. Eldo Blandings was, after all, his only ranking equal as the other Elder Apostle; only Jim-Bob Sinclair held higher rank in the Church of the Prophet's Apostles.

Eldo had seemed all right when Caine began discussing certain of his ideas with him several years ago, but recently he had discovered that Blandings, perhaps in his excitement over the predicted Apocalypse, had begun to lose his grip on reality. At first he seemed eager to "help out" Jim-Bob, who wasn't, Caine told him, able to keep a tight enough rein on things these days unless Caine and Blandings subtly provided him with more help. But now that Hannibal had put together the Special Projects Committee and made Eldo its general, the old war bird was showing his true colors, all of which were shades of yellow.

"Eldo," Caine began brusquely, "what if the world doesn't end Sunday? What if Sinclair is wrong?"

Eldo's jaw dropped. "I don't think you need to worry about—"

"What if the world doesn't end with the eclipse?" he interrupted. Caine couldn't understand how any thinking man could possibly have such blind faith in a prophecy, but all the Apostles seemed to, except for himself and, he was certain, Jim-Bob Sinclair. He didn't know what old Jimmy had in store for the Armageddon, but he suspected it had more to do with taking the money and leaving the country than with helping the masses get to heaven. He did know that if anything happened to the Prophet, the ministry was his, and that almost assuredly meant that from Jim-Bob's Apocalypse on, he'd be in charge.

Still, as the prophesied year approached and the Prophet failed to take him into his confidence about his plans, Hannibal Caine began taking precautions, just in case Jim-Bob dissolved the church and left him high and dry.

He had done his creative accounting slowly, carefully, and now he had a sizable nest egg. There was also the safe in Sinclair's office to which only Sinclair, Eldo and he were privy. And if Sinclair tried to bilk him out of his rightful place before he left, Caine had decided to force Sinclair to share, and share generously, by the use of a little judicious blackmail.

Eldo Blandings crossed his arms and tilted his head back, showing the hairs growing out of his oversized hawkish nose. They were the same steel gray color as the terrible toupee he insisted on wearing. "If you don't believe the Prophet's words, why do you serve him?"

A logical question from an annoying man. Hannibal Caine smiled smoothly and replied the only way he could. "Of course I believe in him, Eldo, but sometimes I lack the strength of conviction you're blessed with." *Schmuck.*

Eldo's sour face split in a grin that made him even uglier, and he patted Caine on the back. "You're a good man, Hannibal. Don't let the devil into your mind and you'll be fine. Just have faith."

"Thank you, Eldo." He nearly choked on the words. Why had he ever thought he could trust this man to lead his missions? If he didn't handle things perfectly, any minute now Eldo Blandings might run to Jim-Bob and tell him about the "good deeds" he and Hannibal had instigated so far: the goat, the mailbox, Corey's precious church.

"Eldo," he began, "we made our little band of helpers swear on their lives that they would never speak of their involvement in our activities. It's for their own good—and ours. Our selfless acts are the kind that could get us in trouble with the law. Not everyone understands the importance of what we've been charged to do. How would it look if the Prophet was privy to our activities? That's why he has asked me to oversee our committee without his involvement."

"But—"

"We are his disciples, Eldo, and we do as he wishes. The Prophet cannot lie; therefore, he cannot know until the day of the eclipse, on the very day the Horsemen ride to glory." Caine stared at Eldo from under his brow. "Telling him now would be against his direct wishes."

Eldo Blandings scratched his chin, obviously unable to separate the nonsense from the truth, especially since there was nothing to separate. "Do you really think so?" he asked finally.

"I *know* so, Eldo." Prior to joining Jim-Bob's church, baby-faced Hannibal Caine had been a used-Cadillac salesman, and he turned on his talents now. "In fact, Eldo," he added with the greatest sincerity, "I guarantee it."

"All right." Blandings hesitated a long moment. "But do we really have the Prophet's blessing for *all* our actions?"

"Absolutely." Caine smiled angelically. Sinclair knew nothing of the Special Projects Committee's true workings and he trusted Hannibal completely. His foolishness would leave him at fault for all the problems. Caine pushed his plate aside. "Eldo, Eldo, Eldo. The

Prophet Sinclair is a very busy man. He's on the radio every day, he leads church services and counsels our members. He's our missionary, the symbol of our faith, and that keeps him too busy to attend to minor details. Look how often he goes into town to spread the word and how regularly he organizes missionary crusades all over Southern California. He is a man of *words*, Eldo. That's his strength. And that's why he chose us to be his Elder Apostles—he needs men of *action* to help him. And you *are* here to help our Prophet, aren't you?"

"Of course!" Eldo cried, and Hannibal Caine felt like he'd just sold him a twenty-year-old pink Caddy with fringe balls and a matching fur-covered steering wheel.

"To my knowledge," Blandings began, abruptly shifting gears, "Chief Baskerville never came out here after the goat was killed. Have you heard any different?" He finished his muffin and began stirring spoon after spoon of sugar into his coffee.

Caine tried not to watch that ritual. "Baskerville hasn't visited." Mel Campbell, one of the people he had handpicked for their Special Projects Committee, had been assigned to keep watch from a distance while the goat was taken and killed. He stayed long after the stoning—out of duty, he said, but Caine knew he'd most likely taken an afternoon siesta. He later reported to him that the animal had been spirited away by Justin Martin, a young man who had been coming to their church meetings lately. Hannibal found this fascinating, but told Campbell to keep his mouth shut about it because he wanted to discuss the matter with Justin personally. The boy, perhaps, had promise.

A sleazy smile creased Eldo's forlorn face. It wasn't a pretty sight, but at least the droopy-eyed coot was getting back into the spirit of the thing. "Baskerville will probably come around asking questions after what we did to the church."

"Eldo, I'm certain he will. The Prophet Sinclair has never made it a secret that he feels the other religions, especially Catholicism, teach heresy. But he'll also justly deny any involvement. All we have to do, if Baskerville makes a pest of himself, is point him in the direction of that little cult that's taken up residence on the other side of the free-way." The cult was nothing more than a bunch of mixed-up idiots running around in black robes baying at the moon. They fancied themselves a witches' coven.

Eldo nodded, a gleam in his eye. "So what's next?"

Though the man had that damnable blind faith in Sinclair, he also had a sadistic streak he could barely keep under control. *That's why I wanted him.* It was Eldo Blandings who had conceived of stoning the goat instead of merely slitting its throat to put it quickly out of its misery. And Blandings was also the one who thought of pouring animal blood all over the crucifix in the Catholic church, instead of merely writing "666" in red paint across the wall. Eldo, Caine reminded himself, had his uses. That's why he had included him in the first place.

Caine sipped his orange juice, then patted his lips with his napkin. "We'll let things cool off for a day or so." He smiled and rose from the table. "Then we'll escalate events." Seeing the psychotic glint in Eldo's eye, he put his hands on the table and leaned down to the man's ear. "We're in the last days of the world, my friend, and we need to save as many sinners as we can, don't we?"

"It's our duty as Apostles." Eldo's eyes flamed with zeal.

"Desperate times, desperate measures," Caine told him. "We're going to pay a visit to the Whore of Babylon herself. The devil's bride."

"Six-six-six." Eldo laughed. It was a thin, papery sound, like dried flesh blowing off bones.

# NINETEEN

# JUSTIN MARTIN

J ustin parked his car near the Haunted Mine Ride at the far end of the lot just as his watch beeped seven o'clock. After the phone call from Hank Marquay, he'd hurried from the house, his mother nagging about his not eating breakfast until he was in his car and out the driveway. He was really getting tired of the old bitch.

Unlocking a back gate, he trotted into the park. The mine ride was built into the upper reaches of the old Moonstone Mine, so it was slightly removed from Madland proper, in the northwest corner of the park.

Justin passed Boot Hill, the nineteenth-century cemetery that Hank Marquay and some of the other old farts claimed contained the bones of their ancestors under piles of colorful rocks, rusted black iron crosses, and a scattering of restored wooden crosses and headstones.

He slowed as he came to Our Lady of Miracles, the little adobe church. Baskerville's cruiser was parked out front and the wimpy young priest was talking to the chief in the shadowy doorway. Justin glanced at his watch: His first class was in twenty minutes, and he had a final he couldn't miss. Still, he wondered what was going on.

He waved at the priest, Corey nodded, and Baskerville turned to look. Justin took the opportunity to veer from his path.

"Hi, Father," he said breathlessly. "Is everything all right?"

Before Corey could answer, the police chief spoke in a low, grouchy voice. "You're the Martin boy?"

"Yes, sir."

"So what are you doing here this time of day?"

Justin smiled winningly. "Mr. Marquay doesn't feel well, so he asked me to stop on my way to school and put a note on the mine ride saying we're opening late today." He pulled the folded note from his shirt pocket.

"He's ill?" Corey asked quickly.

"Just a little stomach flu, Father."

"How's he holding up since Mrs. Marquay's disappearance?" the priest asked, while that old bear Baskerville stared at Justin with that squinty look cops always had, but Justin pretended he didn't notice.

"He's not very happy, Father. He doesn't talk about it much, he just works a lot. Maybe that's why he got sick."

"I'll stop in to see him," Corey said, "after we're done here."

"I'm sure he'd like that." Justin tried to see into the darkened church. "What happened?"

"Vandals," Baskerville said in a dismissive voice. "Aren't you going to be late for school?"

*What do you care, you old shithead?* "Yes, thanks, Chief Baskerville. I'd better run!"

With that he trotted toward the winding dirt path leading to the mine ride.

It was set into the side of a hill and was easily the largest, most impressive amusement at the park. Everything was quiet, the fake mining cars the passengers rode in parked neatly on the entry track. The Marquays were big Disney fans, and instead of sticking with authenticity, they'd constructed a goofy facade depicting caverns filled with colorful stalactites and stalagmites, and phosphorescent eyes peering out from the darkness behind them. The entry doors had a couple tacky dwarfs with pickaxes painted on them. Justin, seeing that nothing was disturbed, let himself in the little ticket office and posted the sign saying they'd open at two. He checked his watch again as he locked up, then ran for his car, relieved that he'd be back early to check on things inside.

## TWENTY

# MOSS BASKERVILLE

M oss Baskerville watched the Martin boy as he tore off toward the parking lot. "It's good to see some kids have a sense of responsibility."

Michael Corey nodded. "Hank says he's a fine young man, that he's been a godsend since Madge has been gone."

They walked back into the church and Baskerville saw the little priest flinch, then look away from the sight of the bloodied crucifix, and felt sorry for the young man. "I'll dust for prints, but it won't do much good unless your vandals were fool enough not to wear gloves. Keep everybody out until Doc Hartman gets here to test the blood. Once we know what kind it is, we'll have something to go on."

"Do you think it's human?" The priest's voice quavered slightly.

"Frankly, no. Probably animal. I'm guessing sheep. Or goat."

Corey studied him. "I heard a rumor yesterday about one of Cassie's goats?"

Baskerville shook his head. Cassie had tried to hide how upset she was about it, but he knew she was very angry and very sad. "It's a damn shame people do what they do. Tom found it, stoned to death, up by the fort. Between the time he called me and I got out there, which was less than an hour, somebody hightailed off with it."

"The same person who did this?" Corey gestured toward the altar.

"Pure conjecture, you understand, but it might be. All you'd have to do is drain the animal, add a little detergent to keep it from clotting, then bring it on in here." Baskerville walked up front and opened his fingerprinting kit. First the goat, then the wreck up on Thunder Road, now this. And worse, as soon as Doc Hartman made a positive identification on the body, the chief was sure he'd be paying the kind of call he hated most on some teenager's parents. The windstorm last night hadn't left any evidence of another car at the scene, but the one that crashed had to have been barreling along to smash the way it did. Plus there was a broken liquor bottle and beer cans in the car.

"Moss."

Baskerville glanced up.

"Do you think this is related to the disappearances?"

"I wish I knew, Mike." Personally, he doubted it, but he wasn't going to close any avenue at this point. "I wish I knew."

The phone in the church office rang, and the priest excused himself to answer it. A moment later, he was back. "It's for you."

In the tiny office, Baskerville picked up the old-fashioned black receiver. "Baskerville. That you, Shirl?"

"It's me, Chief." Shirley Raymond, his dispatcher and secretary, did everything but make coffee, which seemed reasonable since she didn't drink the stuff, and if she ever left, Moss Baskerville was pretty sure the police department would fall apart.

"What's up?"

"I just got a call from Joyce Spelman, over on Cholla Street. Seems her son Rick didn't come home last night."

Baskerville's stomach did a quick twist. Rick Spelman, Madelyn High's star quarterback, was an honor student who wanted to be a cop. He'd gone on a ride- along once during the summer, and Baskerville thought he was a good kid. "Vehicle make?"

"Ninety-six Chevy GTO," Shirley said flatly.

"Damn." He was virtually certain the victim was Spelman. "Tell the doc to check the mouth against Rick Spelman's dental records and get back to me, pronto."

"You got it, Chief." Shirley paused. "And, boss?"

"Yes?"

"Turn on your radio."

He was fine with the car radio, but he'd never gotten in the habit of using the clip-on. Shirley called him a technophobe, quite rightly, he supposed. "Sorry, Shirl. I'll clip it on right now."

As he reentered the chapel, he was embarrassed to see Mike Corey on his. knees, praying. Baskerville cleared his throat softly and Corey quickly made the sign of the cross, then rose and turned to Baskerville, his eyes questioning.

Baskerville briefly told him about the wreck on Thunder Road without mentioning his suspicions as to the victim's identity. Then he suggested that Corey do whatever priests do on weekdays, so that he could be alone with his camera, fingerprinting kit, and his thoughts.

## TWENTY-ONE
# MADGE MARQUAY

"Dear Lord, help me," Madge Marquay whispered through parched lips. She had examined the walls of her lightless prison over and over, stumbling over at least one of the corpses, forcing herself to continue to search for a ladder or a rope or even a handhold, but she had found nothing.

Her perception of time had to be impaired. She had expected the mine ride to open long ago, but she still hadn't heard a thing. It was frightening to think that what felt like days might only be hours.

Now she sat on the floor, legs bent close to her chest, arms encircling them. The rough wall poked and bruised her back, but that was all right because it helped her stay awake. Clutched in her right hand was the only weapon she could find—a foot-long rotting stick of wood. Her wounded arm, hot and tight, throbbed in rhythm with her heart, and the pain, once only below the elbow, had traveled into her shoulder now.

*Hank, where are you? Why won't you come?* A tear rolled down her cheek and she licked it away, grateful for the moisture.

When the trains were running, she remained alert, aware of time passing, seconds, minutes, hours, but for some time she had been fading. Sometimes it was nice. She had relived her first date with Hank, remembered how shy and sweet he had been when he'd asked her to the senior prom in Barstow. She had even relived her first merry-go-round ride—she must have been six or seven years old. It was at the old Pike in Long Beach, a seaside amusement park torn down in the seventies. Her father lifted her onto the magnificent white horse and buckled her in, then stood beside her during the ride, his hand on the small of her back, making her feel safe. After, he bought cherry snow-cones and they sat on a bench, sucking the sweet red syrup and crunching the perfectly ground ice as the huge mechanical fat lady sat on top of the fun house and laughed and laughed and laughed.

Above, she heard the hiss of air as pneumatic machinery came to life. Hank was here at last, testing the doors, the cars, before opening for the day.

"Hank!" she cried as loud as she could, but the word left her dry throat as a bare croak. "Hank!" she cried again, with better results. "Hank, help me! I'm down here!"

There was a moment of silence, then she heard the pneumatic lift traveling down to the levels below the mine ride. He was coming! She was about to be saved! "Hank!"

The lift hissed off, then she had to wait through another agonizing moment of silence. "Hank?"

She couldn't see the face behind the glowing lantern above her. She stared up into it, waiting to see Hank's face, waiting to be rescued: "Thank God you're here, Hank."

"I'm not Hank," came a voice she almost recognized.

She slowly got to her feet, holding her paltry weapon. "Where's Hank?"

"He's home sick today. Mrs. Marquay, are you all right? What are you doing in here?"

Suddenly she recognized the voice—one of her students, Justin Martin, who worked for Hank part-time. Relief swept over her.

"Thank God you're here, Justin! Thank God! Please get me out of here."

"Hang on, Mrs. Marquay," he called. A moment later she heard the slap of ropes against the wall as he threw down a corded ladder. "I'm coming down for you, Mrs. Marquay. Stay right where you are." The light clicked off.

"Be careful, Justin. There are dead things down here. It's horrible!" She knew she was babbling, but couldn't stop. "Someone hit me over the head and when I woke up I was down here. He did things to me, Justin, he hurt my arm. I think it's infected."

"Don't worry, Mrs. Marquay." She heard his feet hit the ground, and now his voice was practically in her ear. "Everything's going to be fine."

"Get me out of here, please, Justin."

"Just a second; let me turn my lantern back on."

"Please, you don't want to see what's down here. I don't want to see." But as she finished speaking, she heard a click and the lantern came to life.

She tried to look only at Justin's handsome young face, but she couldn't do it. She had to look. The room was a mining pit, as she expected, maybe ten feet around. Holding her breath, she let her gaze drop to the floor.

"Dear God," she whispered. "Oh dear God."

First she saw a large white animal, its legs sticking stiffly out at broken angles. Then she forced herself to look at the two human corpses. They were nude, a man and a woman. She recognized the woman instantly—Kyla Powers, her green eyes clouded, her mouth slackly open. Her bloated body lay on its back, and some of the skin was gone—a big circle of it starting just below the breasts and ending just above the pubic area. White flesh remained in a ragged patch around the navel. All around, the red muscles looked dry and shiny. One thigh had been partially stripped as well. Madge glanced at her own arm and knew she had suffered little compared to Kyla.

The man was so decomposed that she wasn't even positive it was

Joe Huxley. The skin had been stripped from his face, giving him a mummy-like appearance. There was an open wound on his distended stomach that looked like a footprint, and intestines oozed out, coiling snakelike on the ground beside him. She looked away, sickened in the knowledge that she had stepped on—*in*—him. She looked up at Justin quickly, knowing that if she didn't, what she saw on her shoes might make her faint. "Please, let's go."

He raised his hands and beckoned her to him. Vaguely she wondered why he was wearing latex gloves, but it didn't matter: All that mattered was that she was being rescued at long last.

# TWENTY-TWO

# JUSTIN MARTIN

*What to do, what to do, what to do!* Justin put his arms around Madge Marquay, turned her towards him, and pulled her close in a comforting hug. He stared down at her matted, dirty hair. *You old battle-ax, how dare you fuck with me!*

He'd taken his time getting here, stopping to flirt with Christie, who was annoyed because her boyfriend, Rick Spelman, hadn't come to school and they were supposed to go on a picnic or some stupid-ass thing like that after class. Justin had been really tempted to ask her out then and there—she would have gone for it—but something told him not to, and Christ, was he glad he'd listened to his instincts.

Instead, he'd arrived at the mine ride at half past twelve, and as soon as he'd let himself in, he'd heard Old Lady Marquay yelling her head off.

Now here he was, patting the old cunt on the back like a knight in fucking armor. None of his victims knew his identity—well, Joe Huxley did, because he had a hard skull and came to while Justin was finishing tying him up, so he'd killed him quickly by taping his nose and mouth shut. It was one of his favorite ways to kill: quick and quiet. He'd first used the method on Old Lady Quigley's yappy cocker spaniel when he was in first grade, and he'd taken out a number of other annoying pets the same way. Dogs were so stupid and trusting, and they flopped around really fine while they were being suffocated. So had Joe Huxley, for that matter.

He'd played with Huxley's fat, flabby body a little, mostly with the face, trying his hand at skin removal. But he didn't do much, because touching a dead body was revolting. Before long, even in the chilly mine shaft, Huxley started stinking, and the last time Justin tried removing a little flesh from the corpse, he'd vomited. The skin had sort of separated from the rest of the body and it slid around against the fat and muscle easily. It also tore easily, and the pus and slime was what made him sick. The instant it touched him—not on his hands because he always wore surgical gloves, but on his face when it squirted out in a big surprise—he'd lost his dinner, lunch, and breakfast.

Months went by and Justin occasionally shined a light down on the body to check out its decomposition, but he did nothing else while he waited to see if the smell would reach the mine ride. To his joy, it never did. Only when you approached the pit levels beneath the ride did it become noticeable in the cold, still air.

About ten days ago, he took his second victim, Kyla Powers. She'd been easy to take and fun to play with. God, those big green eyes when she came to and found herself tied up. She didn't know who he was—he wore a ski mask whenever he came into the pit—and she was so scared, she shit herself when he cut her clothes off her body. It was a kick. She didn't look bad for an older chick, and he'd briefly considered fucking her, but found he was far more

excited by the thought of cutting her, so he stuck with that. He'd taken too much too quickly, and she was comatose in three days and dead in four. *What a bitch.*

He hadn't planned on taking Marquay. She was his history teacher, which was a little close to the old nest, but he didn't like her and the opportunity presented itself.

He got her into the pit, tied her up, and couldn't make himself remove her clothing—she was just really, well, *old*. The thought was disgusting. So he had contented himself with taking an envelope-sized piece of skin from her forearm. He'd been planning on taking another today. He was trying to teach himself how to slide the knife beneath the flesh to separate it from the connective tissue without marring the skin being removed. He just didn't seem to have the talent for skinning.

*The Peeler will teach me.* He smiled, still rocking Old Lady Marquay in his arms. But he had to be good enough for the Peeler to even *want* to teach him. *What to do, what to do, what to do!*

Playing the hero might be hazardous to his health. What if someone remembered seeing him with any of the victims before their disappearances? He could conk Marquay on the head, tie her up again, and practice on her other arm. *But she knows who you are, Justin. Don't be stupid, and don't be greedy. Most of all, don't be impatient. There are lots more fish in the sea.*

In one swift movement, Justin turned Madge Marquay around, yanked her head back under his arm, then grabbed her jaw and twisted with all his might. After an instant, there was a cracking sound and she went limp, her eyes bugging in surprise. *Just like in the movies!* Grinning, Justin let her fall to the floor.

Picking up his lantern, he surveyed the inhabitants of the pit. *What to do, what to do, what to do!* He'd planned on skinning the goat and leaving it on the Peeler's doorstep tonight, but it seemed sort of anticlimactic now. And he'd forgotten to bring his old clothes along so he wouldn't get goat stink, death stink, or body goop on his good jeans and shirt.

He squatted, examining Madge Marquay's body. If he wasn't going to bother with the goat, he had plenty of time to practice on her other arm. Disgust knotted briefly in his belly, then dissipated—she was still warm, possibly still alive. As good old Mom always said, *waste not, want not.*

## TWENTY-THREE
# ALEXANDRA MANDERLEY

It was lunchtime when Alex finally left camp. This morning she and Eric had shared an outdoor breakfast of overdone eggs and burnt toast, then packed up and gone in search of a better campsite. It hadn't taken long to locate a spot on a jeep trail not too far from the main road that afforded them a northwestern view of the Madelyn Mountains and a southeastern one of the park and town and even the interstate. All around lay the high desert, starkly beautiful with patches of brilliant spring wildflowers daubing color against the tans and browns and reds of the desert floor. South of Madelyn, the San Bernardino Mountains rose in a distant blue haze.

After several fumbled attempts to help Eric set up their tents, he had told her that he was a former Eagle Scout and then insisted she go exploring while he set up camp. Setting up would take him most of the day. The easy part was the camp itself. After that, they had mountains of equipment to mount, set, and calibrate. It was just the sort of exacting work Eric loved and Alex despised, so she gladly left the camp in her assistant's capable hands.

She headed out of the canyon, onto Thunder Road, her mission being to check out the town and pick up some supplies. At the huge stand of rocks just before the turnoff for Old Madelyn Highway, a tow truck was hitching up a burned-out wreck of a car—the crash they heard last night. She shivered despite the warm sunshine. No one could have survived it.

She turned south at the intersection and headed toward town. Old Madelyn looked inviting in the daylight, and on a whim she decided to find some lunch in the park rather than in town. She pulled into the parking lot just below the park and started walking toward the entrance.

"Howdy, ma'am."

Recognizing Tom Abernathy's voice, she turned just in time to see him dismount his silver horse. He patted Belle's muzzle, then led the animal up to her. The mare snuffled Alex's hair, and she stroked the velvety muzzle. "She's beautiful."

He smiled. "She knows it, too. Spoiled rotten, aren'tcha, Belle?"

The horse nudged his shoulder, then lowered her head and pushed at his denim jacket. Tom pulled half a carrot out of a pocket and fed it to her. "See what I mean? So did you find a better campsite this morning?"

"Yes." She told him where it was, then asked about the car she'd seen being towed.

Tom's smile faded. "That's what we heard last night. It was a high school kid, crashed into Dead Man's Hill. Chief Baskerville says he'd probably been drinking."

"A shame," Alex said.

"It is. Happens, though. You might want to be careful if you drive that road at night, especially when school's out. Kids race, play chicken, all sorts of horsesh—'Scuse me, all sorts of shenanigans. Watch yourselves up at the camp, too." He told her about the goat and the Church of the Prophet's Apostles. "It might interest you to know," he added, rubbing his chin, "that they're pretty rabid about the UFOs."

"They are?" Alex asked.

"Thought that would make your eyes light up." One corner of

Tom's mouth crooked up in amusement. "Jim-Bob Sinclair comes on the radio every night, and lately he's been preaching about 'heavenly visitations' in the last days of earth. He claims the UFOs are angels giving the faithless —that includes everyone but card-carrying Apostles—one last chance to see the light and repent. He also claims that the Four Horsemen of the Apocalypse will ride on Armageddon, but that before they do, a great army will smite down the heretics."

Alex chuckled. "I see."

The cowboy's look of amusement disappeared. "The thing is, they think the world is ending this Sunday, and we're the tiniest bit concerned that the Apostles might come marching down the road looking for a few heretics to smite."

"Are you telling me I should be careful?"

"I guess I am," he said slowly. "Those people are straight down the road from you and you're pretty isolated. You know how fanatics can get."

"We'll keep our eyes open," Alex promised.

Tom scuffed one boot in the dust. "On the other hand," he added after a long pause, "they could be harmless. We had some vandalism in the Catholic church this morning, and that might mean it's one of those satanist groups behind things."

"Did they hold a black mass?"

He chuckled. "Well, I don't know, though I'd guess not. We had trouble with one of those self-styled devil cults before, but all they did was leave dead chickens on the altar. This time, I'm told, they poured blood all over the Jesus- on-a-stick."

Alex raised an eyebrow.

"No offense meant." He blushed. "It's a crucifix, the padre's pride and joy, too: a life-size antique wooden one, imported. It's big-time vandalism, all right. They wrote 'six-six-six' on the wall in blood, and broke some other things."

"That's terrible! A crucifix like that must be priceless."

"I hear it's worth a fortune. Hope they get the blood out." He gave the horse another carrot. "So are you here for the show?"

"I was on my way into town, but I thought I might look around a bit here first. Are you in the show?"

"Yes, ma'am. The little arena in half an hour. Belle and I are gonna do some fancy ropin'."

"I'll be there," she said as they began walking toward the entrance.

Abernathy started to veer toward the corral entrance, then paused. "You and Eric planning on staying a spell?"

"How long's a spell?" She smiled.

"However long you think it should be," he explained. "It's an easygoing length of time."

Alex laughed. "I guess we're staying a spell. Two weeks or longer."

"Come on, then, let's take care of you." He led her to the ticket window and a moment later she had two long-term passes in her hand. When she tried to thank the cowboy, he just tipped his hat and said, actually said, "'Tweren't nothin', ma'am." He paused. "We're having a little get-together at my ranch Thursday evening about seven o'clock. I'd be honored if you and your assistant would like to drop by."

"Well, I ..."

"Good way to meet people. If you're looking to ask folks about UFOs, well, this would be a good place to do it. Our police chief will be there. I know he's seen a few, if you can get him to admit it. He's looked at some mutilated sheep, too." He stared at her a moment, then laughed. "My Lord, your eyes lit up like Christmas trees when I mentioned the sheep."

Alex felt herself blush and stammered, "Are mutilations a current problem here?"

"You bet. Marie Lopez has lost five of her flock in the last few months, last one just last week. She's got about forty head of merino. Sells the wool. Just losing one of 'em is a huge loss—they aren't your garden-variety woollies."

"Will she be there?"

"Not this week." Abernathy's long, tan face looked supremely sorrowful for a moment. "She's grazing them up in Rattlesnake Canyon."

Alex smiled. "Seven o'clock?"

He nodded.

"I'll try to make it. We can't leave our campsite unattended, so we can't both come, but I'll try to stop by for a while."

"Bring your appetite. My ranch manager's the best barbecue cook this side of the Mississippi. You can take a plate back to Eric."

"I'd be a fool to pass up an invitation like that. Thank you, Tom."

She watched him amble through the corral gate, his horse right behind him, working at getting into his pockets, and realized she was grinning foolishly. She was fairly certain that Tom Abernathy was exactly what he appeared to be, and she wondered how he managed it. As for herself, the thought of socializing terrified her. She was only at home in her own world, and could never find anything to say to people who didn't share her interests. When Abernathy mentioned that she might talk to the others about UFOs, her anxiety decreased enough for her to accept. Still, she didn't look forward to it.

After entering the gates, she forgot her nervousness. Off to the left was the arena where the next stunt show would play in half an hour. Everywhere else were streets lined with freshly painted false-fronted western buildings. Weathered plank sidewalks ran along the storefronts, and wooden hand-railings, small trees, and watering troughs filled with blooming marigolds, daisies, and a rainbow of pansies lined the packed dirt road.

Charmed, she walked up Main Street. Some of the buildings were a blaze of tourist-attracting colors and items, displaying pink and blue-haired Troll dolls, postcards, and cowboy boot coffee mugs. These she passed without a second glance. What held her interest were the shops that were nearly authentic reproductions, in looks and what they sold. She couldn't resist buying herself and Eric each a piece of walnut fudge at Lupe's Sweet Shoppe. Next door was an apothecary shop filled with herbal, homeopathic, and other old-fashioned medicines, and she bought a tube of beeswax lip balm there.

Somewhere between the blacksmith's shop, where she bought a horseshoe with Eric's name on it, and the mercantile, where she found a decent pair of sunglasses and a dozen postcards to send to friends, she realized she'd lost track of time and had missed Tom Abernathy's show. She felt terrible about that and ended up eating Eric's fudge.

Realizing that she'd been in the park for forty-five minutes already and hadn't even explored all of one street, she decided not to go in any more stores today, because she'd end up buying something she didn't need in every single one of them. Well, she had needed new sunglasses, she amended, as she picked up her pace.

At the end of the street, she found several eating establishments, and gulped down a burrito while she explored the nearby amusement rides. Those weren't much: an octopus that was closed and being worked on by a short sweaty bald man with terminal butt-crack; a Ferris wheel, nothing special; and a partially restored merry-go-round. All the restored horses were ribboned off; and people were only riding the faded ones. Alex smiled, wondering if anyone would ride after the carousel was completely restored.

Beyond the rides, signs pointed south toward Boot Hill Cemetery, north to the Haunted Mine, and due east to the Spanish Courtyard, which was, unfortunately, cordoned off with yellow police tape. The area contained a beautiful little church and other adobe structures, and she realized this had to be the vandalized church. It was so beautiful, such a shame to have to close it.

Not that she was religious; she had little use for organized religion, but she loved the feelings the old buildings stirred within her. She found ancient monasteries and pagan structures equally fascinating. The people occupying them had often been ancient astronomers, studying the same things she studied now, and being in such places always imbued her with a sense of belonging and identification. Like them, she had devoted her life to her studies; her work was her love, the only relationship she would allow herself. Hundreds and even thousands of years separated her from these ancestral colleagues, but she could feel them around her in those ancient places, and she wondered if they knew less or more than she did about the universe's secrets.

She checked her watch, then turned and started back down the other side of Main Street. Another day, she would explore the rest: She'd have to thank Tom Abernathy again for the passes. That, and apologize for missing the stunt show, and inquire as to another performance time.

Halfway back down the street, a small, perfect shop caught her eye. The picture window was framed in dark green velvet curtains, and on the glass, in a gentle half circle, were the ornately gilded words SORCERER'S APPRENTICE. A green-clothed table held a crystal ball, two brass candlesticks, an array of wood- cut tarot cards, and a single fresh-cut red rose. A small wooden placard in the corner of the window announced the presence of a fortune-teller.

She bent, cupping her hands around her face to see farther inside. There was a display case, oak-framed glass, that contained an assortment of quartz crystals and other stones. The countertop held displays of tarot cards, jars of incense, and small crystal balls. The walls of the shop were lined with books, irresistible books.

"Hi."

Startled, she straightened and turned to face a teenage boy twirling a large rabbit-foot key chain on his finger.

"Dr. Manderley? I didn't mean to scare you." "Oh, no. You didn't."

"Do you remember me?"

She smiled. "You're the young man who led us into Spirit Canyon last night. Of course I remember you!" But she couldn't remember his name.

"Justin Martin," he said, smiling. "How's the campsite?"

"We had a nice, quiet night, Justin, thank you." He looked so happy that she didn't want to tell him they'd moved this morning.

He seemed to read her mind again. "You might find a much better spot farther from the road if you look in the daylight."

"Thank you, Justin." She would let him think they took his advice. "So are you on Easter vacation?"

"Next week. This week's quarterly finals, so we get out early. I work at the Haunted Mine." He glanced at his watch. "In fact, I'm in charge today and we're opening in about fifteen minutes. Would you like a free ride?"

"Yes, that would be lovely. But some other time? I'm running late today."

His astonishingly blue eyes darkened a moment, then he smiled, all sunshine again. "Sure. Any afternoon." He pushed a stray lock of hair from his forehead and turned to look in the fortune-teller's window. "Have you been inside yet?"

"No." She turned back to the window. "I was just trying to talk myself out of it. All those books. I wonder if they carry anything on local paranormal phenomena."

Toward the rear of the shop, a pale hand appeared from behind a set of heavy dark drapes covering a doorway. It pulled the material back and held it while two little round gray-haired ladies exited. Alex could see them smiling and jabbering, then a tall man, owner of the hand, followed. The ladies stared up at him with rapt attention and he smiled and said something that made them laugh.

She heard Justin Martin catch his breath. "Something wrong?" she asked.

"No," he said quickly, and stamped his foot a couple times. "Charley horse.

From football. That's Carlo Pelegrine, the owner. Would you like me to ask him about the book for you?"

"That's okay, thanks." She gave him an odd glance. "If I decide to, I'll ask him myself." Watching the fortune-teller, she suddenly wished Justin Martin would leave.

Carlo Pelegrine had thick dark hair and pale skin. Patrician features with a strong Roman nose and large dark eyes were framed with fabulously arched eyebrows. He wore an eggplant-colored shirt that had a vague gypsy flair, tucked neatly into dark pants, but she thought that he belonged in a Renaissance painting, perhaps wearing a nobleman's toga, or more appropriately, an astrologer's robes.

Astrologers and astronomers were once one and the same; they were both her ancestors. *You haven't been seriously tempted by a man in a decade, Alexandra. Don't start now!*

But just as she started to turn away, he looked up and their eyes met. Now it was her turn to catch her breath.

# TWENTY-FOUR

# CARLO PELEGRINE

Carlo Pelegrine had many repeat customers, but few came so far or so often as the Katz sisters. Mabel and Missy drove all the way over the Cajon Pass from Santo Verde every Wednesday for an hour-long look into the following week's fortunes.

The sitting had been, as usual, unremarkable but pleasant. They required what they referred to as "the works," and with them, it was an oddly sensual experience. It mattered little what he said because their visits were not for information but for assignation. First came. the crystal gazing, a somber affair wherein he could barely catch either blushing lady's eye. Next there was the tarot reading, a bit more personal, their fingertips brushing his as they picked cards and handed them to him. He used the Queen of Wands, a card depicting a lush woman with a cat in her lap and another at her feet, as the significator in the dual reading, and they never tired of coyly asking him about the traits they shared with the beautiful queen. He always obliged them, speaking in hushed, respectful tones of their virtues.

Today the dark, brooding King of Swords had crossed their Queen, and the foreplay-for that was what the reading was—intensified because they knew that was his card. The ladies blushed and giggled like schoolgirls, and let their fingertips brush his more frequently than usual.

Then came the palm reading, ten minutes for each of them. This was the lovemaking, and because, even to Carlo, this portion was intensely personal, he was always a little ill at ease at the voyeuristic way the waiting sister gasped and cooed with the one whose palm was being examined.

Their creamy, small-pored hands were exquisite. They were always manicured and fragrant with softening emollients: They visited the manicurist before coming to see him. The skin showed little sign of age—the Katz sisters were genteel women, daughters of a citrus baron, and had never had to work for a living. Mabel had a crescent-shaped scar on one palm, and she always trembled when he touched it—he always saved that for last. Missy, who had larger, squarer hands, required a climactic moment wherein he ran his fingers gently across her heart and life lines.

It amused him to think what their reactions would be if they knew that he was celibate and that he enjoyed the sessions almost as much as they did, and in the same way. But, of course, he never told them, just smiled and nodded knowingly, maintaining the cool aloofness of the King of Swords that they expected.

Today he guided them out of the reading room, into the shop, just as he always did. They chattered at him, praising his nonexistent psychic abilities, promising to be on time for their next appointment, and he nodded and said yes, next Wednesday at one o'clock, as usual, and thank you for coming—and at that moment he glanced up and found himself trapped in the eyes of a woman like no other he had ever seen.

"Carlo?" asked Mabel.

"Carlo?" Missy echoed. "Is anything wrong?"

"Is it a spirit?" Mabel asked breathlessly.

"Yes, a spirit." He tore his gaze from the window and smiled at the sisters. "Your aunt Helen sends her love."

Mabel and Missy looked at one another, smiled, and said, "Aunt Helen. Isn't that nice?" simultaneously.

They gazed at him again and he smiled benignly as he urged them to the door. Opening it, he was unable to see if the woman at the window was still nearby. Finally the sisters stepped out onto the recessed porch, then down the three shallow steps. He stood on the porch, as always, because he knew they would turn and wave at least twice. He was at the edge of the steps, and if he turned and looked, he'd know if the woman was there. The old ladies waved. So did he.

"Hi, Mr. Pelegrine!"

He jumped at the sound of the teenage voice at his shoulder. Regaining his outward calm, he turned and came almost nose to nose with Justin Martin. He didn't know the boy well, and didn't want to. Although he was highly thought of by Hank Marquay and nearly everyone else he knew, Carlo didn't like him: He had the cold, soulless eyes of a predator.

"Hello, Justin." Behind the youth, the dark-haired woman stood, looking at her wristwatch far longer than necessary.

"This is Dr. Manderley," Justin said, and the woman looked up. "She's looking for a book and I told her you might be able to help her." He glanced at his watch. "I've got to get to the mine or Mr. Marquay will have my hide!" With that, he turned and trotted away.

Carlo cleared his throat, found himself staring at his own hands, and forced himself to meet her eyes. The effect was staggering. He wanted to get lost in those eyes, with their midnight irises and slight exotic tilt. *Get a grip!* "What sort of book are you looking for, Doctor?" he managed.

She didn't answer for a moment, and he wondered if she was as stricken as he. *It couldn't be. Don't be egotistical.*

"It's rather an odd thing, I'm afraid." There was the slightest hint of England in her voice, which was rich and melodious, pleasantly husky.

"Then you've come to the right place. Come on in."

She entered and he followed, the entry bells jingling as the door closed behind them. "This is a lovely shop."

"Thank you."

"It smells delightful."

"Simmering potpourri. I make it with orange peels, cloves, and cinnamon sticks."

"Do you sell it?"

"Actually, no. It all comes from the market."

"Fresh peels, then?"

"Sure, why not? This way I get my vitamin C and my potpourri."

"You're a practical man." Her smile lit up the room. "I like that." She hesitated, and the smile disappeared. "I'm running a little late. Perhaps I should come back another day."

"Well, at least tell me what you're looking for, and I'll try to find it for you."

She nodded and sucked her lower lip into her mouth for an instant. Carlo realized she was as nervous as a cat. *As nervous as I am.*

"I was hoping to find something on paranormal phenomena in the Mojave."

"Hauntings?"

"I'd be more interested in physical anomalies. Geological oddities, magnetics,

UFOs." She slipped that last one in like a little boy trying to buy condoms. "Things of that nature."

"I believe I have several items here that might interest you." He started toward one wall of books, but she stopped him instantly by laying her hand on his arm for a brief instant.

"I can stop in tomorrow for them," she said, heading for the door. "Or I might send my assistant. He's a tall young man with red hair."

"Very well. I'll put them aside for you. You can look through them and see which you want." He hoped that would cause her to return in person.

"Thank you, Mr... "

"Carlo Pelegrine. At your service."

The door closed behind her, and Carlo just stood there staring at it. Finally he slapped his forehead. "At your service?" he asked aloud. "At your service?" That was something you heard in movies fifty years old, something you said to clients like the Katz sisters, but definitely not something you said to a woman like Dr.— Dr. who? He didn't even know her name, couldn't even recall if she'd told him.

He went to the door, turned the latch and the open sign to closed, then retreated to his reading room. In the last twelve hours or so, he'd begun to lose control of his life. Last night there was the skinned rabbit hanging on the door. It had to be a coincidence, but he couldn't report it, couldn't take the chance. He'd have to wait and see what happened next, and if it wasn't an isolated incident, he'd have to deal with it.

Perhaps his anxiety over that had contributed to the woman doctor's effect on him. He had vowed never to touch female flesh—other than hands—again, yet here he was making a fool of himself, stammering, staring, and wishing his pants had pleats.

Long ago he promised God his celibacy, but he no longer prayed. Instead, he drew his personal tarot deck, a gold-filigreed design with figures from the Italian Renaissance, from a cubby in the rolltop desk and absently shuffled them. He didn't believe in spirits or guides or any of that nonsense, but he did believe in stimulating the subconscious with the images, and he also was forced to believe, because he'd seen it work so many times. He knew a reading shouldn't make sense, but it usually did, and the more important the question, the stronger the answer.

He continued to shuffle. There were cards that turned up all the time, both major and minor arcana. And there were cards that rarely turned up. When they did, it meant something. Synchronicity.

Instead of using the King of Swords as his significator—he didn't feel very kingly right now—he spread the deck out on the table and chose a card at random. He turned it over. The Hanged Man: sacrifice and idealism. Martyrdom. The hairs on the back of his neck prickled up as the image of the skinned rabbit flashed in his mind. Still, being represented as the Hanged Man was not usually considered a terrible thing. He chose another and placed it over the significator. "Hmmm." The High Priestess covered him and meant that he was surrounded by a very strong feminine force, a guardian who brought strength and hope through her revelations. Some card readers described her as the woman all men see when they are in love. All Carlo could think of was the dark and beautiful woman he met today. Since he couldn't get involved with a woman, this might be a forewarning of some kind, a caution not to be party to her influence.

The third card, the influence that would cross his path, was the Devil—lust for power, bondage, evil. "Great, just great."

The next card he turned was one that signified the basis of his question, and told him what his subconscious was really trying to learn.

It was the Tower, the most terrible card in the deck. Its meaning was catastrophe, usually physical and spiritual, and old-time readers usually interpreted it as having supernatural powers.

The card of the recent past was the Fool, and self-explanatory. The card that crowned him was Death, and gave him another chill: It might be literal but usually only meant the death of a way of life. He didn't care for it either way.

The card of the near future was the Knight of Swords, reversed. It signified a young man, fierce but with little real power, who can cause great harm.

Carlo stared at the cards, wondering who the young man was and if the High Priestess was his enemy also. Before he could throw another, he was saved by the rear doorbell. Someone rang it and yelled, "UPS."

"Coming!" He quickly turned the cards over and pushed them into the deck. It was time to get back to the real world.

# TWENTY-FIVE

# JAMES ROBERT SINCLAIR

James Robert Sinclair steepled his fingers and stared down the rectangular meeting table at his top aides. The long meeting, mostly concerned with mundanities, was finally starting to wrap up. Elder Hannibal Caine sat to his right, along with Senior Apostles George Allbright and Lorraine Ferguson. Eldo Blandings was seated to his left, as were the two other Senior Apostles, Steve Clayman and Albert Cramer. They were all long-time and loyal followers, though Sinclair had been a bit uneasy about Eldo lately; he reminded him of a gun ready to go off. Sinclair had spoken to Hannibal about it, but his other Elder didn't think it was anything to worry about, and he was no doubt correct.

"My friends, before we adjourn, I do have one distasteful bit of business to discuss," Sinclair said. "I hesitate to even bring this up, but I think it needs to be mentioned. I had a call from Madelyn's chief of police concerning some acts of vandalism that occurred yesterday. A goat was killed, and a mailbox belonging to the goat's owner was defaced. Also, sometime last night the Catholic church in the park was broken into and major damage was done."

"Why are they calling us about it?" Lorraine Ferguson asked.

"The graffiti was religious. Six-six-sixes were painted in the church and on the mailbox."

"So they automatically ask us about it," Eldo Blandings grumbled. "Why don't they ask the damn Catholics? They probably did it themselves."

Sinclair smiled gently and shook his head. "I doubt that, Eldo."

"*Are* the police accusing us of vandalism?" Hannibal Caine asked in a disbelieving tone. The others' expressions mirrored Hannibal's righteous indignation.

"We haven't been accused of anything." He searched the faces of his aides, letting his gaze come to rest on Eldo. "Do any of you know of any reason we might be accused?"

There were a murmur of no's, including Eldo's. Then the old man cleared his throat. "James Robert, we all know that the Catholics are no better than devil worshipers. And the devil wants to subvert our mission. That papist Corey and his followers are doing the devil's work."

Sinclair studied Blandings. Was the man really losing it, or was he just twisting Sinclair's own words to fit his own narrow views? "We are fortunate," Sinclair said finally, "in that we have found the one true path, and it's our job to help others find the way, not condemn them for their past."

Blandings kept his eyes lowered. "Yes, of course." He looked up then. "In the last days there shall be war," he quoted, his tone almost hopeful.

Sinclair nodded. "And that's why we have an armory." Thoughtfully he looked around the room. "Perhaps Eldo sees something we've overlooked. We *are* in the last days. The very last, and now the police are asking us about these crimes. Perhaps it is beginning."

He shook his head. "Your prophet can be blind at times. I thought we might avoid violence, at least until the day the Horsemen ride, but it seems I am wrong."

"It's a noble hope," Hannibal said.

"You're a kind man. If any of you hear of any more incidents, please notify me immediately."

"Are you thinking of arming the guards?" Eldo asked.

"It's a possibility."

Eldo Blandings smiled, and Sinclair knew that he hungered for the violence.

"That's all for now, everyone." Sinclair rose. "Tomorrow at two, we'll convene again."

Sinclair watched them file out, and wondered again about Eldo Blandings. The man was an old soldier, one who had led men into battle. He took a hard line and understood the art of strategy, which was why Sinclair had chosen him as an Elder in the first place. The man's loyalty to the Apostles was fierce, and although he was extremely prejudiced against anyone or anything that didn't agree with him, Sinclair thought he had enough common sense not to perform acts of vandalism, even if he applauded them.

The preacher smoothed his navy pinstripe jacket and straightened his red tie, then clasped his hands loosely behind his back and walked away from the table. The conference room's walls were decorated with framed photographs showing the history of the Apostles, and Sinclair never tired of looking at them.

The earliest showed him, a youth of twenty-four, preaching at one of his first tent meetings. His arms were raised, his smile brilliant, eyes fiery. The sight of the tacky white suit made Sinclair wince a little now, but it was part of the circus atmosphere back then. The tent was filled with the first faithful, some of whom now lived here at the compound, like Eldo and Hannibal and two of the Senior Apostles, Albert Cramer and George Allbright. Some were still members, others had gone searching for something else.

Today the Church of the Prophet's Apostles boasted two million dues-paying members, though only three hundred lived at the compound. These, the most faithful, were the ones who ran his booming audiotape and publishing businesses, and performed a vast array of office and clerical work required to keep the church going and growing. They donated their time in return for room, board, enlightenment, and the knowledge that they would be the masters of heaven when the Apocalypse came. They knew this because the Prophet had told them so.

Sinclair turned away from the photo, a headache starting to tighten in a band around his head. He had chosen the date of the Apocalypse over a decade ago: May 5, on the day of the last full eclipse of the sun visible in this region in the twentieth century. When he established his church and compound shortly thereafter, he told the faithful it was because the Four Horsemen of the Apocalypse would ride down Thunder Road. The truth was, his funds were modest, the land dirt-cheap, and he knew the remote location would serve him well because he intended to make the most of his fortune through the mail-order business.

The first years were hard, but not too hard. Sinclair had gone out of his way to attract the people who could help get his compound built. He had an architect, plus several other Apostles versed in different phases of the construction business. Under the profession-als' direction, the Apostles carried out the work, and very little had to be hired out or paid for outright.

While the compound was under construction, Sinclair held many tent meetings in the West and Southwest, giving the people what they wanted to hear and, in return, fueling the building fund. At first, everyone lived in temporary structures, tents and discards from California school districts acquired at auction for a song. *For a sermon,* he amended. After the church was completed, a huge second structure was built behind the church. Known as the Fellowship House, it contained a cafeteria, utility rooms, schoolrooms, gym, and infirmary.

It adjoined the church via underground passages. In fact, the church's basement was not only accessible from Sinclair's private office and living quarters, but also held entrances to a honeycomb of passages built beneath the compound. Some led out into the desert. The biggest—an actual road—led into an underground garage where several jeeps and an old army tank—in working order thanks to old army man Eldo Blandings and his band of mechanics—were stored. This, in turn, was adjacent to the underground armory, where an impressive collection of large and small arms and various incendiary devices was stored. These were, in Sinclair's mind, insurance against attack by angry outsiders, and although he had, in the past, preached the kind of aggressive missionary work Eldo preferred, he had gradually ceased talking about actual physical battles.

When he had sermonized about battles, the fire in the eyes of the faithful had shocked him, and at those moments, he had felt true power because he knew his followers would wipe out Madelyn, and more, if he gave the order. For the same reason, he felt fear, especially since the Waco incident.

And so he had played down the Christian soldier angle, although he reluctantly continued to sanction arms training as well as keep a heavy guard on the compound because he recognized that doing so was common sense.

Back in the early years, it had all seemed grand and glorious, from the weapons to the sparkling white cross topping the church. At night it blazed with white light—they called it God's Beacon. He'd had a hard time coming up with an original form that wasn't *too* original, but he'd finally used a traditional crucifix, then added two more short arms crossed diagonally so that the upper portion was more starburst than Christian. Theirs was not a cross-of crucifixion, he told his flock, but of rebirth. It represented the new Star of Bethlehem, and it would shine across the desert as a beacon for the Horsemen and to announce the return of the Living Savior on the Day of Reckoning.

Which would be this Sunday. "So soon," he murmured.

Eight years ago, when the last buildings, the dormitories, were completed, his prophesied Armageddon had seemed an eternity away. In those years, when compound residency grew from twenty-five to two hundred and finally to today's three hundred, he had looked forward to the day he could leave this desert prison behind.

Under another identity, he acquired a large portion of a tiny island in the Caribbean five years ago and, in that time, had a home built and furnished. Not even his Elder Apostles knew that on the day of the Apocalypse he planned to depart the compound via a long passage that ran directly from the bedroom of his luxurious apartment within the church, north to Olive Mesa. They didn't even know the passage existed: He had brought in outside labor. It was a mile-long tunnel, simple and low, but just within the opening was a storage space that held a small electric-powered cart that would take him to Olive Mesa. He smiled. To be reborn.

An old jeep was stored in a hidden garage on the north side, and it was the reason he had instituted his morning meditations—twice a week he traveled out to keep the vehicle in running order.

When the Horsemen were supposed to ride, only Sinclair would be taking a trip. He would drive across an old trail that ran east behind the Madelyn Mountains until it joined with Highway 127 near the California-Nevada border. From there he would return to Interstate 15 and travel on to Las Vegas, hop a flight, and be on the first leg of his journey to his island paradise.

He looked forward to his tropical retirement, though not with the zest he once did. His own sentimentality amused him: He'd grown fond of his church and many of the people in it. He would miss giving the sermons, miss the counseling sessions he held.

He'd changed over the last ten years, there was no doubt about that, and though it amused him, it troubled him as well. He had always possessed the gift of appearing concerned, even empathetic, as well as the glibness to dispense advice, but it used to mean nothing: It was just part of the act. But in the last year or two, he'd actually developed some interest in the things he heard. He'd developed a weakness: He'd come to care about these people, whereas he once thought of them as nothing more than mindless sheep.

*You're developing a conscience, my friend, and that's not healthy in your line of work.* At least he felt no guilt. People who followed, followed, and if it wasn't he who led them, it would be someone else.

*At least I give them something for their money.* Perhaps, after all, there was a hint of guilt, a bit of remorse.

But he wouldn't leave the church destitute after the Apocalypse. Hannibal Caine would inherit control of the organization and would have to explain that the date of the Apocalypse had been wrongly prophesied. Although he didn't have Sinclair's charisma, he had the business sense to keep the ball rolling, and Sinclair was leaving plenty in the church accounts to keep the compound running, its people fed and clothed.

It was something he had never intended to do. What did he care about a group of neurotic, grasping people who couldn't think for themselves?

But over time, the actor had taken on a few of the traits of his character. First he stopped letting women followers seduce him. Now, as humiliating as it was for him to admit, sometimes he felt like he had a paternal obligation to watch over his flock. "You're getting out just in time," he murmured to himself. "Just in time."

# TWENTY-SIX

## ALEXANDRA MANDERLEY

During the day, Eric Watson had set up a campsite for a king, then at dusk, prepared a meal that tasted fit for one as well. Using the groceries Alex brought back from the market, he had roasted foil-wrapped potatoes and fresh corn on the cob to go with the pair of tenderloins he'd grilled to perfection.

A little later, as they'd sat roasting marshmallows over the glowing embers of. the fire, they heard a car pull to a stop up at the roadside, and a minute later, Justin Martin walked into their camp. He said he was on his way to a youth fellowship group at the Church of the Prophet's Apostles and that he'd just stopped by to make sure that everything was going well. Alex thought he was a nice boy, though Eric sat back behind the firelight and watched him, saying very little.

"What did you think of Madland's fortune-teller?" Justin asked after a moment of awkward silence. She'd been glad it was dark because she began blushing the moment the words were out. Eric leaned forward to stir the fire, then asked, amused, "Alex, you got your fortune told?"

"No, no, of course not," she said quickly, and explained about the books.

"What did you think of Carlo Pelegrine?" Justin persisted.

"That's the fortune-teller?" she asked, glad to be reminded of his name.

"Yes, that's him."

"He seemed like an interesting person." "Interesting" didn't even begin to cover Carlo Pelegrine, but she wasn't about to admit that to anyone. Ever since she'd met him, he'd been popping back into her mind, making her stomach do a schoolgirlish little flip each time. She'd decided to send Eric into Madland tomorrow to check on the books, under the guise of giving him some free time, so that she wouldn't run into him again. He was just too interesting for her own good, and she didn't have time for relationships.

Her marshmallow caught fire and she quickly blew it out, then looked at Justin Martin, trying to recover her dignity. "You seem very interested in Carlo," she said in business-like tones. "Is he a friend of yours?"

He nodded. "I'm hoping he'll teach me a little about what he does."

"A churchgoing young man like you wants to learn how to tell fortunes?" Alex smiled. "That surprises me."

Justin smiled back. "I'm full of surprises." With that, he wished them good luck and started walking back toward the road.

"Justin," Eric called.

The boy turned.

"How did you find us?"

"Your lantern light. I saw it from the road. 'Bye." He trotted into the darkness beyond the campsite.

After he was gone, Alex asked Eric why he'd been so quiet; usually he was far more outgoing than she.

"You mean you really don't know what's going on with him?" her assistant asked.

"Don't be mysterious, Eric."

He raised his eyebrows. "Your friend Justin has a crush on you. You didn't notice the daggers he was glaring my way, did you?"

Alex's cheeks flushed again. "Don't be absurd. He was practically forcing me on Carlo—the fortune-teller—this afternoon."

"Well ..." Eric skewered a fresh marshmallow and meticulously began turning it over the coals. "I think he has a thing for this Carlo character, too." He pointed the marshmallow at Alex like a schoolteacher. "There's something weird about that kid. I don't like him." He paused, then grinned self-deprecatingly at Alex. "I'm being dramatic. I guess the Wild West just brings out the hidden cowboy in me. I'm just feeling protective. Forgive me?"

"Forgive you?" Alex started another marshmallow. "I appreciate it. We're out here by ourselves, and we have to depend on each other to keep the wild animals away."

Eric laughed. "And don't forget the coyotes and mountain lions."

"Yes," she chuckled. "Those, too." She knew that Eric had had something of a crush on her during their first years together, but he'd never declared it, and they slowly developed a close platonic friendship based on mutual respect and interests. The young man was engaged to a medical student up north, and his feelings of protectiveness for her were no different from the ones she felt toward him.

They had relaxed another hour and were in the midst of deciding who would take first watch when another vehicle approached. This visitor, unlike Justin Martin, who parked roadside and walked to their camp, pulled his CJ-5 up close, sending Eric and Alex scurrying to protect their equipment from the dust.

"Asshole," Eric whispered, his hand covering the telescope lens.

"You've got that right," Alex told him, recognizing the military officer from the diner the night before. He sat in the rear; a grunt in desert cammies was driving.

The driver stayed at the wheel while the colonel hopped out of the jeep and approached them, a look of distaste smeared on his jowly face.

"Good evening," Alex said coolly. Beside her, Eric had drawn himself to his full height and crossed his arms.

Dole looked around, his eyes finally coming to rest on Alex. "Doing a little stargazing, are you?"

"I hear this is an excellent place for it," Alex replied, allowing herself a tiny smirk.

The officer extended his hand. "Colonel Lawrence Dole, USAF," he said, crunching the bones in Alex's hand.

*You son of a bitch.* "Jane Smith." Alex knew her smooth voice and smile betrayed no emotion. "This is my friend, John Jones." She pushed her nails into Dole's flesh and he promptly set her hand free.

Eric kept his arms crossed, pointedly ignoring Dole's extended hand. "How do you do, Colonel."

"Amateur astronomers?" he asked.

Alex didn't reply.

"Fancy equipment," Dole persisted. "For amateurs."

"Thanks."

"Well, Miss, ah, Smith, Mr. Jones, I hope you know better than to interfere with military business during your stay."

"What's your point, Colonel?" Alex asked sharply.

"Concern for your safety. People get lost up here all the time. They just disappear." Dole rubbed his five-o'clock shadow thoughtfully. "I wouldn't wander too far from my campsite if I were you."

"Is that a threat, Colonel?" Hiding her fury, Alex stepped closer to Dole, her eyes locked on his.

"Of course not." Dole's tight smile looked like it might crack his face. "Let's just call it a friendly warning." His eyes bored into hers with sudden intensity. "People disappear in the desert when they stick their noses where they don't belong. But I don't have to tell you that, do I?"

"We'll keep it in mind, Colonel." The barely disguised reference to her last assistant's disappearance made her stomach turn leadenly. She hid it, wondering if Dole knew what had happened to Jack.

Dole turned on his heel and returned to the jeep. "Be careful, Dr. Manderley," he said. "Let's go, Corporal."

The jeep took off in another cloud of dust. "You smug bastard," Alex said as the taillights disappeared.

"He knew who you were," Eric said.

"If he didn't, he never would have come up here and done his gangster routine."

"Why did you lie about our names, then?"

"For fun, Eric." She paused. "You know my feeling on governmental secrecy."

"You can't be too paranoid, right?"

"Right." She forced a smile. "The fact that he came out here means one of two things. We're either so close to something that he's nervous, or he wants us to think we are so that we don't go where he doesn't want us."

"That's confusing."

"Of course it is. We're dealing with the government." Her smile broadened. "We should be complimented. APRA will be delighted that the military is so concerned." She chuckled. "We're a threat, Eric, and I'm betting we're very close to something they don't want us to see."

"And if we get something, they'll try to discredit us," Eric said somberly. "At the very least."

"Yes," she said. Still excited, she grabbed the cellular phone and called APRA, and quickly recounted the encounter, making sure to mention names and to make several references to the press. She hung up. "I'm certain Dole's people are monitoring our calls, so that should keep us out of harm's way, at least."

"If you say so," Eric said hesitantly.

"After my first run-in with the military, I was a basket case, Eric."

"You mean when Jack was abducted?"

She gazed at the young man. His question was asked lightly, but it still hurt. She'd never said much about Jack Matthews's disappearance, and perhaps she should have, at least to Eric. He was still young enough to feel immortal, and military threat probably seemed exciting to him. "Yes," she replied, then forced herself to look him in the eye. "I don't have any proof—they're very good at covering their tracks," she added dryly, "but who else would the black helicopters belong to?"

He nodded. "Do you think he's alive?"

"I don't know." She doubted it. Jack had been onto something; something that he didn't want to discuss. When she'd questioned him, he'd sheepishly told her that his idea was "so far out" that he wanted to do more research before he told even her. Indulgently, she had backed off.

If she had questioned him, she might have saved him. She still felt guilty, responsible for his disappearance.

"Eric, if you ever have any ideas or theories that are very bizarre, you'll tell me, won't you?"

He looked at her oddly. "Sure. I have no shame."

"Good." Alex allowed a small smile. "Why don't you go get some sleep. I'll take first watch."

"You're sure?"

"Positive. I have some notes to write up and I couldn't sleep now if my life depended on it."

"I don't know if I can sleep either, but I'd sure like to try."

As Eric disappeared into his tent, Alex sat down at the card table and dimmed the lantern. Above, the sky was studded with stars, and the waning crescent moon gleamed white. Elbows on the table, chin resting on her hands, Alex stared into the night. "Where are you, Jack?" she whispered. "Where are you?"

## TWENTY-SEVEN

# JUSTIN MARTIN

"Young man, I'd like to speak with you for a moment. Would that be possible?"

Justin, just leaving the stupid, fruitless youth fellowship meeting, turned to see Hannibal Caine's bald head and candy-apple grin. "Me, Elder Caine?"

"Yes. You're Justin Martin, aren't you?"

"Yes."

"Let's talk in my office, please." He gestured at the corridor adjacent to the meeting room Justin had just exited. "I won't keep you long."

Suspiciously Justin followed him down the hall and into an austerely luxurious office. Caine's desk was polished oak, simple of line but massive, the vast top devoid of anything but a brass pen set and a blotter. Matching bookcases and file cabinets lined the walls to either side, and a large portrait of Caine and Sinclair hung behind it.

"Sit down, son." Caine gestured at one of the chairs facing the desk, then moved to his high-backed desk chair and settled in with a contented grunt.

"Are you thinking of becoming a full-fledged member of our church when you're eighteen, Justin?" He smiled smarmily. "Or have your parents given you permission to join us now? We'd love to see them here, too, you know."

"They're not churchgoing types," Justin said as he settled into the comfortable chair and returned Caine's steady gaze. Of course, he'd never asked his parents for permission to join the church—he was only there to get to know Jim-Bob Sinclair, and maybe test the waters, but he wasn't about to tell that to Caine. Instead he gave him a sorrowful smile. "My parents won't let me join, but I'll be eighteen in six months." *So what's your point, Chrome-Dome?*

"According to the Prophet, the Apocalypse will strike long before that. But even though you're not a member, you can still be saved."

"I can?" he asked, filling his voice with hope.

"Of course, Justin. It's not your fault that your parents haven't seen the light."

Before you could be saved—getting dunked in water just like every other Christian religion—you had to have a counseling session with old Jim-Bob. Justin didn't give a rat's ass about joining the church or being saved, but after trying every other way—such as attending idiotic youth meetings—to get Sinclair's attention, he knew it was time to resort to this. "I can really be saved?" *Don't lay it on too thick.*

Hannibal Caine studied him intently. "Yes, you can be saved!" he said pulpit- style. "Would you like that, Justin?"

"Yes, sir, I would."

"Good. You seem like an ambitious young man."

*No shit, Sherlock.* "Thank you, sir. I am."

"You might be of great help to our cause."

"To the Prophet?"

Caine looked annoyed. "Yes, of course. We're all working for the same cause."

Justin nodded. "And how could I help your cause?"

"We have little time left before the Apocalypse," Caine said slowly. "You believe that, don't you?" He steepled his fingers on the desk, just like Justin had seen Jim-Bob do at the pulpit. *Monkey see, monkey do.*

Caine wanted a certain answer, and Justin took his time before responding. When he finally spoke, he watched the Apostle's reaction to each word. "I believe in everything Prophet Sinclair has to say, sir. I love this church and I think it's the only true church. I do wonder about the Apocalypse ..." He trailed off, waiting for a clue.

Caine nodded almost imperceptibly. "What is it you wonder, Justin?"

"Well, I don't know if ..." He looked at Caine beseechingly. "I don't want to speak out of turn." He thought the man wanted to hear that he questioned the date of the Apocalypse, but he wasn't sure. Caine could also be looking for a comment about the vandalism, and he couldn't risk a wrong answer. He looked at his hands. "I'm sorry. I can't ..."

"Justin?"

He looked up, and Caine was beaming at him. "Yes, sir?"

"Do you believe that great battles will be fought in the last days?"

"That's what Prophet Sinclair says," he replied cautiously.

"With the Apocalypse so close, do you think that sermons alone are enough to sway others to see the light before it's too late?"

"Maybe not."

Caine's smile broadened and Justin knew what to say next. "Maybe we need to have more people on our side before the war against Satan."

"Yes, that's my concern, Justin. We need to bring more sinners into our fold, for their sake and ours, and sometimes it's necessary to shock people into seeing the truth."

"Does the Prophet feel that way?"

There was the briefest hesitation before Caine said yes, and Justin figured that meant that the Apostle was up to something. "How can I help?" he simply asked.

"I have to ask you a question first, Justin, and you're not going to like it."

He sat back and smiled, making a show of his serenity. "Go ahead. I have nothing to hide."

Caine sat forward in his chair. "Why did you take the goat?"

*How's this dickhead know about that?* Outwardly he remained calm. "The goat?"

"You put it in the trunk of your car. Why?"

"I took it to the police station. I didn't think it should be where a little kid might see it."

"Justin, Justin. You're an excellent liar. If our lookout hadn't reported that you were practically dancing for joy when you took it, and if he hadn't reported that the police chief showed up very shortly thereafter and was obviously looking for the animal, I'd believe your every word. Now, please tell me why you took the goat and what you did with the body. I assure you, your reply won't leave this room."

*Jesus fucking Christ.* "I'll answer your question, but then I want you to answer one for me."

"Fair enough."

"I dissected the goat and then I buried it," Justin said easily.

"May I ask why?"

"I'm going to be a doctor. I'm already signed up for some premed courses at college next year, and I thought it was an opportunity that would be foolish to pass up." He paused, then gave Caine a sheepish puppy-dog look. "You won't tell my parents, will you? My mom wouldn't understand."

Caine smiled. "Of course not, Justin. I told you not a word would leave this room, and I meant it. You can trust me, son."

Those words told Justin volumes about the untrustworthiness of this man. "I'll remember that, sir. Thanks. Elder Caine?"

"Yes?"

"I hope you don't think what I did is weird or anything." He applied more sheeps' eyes.

Caine steepled his fingers again, his face serious. "Not at all. I think it's quite commendable. Waste not, want not." He leaned forward. "You're a young man who knows what he wants and has the intelligence, ambition, and resourcefulness to succeed. I wish there were more like you in our church. You look like you have a question."

"Yes, sir, I do." Justin sat up straighter. "Who killed the goat?"

"I don't know," Caine said without batting an eye. "God, I suppose. After all, the animal is a symbol of the devil. We see it as a portent of the coming Apocalypse."

"Did *God* vandalize the Catholic church?" Justin asked, just as smoothly.

Caine's steepled knuckles looked a little white. "I can't say, Justin. But maybe you can have the answers after ..."

"After baptism?"

"Well, no, that's not necessary. What is, is an act of faith toward our church on your behalf."

"What do you mean?"

"You're a courageous young man, and we feel you might be worthy to join a special group who do some specialized work for our cause."

"But if the world's ending next week, what's the point?" Justin was getting sick of the man's runaround.

"There's much to be done in the coming week."

"To spread the word?"

"Yes."

"Does the Prophet oversee this group?"

"In a manner of speaking, but he's not directly involved. I'm in charge of our operations." Caine paused. "It's a high honor to be considered for membership in our little group, Justin."

"I do have other obligations, Elder Caine. School and work, for instance." *And getting to know the Peeler.*

"Of course you do, and our requirements aren't time-consuming. All we would need from you is an act of faith," he repeated.

"Like what?"

"You're not squeamish, I assume."

Finally, something intriguing. "Not at all."

"You will receive instructions to perform a small task. One of our people will be watching, but you won't see this person. If you can perform your assignment without anyone catching you, then all your questions will be answered and you will become a member of a very elite group. I think you might enjoy yourself very much. Plus ..." He paused, giving Justin a twinkly-eyed smile. "You'll have a high place in heaven."

He was tempted to ask what would happen if he told anyone about this so- called elite group or even what would happen if he spoke to Sinclair, because he had a strong feeling the Prophet didn't know. This was, Justin surmised, Hannibal You-Can-Trust-Me Caine's secret baby. "Why do you think this is a group I'd want to join?"

"Think of it as God's Green Berets." Caine gave him a shit-eater grin. "That's something you'd like to be part of, isn't it, Justin?"

Deciding that further questions would do more harm than good, Justin returned the grin. "I'm your man, Elder Caine. Just tell me what to do."

"We'll be in touch, Justin." Caine stood up and put out his hand.

Justin rose and took it. Caine's palm, soft and moist and white, belonged under a rock with other squirming, disgusting things, and Justin controlled the urge to wipe his hand when he let go. "I'll look forward to hearing from you, Elder Caine."

"Good luck with your mission, Justin. Not a word of this to anyone, is that understood?"

"Of course." If he talked, he figured Caine would spill the beans about the goat, which wouldn't get him in any serious trouble anyhow. He'd told people he wanted to be a doctor for years, and it was essentially true. He'd specialize in pathology, and had his sights set on being a county coroner, at least for a start.

"We'll talk very soon." Caine crossed to the door and opened it.

Justin exited. "Thanks again."

"You're welcome, son."

On the way out of the building, Justin briefly spotted Sinclair hurrying toward the church, where resident Apostles were gathering for the nightly sermon. He didn't even consider trying to waylay him now. After he found out what his "mission" was, and knew what Caine's game really was, then he would figure out how to make nice with Jim-Bob Sinclair.

He went out to his Mustang and sat for a moment in the darkened car. Opening the glove box, he removed a blue scarf he'd taken from his mother's dresser drawer and lovingly unfolded it to reveal the rectangles of flesh he'd cut from Old Lady Marquay's forearms.

On the freshest, he'd written in indelible ink, "I know who you are," but now he could see that it, like the first, was rotting, even though he'd done his best to preserve the flesh with table salt. But his methods were crude and the Peeler wouldn't be inclined to do for Justin what he wished: tutor him in the art of peeling flesh from a living human being. He had intended to leave the skin in an envelope in Pelegrine's mailbox tonight, but now he wasn't so sure. He shouldn't, he knew, have left the rabbit—it was too crude to impress an artist— and to follow it up with flesh that was imperfectly taken, with threads of muscle still attached and tears where he'd tried to shave it away, might have the wrong effect. The Peeler would refuse him as an apprentice.

He examined each piece of skin, reminded of Boy Scout camp in fifth grade, when he'd been handed two pieces of leather of similar size, and cord to sew them into a wallet. Maybe sometime he'd make himself a wallet of human hide. The thought made him smile as he wrapped the flesh back up and put it away, then pulled through the parking lot, waited for a couple dweebie Apostles to open the gates, and drove out onto Thunder Road.

He slowed to a crawl just before Old Madelyn Highway met Thunder Road. In the distance he could see Dead Man's Hill, and beyond that, Spirit Canyon. Briefly he considered driving up to see Alexandra Manderley again. She'd been increasingly on his mind since his earlier visit, maybe because Christie Fox wouldn't do anything but cry and whine after she found out about her dead boyfriend.

He quelled the urge, knowing that he should go home and study up on preservation techniques, and decide on a strategy for picking out a fresh victim. He grinned. God knew, he needed the practice.

## TWENTY-EIGHT
# JAMES ROBERT SINCLAIR

The voice commanded him and the light showed him the way.

As if in a dream, James Robert Sinclair rose from his bed. Clad only in blue silk undershorts, his long hair flowing loosely, he crossed the darkened room, going unerringly to the door hidden in one of the oak-paneled walls. He entered the four-digit code and the door slid smoothly away to reveal his secret exit from the compound.

Stepping inside the cool passage, aware of the chill cement under his bare feet, he waited one long moment, then whispered, "I'm here." Another moment passed, and then the light came, swirling to him from the blackness like clear water down a long, dark drain.

Sinclair drew a deep breath, one filled with euphoria and fear, as the blue- white brilliance enveloped him. Then, weightless, he flew along the seemingly endless corridor.

In an eternity, in an instant, he stood bathed in incandescent light so magnificent that tears of joy sprang to his eyes. He fell to his knees, knowing he was in the presence of a God he had dared to doubt.

"Forgive me, Father," he whispered.

The light shone from above and around him, pulsing with life, with love, increasing in its brilliance, blinding him in His glory.

"Forgive me."

*Rise, Prophet.*

Slowly, shakily, he stood and clasped his hands, looking up in supplication. "I am no prophet, Father." Tears of shame streamed down his cheeks. "I am a lie."

*You do not yet know your true nature.*

"What do you wish of me, Father?"

*The time is at hand.*

"The Horsemen will ride?"

*Prepare now, my son, for you shall lead them.*

A pinpoint of darkness appeared in the distance and grew slowly. As it neared it metamorphosed into a near-human silhouette, a dark angel in the midst of the light, brilliance haloing its form, shooting and sparking like the sun's corona.

The angel stepped forward and was terrible to behold, its body gleaming, its huge eyes black and fathomless as it reached out its hand to him.

*You shall be the light.*

"I don't understand," he whispered, and reached out to touch the long-fingered hand of the angel.

SINCLAIR'S EYELIDS JERKED OPEN ON UTTER DARKNESS. HEART drumming against his chest, stomach twisting under an onslaught of adrenaline, he had no idea where he was, why he was standing, or the origin of the pounding that filled his ears. His knees buckled and he sank to the floor as his dream of God and the dark angel returned in a rush.

"Prophet Sinclair!" The voice of Tim Dresner, his personal aide, startled him out of his near faint.

"Yes, Tim, what is it?"

"The angels!"

"Angels?"

"They're here, as you predicted, Prophet."

Stomach knotting, he pushed himself slowly to his feet and groped blindly for a light switch. He wasn't even sure where he was: All he knew was that he should be in bed, and that he'd been dreaming.

"They're at Olive Mesa," Tim called through the door. "Hurry!"

"Just a minute." *What's happening?* Mind reeling, Sinclair crossed to his mirrored closet. As he put his hand on the handle to slide the door open, he caught sight of himself.

"Dear God," he whispered, seeing the red dust on his knees and feet. "It wasn't a dream." Wonderingly he pulled a tiny bit of sagebrush from his beard. "It wasn't a dream!" he shouted.

"Prophet! Is something wrong?"

"No, Tim," he called, trying to quell the trembling in his voice. "I'll be right out."

Quickly he opened the closet, found a pair of trousers and a shirt, and slipped them on. He pushed his sockless feet into a pair of penny loafers, then started for the door, pausing at the dresser mirror to comb his fingers through his windblown hair, snare it with a rubber band, and tuck it beneath his shirt.

When he opened the door, he saw that Tim Dresner's young face was flushed with excitement. The youth wore a windbreaker over his pajamas and was barefoot. "The others are waiting. This way."

Tim led him up the flight of stairs to the main floor of the church, then up to the second. From there they took a narrow corridor that led behind the gallery and back to a door, normally kept locked but now ajar.

Entering, they ascended the long spiral staircase into the steeple. The stairwell was a narrow spiral, white walls pressing claustrophobically on each side. The interior walls housed the huge electric cross, which was lowered from the tower into the church during Sunday services. Finally they reached the doughnut-shaped lookout platform in the top. There, looking out of the windows to the north, were Hannibal Caine and Senior Apostle Steve Clayman. The lights of the cross just above reflected on the glass, making it difficult to see out.

"James," Hannibal said, glancing back.

"Turn off the cross," Sinclair ordered.

Hannibal, Steve, and Tim all looked at him. "But, James," Hannibal protested, "you said it was to stay on all the time until Armageddon."

Sinclair moved to the window and stared at Olive Mesa and the lights moving above it. "Turn it off," he ordered. "When the Angel of God departs, you may light it again."

"But—"

Sinclair drew himself to full height and turned to glare at Hannibal. He summoned his pulpit voice, deep and forceful. "We are humbled to God, Apostle Caine. These are miraculous times, and those are miraculous lights. Ours are nothing in comparison. Turn them off." He turned back to the window as the crucifix lights blinked out.

Two glowing blue-green orbs cavorted beneath a glowing cloud. *I was there,* he told himself with wonder and delight. Still, it had been a dreamlike experience, and try as he might, he remembered little. He had heard God's voice telling him the time was at hand, and something else as well, though he wasn't sure what. Then a dark angel had appeared and reached out to take his hand, then ... nothing.

"What do you make of them, James?" Hannibal Caine asked as he joined him at the window.

The small lights disappeared up into the clouds and, very slowly, the pulsing blue-green light moved westward within the clouds.

"The time is at hand," Sinclair said, and turned to them. "The Horsemen shall ride as I've prophesied. Gentlemen, spread the word. Talk to our Apostles, make them ready to go forth and persuade others to listen." He crossed to the door, then looked back a final time. "I have been to Olive Mesa to commune with God and the angels. God has told me that these are truly the final days of the world."

# TWENTY-NINE

# TOM ABERNATHY

"Tom! Hey, Tom, get out here!"

Davy Styles's urgent call carried in through the night air, drowning out Gary Cooper's voice. Tom reluctantly clicked the VCR remote, stopping *High Noon* at a quarter of twelve, then stood and crossed to the window.

"Something wrong?" he called.

His ranch manager was standing halfway between his cottage and Tom's house, staring at the northern sky. "Come on out here. You've gotta see this."

"Little green men?"

"You got me. Hurry up."

Needing no more prodding, Tom let himself out the den's sliding glass doors and trotted through his patio to join Davy. Styles pointed toward Olive Mesa just as the Apostles' cross was turned off. "Check it out."

"I'll be damned." Tom had seen lights in the sky once or twice before, but they couldn't compare to tonight's show. Low over Olive Mesa, at the western end of the Madelyn Mountains, two brilliant balls of bluish-green light darted and danced. What he'd seen previously, he could write off as military shenanigans or maybe glow-in-the-dark hot-air balloons, weather balloons, for pity's sake, but there was nothing earthly about what he saw now. They flew wide apart, then appeared to come together as one object, only to separate again and perform mad geometrical maneuvers like no aircraft he could imagine.

There were high thin cirrus clouds over the mountains centrally lit by a bluish green glow that Tom wanted to write off to moonlight, but the crescent glowed overhead, slightly to the south.

"What do you say, boss? Davy asked. "Still think those are jets?"

Tom glanced at Styles and saw the humor in his eyes. Davy, whose bloodlines ran back to Cherokee royalty, never had much trouble accepting that there were things in the world that had no easy explanation. Tom envied him that, but wasn't about to say so. "No, not jets. I guess those are spirit lights."

"What?"

"Spirit lights. Last night at the campground, I told the tourists that maybe UFOs are spirit lights, and that the local tribes knew all about them." The two bright balls swooped into the clouds and blue-green light flashed through the clouds, brilliant, startling. Unearthly. In the stables, several horses neighed nervously. Tom glanced at Davy again. "At least now I've got something to spin a story about."

"Look!"

Something darker than the night, something huge, rose out of the clouds, visible only because it blotted out the stars behind it. An instant later, the two orbs reappeared, darting around the monstrous oval.

"Those researchers must be happy as toads in a fly factory," Tom said.

Davy didn't bother to reply, and Tom stood silently beside him as the satellites began to move east with regal slowness, toward Rattlesnake Canyon. Toward Marie.

A shiver shook Tom's entire body. "Marie," he said.

"What?"

"Marie's in the canyon," he explained, doing his best to sound a lot calmer than he felt. "Saddle up Belle while I get my gear, Davy. I think I'd like to pay the lady a visit."

## THIRTY

## MARIE LOPEZ

M arie Lopez awoke, sat up, and grabbed her rifle, all within fifteen seconds of the dogs' barking.

As she slipped from her bedroll and pulled on her boots, she looked for Dorsey and Bill, but couldn't spot them. A moment later, having filled her shirt pocket with extra ammo, she rose, cradling the rifle in her arms.

She'd made camp on a small outcropping above the area where the sheep were grazing. It was one of her favorite places because no one could approach without her knowing about him before he knew about her. The area was protected by a rocky ridge, and she realized that the barking dogs were standing on top of it.

Quickly she climbed onto the cliff with the dogs, and they silenced instantly. Gazing down into the darkness, she saw the dim white sheep gathered in the meadow fifty feet below. Some of them were looking up, no doubt disturbed by the canine alarm, but Rex, her horse, grazed unconcerned, not far from the sheep.

"What's wrong, boys?" she asked, looking at the dogs. Oddly, they weren't homing in on any particular direction. In fact, they, too, were looking up, and with a sudden sinking feeling in the pit of her stomach, she also peered skyward.

The clouds were lit with a blue-green glow that was slowly moving toward her position. Suddenly two bright balls of light swooped out of the cloud to fly so low over the canyon hills that she was sure they'd hit its jagged rim. The darting lights were nothing new to her, though she'd never seen anything quite like these. They halted suddenly right above the sheep. Rex whinnied and trotted out of sight.

Marie raised her rifle.

Bill and Dorsey started barking again, their teeth bared, snarling between the barks. Their tails were stiff and low, their ears back. They were putting on a good show, but she could tell they were scared half to death.

Slowly the two globes descended into the canyon, outlining the sheep with cold bluish light. The animals, almost as one, looked up. Instead of bolting, as she thought they would, they seemed mesmerized by the light.

A straight blue beam suddenly shot from one of the orbs into the flock of sheep. The animals remained statue-still. Marie raised the rifle, aiming at the ball of light, but didn't shoot, afraid a stray bullet might catch a sheep.

The dogs barked hysterically as one sheep, bathed in blue light, slowly began to rise above the others. It wasn't standing on its hind legs, but appeared to be standing normally on all fours. Then its hooves cleared the flock and there was no doubt about it: The sheep was floating upwards in the beam of light.

Wild Bill howled, then Dorsey leapt off the overhang and started down the embankment. An instant later, Bill followed, barking his brains out.

The sheep rose higher. Not knowing what else to do, Marie fired off a shot. It disappeared into the globe without another sound.

As the dogs reached the meadow, she fired again, but with no effect.

The dogs reached the flock and disappeared into it. "Dorsey, Bill, turn!" Marie cried, afraid the dogs would get caught in the light ray too. "Turn, boys!"

The collies reappeared at the edges of the small flock, barking, racing back and forth, nipping at the sheep, trying to move the animals. The sheep that was caught in the beam was more than halfway to the orb now, and Marie shouldered her rifle and started down the embankment, whistling for Rex as she neared the meadow.

Below, the sheep wouldn't respond to the dogs' commands.

Reaching the valley, she heard the black gelding before she saw him. An instant later he appeared, standing still while she grabbed his mane and hoisted herself onto his bare back.

The captured sheep disappeared into the ball of light. Marie dug her knees into Rex's sides, using his mane as reins. "Gee-up, Rex!" She pointed him toward the flock and slapped his rear. The horse neighed, then took off at breakneck speed just as the blue ray cast into the flock again.

In a moment, they reached the flock. Rex halted abruptly, and Marie reloaded the rifle and fired into the light beam, fired again, reloaded, and repeated the process. Despite this, another sheep began to rise above the herd.

"You goddamned rustlers!" Marie cried, loading another round. "Get the hell away from my herd!" With that she fired again.

The sheep, silent, unmoving, continued to rise toward the thing in the sky. Marie, knowing the second animal was lost, began firing rapidly to spook the flock into running. Transfixed by the lights, they remained still.

When the second sheep disappeared into the orb, the blue beam didn't reappear. Marie yelled at the barking dogs to turn the flock, spurring Rex forward at the same time.

Above, the orbs shot up toward the glowing clouds, and in the valley, the sheep, as one, bolted.

Marie and the collies finally herded the flock into a corner of the meadow, where the sheep, being sheep, quickly forgot their fear and settled down for the night. Ordering the dogs to stay with them, she rode Rex back to camp, where she gathered her belongings, then rode back to the flock. She quickly laid the bedroll out, then sat cross-legged, her back resting against a hill. She began cleaning her rifle. There would be no more sleep tonight; she couldn't move the herd back to her ranch until dawn, but she could keep a lookout for any more skyborne rustlers. She didn't know what the hell had happened, and she decided not to think about it, not out there all alone. In the dark.

Above, the glowing clouds moved eastward, toward Spirit Canyon.

# THIRTY-ONE

# JUSTIN MARTIN

*repare yourself!*

P The Voice boomed in Justin's mind as he pulled off the road.

Climbing from his Mustang, his eyes fixed on the lights above, he whispered, "For what?"

*Your destiny.*

"What is my destiny?"

There was no reply, but as he stared up into the night sky, he realized he already knew the answer.

# THIRTY-TWO

## CARLO PELEGRINE

In his apartment above the Sorcerer's Apprentice, Carlo Pelegrine sat by the window and wondered what Dr. Manderley's first name might be. Whatever it was, he thought, she must be in heaven with the light show going on over Rattlesnake Canyon. He got up from his chair and went into his small, neat kitchen, took a wineglass from the cupboard and poured himself a half glass of Merlot, then returned to the living room and settled by the window again.

She hadn't shown up for the books today. Instead, a lanky young man who identified himself as her assistant had picked them up. The realization that he had only imagined a connection with her the day before saddened him. It had seemed so strong that he would have sworn she felt the same electricity between them as he had.

*It's for the best.* He had told himself that all afternoon and evening, ever since Dr. Manderley's assistant left his shop, and intellectually he knew that was the truth, but his emotions weren't convinced.

*And just what the hell would you do if she was interested in you?* That was the thing: There could be no relationship. He had promised God.

*But you don't believe in a God anymore, do you?* He'd been born into a Brooklyn Italian Catholic family, and his youth was filled with the church—confessions, prayers, Communions—and he was even an altar boy for a while. He never questioned the religion, not even after … That's why he had promised God his chastity, among other things.

About ten years ago, when he began working at the restaurant, he first began to doubt his faith. At that time he had started studying other philosophies and religions, which led to his realization that his was an incomplete religion. So much had been removed—reincarnation beliefs chief among them—and replaced with manipulative devices that let the church control its members' actions. It, as most religions, required that a person forever be a child who had to answer to a stern, fatherly God represented, of course, by the church, which required money and loyalty to perpetuate itself and grow. Fear was the best guarantee of these things.

Carlo found that once he thought about it, he couldn't buy organized religion anymore. He believed that a man's relationship with his God—whatever it might be—was personal, and a man's actions were his own responsibility. Asking God for forgiveness was a cheat. The only one who could forgive you was yourself.

How could he keep promises when he no longer believed in the God he originally made the promises to? To Carlo, it was simple: He kept them for himself as well as for the safety of the rest of the world. The monster within him was aroused by lust, and it had to be kept at bay. The only way he could justify his continued existence was to keep his promises.

He swallowed the last of his wine. He could have no intimate relationships, and he knew that if he was ever too tempted to break his promise, he would have to end his life.

The wisest thing in the Bible was in every other religion as well: Do unto others as you would have them do unto you. Carlo believed that what you gave, you received. It was a belief akin to karma, and it meant that if you committed an act against another person, sometime, somehow, the universe would balance itself. He had no doubt that he would pay for his past crimes someday. His acts of atonement would not excuse him from the balances of the universe, nor give him forgiveness, but they helped ease his conscience and his pain.

## THIRTY-THREE

# ALEXANDRA MANDERLEY

"Fantastic! Incredible!" Eric Watson adjusted the zoom on one of the stationary cameras, then returned to the telescope. "I can't believe we're getting all this!"

"Neither can I." Alex kept her eye on the eyecup of her Minicam as she spoke. "We've hit the jackpot, Eric."

She had been controlling the urge to giggle like a schoolgirl ever since the flying objects first appeared over Olive Mesa to the west, nearly an hour ago. Slowly the objects had moved eastward, the largest one unfortunately mainly visible as a glow within the clouds. The objects had loitered over Rattlesnake Canyon for some time, finally moving again shortly after a series of rifle-shots.

Now, as they approached Spirit Canyon, Alex and Eric had caught several glimpses of the huge craft in the sky. Though the UFOs were somewhat north of them, the sky overhead was clear, and Alex's hopes for a clear shot increased with each passing second.

The edge of the huge object moved out of the clouds, a dark mass underlit by a series of brilliant blue and green lights. "Are you getting this, Eric?"

"You bet," he called excitedly.

One of the twin globes swept toward them at terrific speed, then suddenly halted. Silently it hovered, perhaps two hundred yards overhead, and they trained their instruments on it. It appeared to be nothing but a ball of light.

"Look!" Eric called.

The mother craft had come halfway free of the clouds. It was much higher up, and the other globe moved around it like a scavenging fish around a whale. A moment later, the whole of it appeared, a giant elongated oval, moving with impossible silence.

A hot wind swept over them, sending papers flying, rattling their equipment. The charge light on the Minicam flickered, went out, and the ground rolled beneath Alex's feet. As the huge craft drew equal with them, the ground shook harder. A lantern flew off the table and one of the camera tripods fell. The Bronco rocked, and another tripod crashed. Still Alex hung on, and cradling the useless Minicam in her arms, she raced to scoop up one of the cameras.

The ground bucked and Eric lost his footing, going down on his rear, yet managing to hold on to the photo-telescope. "Is the ship doing this or are we having an earthquake?" he yelled.

"I don't know," she called as the shaking subsided. The craft was moving so slowly that it seemed stationary.

Suddenly there was a low roar of engines to the west. A military jet appeared an instant later, flying toward the UFOs. The bright orbs swooped beneath the mother craft and winked out.

A second jet appeared from behind the mountains, and at that instant the UFO stopped its stately, slow movement entirely. A fraction of a second passed and then the craft shot up and away, so quickly that in a heartbeat its lights had disappeared.

The jets circled and flew away to the north. Alex checked her Minicam and found the light was back on. She grinned at Eric. "We got some good stuff."

He nodded, smiling back. "Too bad those moronic flyboys had to come along."

"I'm surprised it took them so long, to be honest." Alex pushed her windblown hair away from her face. "We've got the best that's ever been had, Eric. I'm sure of it."

Eric looked at the eastern hills as another roar of aircraft rose. "Now what?"

Alex readied her camera. "Take more pictures."

Three dark helicopters appeared from behind the hilltops. Insectile, locust-like, they flew over the craggy hills, coming closer and closer, the lead chopper slowly lowering itself until it was within the canyon walls.

Wind from the blades whipped Alex's hair into her face, and she clawed it away, keeping the camera on the aircraft. It was black and slightly different from any other military craft she'd seen.

"What the hell is he doing?" Eric cried over the screaming wind. He grabbed the telescope and shielded it from the blowing dust.

One of the tents ripped free of its moorings and went toppling away like a tumbleweed. Alex kept filming. "Put the scope in the truck. The cameras, too," she ordered, dust filling her mouth and nose. The chopper hovered twenty feet above. Fifteen.

The other tent flew against the Bronco's side, and the card table cartwheeled across the clearing. The other lantern crashed and went out, leaving them in darkness.

The helicopter hovered only ten or twelve feet above them. Alex could almost touch its landing skids.

"You bastards!" Alex screamed as the force of the wind knocked her back against the truck. She fought to keep the camera trained on the aircraft. "You filthy bastards!"

The chopper remained for another twenty seconds, creating a windstorm that destroyed their camp and scratched their equipment before rising to join the other two high above. They circled and flew back the way they had come.

Alex stood up and placed the Minicam in the Bronco. Grimly she pulled out two flashlights and handed one to Eric, who was bemoaning a ruined camera lens. "Let's get this place cleaned up."

"Why?" he asked, staring in the direction the helicopters had gone.

"It was a warning," Alex said briskly. She righted the card table. "If I haven't told you before, I'll tell you now: Where the government is concerned, we have every reason to be paranoid." She picked up a lantern and jiggled it to life. "Bastards." Looking back at Eric, she smiled bitterly. "In a way, what happened is a good thing."

"You're kidding."

She shook her head. "Nope. It means we saw something they didn't want us to see. First thing in the morning, we send our film off to APRA. And not from here. From Barstow, or better, Victorville, where our fine khaki friends won't be able to interfere with the mail so easily."

"Maybe we should use a private courier."

"Good idea," Alex said dryly. "I wonder if Brinks is available."

## THIRTY-FOUR

# TOM ABERNATHY

"Don't move, mister." A rifle cocked.

Tom stayed stock-still and spoke softly. "Marie, your words are music to my ears."

"Tom!" Marie's voice was loaded with relief.

"That's me." He heard the trigger guard snap into place.

"What are you doing here?" She appeared out of the shadowy darkness cast by a huge boulder.

"Saw the light show and thought I might take a look." He didn't dare tell her he was worried about her; you never knew how a woman would take that nowadays, but he'd been worried sick nevertheless, especially when those little shooting stars dropped so low into the canyon, he couldn't see them as he and Belle galloped up the trail. And when he heard all the gunshots ... well, he'd imagined the worst. "I heard shooting," he added, too casually. "Get yourself a mountain lion?"

"Get down off that horse and I'll make some coffee." Marie held Belle's muzzle close to her face while Tom dismounted, nuzzling and being nuzzled. Tom grabbed his saddlebags and two canteens, smiling; Marie and Belle had a little thing going between them.

Belle chuffed, and Rex, fully saddled, trotted up and nudged Marie's shoulder. "Jealous," she chided, but gave him the same treatment.

"Looks like Rex is ready for a quick getaway." Tom got the propane stove going.

Marie poured water from a jug into a pot and set it on the grate. "Lost a couple sheep tonight. Rex is ready to help me get them back."

"Did you see who took them?"

She nodded slowly, taking a pouch of coffee out and watching the water. "I saw them, assuming I'm not losing my mind."

"What did you see?" Tom asked gently.

"You wouldn't believe me if I told you, cowboy."

"Try me."

She shook her head. "Nope. You'll think I'm spinning a windy; next thing I know, you'll be asking me to go tell ghost stories to your tourists."

"That's not gonna happen," Tom said solemnly. He took her shoulders and turned her to face him. "You have a run-in with those UFOs? That what you were shooting at?"

She studied him so long that the water began to boil. She pulled away and dumped too much ground coffee into it. Tom squatted and gave the brew a quick stir.

"Yep, cowboy," she said softly. "I was shooting at UFOs, and if you ever, *ever* tell that to a soul, I'll have your hide."

Tom held up a couple fingers. "Won't tell. Scout's honor." He stirred the pot again, inhaling the fragrance. "Catch yourself anything?"

"Not a damn thing." Marie got a tin cup from her pack and handed it to Tom. "Hope you don't mind sharing. They got two of my flock, and I got squat."

"How?" Tom poured coffee and sipped it. It was so strong, it should have been as thick as molasses. "Perfect," he added, passing it to her. "How'd they take them?"

"Tom, I can't say."

"You don't know?"

"You won't believe me."

"Course I will. I believed what you already told me."

"This is weirder. I don't believe it myself."

"'There are stranger things on heaven and earth ...'" Tom tried to quote.

"Whatever. This was the strangest."

"Give me a clue, woman."

"You'll keep quiet?"

"Yes."

"One of those little balls of light beamed them up."

They finished four cups of coffee between them before Marie finished her story, ending with the jets chasing after the UFOs and the little earthquake. When she was done, he whistled, low. "I gotta admit, Marie, if *I'd* told that story, I wouldn't believe it, but seeing as you're the teller, I do."

"You do?" she asked, her relief apparent.

"Course I do. I don't understand it, but I believe it. What are you aimin' to do about it?"

She shrugged and poured more brew. "Isn't like I can go to Moss and say, 'Chief, little blue men've been rustling my flock,' now is it?"

"I guess that wouldn't be too smart," Tom said, raising an eyebrow.

She smiled back. "Can't you just see the expression on his face?"

"I'd like to see the Wanted posters."

They laughed, and for the first time, Marie relaxed a little, settling back against the hill, right next to him. Dust and all, she smelled wonderful, and he had to resist the urge to move closer.

They sat silently for a while, watching the sky. The clouds had thinned, leaving a clear field of star-dotted black velvet. "Marie?" Tom asked.

"Yeah, cowboy?"

"You bringing the flock home tomorrow?"

"Yep. Figure I'll put the woollies in the barn at night for a while."

"Good idea. Got any other plans?"

"Just to check around in the morning to see if there's any sign of the missing sheep. Alive or dead. Or ..."

"Mutilated?"

"Uh-huh. I've seen those lights zipping around before, along about the time of the other mutilations. Never saw all that I saw tonight, though." She paused. "You have the time?"

Tom lit a match and squinted at his watch. "A little past two."

"I've got more water, but I'm out of coffee."

"I brought extra," he told her, snagging a Baggie from Belle's saddle.

Marie gave him a sideways glance. "What are you smirking about, cowboy?"

He felt himself blush. "I guess I was hoping you'd invite me to stick around."

"Well, I'm glad you showed up, Tom."

"Me too." Her words made his stomach do a little flip-flop, kind of like when he was ten years old and Nancy McLeod had pushed him up against the monkey bars at school and kissed him.

They started brewing more coffee. "If you want some expert advice," Tom began.

"About what?" she asked sharply.

"The sheep rustlers."

"Tom, I told you, nobody's to know. It's too crazy."

"Just hear me out. After you left, this lady scientist showed up. She and her assistant are up in Spirit Canyon watching for UFOs."

"Guess they're happy campers tonight."

Tom chuckled. "Guess so. Anyway, I invited the lady to the barbecue tomorrow night, so if you take a shine to her, you might want to talk to her a little."

"Not likely," she said stubbornly. "I don't need to be written up in some journal."

"Well, it's your call. My lips are sealed."

Marie's expression softened, "Thanks, Tom. I know I can trust you. Water's boiling. Want to hand me that coffee?"

He snagged the pouch and passed it to her. She reached out a little too far and her fingers closed briefly on his. Delighted, he caught her gaze. "You've got the biggest brown eyes," he said without thinking first.

She stared at him. "You're not comparing me to a cow, are you?"

Instantly his face turned hot. "No, no. I was just stating a fact."

"Well, then, thanks, cowboy. You're not so bad yourself." With that, she poured the grounds into the bubbling water. "I'm glad you're sticking around."

For a long moment they stared at each other intimately, then uncomfortably, and Tom was afraid she was going to spook and send him packing. But she didn't. Looking at the simmering coffee, she said, "You're a hell of a lot easier to take than Franklin Hank or little blue men."

"That a compliment?" Tom asked, a half smile on his lips.

Marie studied the coffee some more. "Of course it is. Hand me your cup, cowboy. Coffee's ready."

## THIRTY-FIVE

## JAMES ROBERT SINCLAIR

*I am no false prophet?*

James Sinclair sat propped up and coverless in bed, staring at his dusty bare feet. He had been loath to wash the red dirt from his feet, or throw away the bit of sagebrush that had caught in his beard, because once those were gone, the proof of his sanity would be as well.

He had tried to convince himself he had been sleepwalking and had taken the cart to the mesa and there dreamed of God and the dark angel. But after returning from the steeple, he had checked the cart and found it fully charged and spotless. Besides, he had never had a somnambulism episode before in his life.

*Maybe you were just more inspired than you thought.*

Greed and imagination had always been his inspiration; he had known that from the very first. Until recently, he had counted the days until "the Horsemen rode"—a term that was really a private euphemism for his own ride to his island hideaway.

Had he deluded himself from the first, or was this madness his penance for misleading his followers? Perhaps God, whom he had never believed in before, had chosen him to be on the receiving end of His ultimate practical joke?

He'd never remembered the dream plaguing him before, and he wondered if this new one was the same as the earlier one. He wished he could remember more of tonight's dreamlike encounter. The Voice that had spoken to him had told him important things, but most of them were lost now. And there was the dark angel. Lucifer was a dark angel, but the spirit he had seen was not of Satan. He knew its darkness was an illusion, that its aura had been the brilliant beautiful light in which everything had been bathed. Vaguely he remembered a face he could not look upon. Was it one of God's angels, or God Himself?

And after it had extended its hand to him, what had happened? There was a sensation of ecstasy, and the next thing he knew, he was back here with Tim Dresner pounding on the door.

He had chalked up his recent reticence to leave his flock to the normal human desire to cling to the familiar, nothing more. But now he knew it was born of something more: madness or God, he didn't know which.

"Dear Lord," he prayed, "help me to remember, that I may do Your will."

# THIRTY-SIX

# MARIE LOPEZ

"Thirty-two, thirty-three, thirty-four." Marie Lopez finished counting her flock for the second time, then looked at Tom, who rode beside her. "There were thirty-six yesterday, so even if I imagined last night, *something* happened to them."

"You aren't the sort to hallucinate, Marie." Tom picked a burr out of Belle's silver mane. "Only thing I can think of is that the military is testing some new gizmo and your sheep were in the wrong place at the wrong time. At least we haven't found any bodies."

"Thanks, Tom. You're keeping me sane." Beneath her, Rex snuffled at the spring grasses, looking for something good to eat.

It was barely dawn and rays of sunlight were poking up between the eastern hills, highlighting patches of yellow and blue wildflowers, casting long shadows from rocks and Joshua trees. Marie was glad Tom had stayed the night. She'd taken first watch, and the second: He'd been sleeping so soundly that she didn't want to wake him. Besides, the missing animals were her problem, not his. Now all she wanted to do was get the flock back to her small ranch and catch some shut-eye.

She glanced at Tom. "I'm going to take a ride around the

perimeter of the meadow and make sure the sheep haven't just wandered off." The last time she had found a mutilated animal, it had been wedged between some rocks in an almost impossible position, and that's what she half expected to find again. "You go on home," she added, and to her relief, he refused.

Still, she protested that he had better things to do.

"Nice morning for a ride," he said, shaking his head. Then he paused. "Unless you don't want company."

Tom Abernathy was the most annoying man she'd ever met. He had his laconic, loose-boned cowboy act down to an art, and he had a heart as big as the tall tales he liked to tell, and he certainly knew horseflesh, but in some ways, he was nothing but an overgrown boy. Sometimes she just wanted to punch him in the nose and tell him to say what was on his mind.

She was pretty sure he was interested in her, but he was just too hard to read to be certain. Like last night, when she'd said she was cold, she gave him the perfect excuse to move closer; he'd built up the campfire instead.

Maybe, she allowed, glancing sideways at him, admiring the chiseled, tanned profile under the brown Stetson, she was just as guilty as he was of talking around a subject. Maybe she was as afraid of rejection as she thought he was. For sure, she should have said she was cold and snuggled in closer to him instead of leaving it up to him.

The trouble was, she was afraid of being too obvious because that was liable to scare him off altogether. She suspected a man like Tom might have very old-fashioned notions about women boldly making the first move. Then again, maybe she was just casting her own old-fashioned notions on him. It was all too confusing to even think about anymore.

"Tom, I'd love some company," she said. He looked relieved.

After an hour's search, they found no sign of the sheep. Finally she looked at Tom. "If you want to ride down with me, I'll whip up some breakfast when we get to my place."

Tom nodded. "A man'd be a fool to refuse an offer like that."

"Let's go, then. I'm starving." She whistled for the dogs, wondering if he would have given the same response if she'd asked him into her bed. *You know he would. Maybe he'd take off his hat, though.*

"Marie, that's a devilish smile on your face. What're you thinking about?"

She looked him in the eye. "Nothing fit for a lady to talk about in public." Tilting her hat low over her eyes, she peered across the valley and added, "Ask me in private sometime."

She thought she heard him say he just might do that, but she'd already urged Rex forward so that he wouldn't see her blushing.

## THIRTY-SEVEN

# JUSTIN MARTIN

J ustin Martin left school at eleven-thirty after his last final exam of the. day. It'd been in Old Lady Marquay's history class, though, of course, she couldn't be there since she was busy rotting in the old shaft below the Haunted Mine Ride.

He'd aced the test, no problem, and had encouraged Christie Fox, who hadn't studied because she was *ohh, soo* upset about dead old Rick Spelman, to copy off his paper. Her eyes looked like they needed a bucket of Visine each, but at least she'd smiled at him while he let her cheat. That was a start. In another couple days, he'd ask her to have a burger with him or something equally harmless, and lend her his shoulder to cry on. If letting her sob and whine all over him didn't get him into her pants, he didn't know what would, short of alcohol. And he didn't want to resort to that unless he had to: It seemed unsportsmanlike and he hated to smell it on anyone's breath.

Hannibal Caine had phoned him this morning just before he left for school, and he'd promised to meet the church honcho at Ray's Cafe this afternoon at two. It was a pain in the ass, but Justin knew it could be worthwhile. *God's Green Berets, my ass!* As he turned the car onto Old Madelyn Highway, Justin rolled down the window and spat. He'd have to be careful in dealing with Caine. The thought made him laugh out loud. *What the hell!* He had known how to be careful since he was five years old, when he'd performed his first dissections on his grandmother's stupid lovebirds. He'd taken apart at least a hundred animals since then, not to mention three human beings, and no one had ever suspected. "Careful" was his middle name.

He was on his way up to check on Alexandra Manderley and her nerd-faced assistant before the meeting with Caine. Maybe he'd luck out and Toad-Boy wouldn't be there.

Passing Madland, he grinned at the sight of Police Chief Moss Baskerville stalking toward the entry gate, where a bunch of unsuspecting Apostles were shoving flyers in people's faces as they went into the park. He recognized one of them as Eldo Blandings, even though they were all wearing their Sunday best: white robes and umbrellas.

*What goons!* He'd never seen any of them in robes except on Sunday in the compound. They were supposed to wear the robes so that God would know who they were on the day of the Apocalypse. And they had some bullshit idea about a flood—out here in the desert!—and the umbrellas were to keep "God's tears" off of them.

He reached Thunder Road, then Spirit Canyon, slowing only when he was close to the turnoff for Manderley's campsite. He'd had some really hot dreams about old Alex last night, and he'd awakened with an unrelenting hard-on and a big yen to see her.

In the dream, she was naked, all that toffee-colored skin showing just for him, and she was tied, standing with her arms straight up over her head. Just thinking about it gave him a throbber, big time. He'd had a scalpel and was using it to remove the skin from her back in long thin strips. Lovingly he laid each piece out in the sun to dry like jerky, and the sound of her screams as each strip was slowly, smoothly, torn from her body was sweet music that he could listen to forever. He thought that perhaps the Voice had sent the dream, and with it, a message.

"Shit," he whispered as he pulled onto the turnout edging the camp. He idled a moment, pushing his erection into a more comfortable position, then spent a moment reciting the Declaration of Independence to get his mind off sex—he couldn't pay her a visit looking like that.

After a moment, he got out and walked the short distance around a bend into the campsite. "What the fuck?"

They were gone—the people, the Bronco, the tents and all their junk, packed up and gone. "Son of a fucking bitch," he whispered, walking to the place where the tents had been. "Son of a fucking bitch!"

He stomped around, pissed as hell, examining the area. The bitch had said she was going to stick around awhile, so why the hell was she gone now? How dare she go without telling him? "You goddamned fucking bitch!" He picked up a baseball-sized stone and threw it as hard as he could. It landed with a metallic sound out of sight behind a bunch of rocks and a goddamned fucking cactus.

Fists clenched, he walked over to the rocks and looked around to see what had made the sound. It was a flashlight.

He picked it up. It was dusty as hell, and the lens was cracked, but it still worked. It probably belonged to Ms. Bitch. *I bet she wants it back.*

He stalked out of the camp, jumped into the Mustang, and threw the light on the passenger-side floor. He had an hour to kill and he was going to find Manderley and her twerp. She had to be around here somewhere—probably this campsite wasn't good enough for her either and she'd gone looking for a new one. Women like her were never satisfied. *But I can satisfy her.*

He thought of the dream, the screams, and decided that he'd have to talk to the Peeler about her. Soon.

# THIRTY-EIGHT

# CASSIE HALLOWAY

"I'd kill for some Chinese food," Cassie Halloway told Moss Baskerville asnshe finished off her shredded beef and black bean burrito. She leaned back in the auditorium seat. "Though I guess we should be happy we've at least got a choice here now—burgers or burritos." She fanned her mouth, then took a long drink of iced tea. "I used too much hot sauce again."

Moss laughed. "Yeah, hon, your face is all red. Better be careful or it'll stay that way, then people'll think you've got a gin habit instead of a salsa addiction."

"That's all I need. All the more reason for a Chinese restaurant to open out here."

"I've got tonight off. Want to go into Barstow and eat at the Chinese joint this evening?"

She smiled. "The place where you said the pork tasted more like basset hound? I don't think so!"

"Picky, picky," he teased.

"Besides, Davy's ribs are too good to pass up."

Moss grinned. "You've decided to be sociable?"

"Yeah, I'm going to be a regular party animal. Think Tom'll mind if I bring Eve? I don't want to leave her alone at the house with only a sixteen-year-old baby-sitter. Not after ..."

"Of course he won't mind, Cass."

They were sitting in the front row of the Langtry Theater. When Moss arrived bearing lunch, Cassie had happily given her stagehands an hour off. They'd driven down to Ray's Cafe for lunch, taking Eve along, leaving Cassie alone with her man. They locked the doors and joked about "doing it" center stage, but in the end, decided they were too hungry and too old to make love on the hard wood floor.

"I didn't mean to whine about the food, Moss," Cassie said, then leaned across the armrest and soundly kissed him. He tasted like jalapeño peppers. "Hot stuff." She kissed him again.

"Next free night I get, we're going down to the Red Dragon in Victorville," he declared, "especially if you keep kissing me like that."

"I'll hold you to that, mister." She stared into his steel gray eyes with the deep-set laugh lines in the broad face, then pushed her fingers through his graying blond hair and pulled his face to hers, planting another kiss on him. He was the best thing that ever happened to her. Ten years ago, when he arrived here, she was still wiggling around in a bikini, showing off her tattoos, and when she first laid eyes on the new chief of police standing there in the middle of the audience, she knew she was in trouble. He had looked so straight and stern, so I'm-cleaning-up-this-town-starting-with-you. But after the show, when he inevitably came backstage, he handed her an ice-cold bottle of Coke and complimented her on her body art. She invited him to sit down, and it wasn't a week before the two of them were sneaking around like school kids, making out here, there, and everywhere.

The sneaking had been her idea. She didn't think the chief of police should be seen in the company of the resident tattooed lady. He'd protested a little, but he knew she was right.

When she had Eve, he tried like crazy to get her to marry him, but she kept saying no. For almost five years they'd had a relationship with more fire than anyone over twenty-one usually experienced, and she was afraid that the passion would die—especially since they now had a child—if they married and stopped sneaking around. He'd pointed out that all their friends knew they were a couple, so why not make it official, so she'd told him her fears. He finally acquiesced, and they compromised, spending most nights together at her place because neither of them wanted Eve left with sitters too often.

Right after that, she bought the Langtry Theater, and her life became busier than she ever thought possible. Moss still mentioned marriage about once a month—pointing out that the passion hadn't gone away, even though they rarely coupled in the backseat of a car anymore. He also pointed out that he was a patient man who always got what he wanted, and that he knew she'd come around someday, at least for the sake of their daughter, who would need her legitimate daddy to walk her down the aisle when *she* got married.

Cassie knew Moss was right, and she was finally ready to say yes. In fact, she'd been going to bring it up the other evening, but then her goat was killed and the six-six-sixes were painted on her mailbox. She didn't want Moss to think she was finally saying yes because she was afraid to be alone.

But she *was* afraid. Moss had worked last night, and every little noise she heard had her jumping out of her chair or out of bed, shotgun in her trembling hand, ready to run off any trespassers. She hadn't had any sleep until Moss climbed into bed somewhere around dawn.

Despite her exhaustion, she wanted to go to Tom's tonight because she knew Moss wanted to go, and because she didn't want to deprive him—he'd insist on staying home with her.

"How's the new play coming?" he asked.

"It's shaping up really well." The theater specialized in old-fashioned vaudeville and drama. Each show started with a short melodrama, complete with a live piano player, and the characters were always variations on Little Nell, Snidely Whiplash, and Dudley Do-Right. The audience was encouraged to hiss, boo, ah, and cheer at every opportunity. After the melodrama came the vaudeville acts, always with a western theme, but changing with the seasons. The current show was centered around spring, with mildly naughty double entendres and bad jokes about love, dating, and marriage.

The players were in rehearsal for the summer show, which would begin next week. It featured humor about desert heat, rattlesnakes, and miners. Cassie's favorite, however, was the Halloween show. As soon as the summer show was under way, she'd begin planning it. The ticket taker and the ushers were all dressed as grim reapers, complete with long-handled scythes, and the melodrama was Madelyn's own tale of Olive Carmichael, the Hitchhiking Ghost. Tom Abernathy loved that story, and he'd been the one to suggest it. It'd gone over so well that it had become the traditional feature. After the drama came "The Ghost Town Revue," which was a joy. Cassie and her players went wild thinking up new skits and routines each year.

"What *are* you thinking about, Cass?"

"Huh? Oh, the fall program."

"Work, work, work," he chided as he rose and bent to give her one more kiss. "Speaking of which, I've got to be getting back. Those damned Jim-Bobbers are making real pests of themselves."

"Are they? I haven't been out of the theater all day."

"They're all dressed up in white robes, carrying umbrellas, of all things, and passing out flyers to the paying guests." He grinned. "Or trying to. I'm trying to stop them. Which doesn't leave much time for investigating the disappearances or the vandalism. Goddamned Apostles will be the death of me."

"When are you going to get another officer?" Cassie asked, rising and walking with him to the door.

"That's the good news. Got a young woman arriving this afternoon." He glanced at his watch. "At three."

"Young *woman,* huh?" Cassie poked him gently with one finger. "She's a cop?"

"Of course she's a cop." He grinned. "You jealous, Cass?"

"Maybe," she said, standing on tiptoe to kiss him. "Seriously, Moss, you've really got somebody?" He'd been working such gawdawful hours and looking so tired lately that this was the best news he could give her.

"Yeah, I hope so. She's qualified, and she just moved up to Barstow. She was on the Santo Verde force over the hill."

"She's willing to leave a gorgeous green place like that to live up here? Why?"

"Maybe she's tired of mowing her lawn." He shrugged. "Her former sergeant has nothing but good to say about her." He gave Cassie a hug. "I'm not gonna look a gift cop in the mouth."

She laughed. "Well, good luck. But don't be *too* charming."

He opened the door and they stepped out, squinting in the bright sunlight. Not twenty feet away, five robed Apostles had cornered Eve and the two stagehands by the water fountain. One of the creeps was squatting down talking to Eve, his hand on her arm.

"Hey!" Cassie called angrily as she and Moss strode toward the group. "You get your filthy hands off my daughter!"

The Jim-Bobbers turned to look and, seeing Moss, backed off, barely. The one touching Eve was a scrawny old geezer and he glared daggers at Cassie.

"The Apocalypse is coming," he thundered. "Do you want your daughter to be damned forever?"

"I'll damn you, you dirty old—"

"Cass," Moss said softly, putting his hand on her shoulder. "Let me handle this."

He walked forward until the old man's face was practically against his chest. "This is a private park," he said softly.

"We have our admission tickets," a brick-jawed female Apostle said, waving hers at Moss.

Moss nodded. "You'll be acquiring some other tickets if you don't leave the property, pronto."

The old man backed up and pointed his closed umbrella at the police chief. "You can't make us leave."

"You're disobeying the dress code," Moss said with a nasty little smile.

"There's no dress code."

"There is now. And you better stop pointing that umbrella at me or I'll take you in for threatening a police officer."

"Do you know who you're dealing with?" the old man asked as he lowered his umbrella.

"No, and I don't much care, unless I have to take you in and book you."

"I'm Elder Apostle Blandings, right hand to the Prophet."

"I don't care if you're Jim-Bob himself," Moss said, his smile broadening at the Apostles' scowls. "You're disturbing paying customers and I want all of you out of here now."

Blandings smiled back. "Management hasn't asked us to leave. We're here to save souls until then."

"I'm acting on behalf of management."

"We need to hear from the manager himself."

"I'm management," Cassie told him. "Leave."

"You just manage the theater," Blandings said smugly.

"Miranda," Moss called to one of the stagehands. "Would you mind running over to the arena and fetching Tom?" As Miranda trotted off, Moss turned to Blandings. "You want general management, you got it."

Two minutes later, Abernathy came walking up the street, silver spurs jingling with each step. Miranda had to trot to keep up with his long-legged strides. Tom was in his old West sheriff costume, his face hidden in the shadows of his cowboy hat. He wore a long-sleeved white shirt, black leather vest and string tie, jeans, and a silver-studded gun belt and silver-tipped boots. His gold sheriff's star caught the sunlight and reflected it back at the bad guys. His hand rested lightly on the butt of his blank-filled revolver.

"Chief," Tom said in a slow drawl as he touched the brim of his hat. "What can I do for you?"

Though Blandings stood firm, four of the Apostles backed away slightly. Tom was six four, plus a few inches of hat, and was an even more imposing sight in his lawman getup than Moss. Blandings, however, stood firm. Obviously he hadn't seen *High Noon*.

"You're the general manager?" the geezer asked.

"That's what they tell me."

"Do you have a dress code here?" he asked, shooting an obnoxious look Moss's way.

"Shoes and shirt required," Tom drawled, rubbing his chin and fixing the old man with his gunfighter stare. "You got shirts on under those nighties of yours?"

Before Blandings could react, Abernathy stepped forward and his hand snaked out and snagged the collar of his robe. He looked down the robe, then, fast as lightning, snatched Blandings's hand as it came up. He held the man's wrist, but gave Moss a conspiratorial half smile. "He's got a shirt on under there, Chief." He turned to Cassie, holding the struggling man's wrist. "Cass, you want to take a look down this man's robe?" His eyes danced with glee, but his features were solemn.

"I'll take your word for it, Tom," she replied, barely restraining a snicker.

Tom nodded and released Blandings.

"You want them out of here, Tom?" Moss asked.

Tom stepped back and studied the Apostles like they were ants under a magnifying glass. This time even Blandings, rubbing his wrist, cringed a little. "Well, I hate to throw out paying customers, so we'll give 'em a chance. You throw those flyers in the trash can over there, promise not to do any preachin', and take off those robes so we can see y'all gotcher shirts on, and you can stay. One report of you bothering our guests and the chief here is gonna toss you in the hoosegow."

Blandings tried staring Abernathy down one last time, then gave up. "I won't forget this," he muttered.

"See that you don't," Tom said amiably.

"Come on." Blandings turned on his heel, his group hurrying after him, their robes flying in the breeze.

Tom laughed heartily.

"You went too easy on them," Moss said, chuckling, "but you put Blandings's tail right between his legs."

"Well, Moss, I didn't mean to undermine your authority, and I apologize if I did, but it seems to me you've got too much on your plate to be dealing with those pesty little varmints." He bent and picked up Eve, set her on his shoulder. She giggled and put his hat on her head. It covered her face down to her nose.

Tom ran his fingers through his sandy brown hair. "I'll ask Fred and Becky Anderson to walk around Madland and talk to the shop-keepers and do a little spying. They'll enjoy it."

"I don't believe I know them."

"Tom's a romantic," Cassie explained. "They're newlyweds and they just joined the show this week."

"They've been wanting to get to know the place." Tom put Eve down and took his hat back. "If the Jim-Bobbers act up, we'll detain them and give you a jingle."

"Sounds good to me," Moss said.

Tom tipped his hat, turned, and ambled back down toward the arena.

"He's a character," Cassie said, smiling after him.

"That he is." He bent and kissed Eve's forehead, then rose and did the same to Cassie. "I'll see you two later."

Cassie watched him until he turned the corner. In his own way, Moss was as impressive as Tom. Tall and stocky, he had the shoulders and gait of a bear, and she loved the hell out of him.

# THIRTY-NINE

# JAMES ROBERT SINCLAIR

"He humiliated me!" Eldo Blandings told James Robert Sinclair. The old man standing before the Prophet's desk was so enraged that his entire body trembled with barely restrained anger.

This morning, when he gave the order for the Apostles to do their missionary work in their white robes, Sinclair had feared that something like this would happen. Eldo Blandings was a prideful man with no sense of humor, so when he appeared after lunch, asking for an audience, Sinclair wasn't surprised.

Immaculate in a navy blue suit, Sinclair steepled his fingers and thought about last night. Something had happened, but he was no longer so certain that he hadn't dreamed at least a part of it. Still, it was a sign, and he would have to spend much more time in meditation to try to decipher it. He hoped he could keep this meeting short.

Finally he looked up into Blandings's angry, beady eyes. "Eldo, remember that pride goes before a fall and missionary work is difficult at best. You're dealing with souls who have been misled, some by the devil, some by other people, but always by ignorance." He stroked his beard once, then smiled as gently as he could. Eldo appeared marginally calmer, but the fury in his eyes continued to concern Sinclair.

"Missionary work is a trial, Eldo, a test of our faith; there's no doubt of that. But remember, too, that the more you humble yourself before God, and the more souls you bring into the fold, the greater your reward on the Day of Judgment." He sat back, steepling his fingers once more.

"Thank you, Prophet," Eldo said hoarsely. "Thank you for your guidance."

"It's the guidance of God and the Living Savior," the Prophet corrected mildly.

"He speaks through you, Prophet."

He could see that the anger was all but gone now, though the rapture in Eldo's eyes was unnerving. Sinclair had seen it on others many times during sermons when he was especially eloquent, but then it was transitory; as his sermon wound down, so did the unquestioning look of love. He'd also seen it singularly in the eyes of the women who tried to seduce him. It was fierce and adulatory, and Sinclair told himself he had to be misreading his Elder Apostle's expression. Still, he had worried about the man's state of mind of late, and perhaps he was right to do so: Blandings could be verging on a mental breakdown.

"Sit down, Elder." Sinclair indicated one of the straight-backed chairs before the wide desk.

Blandings sat stiffly and Sinclair was relieved to see the eyes go back to normal: hooded and sullen.

"Eldo, I'd like to hear exactly what happened at the park today." He paused. "But first, do you know where Elder Caine is? He should be here as well."

Blandings looked uncomfortable as he glanced at the glass and copper clock on the wall. He cleared his throat. "I'm not sure if he's in the compound or not," he said hesitantly.

"Is something wrong?"

"No, Prophet."

Sinclair nodded, thinking that Blandings was keeping something to himself. He doubted it was anything important. "Did you have difficulty gaining entrance to the park?"

"Some. The police wouldn't let us in until we bought admissions."

"That's not surprising."

"After we were inside the park we had no trouble until my group ran into the same policeman again. He told us to leave, and I refused, so he called the general manager."

Blandings clutched the edge of the desk, white-knuckled with renewed anger. "Prophet, this man was a messenger of the devil."

"He's the one who humiliated you, then?" Sinclair asked softly.

"Yes, Prophet. He had Satan's own tongue."

"Did he ban you from the park?"

"No. He made jokes at my expense, then he said we could stay as long as we didn't wear robes, or preach, or pass out flyers."

"I see." James Robert leaned back in his chair and closed his eyes, wanting to be done with this meeting. He needed time to think before four o'clock, when he'd tape the sermon for tonight's broadcast.

Finally he opened his eyes. "I appreciate your coming to me with this problem, Elder Blandings. Rest assured that I will take it into consideration." He rose, and Blandings quickly did likewise.

"Thank you, Prophet."

Sinclair nodded and put his hand out to shake Eldo's.

Blandings, the weird adoration slipping back into his eyes, took Sinclair's hand and brought it reverently to his lips. He kissed it, and Sinclair stared at his toupee in the awful realization that Eldo Blandings was truly going mad.

Retrieving his hand, he showed him to the door, then returned to the phone and called Timothy Dresner.

His aide picked up on the second ring. "Yes Prophet?"

"I'm going to meditate, Tim, so please see that I'm not disturbed until it's time to go to the church."

"Yes, Prophet."

"And find Elder Caine and tell him I wish to meet with him in my office immediately afterward."

"Yes, Prophet."

Sinclair hung up and left the office, walking down the hall and entering the key code on a door that opened on a flight of stairs that took him below to his private apartments. With a sigh, he let himself in.

Exhausted, worried about Eldo Blandings, worried about his own mental state for that matter, he walked through the spacious living room and down the hall into his bedroom, where he changed from his suit into tan chinos and a complementary brown pullover shirt. He pulled on a pair of black running shoes, then a brown baseball cap. He was about to slip his ponytail under his shirt, then realized no one would see him and left it out. He smiled, feeling a small sense of freedom.

Approaching the hidden door to the secret tunnel, he punched in the code and waited until the paneling slid open on cool darkness. He shivered with fear and delight at the thought of returning to the site of last night's visitation. Stepping inside, he unhooked the cart from the charger, then backed it out of its parking space and headed into the mile-long tunnel. He began his journey back to Olive Mesa, where he would meditate on the meaning of last night's visions.

# FORTY

# MOSS BASKERVILLE

Moss Baskerville had just settled down at his desk with a cup of coffee and a stack of reports when the intercom buzzed. He punched the button. "Yes, Shirley?"

"Chief," came his clerk's voice, "there's a lady here to see you."

He glanced at the clock. *My new officer's here, and she's an hour early. That's a good sign.* "Send her in."

He rose from his chair as the woman entered. They shook hands. "I'm Chief Baskerville. Please, ah, have a seat." He gestured at the wooden chair before his desk.

"Thank you."

They sat down and he had to remind himself not to stare. She might be a cop, but she looked like a model, tall, dark, with exotically tilted eyes, high cheekbones, and long wavy hair pulled back at the nape of her neck. "You're early."

"I am?" She smiled and raised one eyebrow quizzically.

"Yes. I wasn't expecting you for another hour. Coffee?"

"No, thanks. I should explain—"

Moss smiled. "No need. You probably wanted to get a look at the town first." He searched the stack of papers for her resume without success. "How do you like it?"

"It's fine," she replied slowly.

"Did you have time to get a look at the park?"

"Yes. It's fascinating. Very nice."

"You're not from around here, are you? I can't place your accent." He was glad Cassie couldn't see him stumbling over his words like a schoolboy. The woman was beautiful—*an arresting beauty*—but combined with her composure and air of self-confidence, she was absolutely intimidating.

"I was born and raised in England, but I moved here when I was eighteen."

He nodded. "That makes you more worldly than ninety-nine percent of Madelyn's citizens. You realize what you'll be dealing with here, don't you? It's probably very different from what you're used to down in Santo Verde."

"Santo Verde?"

"Let me explain," he said. Shuffling papers as he spoke, desperate for the resume, because he didn't want her to know he couldn't remember her name. "Madelyn is a fairly quiet place most of the time. Lately it hasn't been. We've had three disappearances. I suspect foul play but can't get a lead. We have teenagers who like to play chicken up above the park. Had a death the other night, in fact. We have tourists driving where they shouldn't, weekends we have drunk trouble at the Mobius Bar, especially when the Santa Anas blow. Sometimes we get calls at Ray's Tavern. Some of those truckers are overgrown redneck cowboys who get drunk and take to jousting each other with the pool cues over the damnedest things. One got his eye put out last month."

"I—"

"Let me finish, then you can tell me if you're interested. We've got extra problems now. Somebody killed a goat, probably the same party that vandalized our church. Might be the local religious cult, might be some rogue satanist. The cult calls itself the Apostles. They expect the world to end on Sunday and they've been hassling our tourist trade and they're getting worse. Also, last night we had a quake that didn't do much damage, but scared folks and kept my only officer and me out most of the night."

"Chief—"

"That's not all," he said, starting on the final stack of papers. "We've got UFOs, and UFO nuts to go with them. Why, I hear we've even got some educated nuts camped out in Spirit Canyon." He flipped one last sheet and found the resume. Breathing a sigh of relief, he looked at his prospective employee. "So, now that you know the truth, Ms. Kellogg, are you still interested in the job?"

She gave him a chilly smile. "My name's Manderley. Dr. Alexandra Manderley. I'm one of the educated UFO nuts camped out in your canyon."

Baskerville, his face flaming with embarrassment, counted silently to three before speaking, which was something he should have done before he ever opened his mouth in the first place. He looked her in the eye. "If I'd had time to get up there and meet you, like I'd intended, I wouldn't have made an ass of myself just now. I'm sorry, ma'am—Doctor. No disrespect meant. I'm hurting for help," he explained, "and I'm expecting a female officer to show up for an interview this afternoon."

"So I gather." The chill left her voice, but she remained reserved. "You're understaffed?"

"Very." He allowed a sheepish smile. "And my lack of sleep is showing. What can I do for you, Doctor?"

"After all you've said, I see I probably shouldn't even be here."

"Dr. Manderley, if you're referring to my calling you a 'UFO nut,' I apologize. I've seen the things myself. It's just sort of a catch phrase."

At last she smiled. "I know. I don't care for the nuts myself. The fanatics give the entire science a bad name with their crazy notions."

Relieved, Moss sat back. "Guess it's the same everywhere. A couple abusive cops can ruin the reputation of an entire department. It's a question of rotten apples. Now, please, what can I do for you?"

"Nothing, probably, but I wanted to report a harassment and, if you have a moment, ask you a few questions about Madelyn's UFOs."

"Shoot," he said, pulling out a report blank. "Who harassed you?"

"The military, I think."

He put down his pencil. "Do tell."

"We were filming the UFOs last night. A couple jets came along and chased them off, then three black helicopters invaded our camp."

"Invaded? Landed?"

"No. One flew down so low, I could have grabbed its skids. The wind from its blades virtually destroyed our camp. Some of our lenses have to be reground, and we had to replace some of our camping gear."

"You can take up costs with the military, but I don't think you'll get anywhere."

"No, I'm sure we wouldn't. That's not why I'm here. Frankly, Chief Baskerville, I'm a bit concerned about our safety. They were warning us off, and I have no intention of running. But we're moving our camp, and I want you to know where we are. Just in case." She took a folded piece of paper from her jacket pocket and opened it, then pushed it across the desk. It was a simple map of Spirit Canyon, taken from a rock hunter's guide, and she'd marked a spot off the main road. "After we cleaned up at dawn, we found this place. It's about an eighth of a mile off the canyon road and it won't be too easy to invade. We're going to be setting up camp under a large overhang, and we're hoping they won't notice us again."

Moss nodded. "I know the place. I or another officer will try to check on you once a day."

"I know you're busy—you don't have to do that. But if we have another UFO event, if someone could make sure we're still there, I would appreciate it."

"You sound like you expect the military to abscond with you."

"I lost a colleague that way several years ago. He disappeared off the face of the earth, as did the film he'd taken of a UFO event in southern New Mexico."

"You're kidding."

She shook her head. "I know it sounds paranoid—government conspiracy plots and all that. But it isn't. You see too much, and something happens. Military pilots sometimes disappear, as do civilians." She paused. "And you'd be surprised at the number of small-town police officers who've disappeared or met inexplicable accidents— always fatal."

Moss said nothing, just shook his head in disbelief.

"Tell me something, Chief. Have *you* ever reported a UFO to the air force?"

"No. I don't see much reason to, and I'm not fond of the air force types around here. They ... kind of ... lurk. There's one colonel—"

"Dole," she said. "He came to our camp and suggested we were wasting our time."

"Did he now? Well, he drives around here like he owns the town, just sort of spying and lurking, and frankly, Doctor, I wish he'd go back to his base and do his lurking there."

"Do you know which base he's from?"

"No. Tried to strike up a conversation a few times when I've seen him in Ray's Café, but his mouth's tighter than a puritan's assh— Excuse me. He doesn't talk much."

The doctor chuckled. "You're not going to offend me, Chief. One thing's for sure, he's here for a reason. How long has he been hanging around?"

"A couple years. He showed up right after we had some UFOs pass over the hills north of us. He's been around a lot lately. You suppose the UFOs are some kind of government experiments?"

"Perhaps. Some of them. The craft we saw last night were so far beyond our technology that I think Dole and his friends are as in the dark about them as everyone else."

"Did you get film?"

She nodded. "We Fedexed it to APRA this morning."

"If the military didn't make the saucers, what do you think did?" He was beginning to really enjoy the conversation. Normally he had to be the voice of sanity, reassure people the things were nothing, but this woman, who didn't seem flighty at all, took the UFOs as a matter of fact, freeing him to do so as well. "Aliens?"

"Possibly. But the craft we saw last night took off at speeds that an organic being couldn't withstand. They're probably unmanned." She paused. "They might be other-dimensional. We have folklore describing such craft that dates back thousands and thousands of years. Witch balls and fairy lights or angels, for example."

The intercom buzzed. "Yes, Shirl?"

"Ms. Kellogg is here to see you."

"Duty calls," Moss said, rising. They shook hands once more. "Dr. Manderley, I'd like to hear more. I'll try to stop by your camp tomorrow, if you don't mind."

"You'll be welcome. It's nice to talk to someone with an open mind."

"Can't help it. I've seen them."

He watched her walk briskly across the parking lot, an elegant long-legged figure in a tan linen jacket and blue jeans, and sighed a little. She would have made a great cop. *Ah, well.*

# FORTY-ONE

# JUSTIN MARTIN

J ustin Martin was pissed. He hadn't been able to find Alexandra Manderley even though he'd searched until twenty of two. Now, at five minutes after, he pulled into the truck stop lot and parked in front of Ray's Cafe, curious about what Hannibal Caine had to say, yet simultaneously resenting the summons.

He got out of the black Mustang and locked the door, surprised at the warmth of the day. At least Old Man Marquay still had a belly-ache and had stayed home again today, so Justin was free to lie to him about opening the mine ride at two. Before school, he'd left a note saying it would open at three. That would give him plenty of time to find out what Chrome-Dome Caine wanted.

Walking into the café, he was assaulted by cool air and the heavenly fragrance of grilled burgers and onions. He glanced around, hoping Christie was back to work, but wasn't surprised that she wasn't around: Spelman's funeral was tomorrow and the blond cheerleader was probably sniveling in the funeral parlor beside his burned-up body.

"Justin, over here."

Outwardly he smiled when Hannibal Caine called his name,

while inwardly he cringed in embarrassment. Waving, he walked across the café and joined the Apostle at a booth under an eastern window, glad that the diner was only a quarter full and no one sat within earshot of Caine's table. Justin slid onto the orange plastic seat opposite the plump man, who was porking down a banana split.

"You were a little late," Caine said, pointing at him with his spoon, "so I started without you." He beckoned to a middle-aged waitress. "This young man would like one of these, too, miss."

He would have preferred a double bacon chili cheeseburger, but Justin just smiled like a good little puppy. "Thank you, Elder Caine."

"You're welcome, Justin."

The man was hard to take seriously. He could have been the twin of the guy on TV who played "The Commish," with his twinkly eyes and round baby face, and it was tough to think of him as anything but harmless. But Justin knew from personal experience that looks could be deceiving: After all, everyone thought he himself was an all-American jockstrap, when nothing could be further from the truth. No, Hannibal Caine would never have risen so far in the Apostolic ranks if he were harmless. Still, he couldn't be as smart as he obviously thought he was.

"How's school, Justin?" Caine picked the maraschino cherry off the top of his ice cream and dangled it by the stem before popping the whole thing into his mouth.

"Fine. Easter vacation's next week."

The cherry stem poked out from between Caine's lips. Plucking it with his fingers, he laid it on the table by his dish.

"I'll bet you're a good student. Smart."

*Get to the point.* "Straight A's." The frowzy waitress set a syrup-drenched split in from of him. "Thanks, miss," he said sweetly. "Thanks, Elder Caine."

"You're welcome." Caine sucked fudge sauce off his spoon, then pointed it at Justin again. "You mentioned last night that you'd like to be a doctor."

"Yes, sir." Justin held his cherry by the stem, focusing on it instead of Caine's intently creepy gaze. "But I guess that's not going to happen if the world's ending Sunday." Caine, he knew, couldn't possibly believe such nonsense, and he wanted to get him to admit it. He needed to know what game the man was playing.

"You sound a bit sarcastic, Justin. Perhaps you're not convinced?"

"Are you?"

"I believe in the Prophet." Caine spread his hands helplessly. "What more can I say?"

*Plenty.* "I'd like to believe, sir. I'm praying for God to give me more faith."

"You just need more time. I'm sure God understands that." Caine stared at Justin, the twinkle in his eyes turning to cold blue ice. "But there is a way for you to find faith, and that is to work for the church. For the Prophet." He folded his hands and the twinkle returned. "And if you're right, if the Day of Judgment is a little slow in coming, your work would still be rewarded."

"You're admitting the Prophet might be wrong?"

Fire blazed in Caine's eyes. "No. I am only saying this because you are still skeptical."

Justin nodded, trying to appear humble. It was hard.

"I'm suggesting that you have nothing to lose and everything to gain by working for me. For the church. Can your parents afford to send you to medical school?"

"No." He didn't bother to mention the scholarships he'd earned, which didn't amount to that much anyway. "But there are student loans."

"The Church of the Prophet's Apostles might be able to help out the right student in a big way."

*Yeah, if I sell you my soul.* "What's required of the student?"

Caine smiled. "Oh, nothing much. We'd have to know that the student is loyal to the church, willing to go that extra mile. We'd want our investment to pay off, of course."

"Elder Caine?"

"Yes?

"If the world's ending in a few days," he began ingenuously, "why are you talking about scholarships?"

"Because *you* are unsure." Irritation showed on Caine's face but was quickly replaced by his smarmy smile. "What I'm telling you is that by working for us, you earn your rightful place in heaven, even though you are not baptized into our church. The Apostles, as you know, are the chosen rulers of heaven."

He sounded so sincere that Justin thought the man should be selling used cars. *Get to the point, Chrome-Dome.* "And?"

"I'm going to be blunt with you, young man."

It's *about time, Your Assholiness.* Justin pushed his ice cream around in the bowl and waited.

"There's a possibility it won't end."

*No shit, Sherlock.* "There is?"

"Let's not play games, shall we?" Caine set his spoon down.

"But your church is centered around the end of the world."

"Every church is centered around the Day of Judgment, young man. I think you know that."

Justin dropped the cherry, and it splashed into the melting ice cream. "Yes, I know that. Not too many have the date picked out, though."

"That's true. Some seers and prophets, such as our own Prophet Sinclair, can predict future events very accurately, except for one thing: timing."

"You're saying Prophet Sinclair is fallible?" Justin asked in hushed tones.

"No, no, no," Caine lied quickly. "It's just that ... time is something we, as human beings, don't comprehend completely." He spread his hands. "Why, even to you or me, sometimes a few minutes seems like an hour."

*Guess you've smoked a little dope in your time.* Justin smiled and nodded. "I know just what you mean."

"Good. Then you'll understand when I tell you that though Prophet Sinclair's prediction is accurate, the timing could conceivably be off, just as it has been with other great prophets. There is a slim chance that we'll have a few more years yet, and we need good, strong members. I think you show promise, young man."

"What do you want me to do?" He pushed his dish to the center of the narrow table so that it trespassed on Caine's territory.

"You weren't frightened or repulsed by the dead goat," Caine said, bulldogging his head forward. "Instead you took it and, ah, put it to good use."

"So?"

"Time is short, Justin, and it's vital that we jolt the sinners into action. Desperate times, as they say, call for desperate measures."

"Is that why you've got your people out in their robes all over the place?"

Caine nodded. "But that's a mere tip of the hat compared to what we must do. We have little time and we must frighten people, make them think, make them realize they need salvation." His voice rose minutely. "It's our duty, as handed down by God to the Prophet, to do everything and anything we can to save all the souls we can."

"Does the Voice tell you to do it?" Justin ventured.

"Yes," Caine said immediately.

"Who is the Voice?" Justin asked.

Caine stared at him before replying. "You know. We all know."

Justin decided not to go further, but he wondered if others heard the Voice as well. "What do you want me to do?" Justin asked instead.

"We might be able to use you on our Special Projects Committee, you know, God's Green Berets."

Caine added that last like the mere words would magically lure him into doing his bidding.

"What kind of special projects?" Nothing was going to get him to wear one of those dumbshit white robes.

"Well, you took the goat before it could have its desired effect, I'm afraid."

"You guys offed it, didn't you?"

"The hand of God killed the goat, Justin. It was a message to the town. A sign."

"Did you do the Catholic church, too?"

"No. I can't answer any questions until you've proven yourself to be one of us."

"So?"

"We want you to kill another goat and display it appropriately."

Justin almost smiled, then caught himself and made his features solemnly serious. Maybe he and Caine could do a little business after all. "Tell me more."

# FORTY-TWO

# JAMES ROBERT SINCLAIR

On the red earth of Olive Mesa, he knelt before God and prayed for guidance. James Robert Sinclair, his shirt and hat tossed aside so that he would feel the full impact of the sun, had been kneeling for more than an hour and a half, the rocks digging into his flesh until his knees first screamed with pain, then went blessedly numb.

Tears streamed down his cheeks. "Dear God," he prayed aloud, "show me some sign that last night was no dream, that I might know I'm not mad." His back burned with the heat, but no answer came. Slowly he unclasped his hands, then stretched his arms out and fell forward, prostrating himself before a God he had only begun to believe in half a day before.

Red dust sifted into his beard. He breathed it and tasted it. He had believed so thoroughly even the night before. For the first time in his life, he had faith in something besides himself. For the first time, he had faith in God.

*Faith. I must have faith in what I saw and heard.* Heart lifting, he realized God was testing him. If he could only sustain faith for a night, then he was unworthy. Still prostrate, he clasped his hands in the dust. "I will prove my worthiness, Father. I will trust in You."

Silently he wept as the sun beat down on him. Slowly his eyes closed.

*You know not yet what you are, my son.*

The Voice exploded in his head, and slowly he opened his eyes to see the Angel of God shimmering before him. Overwhelming love enveloped him as the dark figure with its sunlike corona approached and held out its hand.

Pushing himself up out of the dirt, Sinclair rose to his knees, head bowed, muddy tears of joy flooding his eyes. "You're real," he whispered, coughing on dust.

*You shall lead them to heaven. You shall be the light, and your true nature shall be revealed on the Day of Judgment.*

"What do you mean?" he cried. "I don't understand."

*Look at me and you shall see the truth.*

Trembling, he tried to look into the face of the angel, but could not. "I am weak, Lord, forgive me."

*You are forgiven. The time shall come and you shall know. Abide in your faith, for yours is the greatest of all tasks.*

The angel touched him and he screamed with ecstasy.

# FORTY-THREE

# ALEXANDRA MANDERLEY

"" "You drive like a maniac," Eric Watson told Alex Manderley.

She grinned at him. "I made friends with the police chief; don't worry about it."

They had picked up ice and a cooler full of fresh food, as well as lanterns and flashlights to replace the ones they'd lost the night before. There was nothing they could do about the scratched lenses on some of their equipment, but fortunately, the telescope with its photographic attachment, the video cam, and one camera had suffered no damage. Alex was feeling energized, and as soon as they'd passed Madland, she'd gunned the Bronco and sent them bouncing up Old Madelyn Highway at a gleeful speed.

Approaching Thunder Road, she slowed to make the turn toward Spirit Canyon. "They'll be back," she told Eric.

"You think so?"

"I feel it in my bones. This is big, Eric, and it's going to get bigger."

He laughed. "What happened to the objective scientist in you?"

She smiled. "She's there, but I feel like a kid in a candy store. Don't you?"

"Yeah, I do." As he spoke, he glanced over his shoulder. "Stop the car!"

She stopped so fast, she almost ran off the road. "What?" she cried. "Did I hit something?"

"Look!" Eric pointed to the northwest. "Look!"

She craned her head around and gasped. One of the fiery teal disks hovered low over Olive Mesa. "It might be a reflection," Alex said as she made a U-turn, "but I doubt it."

Eric grabbed the video cam and began taping as they tore down the road. "Keep your eyes on the road!" he yelled when she ran two tires into a rut. "I'm getting this. Just drive!"

She did. They covered two miles in as many minutes, and the disk never moved. Drawing even with the mesa and the UFO, she searched for a jeep trail and finally spotted one. "Hang on!" she cried, and swung the wheel hard right.

"Shit!" Eric screeched, clutching the Minicam to his chest. "You almost put my eye out!"

"Hang on, we're almost to the mesa."

It loomed so close now that they could no longer see the UFO, though they didn't see it fly off, either. Alex drove maniacally, hitting her head on the roof of the Bronco's cab as the trail grew more rutted and dimmer.

"Watch out!" Eric cried as she narrowly swerved around a stone in the road. "Slow down! There's another one!"

She braked just before hitting the second stone, throwing them both forward. The first rock could have taken out a tire, but this one couldn't be passed. It was huge, and had to have been dragged there to block the trail.

"Damn!" Alex glanced at the roadsides, but even the Bronco couldn't maneuver here. She turned off the engine and pocketed the keys, then grabbed the camera and hopped out of the truck. "Let's go!"

Eric, video cam on his shoulder, jumped out and joined her as they trotted toward the mesa. "We're never going to be able to get to the top of that thing."

"Come on," she called, her side already aching, "there's bound to be a trail here somewhere." She sprinted ahead, breathing hard, exhilarated, despite the heat.

At the base of the mesa, she ran to the right a hundred feet, then, finding nothing, turned around and jogged left. "Here!"

The trailhead was hidden in a fold of mountainside invisible from the road. "Hurry!"

She tried to trot up the steep trail, but soon slowed, lungs aching from the exertion and the dust. Eric caught up with her and they kept going, gasping and panting. She wished they'd grabbed a canteen as well as the cameras.

"The UFO's probably gone by now," Eric panted.

"Even if it is, it was practically on the ground. It may have left marks."

Twenty long, hot minutes passed before the winding path finally brought them to the summit. Alex stepped onto the plateau. "You were right," she told Eric breathlessly as he joined her. "It's gone."

"Let's rest a minute."

"Yes, let's." She was exhausted. At home she ran a mile every morning, but it hadn't prepared her for this. She took a few more steps farther onto the mesa, then shielded her eyes with her hand, squinting at something poking up dead center. She barely heard Eric's "What?" as she ran toward the center of the mesa.

On the ground lay a man's brown shirt, sandals, and a baseball cap, nothing more, but the items looked like they hadn't been there long. "Eric!" she ordered. "Stay back a second. Someone's been here." She scanned for footprints and found a few in the red dust, a man's, of average size. Only three were very visible—the desert wind had already erased the rest.

"Aliens?" Eric asked in an amused voice.

She grimaced. "No." After she took photos of the clothing and the remaining footprints, she gestured Eric forward. "Look at this!"

she said, picking up the shirt. She held it near her face and sniffed. "It smells of Aramis. Whoever was here, just left." Next she picked up the cap and detected a faint clean odor of some sort of hair preparation.

"Alex, do you know how weird it is to sniff a stranger's clothing?"

She looked up and saw he had the Minicam trained on her. "The clothes haven't been here long," she said to the camera with all the dignity she could muster, then went on to detail her finds before placing them back on the ground.

"You aren't going to take them?" Eric asked, still sounding amused. "They might belong to an abductee!"

"If they do," she said dryly, "then he'll be wanting them back. Come on, let's see if there are any landing marks."

They searched for half an hour, but found nothing, and at last hiked back down the side of the mesa.

# FORTY-FOUR

# JAMES ROBERT SINCLAIR

"Prophet Sinclair?" Tim Dresner called, knocking on the door. "It's fifteen minutes until taping."

"I need an extra ten minutes," Sinclair called, amazed by his own calm. "Tell the choir to entertain the congregation, will you, Tim?"

"Uh, yes, Prophet. No problem."

Only a few minutes before, Sinclair had opened his eyes to find himself sitting against the tunnel door in his bedroom. He still sat there now, trying to comprehend what had happened, trying to remember it all, wondering if he was going mad.

"I shall lead them to heaven," he said, a vague memory returning.

He rose, his sore knees protesting, and walked across the room to the mirrored closet. "My God," he said, seeing that his baseball cap and his shirt were gone. "It really happened." Red dust coated him from head to toe, and looking behind him, he saw that he'd left red footprints on the powder blue carpet.

He remembered going to Olive Mesa to meditate on the previous night's vision, but he had no recollection of the return trip. The angel had told him to look into its eyes. He could remember nothing after that. *Did I look?*

He thought he hadn't because he was sure he would have remembered. *Look at me and you shall see the truth,* the Voice had told him.

He had proven himself a coward but had been forgiven, perhaps promised another chance.

He stared at his disheveled, filthy body in the mirror and shook his head. "Maybe you're having a nervous breakdown, my friend," he told his image. "You're believing your own sermons."

But as hard as it was for a lifelong skeptic to accept, he did believe in God now. He *knew.* He didn't know how, but he *knew.*

Time was wasting, but before taking a shower, he walked back to the tunnel door and opened it. Stepping inside, he saw that his electric cart was missing. He had walked back. He couldn't believe that, though, because his back didn't hurt and he would have had to remain bent over for the entire distance.

*Then how did I get back?* Amazed, he felt his heart swell with joy: This was further proof that something miraculous had happened to him.

"Prophet?" Tim's voice carried through the locked entry door. "Are you ready?"

"Tim." Full of joy, full of love, he walked to the door and opened it wide.

Tim's jaw worked as he took in the sight of his dusty, half-clothed Prophet, but no words came out. Sinclair laid one gentle hand on the shoulder of his aide.

"Prophet?" Dresner murmured, his eyes wide.

"Tim. Go to the church and tell them there will be no taping today. What I have to say is far too important for that. Tonight's sermon will be broadcast live."

"Y-yes, Prophet."

"I have spoken with God Himself. Tell the Apostles to go forth and spread the word. Tell them to rejoice."

"Yes, sir."

Sinclair closed the door softly.

*The time is at hand and you shall lead them.* The words echoed softly through his mind.

# FORTY-FIVE

# HANK MARQUAY

The tea and toast he'd eaten an hour ago seemed to set well, and Hank Marquay decided to get dressed and go to work. Pushing himself up out of the easy chair in front of the television set, he pulled his bathrobe tighter around him and padded through the darkened living room toward the bedroom.

The place was a mess, and he told himself that when Madge came back, she'd have his hide for letting it get so bad. All the dishes were dirty, piled on the counter and in cold murky water in the sink, and his clothes were everywhere, all of them dirty. Yes, Madge would have a fit.

And he couldn't wait.

He tried to face facts, tried to tell himself that his wife of thirty-five years wouldn't be returning, that something had happened to her, but he couldn't continue to live and think such things. Last night, while he'd still been running to the toilet every ten minutes, he'd told himself that Madge might be dead, and his mood had turned so black that he'd gone into the bedroom and taken his revolver from the nightstand drawer. He had held it up to his mouth, hand trembling, but two things stopped him from pulling the trigger: the hope that

Madge might still be alive, and his gut clenching down in another attack of diarrhea.

Now he changed into his work clothes—a miner's outfit made up of Levi's, red plaid shirt, cap, and boots—then locked up and drove his old Ford pickup from New Madelyn to Old. He parked in the Madland parking lot and walked through the park's back entrance to avoid his well-meaning friends and their words of condolence and support. He just couldn't take it today.

The park wasn't crowded, wouldn't be until the weekend, and he looked forward to the hustle and bustle that would come with the tourists. It would help keep his mind off Madge.

"Hank!"

He looked up to see Father Corey walking down the path from his little church. The young man wasn't in his priest's collar today. Instead he wore an old paint-spattered shirt, cap, and jeans. Reluctantly Hank halted. *No more sympathy, please!* "Hot out today, isn't it?" he grunted.

"Like summer," the priest agreed. "Justin said you weren't feeling well, Hank. How are you?"

"Just a little stomach flu, Father Mike. I'm fine now. Doing a little painting?" he asked before the priest could say something consolatory.

Michael Corey's look of concern turned into a frown. "You must not have heard. Somebody broke into the church and vandalized it. They painted satanic symbols and nearly ruined the crucifix. Gus Gilliam thinks he can get the blood off and restore it, thank the Lord." He crossed himself.

"One of those devil cults do it?"

Corey shook his head. "I don't know. Chief Baskerville is investigating, but I don't expect much to come of it. He's too busy with—with the other problems. Hank, I'm sorry about Madge. If you'd like to talk—"

"Thanks, Father," Marquay said quickly as tears sprang to his eyes. "She'll be back. I've gotta go." He started trudging toward the mine.

"I'll pray for her," Corey called after him.

Hank raised his hand in acknowledgment, not trusting his voice, and continued walking.

"What the—"

The Haunted Mine Ride was closed. He stepped up to the ticket booth to read the note in the window. "Closed for repairs, will reopen tomorrow."

"What the hell?" If something was wrong with the ride, Justin should have told him about it. Irritated, he let himself into the cool interior, sniffing the air as the door slapped shut behind him.

"Holy shit!" No wonder Justin had closed the place down; it smelled like something had curled up and died inside the mine. "Justin? You in here? Justin? Answer me, son!"

# FORTY-SIX

# JUSTIN MARTIN

"Shit!" Justin Martin whispered the word, then yelled, "Be right up, Mr. Marquay!"

He never expected the old man to show up, just as he hadn't expected the goddamned afternoon heat that had made the bodies start stinking. He had to think fast.

"Where are you?" Marquay's voice echoed down into the old pit where Justin was working.

"Mr. Marquay?" he called, shoveling dirt.

"Justin?"

"Wait there! I'll be up in just a minute."

"Hurry!"

"I will!"

Feverishly he shoveled dirt over the bodies in the center of the pit. When he had come at quarter to three, he'd immediately detected the faint but unmistakable odor of putrefaction wafting up from below. He thought the little room at the bottom of the shaft was so deep and the air so cool that it wouldn't happen. After all, Joe Huxley, his first victim, hadn't made much of a stink; certainly not enough to drift upstairs or into the vents. But Huxley had been a scrawny old sun mummy in the first place, without much meat on his bones. His body had swollen, then slowly shriveled until he looked like a real mummy. Justin had been a fool not to take better precautions.

He'd hurriedly put the closed-for-repairs sign out front, then grabbed one of the antique pickaxes and a shovel from the display in one of the ride's exhibits and climbed down into the pit. Lighting his lantern, he saw that Kyla Powers's heavyset and very bloated body had exploded. Fluids and pus oozed from a foot- sized hole in the abdomen. Madge Marquay must have stepped in it. His stomach had turned when he'd seen the maggots swarming in the viscera: He also hadn't expected any flies to come down so far into the earth. *They smelled meat.*

Stolidly he'd gone to work, using the pickax to break up the rocky dirt floor of the chamber. He worked for nearly an hour until, sweating, muscles heavy and sore, he'd managed to make a wide, shallow pit in the middle of the floor. Just before Old Man Marquay showed up, he'd pushed the bodies into it and begun covering them.

"Justin! I'm coming down!"

"No!" he yelled at the top of his lungs. "I'm on my way up!" He threw the last shovelful of earth over Kyla Powers's bubbling abdomen. The bodies weren't entirely covered: He was going to have to do more, maybe bring down some borax or, if he could get it, lime. Taking the shovel and lantern, he quickly climbed the rope ladder out of the excavation, then took the two iron ladders that led to the upper levels, leaving the lift safely below.

"Justin?" Marquay's voice was close now.

Holding up the lantern, Justin stepped onto the tracks that the ride's "mining" cars ran on. "Coming." He started walking toward the exit.

In a moment the ride's hidden lights came on and Marquay appeared in a wide wood-shored doorway. "Hi, Mr. Marquay."

"What the hell were you doing down there?" the man asked, his arms crossed. "What are you doing with that shovel?"

Justin joined him, arranging his features into a look of solemnity. Briefly he considered hitting Marquay over the head with the shovel, but shelved the notion quickly: Others might have seen him come in. Besides, Justin needed the paycheck the old man supplied every other week. "Remember the rat traps you had me set last month?" he asked as they walked toward the ride's main door.

"No. I don't remember anything about rattraps."

"Sure, you had me go all the way into Barstow for those great big ones."

"Oh, yeah, yeah," he muttered.

Justin hid his smile. There had never been any rattraps, but he knew Marquay had too much on his mind already and wouldn't admit he forgot.

Grimly Justin said, "When I got here I noticed the smell, so I went around checking the traps."

"What'd you do, catch a hundred-pounder?"

*If you only knew.* "No, sir, a possum, right under one of the venti-lating shafts.

That's why I put up the closed sign."

"Where is it?"

"I buried it. I didn't know what else to do," he added innocently. "I didn't want to carry it up the ladder, and even if I had, I didn't think putting it in the Dumpster would be a good idea."

"Smart boy."

They stood by the mining cars in the passenger loading area. "You'd better go home and take a shower and change. It still reeks in here, so we'll stay closed, try to get the place aired out for tomorrow."

"Mr. Marquay?"

"What?"

"I have an idea."

"What is it?"

"Maybe I could go down to the store and get some lime to spread on the ground. I couldn't dig very deep," he added, shamefaced.

"Should've used a pickax." Marquay dug in his wallet and

handed Justin some bills. "Get a lot and spread it around. And get rid of those rattraps. They're more trouble than they're worth."

"Yes, sir." Justin opened the door, squinting in the bright afternoon sunlight.

"Justin?"

"Yes, Mr. Marquay?"

"I'm going to go on home. That smell's got my stomach feeling funny again. You'll come right back and do the work?"

"You can count on me!"

"I know I can, Justin, and I appreciate it. I'm leaving the fans on. Turn them off when you're finished tonight."

"I sure will. See you tomorrow, Mr. Marquay!"

## FORTY-SEVEN

# HANNIBAL CAINE

"He wouldn't say anything except that he has spoken to God." Hannibal Caine rubbed his broad forehead. He was developing a whopper of a headache as he sat here in his dining room in his apartment adjacent to the Fellowship House.

"If the Prophet says he's spoken to God, then he has," Eldo Blandings said with finality. "Do you doubt that?"

"No, of course not," Caine said quickly. Eldo might be willing to commit outrageous acts in the name of the Prophet, but he wouldn't blaspheme him. "I just wish he would tell us what he intends to say tonight."

Blandings rose, his gray toupee slightly crooked on his head. "Be patient, Hannibal, and have faith in the Prophet, as you do in the Lord."

Caine walked him to the door. "By the way, you may have a new man for your special projects group soon."

"That kid that took the goat?"

Caine nodded. "Justin Martin. Very smart, very ambitious. I've given him a test. If he passes it, I'll send him to you."

"Can you trust him?"

"Yes," Caine said. "He doesn't want his parents to find out about the goat. He dissected it. Says he wants to be a doctor."

Eldo Blandings laughed. "Speaking of the Committee, I have a special project meeting to chair in a few minutes."

"The whore's theater?" Caine raised his eyebrows.

"Just going to throw a little fear of God into those devil-loving actors." Blandings's dishwater eyes nearly twinkled. "Care to join us?"

"Thanks, but I'll stay here and keep an eye on things." The theater project was purely Blandings's baby: He thought all male actors were homosexual, and the passion of his hatred told Caine chapters about his fellow Elder. At first Caine had gently tried to talk him out of it, but Eldo had promised to keep it mild—a little paint was all—and after the UFO sightings, it seemed somehow more fitting. Also, Caine looked forward to springing his little surprise on Eldo and his merry band.

"Okay, then, I'll see you later." He paused. "There's someone else who deserves some censuring, too."

"There is?" Caine asked lightly. Blandings felt that anyone who looked at him sideways deserved retribution.

"General manager of the park, tall man in cowboy clothes." Eldo's eyes were pinpricks of hatred. "He kicked us out and went out of his way to humiliate me. In front of my people."

Caine nodded. "We'll discuss it later, Eldo."

Blandings started to leave, then turned back. "Remember, Hannibal, have faith in Prophet Sinclair."

"I'll remember."

Closing the door, Caine crossed to a cherry wood hutch, opened the inlaid glass doors, and withdrew a crystal decanter of brandy and a snifter. He poured more than a connoisseur would consider proper, then took the snifter to his creamy leather couch and sat down with a sigh.

As soon as he'd heard that Sinclair wasn't going to tape his sermon but give it live tonight, he'd gone to talk to the Prophet. But

Sinclair wouldn't see him, telling him they would speak in an hour in his office. Caine waited impatiently and when he was finally buzzed in, he was shocked to see James Robert Sinclair sitting behind his desk in trousers and a white button-down shirt without a jacket or tie. Sinclair never appeared in public wearing less than a full suit, even on the hottest August day.

Even more shocking, the ponytail he kept hidden was outside his shirt.

"James, your hair ..." The words escaped before he could stop them.

Sinclair only smiled. "I thought my hair was a vanity, Hannibal. But I've come to realize that my true vanity is in hiding it to maintain the proper image."

Caine could find no answer to that. Finally he spoke. "May I ask why you're doing the broadcast live?"

"I've seen God, Hannibal." Sinclair, the ultimate actor, spoke with the voice of serenity. "And He has spoken to me."

"James, what did He say to you?"

"He gave me news."

"What news?"

"Joyous news, but that's all I will say for now." Sinclair smiled. "Rejoice, Hannibal. We are saved."

Caine nodded and excused himself, his gut as cold as ice.

And now, despite the warm brandy in his belly, he felt another chill. He had been certain, *certain,* that Sinclair was going to disappear on the day of the Apocalypse. All of Caine's own plans hinged on it.

But now he saw that Sinclair either was insane or, more likely, had decided to further milk his ministry. He was going to cancel the Apocalypse with his "joyous news." And that would ruin Caine's plans. He couldn't let that happen.

Hannibal finished his brandy and poured a little more. Maybe Sinclair wasn't tired of playing at religion, but he was tired of living in his shadow. Once he was sure that Sinclair was veering off his path, then he would take action.

The world of Jim-Bob Sinclair was going to end, all right. Of that, Hannibal Caine had no doubt, because he intended to see that it happened.

# FORTY-EIGHT

# ALEXANDRA MANDERLEY

At dusk, Alexandra Manderley passed through the open wrought-iron gates of El Dorado Ranch Road and drove the narrow mile-long private road to Tom Abernathy's sprawling Spanish-style ranch house, cream-colored stucco with an adobe tile roof. The courtyard was enclosed by stuccoed pillars holding black iron fencing, and as she opened the gate and walked under the arch into the patio, she felt as if she were in the dry, hot desert no longer. The front courtyard was paved with flagstone and lined with potted palms and cacti. Low round adobe bowls filled with yellow and orange marigolds lined the walkway to the house.

She stepped onto the veranda and rang the bell beside the carved wooden door, feeling guilty for leaving Eric behind; feeling guilty for being here at all.

After the sighting at Olive Mesa, the pair had headed back down to the Old Madelyn Campground, where they took much-needed showers at the campground's central facility. After that, refreshed, they drove to the new campsite and set up, or rather Eric did while she busied herself cleaning the equipment. Finally, leaving the cellular phone with Eric, she made him promise to call her if he spotted anything unusual overhead, and told him she'd be back by ten.

"Why, howdy, Doc. Come on in." Tom Abernathy pulled the door wide and stepped back, gesturing her inside. As always, he looked like a cowboy, in boots, jeans, and a light blue shirt, the sleeves rolled up in deference to the balmy night.

"What a beautiful home." The sunken living room was open and airy with gleaming hardwood floors and Navajo rugs, while the white rough-textured walls were decorated with western art and native weavings that went perfectly with the heavy leather and wood furniture. An arched fireplace took up most of one wall. At the rear of the room, wagon-wheel-style railings separated this room from the rest of the house.

"Everyone's in back." Tom hung her jacket on an old-fashioned bentwood coatrack and led her up the steps past the walkway, through an archway, and down a short hall lined with Remington prints. Despite the thick walls, she finally heard voices and a few guitar chords. Nervously she followed Tom around a corner, and found herself in a huge room with another fireplace, full of people and the heavenly odor of mesquite and ribs. Nearby, a long buffet table held covered dishes, some nestled in ice, others on warming trays. A stack of thick cobalt blue plates sat near a large empty expanse at one end, and at the other were condiments, utensils, napkins, a coffeepot, and an ice-filled cooler loaded with sodas, bottled waters, and beer.

Tom nodded at a small dark man in jeans and a bleached denim shirt who sat by the fireplace brushing sauce on a rotating spit of ribs. "We turned the fireplace into the kind you can cook in because it's just too dang hot here come summer to cook outside."

"It's nice out now," Alex said, glad no one had noticed their entrance. Sliding glass doors were wide open on a rear courtyard, this one lit with luminaria-style paper lanterns strung amidst a plethora of greenery. Small candlelit iron and glass tables with matching chairs were grouped close together under a redwood lattice woven with philodendron, and a tiered tile fountain bubbled invitingly nearby.

"It'll get cold in an hour or so," Tom said. He pointed at the court-yard. "Plants like it better if we cook in here and eat out there. They don't much care for the smoke, but they like the company."

Alex smiled at him. "You're full of surprises, Mr. Abernathy."

"Just Tom. Let me introduce you around, Doc."

"Alex," she murmured as he took her arm and led her toward a conversation area at the far end of the room. Several easy chairs and a sectional couch were gathered around a bark-edged coffee table obvi-ously hewn from a single huge tree. Tom saw her looking at it. "It's better'n a century old. I didn't kill any giant redwoods, don't worry."

On the wall facing the conversation pit stood a massive oak enter-tainment center, which held a twenty-five-inch television, turned off, a stereo, and, behind the glass-front cabinets, row after row of video-tapes, mostly westerns like *Broken Arrow, El Dorado, and High Noon.*

"Folks," Tom was saying to the people on the couch, "this here's Dr. Alex Manderley. She's here studying our UFOs."

At Tom's voice, the two people on the couch turned around. One of them was Moss Baskerville. He rose, along with a copper-haired woman whose sleeveless cotton shirt revealed a number of colorful tattoos. "Cassie," the cop said, "this is the lady I thought was my new officer."

The willowy redhead grinned at her. "Pleased to meet you." She poked Baskerville's ribs companionably. "I'm glad you were wrong, Moss." She stuck out her hand and shook Alex's with a firm dry grip. "That's Eve, over there with Davy," she said, pointing at a little blond girl who had joined the man basting the ribs.

Tom next introduced her to Michael Corey, a pleasant, timid-looking young priest who was picking "Home on the Range" out on a guitar, to Ray Vine, whose deep voice was just as commanding now as it had been when he'd told the truckers in the diner to back off, and his wife, Rosie, who had a pleasant open face and a marvelous laugh. At last he came to Davy Styles.

"Ma'am," Davy said, rising. His straight black hair was thick and brushed the back of his shirt collar. High cheekbones and a square jaw told her his heritage.

"Alex," she said. "Are you Cherokee?"

The serious face split into a dimpled grin that made him look very young. "You're only the second person to guess right the first time."

"I was the first," Tom said proudly. He glanced at his watch. "A few more ought to be showing up any minute now. You might've met a couple of them already."

Immediately she thought of Carlo Pelegrine, and a little thrill of pleasure and fear coursed through her. Just then the door chimes rang. "Excuse me a minute."

# FORTY-NINE

# TOM ABERNATHY

"I hope I'm not late, cowboy."

Marie Lopez's smile made the evening complete for Tom Abernathy. "Not at all. Davy's still working on the ribs." He hadn't seen her since breakfast this morning, but it seemed much longer than that, and he had to control his urge to grab her up and give her a squeeze. As she passed him he caught a whiff of her; no lanolin tonight, only the clean scent of shampoo and a delicate flowery fragrance that reminded him of the star jasmine blooming in his back courtyard.

"My goodness, Marie, look at you! I don't think I've ever seen you in a dress before."

She twirled, showing off the flowing turquoise dress belted with a striped sash. A teardrop of turquoise on a silver neck chain nestled just where Tom wished to do the same. "My aunt sent it to me for my birthday. Is it too much?" She began to look embarrassed. "Maybe I should go home and change."

"Absolutely not. It's prettier than sunrise." He paused, admiring her. "You never mentioned your birthday before."

She shook her head and smiled. "Everybody has them."

"When's yours?"

"I'm not gonna tell you, Tom, because I don't want any fuss."

He grinned back. "Then how old are you?"

She punched him in the arm, fairly gently. "I thought you were a gentleman, cowboy."

"I thought liberated women didn't mind telling their ages."

"Touché. Let's just put it this way: Aunt Carmen also sent a note saying that I was getting too old to be single and I should use this outfit to catch a man's eye." She hesitated, and even in the dim light, Tom caught her blush. "Aunt Carmen's old-fashioned," she added quickly, "and my legs are cold in this getup. I'll be back in twenty minutes."

Marie turned and made for the door, but Tom caught her elbow, turning her toward him. "Don't leave, Marie," he said softly, "please?" Amazed, he watched himself reach out and take her other hand. "That dress is real pretty, but you don't need it to attract a man."

"What are you saying, Tom?" she asked, staring at their joined hands.

His stomach did a flip-flop. He was more than a foot taller than her, and he wished he could see her eyes instead of her glossy dark hair. Hell, he might've even kissed her if she'd been in easy reach. "I'm just saying ... well, what I mean is—"

"Tom?" Alex Manderley hesitated in the doorway. "I'm sorry. I didn't mean to interrupt—"

Tom and Marie let their hands drop. "No problem, Doc. What can I do for you?"

She stepped forward. "I just wondered if it would be all right if I called Eric and left your number with him."

"Of course." He pointed her in the direction of the kitchen. "Nearest phone's right through there."

"Who's that?" Marie asked after Alex disappeared.

"Alex Manderley. She's the UFO researcher I was telling you about." He paused. "You know, it wouldn't be a bad idea for you to tell her about the missing sheep. She'd be interested."

"Don't start again, cowboy. I don't care to be written up in some book or something." She gestured down at her outfit. "I've already made a big enough fool of myself as it is."

"Marie, I—" But the moment was gone. "You're as far from fool as I've ever seen," he finished weakly.

"Thanks." She fixed him with a look. "Not a word about the sheep. Promise."

"Cross my heart."

Finally, assuaged, she gave him a little bitty smile. "The smell of Davy's cooking's making my mouth water. Let's go take a look."

Tom followed her into the den, feeling just a little shaky. He didn't know why he was so sure Marie would turn him down if he declared himself; after all, he'd never had trouble of that nature back in his youth. Maybe, he thought as he watched her go up to Davy and exchange hugs, it was because he'd never fallen in love before.

Marie moved through the room hugging everyone hello; Cassie, Moss, Eve, Mike Corey. He was the only one she never hugged, but then again, he wasn't the huggy type, and maybe she realized that and was just respecting his style. The way she hadn't drawn away when he took her hand, though, made him hope it was possible she was timid around him for the same reason he was shy with her.

## FIFTY

# CARLO PELEGRINE

The scientific name was doraphilia, a term that Carlo Pelegrine thought sounded more like a preoccupation with women of a certain name than a fetish for skin.

Carlo stood under the shower's hot spray, scrubbing his own skin with a soapy loofah. He'd had a last-minute appointment with Ann Quigley, a frail, middle- aged resident of New Madelyn. She was a sweet woman who had had an unbearably sad life, and when she called, Carlo couldn't turn her down, even though it meant he'd be late for Tom's barbecue. All Ann wanted was a little sympathy from someone who would listen to her and reassure her that she hadn't been a bad wife because her husband had died of a heart attack ten years before, or that she hadn't been a bad mother because one of her children drowned in a neighbor's pool shortly thereafter, or because her other had been killed last year by a hit-and-run driver. Then there were the dogs. Having lost her family, she lost one cocker spaniel after another. Some disappeared, others met with accidents. The woman was so full of guilt, yet she was guiltless.

He had sat with her in his reading room for over an hour, listening, comforting, finally reading her palm. Rinsing the shampoo from his hair, he thought about her skin. It was very light and fine-pored with a light sprinkling of freckles. She had a scar like a crescent moon on one index finger that fascinated him. When he asked her about it, she told him that when she was ten, she and her best friend used a jackknife to cut themselves so that they could become blood sisters. So romantic in its way. Nostalgic. That was something one couldn't do anymore. He'd run his own finger over the scar once more than he should have, and still felt guilty for it.

He turned off the shower and stepped out onto a terry bath mat, then began drying with a thick white towel. He rubbed hard, just as he scrubbed hard, a neurotic habit that had begun after the murders twenty years ago. In the first years, he'd had something of a hand-washing compulsion, but recognizing it helped him overcome it. Now he was merely a little obsessive about cleanliness in general, and that, he could live with.

He tossed the towel in the hamper, then padded into his bedroom to dress in the clothes he'd already laid out. His choice of clothing amused him because it harkened back to his Brooklyn youth: tight jeans over ankle-high black boots, a white long-sleeved shirt, and a black leather bomber jacket. It was close enough to what everyone else wore to allow him to fit in, but personal enough to make him comfortable.

He buttoned the shirt up to the neck, as he always did, to prevent his chest hair from showing. He rarely looked at himself shirtless because he disliked the hair: It detracted from his skin. At least there wasn't any on his back. There his light olive skin was as smooth as it had been before he hit puberty.

As far as Carlo Pelegrine knew, he had been born with his skin fetish. Try as he might, he could find no psychological cause, though he had no doubt one existed. But the obvious one, that he hadn't been touched or cuddled enough as a child, was certainly not the problem: His entire family hugged and kissed one another in totally normal, familial ways.

He had been no different. Little Charles Pilgrim, named for his grandfather (who had been Carlo Pellegrino before coming to America), had hugged and kissed his mother and father, roughhoused with his brother and friends. But then he began to sense something about himself, some difference between him and his family and friends.

It began with a bottle of Elmer's Glue All. One day he and his brother smeared it on their palms and let it dry, then peeled it off, just as every other kid in the world had done. But Carlo couldn't stop. He kept a bottle of glue out in the backyard, and sometimes he'd spend hours spreading it on and peeling it off.

That summer he got a bad sunburn at Brighton Beach and he watched, fascinated, as the skin on his abdomen and shoulders blistered. Hidden under his bedspread on a hot July night, holding a flashlight, he stuck a pin in the blisters and gently compressed the serum out.

And felt dirty for doing it, even though he was never caught. To him, it seemed a sin as bad as masturbation, and he never confessed to the priest because, even then, he knew it couldn't be forgiven.

Then the skin dried and began to peel. Slowly, carefully, he learned to peel the dead skin off, rolling it gently down, trying to keep it intact. He'd hold it up to the light, studying it with endless fascination. And with each burn he got—and he had several that first summer—he peeled his skin and folded it neatly and put the pieces in individual wax paper sandwich bags, each dated and hidden away.

His collection grew summer by summer, until he turned sixteen and grew handsome. Until the high school girls noticed him.

And he noticed them.

He was afraid of his new feelings, and afraid of the opportunities that kept presenting themselves. Even before anything happened, he sensed that his lust for them was dangerous, and though he dated, he refused to let himself go very far. Fortunately, just the feel of feminine lips against his, the taste and incredible pliant softness, was sweet torture.

During the summer of his seventeenth year, he began to learn the rudiments of self-control, but they weren't enough to prevent what happened a week before his birthday.

Carlo grabbed his keys and trotted downstairs, going out the back door and wheeling his motorcycle out of the little shed behind his store. He swung onto the machine and turned the ignition, then rode slowly down the narrow access road until he reached Old Madelyn Highway, where he turned south, toward Tom's ranch.

Tom once told him that he measured a man by what he saw, not by what he had done in the past, and that helped Carlo accept the rancher's friendship, and the friendship of the others. But even with Tom, he remained distant, knowing that his past would be unacceptable, even to a man who seemed to accept everything and everyone. Carlo's secrets were beyond comprehension. Even his own.

The first victim, whom he took on a chill, foggy October day, was a prostitute, just as his later victims would be.

It was Saturday, and he and his friends Glen MacIntyre and Ted Furillo had taken the B Train to Coney Island. The place was cold and deserted, the parks nothing but ancient dinosaur bones rising in the mist.

Carlo loved the derelict amusement parks, loved sneaking inside and walking among the skeletal remains. He always imagined he heard the ghosts of the past, childish screams as roller coasters groaned and whooshed, blasts of air and young girls' giggling shrieks as they tried to keep their skirts down, the carnies seducing quarters and dollars from the pockets of young men who wanted to impress their girls. Those sounds mixed with the ocean's endless roar and the wind whistling through coasters and past boarded-up buildings to give Carlo a sense of peace and wonder.

Glen and Ted wouldn't have understood. They loved to go into the parks, but were interested in petty acts of vandalism, not sitting quietly and soaking up the atmosphere. Now, as the three of them walked along the deserted boardwalk, Ted and Glen were one-upping each another with tales of their lovemaking prowess. The trio had gone out with three cheerleaders for pizza and a movie the night before. After, they split up. Carlo took his date to a coffee shop, then straight home. The girl had been willing and he knew he'd disappointed her, but each time he looked at her, each time he felt her shoulder against his in the movie theater, frightening images filled his head, visions of him touching her skin, petting it, filling him with such lust that he wanted to devour her. He barely made it through the evening.

Glen and Ted had no such problems, but ruined the other girls' reputations with every word they uttered. Now Ted turned to Carlo, who was still Charles Pilgrim. "Hey, Chucky, did Laurie put out for you last night?"

"Does she play the skin flute?" cried Glen.

"The mouth organ?" Ted added.

"I know, I know," Glen screeched. "The sexaphone!"

Carlo just looked at them, smiled, and the pair nodded at each other.

"He ain't talking, Ted. He *really* got laid."

"You mean you didn't?" Carlo asked innocently.

Glen and Ted responded with obscene descriptions of the powers of their cheerleaders' oral abilities. Carlo didn't believe a word of it.

They walked a little farther and were just beginning to discuss the best places to climb over one of the park fences when they saw the girls. The women. Glen and Ted's hoots silenced as the miniskirted, heavily made-up females walked toward the boys, their hips moving as if they were full of ball bearings.

"Silicone tits," Glen hissed, seeing the unmoving oversized breasts on a dark- haired woman snapping gum as if her life depended on it.

"I hear silicone tits are as hard as rocks," Ted told him.

"Oh, yeah? Well, so am I." Glen glanced at Carlo, who was considered the brains of the trio. "You think they're whores?"

"Could be." The other two girls, both bleached blondes, wore form-fitting sweaters and almost nonexistent skirts, just like Silicone Tits. Tits had black mesh nylons, as did one blonde. The other wore white nylons, the opaque tops showing slightly from beneath her purple skirt each time she took a step.

"Hey, boys," said the brunette as they came face-to-face.

"Hey, girls," Glen said in a goofy tone.

"You looking for some fun?"

The other boys glanced at Carlo. He nodded slightly, meaning that he was sure these girls were hookers, but the other two obviously thought he meant "go for it."

"Sure," Ted said. "We're looking for fun."

"Got any money?" asked the black-stockinged blonde.

Ted and Glen nodded enthusiastically.

"Do you?" White Stockings asked Carlo, licking her lips. He was staring at her peeling, sunburned shoulders.

He nodded hesitantly.

She giggled and whispered in his ear. Did he want a blow job?

You bet. This, he thought, might be safe. He told himself his fantasies wouldn't take control of him if he didn't touch her, if she only touched him.

"See you guys later," Ted called as he strolled toward an abandoned pier with Silicone Tits. Glen put his arm around one of the blondes and they took off in another direction, leaving Carlo with White Stockings. "My name's Lola," she told him, "And you know what they say?"

He shook his head.

"Whatever Lola wants, Lola gets," she told him. "Come on, cutie."

She led him toward the old amusement park and in through a well-disguised break in the chain-link fencing. Keeping to the shadows, disguised by the fog, they were invisible. Lola took him deep into the park, farther than he had ever dared go before. She obviously knew her way around, and soon they entered a large building. The House of Mirrors.

Producing a flashlight from her voluminous purse, she took his hand, warning him to watch his step, that there was broken glass everywhere. As they moved, he caught brief, crazed images of himself in the distorted mirrors. He thought he looked like a monster.

Finally they came to a small room with mirrors everywhere, reflecting their faceted images from all around and even above. Few of the mirrors were broken here, or even cracked. Probably, thought Carlo, because the place was so hard to find.

In the middle of the room lay a pile of old canvas tarps and a kerosene camping lantern beside them. Lola used a cigarette lighter to light it, then turned toward Carlo, licking her lips and folding down to her knees on the material. She took his hand, and Carlo, trembling with desire, nearly overcome with it, let her pull him forward.

She looked up at him. Mascara had smeared under one eye. "You're a real hunk, you know that?"

He shrugged.

"How old are you? Eighteen? Nineteen?"

"Nineteen," he lied.

She began to tug on his zipper. "How much money you got?"

Trembling, he pulled out his billfold, looked inside. "Forty dollars."

At that, she let go of his belt and grabbed his hands, pulling him down beside her. "For that, we can go all the way, sweet thing." She pulled her sweater over her head, exposing peeling, sunburned flesh and a black lace bra. "Would you like that?"

Dumbly he stared at her as she unhooked her bra, revealing heavy breasts, pale white with a delicate tracery of blue veins around rusty-rose nipples.

"Get undressed. What's your name?"

"Charlie," he said, unbuttoning his shirt, thinking about feeling his skin against hers, frightened, excited.

She stood up and unzipped the skirt, let it fall to the ground. All around, images of her flickered in the mirrors.

"Let me," Carlo whispered as she hooked her thumbs into her white panty hose.

"Sure, babe." With trembling fingers, he slowly, oh so slowly, peeled the panty hose down over her hips, thighs, calves. He stared up at her as she reached down and pulled them off. The soles of her feet were filthy.

"Like what you see?" she asked, running her hands over her ribs.

Swallowing hard, he nodded. Her breasts and pubic area stood out in stark contrast to the tanned and burned flesh. A tiny strip of peeling skin at her bikini line caught his eye. He stared at it and his hand went out and touched it. Delicately he pulled it away, then gazed at it on his fingers.

"Hey, Charlie, let's do it. Take off your pants."

Mesmerized by her skin on his fingers, he didn't move until she pushed his shoulder. "What's the matter? You never seen a sunburn before?" She got to her knees and undid his belt and zipper, pushing his jeans down around his knees. She grinned. "Well, you're ready," she said. With one hand, she dug in her purse and pulled out a condom. Tearing the package open with her teeth, she slipped the condom on him and pulled him down on top of her, guiding him with her hand.

His hands roamed her body and he was barely aware that he was making love to her. The sensations he concentrated on were in his fingers as he touched, sometimes plucking at her peeling skin, moving his hands low over thighs, up over the curves of her waist, around her breasts, kneading, patting, stroking.

He still remembered the desire, a need so strong that it finally overtook him. He remembered being hypnotized by the mirrors, watching his hands as they moved higher and higher, up to her shoulders, his fingers digging into her flesh, her screaming and flailing, cursing him as his nails drew blood.

And that was all. He remembered no more until he found himself dressed, wandering aimlessly around the abandoned park. The sun had moved westward and at least two hours had passed.

He saw blood under his nails. And skin.

Shocked, he ran, searching for the House of Mirrors. When he found it, there was nothing within but darkness, and he knew it would be useless to try to find the room of faceted mirrors. He called and called, but there was no reply except for the echo of his own voice. In his gut, he knew that the prostitute was dead.

Back out in the hazy sunlight, he remembered his wallet and began to panic. But amazingly, it was in his back pocket. Everything but the forty dollars was there. He'd left her with that, at least. Checking himself further, he found that he had left nothing of his belongings: His comb and jackknife were in his pants pockets.

Yet he remembered nothing. All he could think of was how silly he thought *The Wolfman* was when he'd watched it late at night a few months before. It didn't seem so silly anymore.

But then, as he made his way through the deserted amusement park, it all began to seem like a dream, a nightmare. Finally he located the camouflaged hole in the fence and climbed through, grateful that no one was on the boardwalk.

Numb, in shock, trying to comprehend the incomprehensible, he walked down onto the beach. The ocean looked chill and dark, and smelled of rotting seaweed. Gnats swarmed around his feet as he walked. When he reached the hard-packed sand near the water's edge, he walked slowly along the deserted shore, turning his jacket collar up against the cold wind.

Winter was coming. He could see it in the color of the sky, hear it in the crashing waves, taste it on the air. He approached a mass of seaweed, recoiling slightly when he spotted a dead seagull twisted in the vines. The body crawled with insects and a tiny crab scuttled out from beneath it. Disgusted, he stepped widely around it, and shoving his hands in his jacket pockets, he moved on.

Something slimy was in the right-hand pocket.

His stomach cramped as he felt the slippery mass around his fingers. He didn't have to look to know what it was, but he stopped walking and grimly pulled the piece of flesh from his pocket.

Carlo turned his motorcycle down the ranch road, remembering, trying to forget. He had been tempted to keep the skin. It aroused the dark thing that lived inside him. Instead, tears in his eyes, almost grateful he couldn't remember what had happened in the House of Mirrors, he flung it into the sea, food for the fishes. Then he approached the water and squatted, letting the salt water wash away the blood. He had no criminal record, had never been fingerprinted, and the body wasn't found until six months later, just after he committed his second atrocity.

As he pulled up next to Cassie's Honda Civic and killed the engine, he looked up into the night sky. The stars were clear and bright, the moon, a brilliant crescent border on a nearly invisible disk. To this day, he didn't know exactly what happened so long ago in the abandoned amusement park on Coney Island, any more than he remembered the bloody details of the other murders.

He remembered only that all three victims had been prostitutes, and the police theorized that their profession was his reason for the kills. But that was untrue: He had no grudge against them. It was simply because they approached him first and whispered things in his ear that made his blood boil, and then made him forget everything.

Checking his watch, Carlo saw that it was well past eight o'clock, so he walked directly around to the back courtyard. As he approached, he heard people talking and, as always, experienced an instant of self-hatred. None of these people would want to have anything to do with him if they knew what he had done. And rightly so. He was a living, walking lie, an unworthy were-creature only pretending to be a normal human being. Opening the gate, he resolutely pushed the dark thoughts from his mind.

"Hello, pilgrim."

Carlo, stunned by the name, stopped dead in his tracks, but Tom Abernathy just grinned at him from halfway across the patio. "Is my John Wayne impression that bad?"

Carlo managed a smile. Abernathy had used the same John Wayne line on him numerous times, but never had it shocked Pelegrine like it did now. "I've, ah, heard better," he said, returning Cassie's wave.

"Come on over here," she called. "We've got fresh blood."

He controlled a flinch, grateful he was rarely this sensitized.

"Go on," Tom echoed, leading him toward the group. "I'll tell Davy you're here so we can get down to some serious eating."

Approaching Cassie, he saw a woman beside her who was turned away from him, talking to Marie Lopez.

"Carlo Pelegrine, this is Alex Manderley," Cassie said.

At her name, Alex whipped her head around, her dark eyes wide and bright.

"Alex, this is Carlo, our illustrious fortune-teller."

Carlo stared at her, his throat dry.

"We've met," Alex said softly, her eyes locking on his. His heart skipped a beat.

And then she smiled, and it skipped another.

# FIFTY-ONE

# JUSTIN MARTIN

*Easy pickings.* Justin Martin cruised past Cassie Halloway's place and grinned, seeing that the house was dark and that neither her car or Baskerville's cruiser were there. Just to be safe, he turned around and drove south until he could see Tom Abernathy's brightly lit ranch house in the distance. Grabbing a pair of binoculars from behind the passenger seat, he trained them on Abernathy's place.

"Yeah, good," he whispered, picking out a yellow auto and a police cruiser parked at the cowboy's house.

It was about time something went right today. Justin had spent hours getting rid of the death stench in the pit below the Haunted Mine Ride. First he bought a bag of lime in Madelyn, just like Old Man Marquay expected him to, then he had driven into Barstow and bought four extra bags out of his own money.

Happily, by the time he returned, the park had closed for the day, which meant he didn't have to risk lugging the bags from the parking lot. Instead, he unlocked the big delivery gate and drove in, a legitimate delivery to make. No one had asked him what he was doing, and, in fact, the only person he thought even noticed him was Carlo

Pelegrine, who had been in front of his shop sweeping the sidewalk, still in his gypsy clothes. Justin had been tempted to stop and shoot a little shit, but decided against it since he had so much to do and so little time. Besides, he didn't want to arouse Pelegrine's suspicions by being too friendly too suddenly, so he proceeded straight to the mine.

The entire time he'd swung the pickax and wielded the shovel, Justin considered his options with regard to that asshole Hannibal Caine and his idiot "God's Green Berets." If the so-called test Caine had cited hadn't been so intriguing, he would have told the guy to fuck off, but by the time he was three- quarters done with the job in the mine, he had decided to go ahead and do the dirty deed.

After all, it couldn't hurt and it might be fun. Then, later, after he did a little investigating, maybe he'd turn tables on Caine and go to Jim-Bob Sinclair and tell him how Caine had blackmailed him into participating—which, to some extent, was the truth. After all, the way Caine talked, he suspected Jim-Bob didn't know anything about Caine's terrorist activities. *Trouble in paradise.* That tickled the hell out of Justin, and by the time he stopped home to shower and change, he was enthusiastic, and eager to get going: It was a situation that could be used to his advantage any number of ways.

He swung the Mustang around and cruised back to Cassie Halloway's with his lights out. He passed the house and pulled the Mustang to a stop behind some mesquite bushes that partially hid the vehicle.

Tugging on a pair of latex gloves, he grabbed a knapsack containing the items he would need, then locked the car and pocketed his keys. Everything remained quiet and dark. Pleased, he trotted across the road, then down to Halloway's front door, and opened the screen, letting it rest against his back.

He used his Swiss Army knife to pry the lid off a pint of red paint. This junk was a pain in the ass, and he'd wanted to use spray paint, but Caine, rightly, had told him that the police would write off the graffiti to high school punks if he did.

He placed the paint lid on a paper towel, then wiped his knife off and slipped it back in his pocket. Finally he dipped a brush in the paint and slapped "666" down the door, one giant dripping "6" in each of the three panels. Finished, he wrapped the brush in the towels, capped the paint, and stuck it all back in the knapsack.

Stepping back, he admired his work by the glow of his small penlight. At first glance, the numerals appeared to have been painted in blood.

Slinging the pack over one shoulder, Justin walked up the side of the house, keeping to the shadows. About ten feet from the cottage's back door, a narrow moonbeam highlighted a four-foot-high wood and wire fence enclosing a yard containing a tiny barn that was really nothing more than a large shed.

Justin opened the gate and went into the yard, turning on the penlight as he entered the little barn. It only took a moment to locate the single white goat.

"What to do, what to do, what to do?" he whispered, studying the goat. Caine wanted it killed and prominently displayed in front of the small Presbyterian church in New Madelyn, but Justin found the idea boring, unimaginative, not worth the risk.

He took his coil of rope from the knapsack, made a slipknot, and dropped it over the animal's head. There had to be something easy and imaginative he could do: something much better than leaving it on the church steps. Something with flair.

A slow smile spread across Justin's face. "Come on," he whispered, and led the goat toward his car.

## FIFTY-TWO

# ALEXANDRA MANDERLEY

They had piled their plates high with ribs, coleslaw, baked beans, and sourdough bread, and now Alex Manderley sat back in the metal patio chair and patted her stomach. "I've never eaten so much in my life!"

Cassie Halloway finished off her last rib. "Davy's cooking has that effect."

She, Eve, Carlo, and Alex shared one of the tables, and in a way, Alex was grateful for that. Although she wanted to be alone with Carlo, she was afraid of getting involved. Just as had happened two days ago at his store, his eyes, the color of bittersweet chocolate, seemed to burn into hers with an almost unbearable intensity. She couldn't look away, and didn't really want to because his gaze aroused in her desires that she had repressed for many years. The force of those feelings had been terrifying yet exhilarating when Carlo had followed her to the table after they filled their plates. They had exchanged a few words, about what, she had no idea, then Cassie approached and asked if they'd like to share the table. In unison, Alex and Carlo had said yes.

The fortune-teller had sounded as relieved as she felt, and that just served to make him all the more interesting. While they ate, Alex carefully avoided locking eyes with him, and the conversation stayed light as Cassie chattered about the new show opening at her theater. Now she pushed her plate back and excused Eve to go play, then leaned forward. "So how'd you like our UFO show last night?"

"Spectacular," Alex said.

"You think they're really from outer space?"

Alex glanced at Carlo and saw one corner of his mouth crook in amusement.

"Well," Alex began slowly, "from a purely skeptical point of view, there's a well-known weather phenomenon that occurs over Mount Shasta in Northern California. When hot and cold air flow together in a certain way, the results are saucer-shaped clouds the same blue-green color as we saw last night."

Cassie rubbed her chin. "You think they're just clouds?"

"No." Alex smiled. "I've seen the infamous Shasta 'saucers.' They're impressive, but they're just clouds. Yours aren't." She paused. "In my opinion."

"What do you think they are?" Carlo asked softly.

She tried to focus on the dark curl of hair that had strayed onto his forehead when she turned to him. "I don't know."

"Sometimes it's the not knowing that's best."

His soft-spoken words sent heat to her cheeks, but when she let her gaze meet his, his dark liquid eyes were guileless. She blushed again. "I agree." Clearing her throat, she looked at Cassie. "That's the beauty of life, I think. The more you learn, the more there is to learn."

"The possibilities are endless," Carlo responded.

Tom Abernathy chose that moment to stroll over to the table. "Folks, some of us are going inside to see if the end of the world is still scheduled for Sunday. Care to join us?"

"What?" Alex asked.

"It's almost time for Jim-Bob Sinclair's radio sermon," Cassie explained, rising. "He's a hoot."

Alex nodded. "I'll be along in a moment."

She watched the others drift into the house, acutely aware that Carlo Pelegrine remained seated. His neatly manicured hands, folded before him, were long-fingered with a sprinkling of short dark hairs between the first and second knuckles. On his right index finger, he wore a silver ring with an unusual onyx and carnelian inlaid setting.

"Your ring," she ventured. "Is it handmade?"

A slow smile gave him a boyish look. "Yes. It's Navajo. It means 'He who walks alone.' Before I came here, I spent a little time in Santa Fe and I met a medicine man. He taught me something about Navajo occult traditions," he explained. "Just before I left, he blessed the ring and gave it to me." He paused, spreading his hand to better show the ring. "A shaman's ring, very old." Chuckling self-deprecatingly, he added, "He told me I had the calling. In a way, I suppose he was right."

"What a lovely story." Alex reached out to touch it, then pulled back self-consciously. "And are you?"

Carlo raised his eyebrows questioningly.

"A man who walks alone?"

He stared off into the night for a long moment. "Yes," he said sadly. "I suppose I am."

"I understand," Alex murmured.

"I believe you do." He gazed at her intently until goose bumps rose on her flesh.

The quiet between them was comfortable but charged with electricity. She remembered the force of a pubescent crush, and the force of raw desire, but this was different, almost as if she could read his mind if she dared to touch his hand. As if he might read hers. The thought frightened her. "Sinclair," she said quickly, "must be something special for people to drop everything to listen to his sermon."

Carlo chuckled. "He's charismatic and outrageous, but there's more to it than that." He told her about Cassie's goat and the vandalism at Michael Corey's chapel.

"Tom mentioned the Apostles are suspect."

"Yes, particularly by Tom. He doesn't care for them. The Apostles' land butts up to his and he worries about his horses."

"They're nowhere near his stables, are they?" Alex had noticed the outbuildings south of the ranch house when she arrived.

"No. It's not the purebreds he's worried about. He's adopted quite a few wild mustangs and burros, and they have shelter and feed out that way."

"Does he think they'll steal them?"

"No. Marie Lopez has a small sheep ranch that also backs up to the Apostles' land. She's lost some sheep under mysterious circumstances recently."

"Lost?"

"Killed. And mutilated."

"Mutilated?" Alex asked, her interest sparked. "Were any photos taken?"

"I don't know. You could ask Moss." He smiled. "Are you thinking the UFOs might be involved?"

"Not necessarily, but UFOs are often sighted in the vicinity of animal mutilations. I'd like to talk to Marie."

Carlo nodded. "She insists it's a mountain lion, but it can't hurt to ask."

Alex laughed. "And she's probably right."

Inside the house, organ music swelled, then a man's distant voice clearly asked, "Are you washed in the blood of the Lamb?"

"Shall we hear what the man has to say?" he asked, rising and extending his arm to her.

She took it, fighting down a swarm of butterflies. "I wouldn't miss it for the world."

# FIFTY-THREE

## JAMES ROBERT SINCLAIR

"Are you washed in the blood of the lamb?" James Sinclair thundered as he stood at the pulpit and looked out upon his white-gowned flock. He raised his arms, and the organist played several full chords as the lighted cross on the church steeple began its slow descent into the church. Normally the ten-foot cross was only lowered on Sunday, but tonight was special, and now it settled between two permanent smaller crosses, its adjustable lamps lowered to a soft level that made Sinclair, standing some twelve feet in front of it, appear to be surrounded by a glowing nimbus. At the end of the service, when Sinclair raised his hands and cried "Hallelujah," that would signal the operator to make the lights blaze, half blinding the audience, as the cross disappeared back up into the sky. Now it seemed very nearly a cheap trick, and that surprised him: He'd never felt that way before. *Live and learn.* He opened his mouth to speak.

"Before the Lamb's blood is spilled once more, you must give yourselves to Him that you may be allowed to enter Paradise!"

He motioned the choir to rise as the organist played the first chords of "Onward Sinclair's Apostles." This had always been

Sinclair's favorite song, but now it sounded cheap, a tawdry ode to himself, not a praising of God.

Normally he relished the moments of rest the choir's performances gave him, but tonight he waited impatiently, filled with urgency. He glanced at the notes for the sermon he had planned. It was days-old rhetoric, and disgusted, he ripped the notes in half and let them drift to the floor. In the front row of the church, Hannibal Caine stared in surprise at the fluttering papers, and perversely, Sinclair enjoyed the shock in his face. He searched in vain for Eldo Blandings, curious about his reaction, but the older man was not in his accustomed place next to Hannibal in the front row. Sinclair realized that Elder Blandings had missed many of the sermons, and he resolved to ask him why. At a time when he felt the most control, he also felt the least, and he couldn't help but wonder about the loyalty of one of his highest-ranking men. He had seen a certain hunger in the man's eye.

The organist played the ending notes and the choir sat down. Sinclair gripped the edges of the pulpit and, for a long moment, remained silent despite the sound engineer's urgent gestures. At last Sinclair cleared his throat and leaned toward the microphone.

"I have seen the Angel of God," he said softly. "I have seen the Angel of God!" he thundered. "And I have spoken with God Himself!"

Adrenaline filled him until he thought he might burst. "And do you know what God said to me?"

He waited, one beat, two, listening to the silence. "He told me that I have been chosen to lead you through the Apocalypse and unto Heaven!"

Softly now. "He told me that I am the Light." Again he paused. "In a few days' time the true signs shall begin. Fire! Floods! The earth beneath your feet will shake and the moon will turn to blood. And when the sun is blotted from the sky, the Four Horsemen shall ride!

"And when they ride, Armageddon will be at hand. Salvation shall not be possible." He grabbed the mike and took it with him as he strode across the rostrum, his gold-trimmed white robe billowing around him. "My friends, it is up to you to save the souls who have yet to give themselves, to God. To help them find their salvation. Go forth in your robes, that they might know you, for there is no more time for subtlety. Hundreds and thousands—no, *millions*—of souls are depending on you to save them!"

# FIFTY-FOUR
## ALEXANDRA MANDERLEY

"Inciting a riot," Moss Baskerville said gruffly as Tom Abernathy turned off the radio, the sermon barely begun. "Sinclair's inciting a riot."

"Moss," Cassie soothed. "He's always spouting that stuff."

Moss shook his head. "Not like this. He obviously knows about the run-in Tom and I had with those damned Apostles in the park today, and he's telling them to go out and do it again."

"Well, at least you hired another deputy," Mike Corey said. "Didn't you?"

Baskerville's laugh was harsh. "Yes and no. She can't start until Monday. We're going to have to ride those bastards without an extra hand until then, and that doesn't leave any time for real police work."

"Well, don't worry about the park," Tom said. "The stunt people loved playing posse today and they'll love it tomorrow."

Moss cocked an eyebrow. "Abernathy, I do believe you're enjoying this. How about I deputize you?"

Tom shook his head. "No, thanks. I just like *playing* sheriff. The shopkeepers are all set to phone over to the arena at the first sign of trouble. The posse will herd up and escort out any stray Apostles, and we sure as heck don't need any real deputies for that, Chief."

"The park is private property," Cassie chimed in. "We have every right to kick them out."

Moss eyed Tom. "So I guess you're saying you don't need no stinkin' badges, is that it?"

"That's right."

"I don't know." Moss shook his head. "I just don't know. You and your cowboys seem to think this is a game."

"Life's a game," Tom said, and everyone in the conversation pit laughed except Moss Baskerville.

"Those people are getting crazy."

"Zealots," Ray Vine added somberly.

Baskerville nodded. "What are you going to do if they go after you?"

"A showdown at the Madelyn Corral?" Again Tom's face spread in a slow, calculated grin. "You saying they're gonna be fool enough to attack a bunch of big tough wranglers? Why, Mad Dog Steinberg could scare them all out of town with just one of those snake-eyed looks of his. Besides, we all carry pieces. Those Apostles can't be sure they're loaded with blanks."

"Which gives them reason to go ahead and shoot at you, if they get good and rabid." Moss glared at him, but it didn't faze the cowboy.

"Moss," Carlo said quietly. "I agree, the Apostles are a problem, but I don't think you have to worry. If several stunt people approach them at once, they'll go quietly."

Baskerville still looked unhappy, but he finally nodded. "Well, I guess we'll do it your way, but I'll cruise through every hour or two just to keep the fear of the *real* law in them. And you'd better call the station at the first whiff of real trouble."

"You betcha, Chief." Tom looked around. "Any of you want to hear any more of Jim-Bob's preaching?"

After a chorus of no's, Moss looked around. "I sure wish old Joe

Huxley would drag his sorry ass back into town so we'd have a night watchman again."

"It's looking like he's not coming back." Cassie shook her head. "Not him nor Kyla, nor Madge."

"How's Hank holding up?" Ray asked.

"Not too good," Cassie said. "On top of everything else, he's been sick as a hound with stomach flu. It's a good thing he's got that high school kid working for him."

"You mean Justin?" Alex asked.

Cassie nodded, showing surprise. "You know him?"

"He led Eric and me into Spirit Canyon when we arrived, and came back to visit us the next day."

"He also introduced Alex and me in town," Carlo said, then paused. "He drove into the park after closing tonight, heading toward the mine."

"He *drove* into the park?" Moss asked.

"I'm sure he was making a delivery at the mine for Hank."

"He sure gets around," Ray observed. "He's courting one of my waitresses." He chuckled. "He's not getting very far, though."

"Well, it's a good thing Hank's got him," Cassie said, then turned to Alex. "So. What do you think of Jim-Bob Sinclair? Think those UFOs are some of his so-called signs that the world's about to end?"

"We had a couple little shakers a few days ago," Tom added, grinning. "And that strong one last night, while the flying saucers were doing the two-step up there. Maybe Jim-Bob thinks they go together."

"Earthquake lights are fairly common," Alex said. "They're usually flashes of light accompanied by a cracking sound, rather like thunder and lightning. Last night's phenomena might have something to do with the atmospheric conditions surrounding the quake." She hesitated, then saw that everyone was watching her eagerly. "The thing about UFOs is, they aren't anything new. We just think they are because we're in an age where every mystery is interpreted technologically. Today's flying saucers are yesterday's chariots of fire. Aliens used to be called angels. Or devils"

"Really?" Cassie asked.

Alex nodded. "And it goes back much farther than biblical times. There are stories about flying disks hat date back to China three thousand years before Christ. And that probably means the sightings go back as far as man. Or farther."

"And you folks accuse me of telling tales," Tom said.

She looked at him. "We see UFOs in the context of our own society. In the mid eighteen hundreds there was a series of midwestern sightings that ran in a nearly straight ne down the United States, from Canada to the Gulf The farmers who reported them claimed they saw a huge steamboat-type craft in the sky, and the close encounters reported were with men from these steamboats who came down to fetch water." She glanced at Marie. "And frequently they took away animals. It's a pattern that has repeated throughout history, all over the world."

"Why do we hear about little blue men if those farmers saw something different?" Tom asked.

"And why do other people, like Sinclair, see angels?" That came from Ray.

"It's what they expect to see. Joseph Smith claimed that the Book of Mormon was given to him by a godlike creature from a planet that orbited a star called Kolab. Smith evidently believed what he preached, or at least ended up believing it. Sinclair sounds like he believes what he preaches as well."

"It awful hard to swallow," Tom said, rubbing his chin.

"The biggest tale-spinner of all time is our biggest skeptic," Cassie said wryly. Tom shrugged. "Nothing wrong with a little skepticism."

"I agree," Alex said. "I'm a skeptic myself. If I weren't, I might buy into the notion that UFOs are simply aliens visiting from another world and that they first arrived in the nineteen forties. But that seems too ... pat, I suppose. I believe we should always look to history for clues about the present. Even when it comes to aerial phenomena, history repeats itself." Suddenly self-conscious, she glanced around. "I'm sorry, I didn't mean to talk shop."

"Honey," Cassie said, "you're a breath of fresh air. Usually the only person around here who can tell a story is Tom, and his are always made up."

"Ah, Cass, you know everything I say's the gospel truth," Tom drawled. He smiled at Alex. "Doc, you can't leave us hanging now."

The room suddenly seemed far too warm, and Alex hesitated, embarrassed. Seated beside her on the couch, Carlo lightly touched the back of her hand. "Please."

She stole a glance at him, at those incredible eyes. "We see what we expect to see," she said, launching back into shop talk to protect herself from the overwhelming feelings this man stirred in her. "That's what one of the most respected researchers suggests, and I agree with him. It may be that *we* decide what form this energy or life-form, whatever it is, takes. Perhaps it's the result of a given society's collective unconscious.

"Think of all the stories about leprechauns in Ireland, trolls in Scandinavia. There are fairies and elves, the Gentry of the eastern United States, and Green Men, who are earth spirits, part man, part plant. Also, there are the elemental spirits of the American Indian, right, Davy?"

Styles nodded. "We have a legend about a red sun that rises straight up in the air. I don't recall the details."

"The Zulus have a corresponding story," Alex said, pleased. "The red sun descends to devour cattle, then rises straight up afterward." Alex saw Marie flinch slightly, and hoped the woman would be willing to talk to her later.

"What it boils down to," Alex continued, "is that yesterday's fairy circles are today's saucer landing sites. You'll find stories about lights in the sky like the ones we witnessed last night in every culture's folklore. There are certain commonalities in all of them. Only the window dressing changes.

"At one time, there were stories about fairy folk abducting

humans, usually via fairy circles. What's left out of the version we tell children is that they were abducted for breeding purposes. These days, aliens supposedly do the same thing. But I'm not so sure any of these creatures are aliens."

"But that's such a big deal in books and on talk shows," Cassie protested.

"Aliens with the ability to travel to earth wouldn't need to mate with humans to improve their genetic stock. It's illogical. We're close to re-creating life with our own DNA experiments. Certainly creatures capable of interstellar flight would have already mastered the techniques."

"So what's the bottom line?" Ray asked.

"UFOs might be of the earth," Alex said promptly. "They're certainly an important part of our mythology. Yesterday's and today's."

"Isn't it possible they're from another world?" Cassie asked.

Moss nodded. "I saw them last night, and they didn't look like anything from around here."

"The possibilities are endless, but whatever they are, the only thing I'm sure of is that they shape our myths and our history. UFOs, angels, spirit lights, whatever one calls them, they loom very large."

Enthusiastic now, she leaned forward. "For example, Eric and I were driving back to camp today when we saw one of the small round UFOs over Olive Mesa. We hiked up, but it was gone by the time we arrived. However, we found some clothing, and it hadn't been there long. I'm willing to bet Sinclair was up there speaking to his Angel of God."

"And whatever he heard, it reinforced his belief that the Apocalypse is coming," Carlo finished.

She smiled. "Precisely."

"And that raises lots of questions about destiny and fate and prophecy." Carlo shook his head. "Is it self-fulfilling? Do we make our own destiny or does some other force—God, aliens, elves—guide us?"

"I used to believe all prophecy was self-fulfilling and that it was of wholly human creation," Alex replied, "but now I'm inclined to think that something plants ideas and attempts to guide our destiny. And the fact that most prophecies concern the end of the world or lesser disasters, all negatives in any case, tells me that it's not some wise, all-knowing, and loving God behind it all. It's something with a terribly wicked sense of humor." She smiled then, aware of how ridiculous she probably sounded. She turned to Mike Corey. "Father, I hope I'm not insulting your religion."

"If I were thin-skinned, I wouldn't hang around with this bunch." The young man smiled and pushed a stray lock of light brown hair off his forehead. "From a purely Catholic point of view, I'd have to say the things you're speaking of are the work of the devil." He smiled. "Thereby proving your point about various interpretations."

"I take it Sinclair hasn't been this frantic about the Apocalypse until now?" she asked, looking around at the others.

"No," Ray Vine said, "although he's always very dramatic."

"He really did sound different tonight," Cassie added. "Usually he just chews the scenery."

"He was like the Dutch boy with his finger in the dam trying to sound the alarm," Mike Corey added. "He sounded almost frightened."

There was general agreement, then Tom Abernathy said, "Maybe he's just gone off his rocker."

That broke the intensity in the room. Even Alex laughed and agreed that was probably the case.

"You know," Tom said thoughtfully, "if the Four Horsemen of the Apocalypse really did come riding down Thunder Road, I'd purely love to see the look on Jim-Bob's face. Now, who wants apple pie and ice cream?"

# FIFTY-FIVE

# ELDO BLANDINGS

E ldo Blandings checked his watch and grimaced, which was as close as Eldo ever came to smiling. It was nearly twenty-one hundred, and Prophet Sinclair would be nearing the end of his live broadcast. It was time to strike a blow for the Prophet. Another grimace. Tonight, they'd teach that devil-worshiping whore and her queers at the Langtry Theater a little lesson, and that pleased him almost as much as pondering what he would do to Tom Abernathy for the humiliation he'd suffered at that godless bastard's hands earlier in the day.

He and his gang of four had driven out of the compound an hour before. After they were out of easy sight, he left Thunder Road to take a jeep trail up behind Dead Man's Hill. They parked the vehicle in a shallow cavern formed by the rocks, then stripped off their loose outer clothing, leaving them dressed in brown and tan camouflage fatigues. After stowing the clothes, they piled tumbleweeds in front and over the little jeep, just to make sure no one would notice it.

His Special Projects Committee included two of the Senior Apostles, a broad- shouldered bitch named Lorraine Ferguson who was also a white supremacist, and granite-jawed ex-marine Steve Clayman, who didn't know why he'd joined the Apostles. Blandings knew exactly why: He needed to have someone tell him what to do. Another member of his elite group was Mel Campbell, a former cop who had been run off the force for applying a nightstick too frequently. By the time he joined the Apostles, he was a speed freak, buying and selling through his old contacts from his legitimate days. The Church of the Prophet's Apostles had saved his life, cleaned him up, and given him purpose again. The fourth was Corky Deitz, a hard little woman, a former cheerleader at Madelyn High, and she was as full of loyalty to the Prophet as she was full of hatred for people who refused to listen to his word. All had been handpicked and tested by Eldo and Hannibal. As Apostles, each was very flawed in his or her own way, and perfect for the Special Projects Committee.

They had traveled the last miles to the theater on foot, keeping to the trail above the road, only crossing Thunder Road when they were even with the theater. There, they quickly climbed the high chain-link fencing and spent the last fifteen minutes waiting while Steve Clayman reconned the theater and adjacent buildings. Now Eldo stepped forward as Clayman's dark form approached.

"All clear," he said softly. "No one's around."

"Good work." Eldo checked his watch again. "Top of the hour," he whispered. He shined a penlight all around, checking to make sure his people were wearing gloves and had their equipment ready. Finally he nodded. "We meet back here at twenty-one twenty. You know what to do. Let's go."

They approached the deserted theater quietly, each going to his assigned position. Lorraine Ferguson and Steve Clayman went to work with a pint of red paint and a brush, painting "666" on the windows, while ex-cop Mel Campbell and Corky Dietz went to work spraying the flower beds with a jug of herbicide.

Suddenly Eldo heard a vehicle approaching. "Everybody down!" he hissed as he crouched in the shadows. The car was dark, its lights out, and it rolled to a stop not ten feet from him, right near the flag-pole by the steps to the building.

The driver's door swung silently open, and for a brief instant before the driver clicked off the interior light, he had a look at the man. It was Hannibal's green recruit, Justin Martin, dressed in black. Eldo breathed a sigh of relief but remained hidden. Hannibal had told him what the boy had done with the goat—a sick kid, no question —and had added that the boy didn't want his parents to find out. Nothing would go wrong, but maybe he'd get to test the kid's nerves. He waited.

The boy opened the trunk of his car. Eldo heard him grunt, then the youth lifted something out. Eldo started counting, and at five seconds, the kid came staggering around the side of the car carrying something large wrapped up in a blanket. The youth was wearing gloves. *Smart kid.*

He came closer, closer, and Eldo held his breath. Then Justin stopped at the flagpole, bent, and dropped his burden at its base. The boy stood and Eldo heard him sniffing. He'd caught the odor of the herbicide.

Justin grabbed the rope line on the tall flagpole. He tested it, tugging hard, then squatted and uncovered his burden. He started working with the pole rope, wrapping it around whatever it was he'd taken from the trunk.

The boy stood up and took the rope with both hands. He began hoisting something up the pole.

It was another goat. *Of course.* A happy grimace etched in his seamed face, Eldo watched the animal, tied by the hind legs, as it slid jerkily up the flagpole. As soon as the rope was tied off, the goat hanging at full mast, he softly said, "Justin Martin!"

The boy didn't react as Eldo expected—he didn't run or even look. Instead he slowly turned, head cocked, listening. Justin slid his hand into his pants pocket, then withdrew it quickly, holding something.

*A gun?* No. Eldo heard the snick of a jackknife opening, then saw an oversized blade as the silver steel caught the moonlight. Eldo rose and drew his own .38, aimed it at the kid. "Drop the knife," he hissed.

The kid homed in on the sound of his voice and, fearless, stalked toward him, knife ready.

"I said drop the knife." Eldo cocked his gun, and that sound halted the boy.

Slowly, coolly, Justin bent and placed it on the ground, the blade pointed toward Eldo. Blandings was impressed. No doubt the kid was as deranged as they came, but he had the right kind of mettle for this operation.

"Boy," Eldo began, still keeping the gun trained on Justin. "I'm impressed. Did Hannibal tell you to kill the goat?"

Silence.

"You're among friends, boy. Answer me. Are you acting under Hannibal's orders?"

"Yes," Justin said, squinting into the darkness. "Are you Eldo Blandings?"

"Did he tell you to come here?" Hannibal knew Blandings and his crew were coming here, and to send the boy here would endanger the mission. Suddenly suspicious of Caine, he said louder, "Answer me!"

"No. He said to display it prominently. I thought this was the perfect place," he added, a note of arrogance in his voice. Are you Eldo Blandings?"

"I'm your new boss, boy, and if any of this gets out, we'll lay the blame for everything we've all done here tonight right on your doorstep. Do you doubt me?"

"No, sir." The tone was humble, but Blandings knew this kid didn't know the meaning of the word.

"Good. Now get out of here. Get that car out of here. We'll be in touch."

Silently the boy bent and retrieved his knife, then turned and walked down toward his car.

"Boy!" Eldo's quiet voice carried easily in the desert night.

Justin turned, saying nothing.

"Good work."

The boy nodded, then went to the back of his car and closed his trunk before getting in the car. Lights out, he drove away.

# FIFTY-SIX

# MARIE LOPEZ

"They stopped in at Madland to inquire the way," Ray Vine sang as he strummed Tom's guitar. "And Jim-Bob saw Cassie and declared he would stay. Sweet Cassie got frightened and ran like a deer, while Jim-Bob Sinclair pawed the ground like a steer." The guitar notes trailed off very nearly the way they were supposed to.

Marie laughed, wishing she had the nerve to sing in front of company. "A steer?"

"Frustrated, you know," Ray explained, setting the guitar down and smiling at Cassie. "He knew she'd turn him into a steer if he got too close."

Cassie laughed her head off, just like she always did. "Thank you, Ray." "Mommy, what's a steer?" Eve, who had been sleeping curled up in Cassie's lap, rubbed her eyes.

"Well, it's ... Tom? You tell her."

"Why, Eve, it's just a bull with no ... It's a gelded bull," he finished lamely.

Sure enough, the next question was, "What's gelded?"

"Honey," Cass said, "it's way past your bedtime. Maybe we better get on home."

"Can I have a soda?" the child asked, bouncing from her mother's arms.

"Course you can," Tom said, ignoring Cassie's glare.

"You go on ahead."

Marie knew that Tom hated having the evening break up, and ten-thirty was far too early for anyone but Mike Corey, who always left early, to say good night. Though tired, and still a little embarrassed about her attire, Marie was glad he was keeping things going: She was enjoying herself more than she had in ages, mostly because Tom had nearly declared some feelings for her. The other reason was that she had decided that she wanted to talk to Alex Manderley after all, but hadn't found the right moment to do it. Now Alex was off sitting by the fireplace with Carlo, and Marie swallowed and decided she could speak in front of Pelegrine.

"Hi," she said uncertainly as she approached Alex and Carlo.

Alex smiled. "Please, join us."

"Yes," Carlo said, patting an empty chair.

"Thanks." She sat, then fiddled nervously with her hands.

"That's a beautiful outfit," Alex told her.

"Oh, ah, thanks. I ..."

"Yes?" Alex prompted.

"Tom's been after me to talk to you. About my sheep, the ones that were killed." The words poured out in a rush. "I feel ridiculous, I mean it's probably just a mountain lion, and I told Tom to forget about it, but, well, I just feel ridiculous."

"Will you ladies excuse me for a minute?" Carlo asked, rising. He smiled gently at Marie, and she smiled back, grateful that he'd realized she wanted to talk to the scientist alone.

Instead of joining the others, Carlo walked onto the patio and out beyond the guttering candlelight, until he was only a shadowy figure staring up into the night sky. Marie looked at Alex and was amused to see that the woman was still watching Carlo, an enigmatic expression on her face. The first time Marie had seen them together tonight, she thought something was brewing between them; now she was certain.

"Carlo's very nice," she said softly.

Alex quickly turned to face her, a slight blush coloring her cheeks. "He does seem nice," she said. "Of course, I don't really know him."

Marie smiled. "No one knows Carlo too well. I guess being mysterious goes with his profession."

"Yes." Alex cast one more glance his way, then focused on Marie. "I was hoping you'd talk to me."

"Did Tom tell you?" she asked, perturbed.

"He only said something in passing. So did Carlo."

Marie shot a sharp look across the room at Tom. He saw her and raised his eyebrows in a what-did-I-do expression. She turned back to Alex. "Tom didn't say anything about last night, did he?" From the moment she'd told Tom about the evening's events, she'd regretted it, certain he would spin it into one of his tall tales.

"No. What happened last night?"

"I was up in Rattlesnake Canyon with my flock, and I came out with two less sheep than when I went in."

"They were killed?"

Marie shook her head. "I don't know. I think I hallucinated or something."

"The UFOs were over Rattlesnake Canyon for a long time," Alex said. "You certainly didn't hallucinate those."

"Earlier you said something about UFOs taking animals?" Marie began, still loath to admit to what she imagined she'd seen.

"It happens frequently, particularly in conjunction with mutilations. As I mentioned, it's gone on for centuries." She paused. "It's been epidemic in the States since the mid-seventies."

"It has?" Marie felt better knowing that. "Three of my sheep, two the same night, were mutilated recently. I've never told anyone this, but I saw— something—the night before the first two were killed."

"A UFO?"

"I guess. I was up on the range, near where I was last night. There were four of those little bright disks shooting around, very high in the sky. It wasn't like last night, though; they were so far away that I thought they might be air force jets on maneuvers."

"Did they move like the ones last night?"

"Yes."

"Then they weren't jets."

"I was afraid you'd say that." Marie shook her head. "I didn't know anything was wrong until the next morning, when I found them. They were cut up just like the first one. She was killed right on my property."

"What was done to them?"

"An ear was gone, and the tongue. It looked ... cauterized. Their abdomens were cut open and some of their organs were gone."

"Which ones, do you know?"

"The genitalia, both sexes. The stomach on one. Two of them had perfect circles of hide cut away. I know a predator couldn't have done that ... But the strangest thing of all was that there was no blood, around the bodies or on the ground, but there were drops of a blue fluid, sort of a gel, on the wounds. Have you ever heard of that?"

"Once," Alex said excitedly. "The report was in conjunction with UFOs and a Bigfoot sighting, so it's never been taken seriously."

"Bigfoot?" Marie asked, disbelieving.

"You'd be surprised how many Bigfoot and UFO sightings occur simultaneously." She smiled. "It rather stretches credibility, doesn't it?"

"It all does. I don't feel very credible myself right now."

The scientist patted her hand. "You're very credible, don't worry. But tell me, do you have any photos of the animals? Or did you take samples of the fluid?"

"I took pictures of the animal at my ranch and gave them to Moss. We both figured it was some sort of horrible practical joke." She paused. "I took a camera back to the canyon the next day after the two sheep were killed, but the bodies were gone."

"Any tracks?"

"There'd been a dust storm."

"Oh, well. Would you ask Moss to let me see the photos you did get?"

"I would, but they disappeared, right out of his files." She shook her head. "I had the negatives, but they disappeared too. From my trailer."

"I'm not surprised. That happens frequently too."

"You know what?" Marie pushed her hair back from her face.

"What?"

"This sounds crazy, but I've always suspected that military type who hangs around here is behind it somehow. The mutilations, the missing photos, I'm not sure exactly what. Does that make sense?"

"Absolutely. I'll lay odds he had the photos and negs taken," Alex said. "As for the mutilations, occasionally there's been evidence of military involvement. At one site, an army scalpel was found, and helicopters are often spotted in the vicinity. On the other hand, the military is a victim too."

"What are you ladies so deep into?"

Marie jumped at Moss's voice. She'd been so involved in the conversation that she'd forgotten about everyone else. Tom. and Carlo had also approached.

Alex looked surprised as well. "Just this and that," she said.

"It's okay, Alex," Marie said, no longer feeling awkward. Of course, she hadn't gotten to the part about last night's floating sheep, but right now she felt like she could handle anything. The three men sat down, Carlo close to Alex on the fireplace steps, while Tom perched his butt on the arm of Marie's chair. Briefly Marie and Alex brought them up-to-date on the conversation.

"You were saying the military is a victim of mutilations?" Marie prompted at last.

Alex nodded. "The big thing about mutilations is that they don't make sense. If aliens needed to take animals—and that makes no more sense then them needing to mate with human beings, and I don't buy that for an instant—but if they did, they could take them from places where they wouldn't be missed, or even found. Rustlers, same thing. Most of these are taken from small herds, like yours, Marie, and from corrals like yours. Many are in conjunction with UFO sightings, and I think it's possible that some of these are staged to draw attention away from one thing or the other. At any rate, a good percentage of the mutilations are real, and many can't be accounted for as the work of cults—or coyotes. In fact, in many cases, carrion eaters won't touch a mutilated animal."

Marie nodded. "It's like they know something's wrong."

"Exactly. I don't know what the purpose of mutilations is, or who or what performs them. There's evidence of something similar to laser surgery, and often the bodies are entirely drained of blood. All I'm sure of is that mutilations are manipulations."

"What do you mean?" Moss leaned forward, hands on his knees.

"The mutilations occur where they will be noticed. It's mass manipulation at its best because there's very little as effective as a terrorization technique as the mutilation or torture of people or animals. It's an ingrained terror that goes right to the heart and talks to the caveman within."

"The Nazis figured that out," Tom said.

"Along with thousands of other cults and societies," Alex agreed.

"What about the military?" Moss asked. "You said they're victims, but it sounds more like they're behind it."

"Maybe a little bit of both. There were a lot of mutilations in Colorado right next to Cheyenne Mountain, where NORAD's Combat Operations Center is housed. The center is inside the mountain, built of steel, and its purpose is to analyze anything in our air space. You can imagine the safeguards on the mountain, and surrounding it. The perimeters of the military land are guarded with everything from motion detectors and cameras, radar and human guards, to sensors that can detect the small amount of ammonia in human skin. You can't get in there without being noticed.

"But someone or something did. The Cheyenne Mountain Zoo is on the north side of the mountain, on military land. In 1975 a female buffalo was mutilated. She weighed fifteen hundred pounds, and an udder, an ear, and the vagina were removed. Also four square feet of hide. The dissection was done with some sort of very sharp instrument. The hide was removed without puncturing the underlying tissue. The surgery was said to be cleaner than even a coroner could have accomplished."

"Christ," Tom said.

"Christ indeed. The next year, right next to a NORAD entry gate, near a road not shown on most maps, a cow about to calve was mutilated. The sex organs were removed, including the calf. It was never found."

"Why?" Marie asked.

Alex shrugged. "No one knows. I doubt that the military knows, except for whatever mutilations they might indulge in themselves. The first rule of espionage is to always act like you know everything—so they're not going to admit they don't. I'm sure that's a major reason the entire UFO business is so hush-hush with them. They actually know very little about it. I think that mutilations are terrorist tactics by unknown persons meant to deliver some kind of message to our society, or the government or the CIA or whatever secret government is trying to run the more public one at any given moment."

"That Cheyenne Mountain business," Tom began.

"Yes?"

"If no one can get in there, then I'd guess the military did the dirty deeds themselves so they'd look like victims as well."

Moss pointed at him. "Give that man a cigar. It's that old Sherlock Holmes thing. You eliminate everything and what you've got left, no matter how confounded, that's your answer. So the government or the intelligence community commits the mutilations and throws in a few on military land to make themselves look innocent."

"I'd imagine a good deal of what you say is valid," Alex replied. "But phenomena that occur with some of the mutilations are either the stuff of aliens or folklore. I favor folklore."

"Like what?" Marie asked.

"Levitations."

"Ah, come on," Moss said.

Marie shivered as goose bumps prickled her skin. She looked at Tom, and they locked eyes for an endless instant, then he reached down and touched the back of her hand. He started to withdraw, and without thinking about it, she turned her wrist and entwined her small fingers with his, twice as big. He squeezed very gently and suddenly she felt much safer.

"Marie?" Alex asked. "You're dead white."

"That's what I saw last night. The big UFO came down. There was a blue light and first one sheep, then another, just floated right up into this huge, this huge *thing*. I thought I was losing my mind."

"The sheep were still missing in the morning," Tom added.

Moss looked at Tom. "You're in on this, aren't you, cowboy? This is all set up to get my goat."

"He's not in on anything," Alex said, surprisingly stem. "I can show you reports from sheriffs and police officers across the country wherein they recount seeing levitations. For instance, not one, but two officers were in a patrol car in the Midwest, driving in ranch land. They had to slam on the brakes when they realized they were about to hit a cow crossing the road ... four feet off the ground."

Moss laughed, then cut it short under the researcher's glare. "You're serious, aren't you?"

"Utterly. If you'd like copies of the reports, I'd be glad to get them to you. I have them in my car outside."

"Ma'am, I'd love to read those. I believe you because you seem like an intelligent, rational person, and I believe you, Marie, for the same reasons, but at the same time, I'd have to see it for myself."

"That's reasonable," Alex said serenely. "Any intelligent, rational person would say the same." She stood up. "I've left Eric alone long enough, and it's about the right time of night for, ah, aerial activity. Thanks for a lovely evening, Tom." She shook his hand, then turned to Marie. "May I come and see you tomorrow or the next day? I'd like to go into the canyon with you and see where it all happened."

"Can you ride a horse?"

"With the best of them."

"Good," Marie said, smiling. "I'll take you out there, but it has to be Saturday. I've got a full day tomorrow." She looked at Tom. "Can we borrow a horse?"

"I've got a quarter horse named Tess who would love some exercise," Tom said. "She's a new mama and really needs to get away for a few hours. I'll bring her up to Marie's Saturday. Just let me know what time."

"You inviting yourself along, cowboy?" Marie asked, pleased that his hand still enveloped hers.

"Wish I could, but duty calls."

Marie tried not to let her disappointment show as she and Tom rose and let their hands part while they waited for Alex to say her good nights.

Outside, Moss cleared his throat. "It's a long ways up there in the dark. You want an escort?"

"No, I'll be fine," Alex said, looking at Carlo instead of the Chief.

"We've had some nasty types roaming around lately," Moss reminded her. "People have disappeared. I'd feel better if you let me lead you up."

"It's not necessary."

"How secure is your new camp?"

"Very. It can't be seen from the road."

"Alex," Carlo said quietly. "You have a motorcycle rack." He pointed at the back of the Bronco.

"We'd intended to bring a dirt bike for exploratory purposes, but we couldn't get the funding in time."

"I'm going home now, too," he said, slowly. "And I have a motorcycle. I'd feel better knowing you got to your camp safely. I could ride up with you in your truck, then ride my bike home."

"It's not necessary," she said, now sounding regretful. "But if you'd like to see the camp ..."

"Yes, I would."

They said their good nights, then after Alex and Carlo drove off, the three went back inside. "Penny-ante poker, anyone?" Tom asked. It was the last Thursday night ritual, besides whatever whopper Tom would decide to tell. He never failed, and Marie figured it would be a doozy tonight: He hadn't spun a windy all evening.

"Poker?" Ray called as he and Rosie helped Davy set up a round card table. "That's my middle name."

"Then we got the same middle name," Tom said, getting the cards out of a drawer in the entertainment center.

# FIFTY-SEVEN

# JUSTIN MARTIN

"'We'll be in touch.' Oh, yeah, we'll be in touch, you fucking asshole!"

Justin Martin repeated Eldo Blandings's words, relishing the cold rage they brought. That holier-than-shit asshole's condescending attitude had really pissed him off, and now, as he slouched behind the steering wheel, his car concealed behind a mound of gravel in a turnout in Spirit Canyon, he thought about how fun it would be to kill old Eldo Blandings. He'd sneak up behind him and pull him backward, knocking the old man's knees with his own to throw him farther off balance. Then, quick as a wink, he'd yank Blandings's head back to expose his throat and draw a sharp knife across his neck, cutting skin, muscle, tendons, veins, and arteries, hearing the crunch of gristle as he broke the Adam's apple and severed the windpipe, cutting all the way back to the bone, giving Eldo Blandings a certified flip-top head. Justin grinned in the darkness, imagining the sensation of the old man's hot blood cascading over his hands, spurting between his fingers ...

In the distance, an engine growled—a car was beginning the climb into Spirit Canyon. Justin sat up, rolling the window down farther, the better to hear. He wasn't sure it was Alexandra Manderley's Bronco, but he had a hunch that tonight's wait was about to pay off.

Justin was sure she hadn't left town—not with all the UFOs doing their thing last night—but he still hadn't been able to find her camp, even tonight, in the dark, when he'd expected to be able to catch the reflection of camp lights against the hills. That had further pissed him off. He'd decided to sit and wait for a while: He didn't want to go home—he couldn't stand the thought of hearing his parents snoring away in their bedroom, or finding his mother's cutesy little notes to him all over the house. *Justin, there's leftover lasagna in the refrigerator; Justin, please make your bed; Justin, have some milk, it's good for you; Justin, fuck me up the ass.* Christ, who could stand it? He sure as hell couldn't. He also knew that Christie Fox would still be blubbering over Rick Spelman and wouldn't want to go out—shit, had that ever backfired—and there just wasn't anyone else from school that he wanted to fuck: He'd already nailed anything worth screwing.

So, for lack of anything better to do, he'd stayed here for an hour, fueling his anger at Caine, Blandings, and Manderley, occasionally peppering his murderous fantasies with sexual ones as he saw himself on top of Manderley drilling her brains out and slowly squeezing her throat, tighter, tighter. She'd be so turned on that she couldn't even fight him. He had stayed here, daydreaming, and hoping that Manderley was out and would return. He'd figured chances were good she was down there at that overgrown cowdick's house, along with the others, and as he watched the approaching headlights, he was sure he was right.

His smile as he recognized the Bronco turned to a frown when he spied the motorcycle mounted on a rear rack. He didn't remember seeing it before, and it upset him to think he might have missed it.

Justin pulled onto the road, lights out, staying well back from the truck. About midpoint through the canyon, after the road climbed to its highest point, the Bronco's taillights disappeared down a narrow road sandwiched between the mountaintops. He drove past and pulled over at the next wide spot in the road and got out.

Sound carried easily here, so he closed the Mustang's door very quietly, then he walked to the narrow cutoff, which was angled so that it was difficult to see, even in the daytime.

He started down the jeep trail, walking as quietly and quickly as he could in the darkness. After walking perhaps an eighth of a mile or more, he rounded a bend and finally spotted the camp. It was hidden in the shadows of a granite overhang, as was the Bronco, and it all would have been invisible except for a pair of kerosene lanterns. Staring, he made out two tents, a table where one, two, no, *three* people were sitting around talking.

*Who the hell is that?* Justin hugged the mountainside and moved closer, edging around a hill, then crawling on his belly to a small mound of rocks no more than fifteen feet from the campers.

Justin recognized Eric Watson as he stood and stretched his long bony arms. Lamplight glossed his red hair. "I'm going to catch a couple hours of sleep," he announced. "I'm bushed."

"Go ahead, Eric," Alex said. "You've done more than your share of the work today."

"Be sure and call me when you're tired of keeping watch."

"I will. Good night."

"Good night," echoed the stranger. The voice sounded vaguely familiar.

Eric disappeared into a tent, and Alex and the other man sat without saying a word for several minutes. Finally Alex spoke. "Would you like to take a look through the telescope?"

"Very much."

*The Peeler!* He should have known when he saw the motorcycle. Excitedly Justin squinted at the couple as they rose and walked toward the cliff. What was Carlo doing here? Was he getting ready to do Alexandra Manderley? To *peel* her? Suddenly a hard-on pinched painfully in his shorts. *Goddammit!* He adjusted himself, never taking his eyes off Carlo and Alex as they walked to the cliff and took turns peering into the scope.

"They've turned the cross back on," Carlo said. "Gaudy, isn't it?"

Alex laughed. "That it is."

Justin felt a surge of anger: He could tell by the scientist's tone that she was flirting with the Peeler. *Slut. You deserve what's coming to you, bitch!*

Soon the pair returned to the encampment. "I should be getting back," Carlo announced.

"Wouldn't you like some coffee first?"

He hesitated. "Yes, that would be very nice."

Justin could hear Carlo's unspoken interest in the woman and determined that he would be witness to the Peeler's greatest act, one way or another. Maybe he'd even be allowed to participate.

Justin knew he should get out of the camp immediately, just to be sure Carlo didn't see his car up the road, but he lingered a few moments, listening.

"Tomorrow," Carlo said, "about one o'clock, I could show you around Old Madelyn if you like."

"Close your shop?"

"I usually do, an hour each day. My profession is very draining, and I need time to recharge my batteries."

"Then you shouldn't waste your resting time."

"Alex," he said slowly, "showing you around the park would recharge my batteries far better than reading a book or taking a nap."

"Well," she said doubtfully, "I've been leaving Eric here alone so much, I don't know ..."

*She wants him to talk her into it. Slut!*

"An hour?"

"Well, if I'm back here by two-thirty, I could give him the afternoon off." She paused. "Carlo?"

"What is it?"

"There are things about me that you don't know."

He chuckled, a bitter sound. "I have secrets you don't want to know."

Fascinated, Justin leaned forward, trying to see their faces.

"I guess we all have secrets," Alex replied at last. "Carlo, what I mean is, well, to be blunt, I'm very attracted to you ..."

Justin's hard-on became achingly apparent.

"But I can't get involved. I'm afraid I'm sending mixed signals."

"Is there someone else?" he asked.

"No. No one. I can't explain. I just can't get involved with anyone."

"Alex, don't worry. I don't know what I'm doing here. I shouldn't be here. I can't go farther than friendship, and I can't explain. But, Alex, could we just be friends?"

She didn't speak for a long time, but when she finally did, her tone was lighter. "Yes. We can do that. I'll meet you."

"Good." He refilled their mugs. "How did you like those books?"

"Wonderful. Especially the one on magnetic ores."

They launched into a technical discussion and Justin took the opportunity to belly-crawl back to the hillside and inch away out of sight. When he was around the edge of the mountain, he began walking quickly. Hoping Pelegrine wouldn't leave too soon.

He tripped twice in invisible potholes as he hurried down the trail, but finally made it, dusty and dirty, back to his car. As he dug in his pocket for his keys, he heard the roar of Carlo's motorcycle. He cursed himself: He might have heard it sooner if he'd been paying attention.

"Shit." His keys weren't in his pocket. Frantically he tried the other one, but they weren't there either. The motorcycle was almost to the main road. "Shit!" Justin squatted between the car and the hillside. They were midpoint in the canyon and it was a fifty-fifty chance that Carlo would turn right and go back via Thunder Road. If he did, he was safe from discovery.

The motorcycle appeared. Carlo sat at the junction a moment, then revved the engine and turned left.

"Shit!" As the cycle's headlight shone on the car, Justin slid down to the ground on his ass, his back against the hillside, and feigned sleep as Carlo slowed, then stopped beside the Mustang. *Shit.* Footsteps approached, stopped in front of him. *Busted. By the Peeler.* The thought gave him a little thrill.

"Justin?"

He opened his eyes and stared up at the helmeted man, pretending he didn't know who he was. "Who? Who's there?"

"Carlo Pelegrine," the Peeler said, removing his helmet.

"Thank God!" Quickly Justin pushed himself to his feet and stepped around the Mustang, a big relieved smile plastered on his face. "I didn't think anyone would come along tonight! Boy, am I glad to see you, Carlo. My car broke down."

Pelegrine studied him. "What are you doing up here this time of night?"

"I was on my way home from church. I guess I shouldn't have taken the long way."

"I guess not."

Carlo didn't sound too friendly, but Justin pushed ahead. "Can you give me a lift?"

"What's wrong with the car? Maybe we can get it going." Justin shook his head. "The fan belt broke."

Pelegrine looked doubtful. "You're sure?"

"Positive. I can fix it myself tomorrow. After school," he added, looking worried. "I have a math final in the morning, and I have to study."

"Is the car locked?"

"Uh-huh." Justin tried the driver's door to prove it. "Locked up tight."

"Okay." Carlo put his helmet on and straddled the Harley. "Climb on."

Justin did, then put his arms around Carlo's waist when the man told him to do so. Although the Peeler drove slowly, it was still a thrilling ride. He could feel Pelegrine's back muscles move through his black leather jacket as he piloted the cycle through the curves, and with each tiny movement, Justin imagined that the Peeler was peeling Alex Manderley, and that he was helping.

By the time Carlo pulled up at his house, Justin had a hard-on that wouldn't quit. He was careful to keep his crotch out of Carlo's sight, worried that the man might think it was for him. It wasn't. It was for the kill.

# FIFTY-EIGHT

# TOM ABERNATHY

"I fold," Tom said, throwing in his cards. He got up from the table, stretched, then fetched himself a beer before returning to the table, where Ray Vine was just showing four kings to the others. Grinning, he pulled the pot, all ten dollars, toward him.

"I'm a rich man," he announced, and laughed.

"Well, you won most of that from your wife," Rosie said dryly.

"So, Tom," Moss began, "what'd you think of Alex's stories about. aliens and elves and all that stuff?" He chucked. "You're going to have a hard time out-telling her tales."

"Oh, well, I don't know about that," he drawled. "I didn't want to steal her thunder, her being my guest and all." He paused, looking from face to face. All but Marie were smiling; she looked wary. Marie might be a little touchy, especially after spilling her guts about the mutilations, so he resolved to say nothing that might offend her.

"Did you have yourself a close encounter, Tom?" Cassie asked, egging him on.

He glanced over at the couch, saw that little Eve was fast asleep, then looked at her mother. "I sure did, Cass. *Real* close."

Ray and Moss both groaned.

"It was on a night kinda like this, in the spring about, oh, three years ago. Belle and I were having ourselves a midnight ride up to Olive Mesa. There we were, just looking out at Madelyn, listening to the silence, when all of a sudden the night turned bright as day and I saw this great big old flying saucer right over my head. Belle, she was as stunned as I was. Then I heard this lady's voice say, 'Howdy, Tom.'"

"That was me," Cassie snickered. "I was up there moonbathing."

Tom made a show of rubbing his chin, then finally shook his head. "Nope, wasn't you, Cass. You have red hair. This lady had green. And three of everything. Three eyes, three ears, three mouths, why, she even had three—"

"Tom!" Rosie hissed. "There's a child sleeping in here."

"'Sleeping's' the key word," Cassie said. "Don't worry about it."

"I was gonna say 'arms,'" Tom said, with a falsely hurt sniff. "Well," he continued, leaning forward, his tone conspiratorial, "I can tell you, I was in shock, seeing this curvy green-haired lady alien just suddenly standing in front of me."

"I'll bet she was naked, too," Moss said, laughing.

"Oh, nooo." Tom shook his head. "She had on this see-through space suit. Ever wonder where all those tubes on an astronaut's space suit go? Well, let me tell you, it's *real* interesting. And not worth going through for a walk on the moon, take my word."

Even Marie was starting to smile now. He wasn't sure what had gotten into him tonight—he rarely told even mildly bawdy stories, at least not in mixed company, but now he was being positively racy, and he just couldn't seem to stop. He guessed that seeing Marie in that pretty little dress all night and getting to hold her hand for a while must have had its effect. He hadn't been that close to a female for some time and he felt like it had turned him into a sniggering adolescent. But he was having too much fun to care.

"So what'd she want?" Moss asked. "As if I didn't know." He poked Cassie and they both chuckled.

"Why, she wanted to buy Belle right out from under me." Tom

smirked at Baskerville. "I didn't care whether she wanted her to ride or to experiment on, I wouldn't sell my horse for all the cheese on the moon, and that kinda riled the green lady up and she pointed a ray gun at me and ordered me off my mount." He paused. "That alien was nothing but a low-down, belly-crawling horse thief, and you know what we do with those?"

Davy grinned. "Necktie party?"

"Yep. Code of the West. I threw my rope and lassoed that pretty green neck of hers, but she had that dang space suit on and it didn't faze her a bit. Instead, she blasted me with her ray gun. I went flying out of my saddle, and Belle, being the smartest horse that ever lived, she took off as fast as she could, so the space alien wouldn't get her. The last thing I saw was that three-legged space woman standing over me, staring at me with those creepy eyes of hers." Frowning, he shook his head. "That one in the middle was especially unsettling."

"I take it you escaped, since you lived to tell the tale?" Cass prompted.

"I did, but that devil-woman almost sent me to the last roundup. You see, I woke up with a whopper of a headache, not knowing where I was. It was only a minute before I realized I couldn't move a muscle, and I looked around. I was tied down to a table in a big white room with all sorts of buttons and computers and *pingy* noises all around. I thought I was dreaming, but I couldn't wake up. Then that space lady came in, followed by a whole passel more of them, all with three of everything. The first alien, she told me that all the men on their planet had gone off to live somewheres else—"

"Sounds like she probably ran them off all by herself," Ray observed.

"I wouldn't be surprised," Tom replied, smooth as you please. "However it happened, I guess those stories about aliens abducting people and making babies with them is true, even though Doc Alex says it isn't."

"How was the ride?" Ray asked. Rosie shot him a long-suffering look.

"Why, I guess I don't know," Tom said, shrugging. "I refused."

"From what I've heard," Cassie said, smiling, "you *can't* refuse."

"Maybe those other fellas never tried," Tom drawled. "Those green ladies look like quite a treat."

"So they just let you go?" Davy asked.

"I had to fight those ladies off, which was hard, seeing as how they had lots more limbs than I did, and in the most peculiar places.

"What I did was tell 'em I'd do the deed, and I convinced 'em to untie me so I could do it right. As soon as they did, I skedaddled, ran all over that spaceship of theirs, looking for a way out, those crazy space women on my tail. All the doors were *whoosh-whooshing* as I ran from room to room, just like in those science fiction programs. I was getting really nervous about then, thinking I was doomed, but then another door *whooshed* and I ran into a room with nothing in it but this weird blue light. It was a column, ten feet around, and it seemed to come out of the ceiling and go down right through the floor.

"Well, I was staring at it, not knowing what to do, and the door *whooshed* open and those three-eyed women came rushing at me. I ran right into the light, and I couldn't see 'em anymore. All I could see was blue, and it felt like I was in an elevator, going down.

"Finally the going-down feeling stopped, but all I could see was blue. Then I looked down and saw the good red earth under my feet, so I started walking. A second later, I was out of the blue column, back on Olive Mesa. I gave a whistle and Belle came running. I hopped on and then she hightailed it out of there like the devil was on her tail." He paused. "Which maybe he was, considering what the doc said."

He sat back, eyes closed, soaking up the groans and smattering of applause from his little audience. A chair scraped back and he opened them to see Marie standing up. She didn't look happy.

"Thanks for dinner. I've gotta go."

"Marie?" he asked, rising. "Something wrong?"

She paused, looking at him. "No. It's late and I'm tired."

"I'll walk you out."

She didn't object, so he trailed her to the front door. Snatching her coat, she slipped it on before he could help, then pulled her keys out of her pocket.

"Marie?"

She opened the door and stepped out, before turning to face him. "Yes?" Her eyes snapped at him.

"What's eating you?"

"You expect me to believe you, don't know?"

"I'm afraid I don't," he replied, completely confounded. He'd made sure not to say anything about sheep when he told his tale, so it couldn't be that.

"Well, you think on it, Tom. Good night." With that, she whisked off to her mini-truck and sped away.

"Women," Tom said, scratching his head.

# FIFTY-NINE

# HANNIBAL CAINE

"He's mad," Hannibal Caine said as he paced back and forth in his office. "He's completely insane!" He stopped mid-step. "And here I am, talking to myself!"

But who else did he dare confide in? Not Eldo Blandings, lost in a sadistic madness of his own. Not the Senior Apostles, two of whom were part of Blandings's terrorist group, which meant they weren't to be trusted on general principles. As for the other two, Caine had seen the rapturous looks on their faces tonight as Sinclair had ranted and raved about talking to God. They were sold on the Prophet.

No, Hannibal Caine would keep his own company, just as he always had. Caine dropped into his chair with a sigh. Sinclair had a glint in his eye tonight unlike any he had ever seen before, and afterward, when Caine had insisted on a private meeting, all he did was go on about "seeing the light." Unless James Sinclair was a better actor than Caine gave him credit for, the man truly believed the Apocalypse would happen just as he prophesied.

Either that, or Sinclair was preparing to leave after all, and with a real bang.

Unfortunately, Hannibal Caine thought as he poured himself a brandy, that was highly unlikely. Still, he would help things along, to make sure Sinclair would be out one way or another. First there were the terrorist tactics, which would inevitably be blamed on Sinclair himself, escalating his downfall. Caine thought Sinclair's assertion that he'd been talking to God might just help things along tremendously, turning him from charismatic preacher to crazed zealot without too much help. Caine might have to do very little more than plant a few ideas in the police chief's head. And if that didn't work, he could engineer another Jonestown massacre.

"Insane," he said, and gulped the brandy. Smiling, he poured another. "Completely, totally insane."

# SIXTY

# MOSS BASKERVILLE

"Is Eve asleep?" Moss Baskerville asked as he came in the back door.

Cassie nodded and laid her hand on Moss's arm. "Is Iris all right?"

The minute they'd come home and found the huge "666" painted on the front door, Cassie had started worrying about her remaining goat. Moss had told her he'd go out and check while she put their daughter to bed.

"Moss?"

"Iris is missing, Cass."

Her eyes glossed with tears and Baskerville pulled her to him and hugged her fiercely. "I'm sorry, Cassie. I'm really sorry."

"I know." She pushed away from him and roughly wiped away her tears. "Do you think she's ..."

"I hope not, and I'm gonna go look for her in just a minute." He crossed to the phone and called the station. His officer, Al Gonzales, was down at the Cactus Flower Bar getting ready to haul in a couple drunken disorderlies, but otherwise, everything was quiet. Moss told Ken Landry what had happened at Cassie's and that he'd be coming up on the radio shortly, then asked him to have Al cruise town with an especially watchful eye for vandals.

Hanging up, he fetched his gun belt from the bedroom, then returned to the living room, buckling it on. He checked the clip in his .38, then grabbed his leather uniform jacket from the coatrack by the door.

"Moss, what are you going to do?"

"I don't know," he said honestly. "Guess I'll check around the fort, to start with." He pulled the jacket on.

"Be careful, babe," she whispered, her eyes starting to glisten again.

He bent down and kissed her. "Don't worry, and keep everything locked up."

Outside, he climbed in the cruiser and headed up Old Madelyn Highway. At the junction, he slowed and shined his light around the fort. No goat. For the first time, he thought the animal might really still be alive.

He turned east on Thunder Road, driving slowly, playing the spotlight over Dead Man's Hill on the north side, then on the backside of the fort. Nothing. He turned around and started back down the highway, passing Cassie's and turning in to Madland. He cruised the streets of the park, seeing no one and nothing amiss until he turned onto the northernmost road and spotted the Langtry Theater.

"Shit." He played the spotlight over the building. The vandals had painted 666s and obscenities all over the white clapboard building. One window was broken on the first floor. He moved the light to the second story and saw it was untouched. Getting out of the cruiser, he trudged up to the front doors, examined them. They were locked. Quickly he rounded the theater and found the back door intact as well. Extracting a key, he unlocked it and stepped inside, switching on the lights. Nothing had been disturbed. *Thank God for small favors.*

He locked the back door and returned to the cruiser, pausing as he caught an oily scent around the flower beds. As he picked up the radio receiver to call in, he glanced up. There, hanging at the top of the flagpole, was Cassie's goat.

"You sick bastards," he growled. "You goddamned sick sons of bitches. I'm gonna get you and you're gonna be sorry you were ever born."

Later, driving back to Cassie's after he'd cordoned off the theater with police tape, he tried to fit the clues together. The vandals had attacked Cassie's house and theater, and she was a woman who might be considered evil by a religious nut.

The vandalism seemed too directed and too complicated to be the work of the local high school punks. It was probably the work of more than one person, considering the extent of the damage at the church and at the theater, and it was religious—and prejudiced—in nature. Everything led to fundamentalist fanatics—or a cult of some kind. Baskerville was guessing the latter. Sinclair's cult.

Heaving a sigh, he headed back to Cassie's, not looking forward to giving her the bad news.

## SIXTY-ONE

# JUSTIN MARTIN

It was nearly three in the morning and Justin Martin was exhausted after bicycling all the way from New Madelyn back to his car in Spirit Canyon. He dragged himself off the bike and walked it to the trunk of the car. Withdrawing the spare key he'd brought back with him, he opened the trunk and stowed the bike. He hesitated, then opened the small plastic toolbox he always carried. In it was a single goat's ear, cut from the animal before he'd run it up the flagpole. He wrapped it in a paper towel, slipped the packet in his pocket, then quietly shut the trunk. Next he unlocked the driver's door and slid into the seat. He rested a moment, then fished around in the backseat until he found half a bottle of Evian. He chugged it, then sat back for one more minute before grabbing his flashlight and exiting the car again.

He would have liked to rest longer, but dear old Dad would be up in less than an hour, and all hell would break loose if the Mustang was gone when he went to work, and Justin didn't care to get stuck making up any fancy explanations. He began searching for his lost keys, running the light back and forth over the dirt road as quickly and methodically as possible.

By three-thirty, he was nearly to the camp—as far as he could go because he didn't dare take a chance on shining the light where it might be seen. Even though the night sky had remained silent, one of the scientists was probably up. He turned and went back to the car. Tomorrow, as dear old Mom always said, was another day.

# PART THREE

# REVELATIONS

Thou shalt ascend and come like a storm ...
—Ezekiel 38:9

When the right combination of social and psychological conditions is met, when the phenomenon finds in a witness a ready believer, then revelation takes place.
—*Jacques Vallee, Dimensions*

The people that walked in darkness have seen a great light ...
—Isaiah 9:2

# SIXTY-TWO

# JAMES ROBERT SINCLAIR

### FRIDAY

James Sinclair had slept blissfully after his sermon, and this morning as he sat in the meeting room with his Elders and Senior Apostles, he felt well rested and enthusiastic. And more. He felt love for these people, for each and every one. It was new to him, enlightening and wonderful, and he knew that, whatever happened, he and those they could reach would be at peace.

"My friends," he began, "in a little over forty-eight hours, the Four Horsemen will ride and the world as we know it will end. We have much to do in the next two days, and that's the reason we're here. Are there any questions?"

He gazed at each of his Apostles in turn—Blandings, Caine, Allbright, Cramer, Ferguson, and Clayman—and each murmured no. Satisfied, he passed out special agendas for the last two and a half days of the world.

"Tonight and tomorrow night at seven P.M., we'll conduct special baptisms for new members. There will be a final baptism Sunday morning as well. We want to save as many souls as we can, so today and tomorrow I want all our Apostles out spreading the word and inviting everyone to the service. Eldo," he said, looking at the hawk-nosed old man, "you're in charge of Madelyn. George, you take a van of Apostles to Victorville and Hesperia. Lorraine, you do the same for Barstow." He turned to the last two senior Apostles. "Corky, you lead a van to San Bernardino, and Mel, take as many people as you can to Palmdale and Apple Valley."

His gaze fell on Caine. "I need you here, Hannibal, but I'd like you to arrange for car pools to the outlying regions. Send people to shopping centers in Santo Verde, Fontana, Yucaipa, Ontario, Upland, and Montclair. If there are more cars available, use your own judgment as to where they would best be sent."

"Yes, Prophet," Caine replied somberly.

"One caution to you all, especially you, Eldo, since you're in charge of Madelyn. If you're asked to leave private property, please do so immediately. We won't get converts by antagonizing people. Is that clear?"

He studied Eldo Blandings. He had decided to keep the Elder here to better control him. Since he'd already had one run-in with Old Madelyn's management, he would probably refrain from zealousness there. And if he did get carried away, he would be easy to remove.

"Yes, Prophet," Blandings said, rather glumly. "We'll wear our uniforms and carry our umbrellas, I assume?"

When he'd begun his religious movement, Sinclair had declared that the Apostles would wear white robes when Judgment Day came, in order to identify themselves as God's chosen ones, and carry white umbrellas to shelter themselves from the great floods that would come at the end. Now the umbrellas seemed embarrassingly dramatic, but to say so would do more harm than good. "Yes, wear your uniforms," he said at last.

"Now, let's talk about Final Communion. Sunday morning, after the final baptism, we'll prepare the Communion service. It will coincide with the eclipse ... with the ride of the Horsemen. The eclipse begins at eleven-thirty in the morning and ends an hour later. We will begin our services at eleven-thirty and commence the Communion at noon, exactly. It will be complete in fifteen to twenty minutes, and I will resume services and continue until the Horsemen ride."

Beside him, the intercom buzzed. "Yes, Lily, what is it?"

"Prophet, the New Madelyn chief of police is here. He wishes to speak with you."

He watched his advisors' faces as they heard the secretary's words. He thought he saw Lorraine Ferguson's eye twitch once, but that might have been a coincidence.

"Very well. Tell him I'll see him in a few moments. I'll buzz from my office when I arrive there."

He switched off the intercom. "Do any of you have any idea what Chief Baskerville wants?"

They all looked blank, except Hannibal Caine. "He's probably here about the incident at the park yesterday," he announced. Eldo Blandings glared at him.

"I see," Sinclair said, rising. "I'd like you all to join me tomorrow night for a special dinner to celebrate the coming of the Living Savior. Is that amenable to you all?"

"We'd be honored, Prophet," Hannibal said. The others nodded.

"We will meet in the private dining room of the Fellowship House at the usual time," Sinclair said. "Senior Apostles, you're dismissed."

He waited until all four left the room before turning to Hannibal and Eldo. "I fear some of our Apostles may become overzealous, so make sure the groups are made up of our most levelheaded members. Hannibal, I want you to talk to everyone before they leave. You have a calming influence that will be beneficial." He lowered his voice. "I've overheard some of our faithful talking about the weapons, wondering when we're going to use them, and I'm a little concerned."

"*Aren't* we going to use them?" Eldo asked, dismay in his voice.

"No. I've decided that there will be no violence, not even on Judgment Day."

Eldo looked up. "But what about the Special, that is, the armory?"

Sinclair smiled gently. "It will all be over in three days' time. What does it matter, Eldo?" He paused. "Violence isn't the way."

"But, Prophet," Eldo began. "You said to go forth and—"

"Not now, Eldo." Sinclair glanced at his watch. "I'll try to explain it to you after I speak to Chief Baskerville."

He turned on his heel, straightening his blue suit, and headed out the door.

"James!"

He stopped. Caine was chasing after him. "Hannibal?"

"Excuse me, James, but I just wanted to tell you that I know you're very busy. I think I can make Eldo understand your new position on violence without your using up your valuable time."

Sinclair smiled. "Thank you, Hannibal. I'd appreciate that." He turned and strode down the hall, thankful for Caine's services. Whereas he had doubts about Eldo, and even some worry about his two most zealous Senior Elders, Hannibal Caine was a rock. A man he could trust. "Thank you, Lord," he prayed softly as he entered his office through the back door, "for giving me Hannibal as my good right hand."

He sat down at his desk. He continued to dress in a suit, not robes, but his ponytail had remained prominent as it fell down his back, cool and comfortable above his clothes. He'd never known how much it itched before, and he enjoyed the new freedom he felt. He smoothed the jacket, ran a hand over his beard, then pressed the intercom button. "Please send in Chief Baskerville, Lily."

## SIXTY-THREE

# HANNIBAL CAINE

Eldo Blandings stopped pacing back and forth and turned to face Hannibal Caine as he reentered the meeting room. Blandings's squinty blue eyes were ablaze. "Hannibal, did the Prophet explain why he's condemned using weapons?"

"Yes, Eldo, calm down," Hannibal soothed. "Have a seat, and I'll tell you what he said."

Eldo eyed him suspiciously, than sat. Hannibal pulled a chair out, turning it to face Blandings, then smiling broadly, seated himself. "Eldo, nothing has changed."

"Then why did the Prophet say those things? We planned on using force. Hell, we *are* using force," he growled. "It's the only way to win a war!"

Blandings, Caine thought, was like a little boy afraid his parent was going to take away his toys. His expression turned soothing, conspiratorial. "Eldo, right now the Prophet is speaking to a policeman. He's likely to do so again. Remember, I explained to you that he gave us the freedom to form the Special Projects Committee, but that the Prophet didn't want to know what our activities are?"

Eldo nodded grumpily.

"It's the same with the weaponry. He can't know. He's a holy man, Eldo, and he cannot lie. If the police asked him about our activities and our use of weapons, he would have to tell the truth. So he *cannot* know. His instructions are to be subtle in our dealings with the public and to use our own best judgment. Today we do missionary work without weapons. Tomorrow we use them if we must, to convince people to see the light."

Eldo relaxed a little. "An army's got to have weapons."

"He wants us to take prisoners tomorrow," Hannibal said quietly.

Eldo's eyes lit up. "He does?"

"Yes. It shall be as it was planned. We're going to have our last Communion, Elder Blandings, and we have to do it right. There must be sacrifices."

"Sacrifices?" Eldo repeated the word reverently. "What kind of sacrifices?"

"Human, Eldo, human. The dregs of society. Those who deserve to die." Caine repressed a smile: Blandings was eating this stuff up, driven by his bloodlust, his power lust. "How many crosses have we on our rostrum?"

"Three, when the great cross is lowered from the tower."

"We must have three prisoners, then."

"Heathens to serve as symbolic sacrifices?" Eldo asked, eyes gleaming.

"Perhaps. The Prophet has asked me to decide who it should be. These people will be greatly honored and hold high places in heaven," he added, his voice full of awe. "But, Eldo," he cautioned, "I've told you more than I should. You must swear to me to keep this to yourself."

"I swear," Eldo said, his voice hoarse.

"The Prophet wants to hear nothing of it. He has plans of his own he hasn't told you about yet."

"He has?" Eldo asked hopefully.

But Caine only smiled. "You'll know soon enough, my friend.

Now, tell me what the Special Projects Committee will be up to today."

He sat back, listening to Eldo with only half an ear. Things were falling into place more easily than he had ever expected, and soon Jim-Bob Sinclair would only be a memory.

## SIXTY-FOUR

# MOSS BASKERVILLE

"So, you can see my problem, Mr. Sinclair." Moss Baskerville leaned back in the cushiony leather chair before Jim-Bob's desk and tried to appear completely at ease. But he was nervous as a cat. The preacher's eyes bored into his, which wouldn't have bothered him if they had been filled with that cold criminal look that Baskerville knew so well. No, Sinclair's eyes were fathomless, and Moss couldn't read what was in them.

What seemed to be in them was, of all things, genuine sincerity. He exuded trustworthiness, and for that reason, Baskerville's hackles were up.

"I assure you, Chief," Sinclair said in a voice as riveting as his eyes, "I know nothing about vandalism in town. I am truly sorry that it happened and I'll help you any way I can."

Baskerville believed him, despite the hackles. "Do you think some of your members might be getting a little carried away? Behind your back?" he added, no menace in his voice. The man amazed him and he understood for the first time the true meaning of the word "charismatic"; it meant unnerving. This man could take nearly anyone's free will, yet he gave off not a whiff of criminality. For the first time, Moss wondered if Sinclair truly believed he was what he claimed to be. *No, the place is too expensive ... The furniture, the paintings, the suit. He knows exactly what he's doing. Money doesn't lie. A prophet should be dressed in rags, and barefoot.*

"Chief?"

"Sorry, Mr. Sinclair. You were saying?"

"After your phone call, I spoke to my advisors, and they assured me our people had nothing to do with Miss Halloway's problems or the vandalism of the church. But you are welcome to question anyone here."

That surprised Baskerville. "That won't be necessary for now, Mr. Sinclair."

"Chief Baskerville, I also wanted to apologize to you for the invasion of the park the other day. I understand there was some commotion."

"Nothing to worry about." Moss heard himself say this when what he meant to do was give Sinclair a stern warning about trespassing on private property. But for some reason, he couldn't.

"We believe the Four Horsemen of the Apocalypse will ride this Sunday, Chief Baskerville, and we believe that the more souls we can rescue before they come, the better. We will be out doing missionary work, but I've asked my people to stay off private property and be polite at all times."

"Thank you." Sinclair's voice mesmerized him, and Moss continued to stare into those dark brown eyes. *This guy ought to be put away for the safety of everyone.* He wondered if Hitler and Napoleon had possessed such charisma.

Sinclair rose and Moss followed suit. "Thank you for coming to see me," the preacher said, sounding utterly sincere. "If you change your mind and want to talk to my people, you're quite welcome. You're also welcome to come to our services and join us in celebration of the Living Savior."

"The Living Savior," Moss repeated. "That anything like Jesus?"

Sinclair nodded. "The Second Coming. He'll walk among us soon."

Moss felt himself returning to earth, despite the man's charm. "Caught a little bit of your sermon last night, Mr. Sinclair."

Jim-Bob smiled. "You did?"

"Um-hmm. You said you talked to God." Now his feet were firmly planted back on earth. "Did you mean that literally?"

Sinclair tried to pull him back in with his hypnotic gaze. "Yes, quite literally. I was praying on Olive Mesa the last time He came to me." He extended his hand.

Moss was unnerved by the eyes, the voice, and now the touch of the hand. It was supercharged, almost electric. *You're imagining things, buddy. He's doing his voodoo on* you. Moss pulled his hand back quickly, but Sinclair didn't react. "You know, that's interesting about Olive Mesa. A scientist friend saw a UFO over the mesa yesterday afternoon."

Sinclair's eyes moved rapidly, taking in all of him, fascination obvious. "That's amazing," he murmured. "A true miracle. What time did this occur?"

"Around three or four, I believe."

"Tuesday night was my first visitation. The newspaper mentioned several UFO sightings that evening ..." Sinclair's voice trailed off, but his eyes kept Baskerville imprisoned.

"We had all sorts of reports that night," Moss said.

"What we once recognized as angels," Jim-Bob Sinclair mused sadly, "are now mistaken for little green men from Mars." He broke eye contact.

"Funny," Moss said, studying the preacher. "That's exactly what my scientist friend said."

"Really?" Sinclair's voice was almost a whisper as he guided Moss to the door. "Please excuse me now, Chief Baskerville. I need to meditate. To think." He opened the door to the outer office and guided him past Lily and out the hallway. "Please come to our services, my friend," he said in a soft voice. "You're a good man, and I'd like to share heaven with you." With that, he turned and disappeared back into his office.

# SIXTY-FIVE

# ERIC WATSON

"Will you stop feeling guilty, Alex? It's nice to see you having a social life for a change!" Eric Watson pushed the Bronco's door shut, then leaned in. "Take your time. I have a pile of work to do." He smiled at his boss. "Stay out all night if you want to."

Alex made a face. "It's just lunch, Eric. "I'll be back by three." She started the engine.

"Have fun," he called as she drove away.

In the three years that he had been her assistant, he'd never seen her show any interest in a man. Once, she even admitted to him that she had no close friends outside of the institute. She was, she joked, married to her work.

Eric walked across the camp to the cliffside and checked the instruments. He'd had a small crush on her that first year, but fortunately, that had mutated into a solid friendship that he valued more than anything else. He smiled to himself as he sauntered toward a pile of boulders edging the dirt track that led to the campsite. He still enjoyed the frequently voiced envy of the other young men who worked at APRA. He climbed up the rock pile and sat on a flat-faced stone, knees up, his arms wrapped around them. He'd been in a barely controlled state of euphoria ever since the UFO show Wednesday night. To be part of the team that got the footage of the phenomena was the chance of a lifetime, and the work done here was going to make his doctoral thesis something very special. Something publishable.

"Life is good," he said, staring at the beautiful red desert. Overhead, huge powder-puff clouds dotted the deep blue sky. In the northwest, darker clouds hung ominously low against the stark mountains. The day was mild and magnificent, and briefly he considered taking a hike, but his guilty conscience insisted he get to work on his thesis.

Eric stretched and lowered his legs, then slid off the boulder to the ground. The toe of one Reebok hit something that made a metallic sound.

"What the hell?" He bent down and came up with a set of five keys and a rabbit's foot on a key chain. "Christ," he said, holding the set by one key so that the foot dangled away from his hand. Usually a rabbit's foot was dyed green or red or blue, but this one was natural black and white speckles on gray, its tip wrapped in leather binding. "Homemade." Dyed feet were bad enough, but to Eric, this was disgusting. Why anyone would kill an animal for something like this was beyond his comprehension.

Then he noticed that the keys hadn't been there long: The metal was shiny under a very thin layer of dust. Mystified, he carried the key chain back to the camp and laid it on the card table between a couple stacks of books, so that he wouldn't have to look at the disgusting thing.

He flipped on the radio just as a tune ended. "This is Holly Ray with you on Y-102," the female jock purred. Her voice was smoky velvet and he listened, wishing she'd magically appear to sweep him away from his studies and whisper sweet nothings in his ear. Instead, she announced ten hits in a row, and Eric hit the books.

# SIXTY-SIX

## CARLO PELEGRINE

The second victim of Charlie Pilgrim's lust had been an aging prostitute who tried to pick him up after the homecoming game of his senior year in high school, and Carlo remembered very little about that night. He, Glen MacIntyre, and Ted Furillo had been drinking beer in a small park near the school, and it was well past midnight when Ted announced that his old man would kill him if he didn't get home. Glen left with him, but Carlo had stayed behind, ostensibly to finish his beer, but in truth because he wasn't used to drinking and wasn't sure he could walk.

After a while, he felt better and stood, shakily at first, then with more confidence. He remembered giggling like a little kid while he peed in the bushes, then walking across the park and out to the street, disoriented even on the outskirts of his own neighborhood. He walked a long time, keeping to the shadows, not wanting to go home until he was sure he could pass for sober, not sure he could find his house or even his own street.

About three A.M., he found himself in a seedy part of town, far from home. He had no idea how many miles he'd walked in the last hour or two, but the drunk had dimmed to a haze and a dull throb in his head, and he knew he could find his way home.

That was when she came along.

"Hi, handsome."

The voice called to him from the shadowed doorway of the Geldorf Hotel, and a second later, a tall thin woman with hair the color of carrots came into view. She was far older than he, and had tried to hide her age with caked-on makeup, mold blue eyeshadow, and false eyelashes. Her fingernails, as her hand touched his, were painted the same orangey-red as her hair.

"You looking for a good time?"

Until that moment, he'd managed to blot the memory of the first incident on Coney Island, but now it all came rushing back—the blond hooker taking him into the House of Mirrors, stripping, his touching her skin, then finding himself outside, blood under his nails.

"No," he said, and tried to walk away.

But she wouldn't let him. Grabbing his arm, she pushed him up against the wall, rubbing her body against his, arousing him until he wanted her. Wanted to touch her, feel her.

"You got enough for a hotel room?" she asked, nodding in the direction of the Geldorf.

He shook his head no, and as much as he wanted her, he felt relief. She'd reject him now, he'd thought, but he was wrong.

"Well, how much you got? Twenty?"

He dug in his wallet, came up with three fives.

"That'll do," she said, snatching the bills from his hand. "Hard times. Come on."

She led him down an alley of apartment buildings and unlocked the door of a basement room. "Come on, sweet stuff," she said. "I don't usually bring customers to my own place, but you look like a sweet kid."

The one-room apartment was dingy and water-stained and smelled of dirty clothes, stale cigarette smoke, and spilled booze. She led him to the bed. "Take your clothes off, sweetie," she said, as she began to strip. Slowly he followed suit, folding his clothes over the back of a wooden chair.

"My, aren't you the neat one?" She laughed as she tossed her bra on the floor with her miniskirt and tank top. Finally she peeled off her red bikini panties and threw them at him. At once, he was repelled and excited.

She went to the bed and reclined on grungy yellow-gray sheets, posing so that her sagging breasts looked firmer, spreading her legs so that her sex peeped out from a thick brown bush of hair. "You like?" she asked.

Dumbly he nodded. *Get out!* But he was paralyzed.

"Then come here. Fifteen bucks doesn't buy that much time, you know."

He approached, standing over her, rock-hard as he stared at three small strawberry moles on her midriff. They looked like extra nipples against her white flesh. Whereas the first girl's skin had had a bluish undertone, this woman's was yellowish. Her belly, though flat, had shiny stretch marks, her breasts, too, and they were the first—and last —that Carlo had ever seen. He reached down and slowly ran his finger over one of the shiny flat marks.

"What the fuck are you doing?" she asked, pissed. "Let's get going." She spread her legs farther. "Into the saddle," she ordered, dangling a condom at him.

He did as he was told, climbing on, pumping, running his hands over her skin, across her shoulders, up to her neck, around it.

And that was all he remembered until he found himself lying on top of her, her dead eyes bulging blindly. There was blood under his nails. Horrified, he rolled off of her, and seeing blood on his abdomen, thought he was hurt. Then he looked at her. The skin from the pubis up to the rib cage had been hacked away. His jackknife lay beside the corpse and he snagged it up, tears streaming down his face. Somehow, he'd made it into her shower, washed and dried and dressed, then went around the room, wiping everything down, carefully keeping his eyes off the corpse.

Two days later, he'd been dubbed "the Peeler" by the newspapers. By that time, the other prostitute's body had been found and he was now considered a serial killer. Lurid stories in the *Daily News* reported outrageous lies about the extent of the skinnings, the expertise, and those stories were still told to this day.

The ragged square of missing skin was gone, and never found. Even he didn't know what had happened to it, and he never dared consider the possibilities.

Like Alex's UFOs, the Peeler was mythology in the making. He smiled bitterly and wondered what he was doing, seeing her again, even for lunch. He had no right.

The bell over the front door rang and a flurry of butterflies battered his stomach. Quickly he ran a comb through his hair, then, swallowing, left his reading room and entered his shop.

Justin Martin was standing there. "Hi!"

"Hello, Justin. What can I do for you?"

"I just wanted to thank you again for giving me a ride home last night."

"You're welcome."

Behind Justin, the door opened and Alex Manderley stepped inside. "Hi, Carlo," she said. "Am I too early?"

Carlo saw the briefest look of surprise on Justin's face, then it disappeared into a polite smile.

"Hi, Dr. Manderley. How are you?"

"Fine, Justin." She smiled. "Getting your palm read?"

"Uh, no."

"Justin's car broke down in the canyon last night," Carlo explained. "I gave him a lift home." He glanced at the youth. "Did you get it going all right?"

Justin grinned, but it looked false. "Just fine. My dad took me to it this morning. It was a snap." The kid appeared to be at ease, but his gestures and tone were too studied.

"Good." Carlo walked to the door and turned the OPEN sign to CLOSED. "Do you like Mexican food?" he asked Alex.

"Love it," she replied.

"I've gotta go," Justin said, passing Carlo and Alex, to quickly stride out the door and down the steps. "Thanks again," he called, and dashed off in the direction of the mine.

He and Alex stepped out onto the porch. "He broke down right at the trail to your camp."

"You're joking!"

Carlo locked the door. "Strange, huh? He claimed he was going home the long way. I doubt that he knew you were even there." He paused. "Though he probably wonders what I was doing, coming out of nowhere like that."

"I didn't tell him where our new camp was. I suppose I should have."

Carlo paused at the foot of the steps, studying her. "I wouldn't do that."

"Why not? He seems like a nice kid."

"You didn't notice the way he was looking at you?"

Alex laughed. "How was that?"

"With lust."

"You sound just like Eric." She laughed again. "That's very flattering, but ... I don't think so."

Carlo shrugged. "Let's have a quick bite, then we'll come back here and I'll read your palm if you like."

"I'd love it."

Her smile made his butterflies take flight again.

SIXTY-SEVEN

# MARIE LOPEZ

"You're the only male worth knowing, Rex." Marie Lopez patted the black gelding's neck affectionately, then urged him up the trail toward Rattlesnake Canyon. She smelled rain in the air, but the storm clouds were still many hours north, maybe even a day or two if they didn't pick up speed. With her luck, they'd come in just in time to ruin the eclipse.

Marie had spent the morning fuming, picking up hay at the feed store, fuming some more, checking wool prices, fuming, and mucking out the stable. And fuming. Finally she decided the only thing that would help was a ride, just like Tom always said. *Tom, you turkey!*

She made herself stop thinking about him, thinking instead that it was good to be out here, just her and her horse, no sheep, no dogs, no people. No men. *No Tom Abernathy!*

She couldn't get away from it: She was pissed. She'd made a fool out of herself last night in that stupid dress, in high heels, for Christ's sake! Clothes like that made her feel vulnerable, and now she couldn't even figure out what had possessed her to wear that getup. *Tom, that's what.* She grimaced. He'd been getting into her dreams lately, touching her everywhere with those big long-fingered hands of his, kissing her neck, her breasts ... She guessed the sexual tension that spilled over into daytime had addled her senses, turned her into a stupid, flirtatious little female. Exactly the kind she hated.

"But you loved it when he held your hand." Rex's ears twitched at the sound of her voice, so she patted his neck and urged him on up the rocky ridge.

The trouble with Tom Abernathy was that he moved too slow and she was damn well tired of waiting. And just as things finally got promising, he'd taken her story about the floating sheep and humiliated her by twisting it into one of the worst tall tales he'd ever told. *You bastard, Abernathy!*

What really galled her was that he acted like he didn't even know why she was angry. How could he be so dense? She couldn't get any satisfaction. The man couldn't be confronted because he wouldn't respond. That damned cowboy had just two talents: a way with horses, and a way with his mouth. He could talk his way into or out of anything without ever getting riled. Her own temper was hair-trigger, and Tom's ability to control his sometimes made her want to shoot him.

There was one more thing pissing her off, and that was her own anger. *Marie, you're too touchy.* That's what Aunt Carmen would tell her if she took this problem to her, and she knew it was true. As angry as she was, she knew Tom hadn't meant to humiliate her. She knew his confusion last night was real. *But damn him, he ought to have enough common sense to know what he did!*

Rex gained the ridge top and they stayed there a few moments while she gazed across the mountaintops and down into the circular valley where she'd lost her sheep.

Suddenly she noticed a white splotch half-hidden by a granite outcropping on the southwestern side of the valley. "I'll be damned," she whispered as she tilted her Stetson down to keep the sun's glare out of her eyes as she searched. Sure enough, at the other side of the round valley, there was the other sheep. Dead, she thought, wishing she'd brought her binoculars. There was no way that she and *Tom—Tom again!*—could have missed them yesterday morning.

Excited, she started to give Rex the order to descend into the valley, then remembered Alex Manderley wanted photos and samples. Glancing at her watch, she saw there was plenty of daylight left, so she turned Rex back toward her ranch to fetch her camera and some Ziploc bags for samples.

# SIXTY-EIGHT

# TOM ABERNATHY

*What the hell do women want, anyway?* Tom Abernathy leaned against the corral fence of the little arena in Madland and pondered Marie Lopez and her gender in general. He'd hardly slept last night, wondering just what he'd done to make her run off like that. *Women!*

In ten minutes he'd be out in the arena himself, playacting Madelyn's old-time sheriff up against the bad guys. Beside him, Belle knickered softly and nudged his shoulder, telling him she needed a carrot. "You know I've got no pockets in this costume, Belle," he said, scratching her muzzle. "You just wait a few minutes."

Behind him, Fred and Becky were calf-roping to the cheers of the crowd in the stands, and in front of him, tourists strolled along the wooden sidewalks looking in windows, going in shops. Then he spied four men carrying shopping bags as they disappeared into the rest room kitty-cornered from the sweet shop. That struck him as kind of odd, and he casually took to watching the door.

"Hey, Tom. How they hanging?"

"Hey, Shorty. Hanging just fine."

Shorty Sykes was even taller than Tom, six feet five inches of broad- shouldered stuntman. He was dressed in his bad-guy duds, and in the upcoming show, Tom would shoot him off the top of a barn. Shorty loved doing falls more than just about anything, even though he'd broken enough bones to construct a whole other man. Just then, Mad Dog Steinberg, who'd proclaimed himself "the orneriest Jew in the West," ambled up. He was short and dark and could stare down a rattler at five paces. His bad-guy duds included a bullwhip, and Tom was glad it wasn't ever applied to him—he was no stuntman, after all— even though Mad Dog and his stunt-riding victims all said he wrapped that leather around you as sweet as you please.

"What are we doing about the eclipse?" Mad Dog asked.

"Why," Tom drawled, "I guess we can't do much of anything about it."

Mad Dog started to smile, then tried to look surly instead. "Do we wait till it's over and start the afternoon show late?"

"I dunno. Shorty? What do you think?"

Shorty shrugged. "I dunno. Ask Hank Running Deer. He's the organized one around here."

"Hey, Henry!" Mad Dog yelled. "Getcher keister over here!"

Henry came out of the corral. Even though he had his long black hair pulled back in a low ponytail, it was flapping in the breeze. "Rain's coming," he announced, joining them. "What the hell do you want, Steinberg?"

Mad Dog told him, and Henry, who liked to decide things like that, announced they'd start the stunt show at two instead of one on Sunday. Everyone thought that was a good idea.

"So, Tom," Henry said. "How come you're staring at that men's room door?"

"There somethin' you want to tell us?" Shorty asked, poking him painfully in the ribs.

"Yeah, I guess I do. Saw four men go in there with shopping bags right before you showed up. I'd swear one of them was that damned

Apostle with the bad rug—the one that gave Moss and me all that lip yesterday."

"You think we got trouble?" Henry asked.

"They're probably in there blowin' each other," Mad Dog announced.

Tom ignored Mad Dog. "I'm really beginning to wonder what they're up to."

Just as Henry, the worrier of the group, suggested they were planting bombs in the toilets, the door opened and out came the four, all decked out in their crazy white robes and carrying those long white umbrellas under their arms. One of them had a stack of fluorescent pink flyers.

"I told them they couldn't do that," Tom said softly. His consternation over Marie was making him feel unusually peevish.

Mad Dog checked his watch. "We got just enough time to roust them." He stepped forward, but Tom put a hand on his shoulder and stopped him.

"Let's wait a minute and see what they're gonna do. Show never runs on time anyhow."

The four white-robed men started handing flyers to the tourists, sermonizing in loud voices about the Living Savior and the Four Horsemen of the Apocalypse, telling everyone they'd pray for them to see the light. It was disgusting, and they were approaching fast.

The Apostles were only six feet from them, either unaware of them or flaunting their trespassing. "You know, boys," Tom drawled in his best booming cowboy tones, "those guys in those white dresses are really something."

The Apostles turned to look at him, and he saw that he was right. Old Beaknose was back, glaring at him. Tom smiled as he locked eyes with another man he'd seen yesterday, a fellow in his thirties with a powerful build, short hair, and the face of a hardcase.

"I kinda like those umbrellas they got, though," Tom told his buddies. "In those getups, don't those Apostles just sorta remind you of a big old herd of Mary Poppinses?" Laughter came from a growing crowd of onlookers.

The hardcase's umbrella came up, its silver tip pointing at Tom. "You take that back!" he growled.

The umbrella's tip was within six inches of Tom's chest, and he had to put his hand on Mad Dog's arm to stop him from pushing it away.

"Campbell," warned Beaknose.

The hardcase didn't move. "I said, you take that back."

Tom smiled, wide and tight-lipped, then turned his slow, unconcerned drawl back on. "If you boys want to look like girls, that ain't nothin' for *me* to apologize for, mister."

"Tom, what's gotten into you?" Henry hissed in his ear.

"Did I say 'mister'?" Tom asked, winking at Henry. "I meant to say 'miss.'"

"Why, you cocksucking son of a bit—" Campbell lunged the umbrella at him, but Tom was the quickest draw in Madelyn, and his hand was up and wrapped around the tip before it could touch him.

"Better smile when you say that, friend," he said slowly. He looked at Beaknose. "Better wash this boy's mouth out with soap. Got a real stinkin' load of garbage in there."

Campbell, red-faced, was still hanging on to the handle end of the umbrella. "I'm gonna kill you—"

"I said, *smile.*"

Before the Apostle could react, Tom moved, yanking the umbrella from Campbell's hands and giving it to Shorty Sykes. "Take care of that for me, will you?"

"Pleasure." Shorty promptly bent the thing in two, smiling the whole time. Mad Dog was also grinning, and even Henry looked vaguely amused.

"Now, you boys better get on outta here."

"We've been sent by God. His law supersedes Baskerville's!" Beaknose intoned.

Tom put his hand on his blank-loaded gun. The one called

Campbell was about ready to spring, and Tom didn't care to get in a scuffle. The gun's blast would confound the guy long enough for the stuntmen to grab him. "Well, maybe God's law supersedes the chief's; I just don't rightly know. I'll have to ask him. Here, I'm in charge, and you're gonna have to abide by *my* laws. Me and my deputies here will be seeing to it. That's a fact." He heard applause all around and couldn't help smiling. He loved a good show as much as the next man. More, maybe.

"You will pay for this," Beaknose hissed.

A vein was popping rhythmically on Campbell's temple, but he made no move. Tom thought maybe he wouldn't try anything now, especially if he made himself scarce. "Boys," he said to the stuntmen, "I got to get to the show. You three still got a couple minutes. How about seeing these gals to the gate?" Calmly he put his foot in Belle's stirrup and swung into the saddle. He tipped his hat. "Afternoon, ladies."

Belle stepped toward the Apostles, and that's when Campbell grabbed at Tom's leg. Shorty made to move on him. "No!" Tom ordered, grinning and doing snake-eyes as well as Mad Dog as he kicked the man's hand away. "This one's mine." As he spoke, he took his lariat from the saddle and moved out into the wide dirt street; getting it ready.

The crowd lining the sidewalks cheered wildly.

"You want me to rope all of you at once?" he asked, kicking Campbell away again. "Might make your hair fall off your head," he added, looking at Beaknose. "Toupee ain't worth a horse potato once it's been roped off and stomped."

Belle backed up, making enough space to throw the rope, just like she would in the show. Tom glanced up and saw that Henry was clearing the street of tourists, sending them all up on the sidewalks. Henry always thought of things like that, thank heaven. "You all back off," he told Beaknose and the two others. "You, Campbell, I'm a sporting man." He looked down the empty street, at all the tourists waiting for a show, *needing* a show, and decided that, by golly, that's what they were going to get.

He urged Belle around, cutting Campbell out of the flock. "You get runnin', right down the street. And if I don't catch you by the end, why, you boys can walk around the park in your dresses."

"I'll see you burn in hell," roared Beaknose.

"Not if I see you first. Yeehaw!"

The whoop set Campbell into motion, and the crowd went wild as he ran the gauntlet. When he was halfway down the block, Tom signaled Belle to take off.

Holding the lariat up, sighting on Campbell, who didn't even have the sense to zigzag around a little bit, Tom waited until he was fifteen feet away, then let the circle of rope fly at its target. It lassoed Campbell like a dream, and the crowd yelled and applauded as Tom cinched him tight and reeled in the rope, snugging it over the saddle horn when Campbell was nice and close. "Now, miss," he drawled, "you gonna come along quietly? 'Cause if you ain't, I'll just hog-tie you right now."

Silently Campbell walked alongside the horse, eyes forward, giving off such strong sparks of anger that Belle kept shying away from him. Tom rode back to the arena, tipping his hat, loving the cheers, and reminding everybody to come to the stunt show. When he arrived back at the arena, the other three Apostles were nowhere to be seen.

"They're waiting outside the gate," Shorty said.

"You want to give this one to Baskerville?" Mad Dog asked, grinning at the fallen Apostle.

Tom rubbed his chin. "I guess not. Moss's got plenty to do without having to take out the trash, too. I don't think these boys'll be back any time soon, anyway. Ain't that right, Campbell?"

The man didn't answer.

"Tom," Henry said. "They're cueing you."

"Well, hell's bells, Campbell, I got to go." He waited until Henry removed the rope and Mad Dog and Shorty had the guy by the elbows. "Come on, Belle," he said. As they trotted into the arena, he felt much better, and hearing the applause made him feel downright fine. He took his Stetson off and waved it at the crowd, who cheered louder and waved back. *My Lord,* he thought, *there's nothing better than a good audience.* And as he dismounted in front of the false-fronted western town set, that little voice came back to annoy him by adding, *Nothing better except for a good woman. Like Marie.*

# SIXTY-NINE

# JUSTIN MARTIN

After seeing Carlo and Alex Manderley enter La Panza Roja, the nicest restaurant in Madland, Justin Martin hurried to the Haunted Mine and told Old Man Marquay that he had to run home and change a flat tire for his mother. Marquay was understanding even though the park was teeming with people this Friday afternoon. Justin thanked him and promised to return as quickly as possible, then he ran for his car.

He drove south, toward home, just in case Marquay noticed him. He crossed through New Madelyn, then turned up Ghost Town Road, the long way into Spirit Canyon. He finally got back up to the Madland fork, where he turned right onto the dirt track that led into the hills. He'd last traveled this way in the wee hours on his bicycle, and as the road began to climb, he marveled that he'd made it.

A few minutes later, he found Alex's turnoff and nosed the Mustang along the tight hillside road, driving slowly, watching for the glint of his keys. He finally rounded the last bend and drove onto the broad flat, and parked just past the mound of rocks he'd hidden behind the night before. His keys had to be here somewhere.

"Hi!" Eric Watson ambled toward him, a red-haired scarecrow of a guy, pure nerd from his glasses to his goofy grin.

"Hi, Eric!" Justin slipped his spare key in his pocket, then pulled one of his shoelaces loose before climbing out of the black Mustang. "I just stopped by to see how you guys are doing." He scanned the ground at the back of the boulders, but saw nothing. *Damn!*

"Come on over in the shade," Eric invited. "Want a Coke?"

"No, thanks. I can't stick around." He walked over to the rocks, surreptitiously searching for the lost keys. "Could I take a look through your telescope, though?" That would allow him to walk closer to the road.

"Sure. Come on."

"Go ahead, I've gotta tie my shoe." He bent down. The fucking nerd didn't go ahead but waited until he was done. Still no keys. "Let's go," he said, ready to put Plan B into effect.

After staring through the scope at the storm clouds and mountains far to the north—*big fucking deal*—Justin checked his watch. "I'd better get to Madland. Don't want to be late for work." He began walking back, purposely veering over to the road as he moved. The nerd came along with him.

"So where's Dr. Manderley?" he asked as they approached the car.

"She's having lunch with a friend." Nerdman paused. "Say, how'd you find our camp?"

"Oh, Carlo told me." Digging in one pocket, then another, he asked, "How come you moved again?"

"Military harassment," Nerdly said, his nose wrinkling.

"Can they do that?"

"Helicopters can do anything they please. They practically blew us out of the canyon. What's wrong?"

"Can't find my keys. I put them in my pocket when I got here. There's a little hole in it—they must have fallen out." He started searching in earnest.

"That's a coincidence," Eric said.

Justin looked up. "What do you mean?"

"I found a set of keys right by that pile of rocks this morning." Eric's lip curled. "On a rabbit-foot key chain. But you just lost yours, right?"

*Goddamn son of a bitch!* "Yeah. Just now." He turned away from Eric, slipping the spare key from his pocket, then bending down and pretending to pick it up. "Found them," he called out.

"Great," Nerdface said.

Justin opened the car door and sat down, then flashed a shit-eater. "Say, would you like me to drop those keys off at the police station?"

"No, thanks. It's possible that Alex dropped them. I'll have to show them to her first."

*Fuck!* "You know, if you and Dr. Manderley want to go into town together, I'd be happy to watch the camp for you."

"That's nice of you, but I don't really think I'll be leaving the camp for a while." Eric smiled tightly. "I'm working on my thesis, and this is the perfect place to do it because there's nothing to distract me."

"Okay," Justin called as he began to pull away. "But keep it in mind." *You fucking asshole nerd!*

Enraged, Justin drove down the narrow jeep trail and pulled out on the road, turning to go back the way he came. He was pretty sure Alex Manderley would recognize his key chain, with its dangling rabbit's foot.

Justin screeched down the canyon's back road, only slowing when he reached the fork. He turned sedately back onto the paved road that wound toward Madland. At the camp, he'd almost offed the nerd right then and there, but he'd stopped himself, knowing it would be a good idea to consider his options. The key chain was his and he wanted it back, especially because if Alex recognized it, she'd know he'd been up there. Though it meant nothing in connection with anything serious, like murder, it meant humiliation, and he couldn't stand that.

He decided he would have to wait and see if she knew the keys were his. If she did, he would do something about it. Or maybe ask the Peeler to handle it. After riding down from the canyon on the back of his motorcycle, Justin felt a stronger kinship with him than ever and knew that he would tell him the truth very soon. But he needed to give him at least one more gift first. The goat's ear wasn't much, but unless something better came along, it would have to do because the rectangles of skin he'd taken from Old Lady Marquay had gone bad. The goat's ear made him think of that fucking Eldo Blandings, the high-handed Supreme Asshole of the Apostles. He hadn't heard a peep out of him or Caine yet, and that was really grinding his ass. *Ungrateful motherfucker!*

A half mile from Madland, Justin saw movement near the roadside, a flash of blue, and slowed, peering into the brush. A boy, no older than eight, was sitting on the ground. Beside him lay his bicycle, a little motocross number.

Something better had come along. Justin stopped the car and rolled down his window. "Hi!"

The boy glanced his way but didn't answer.

"Is something wrong?" Justin hung his arm out the window so the kid could see the "M" on his varsity jacket sleeve.

"Got a flat," the kid called glumly.

"You want a ride home? Your bike'll fit in my trunk." The kid almost smiled, but still seemed unsure.

"I go to Madelyn High," Justin told him. "What school do you go to?"

"Madelyn Elementary."

"Then we're neighbors." Justin smiled broadly. "Madelyn's so little that everybody's a neighbor here."

Finally the kid smiled. "I'm Billy Cole. I'd like a ride, I guess."

"No problem." Justin pulled to the side of the road and turned off the engine. Looking in both directions, he saw no people, no cars, nothing. Perfect.

He walked over to the kid and picked up his bicycle and carried it back to the Mustang. The kid trailed along right behind him, a good little puppy. Justin smiled again and set the bike down and opened the trunk, then turned to study Billy and his bike. *What to do, what to do, what to do?* Should he put the boy or the bike in first?

"I need to move a couple things around." He rummaged around in the trunk and pulled out his crowbar and showed it to the kid. "Wouldn't want this to mess up your bike. That happened to me once. Let's put the bike in."

He glanced up and down the road. Deserted. "You get that end."

As the boy bent and picked up the back of his bike, Justin pivoted on one heel, bringing the crowbar up, then slammed it against the back of the kid's head. Billy went down like a sack of sand, blood trickling from the base of his skull.

Smiling, Justin pulled a black plastic trash bag from the trunk and tucked it around the kid so that he wouldn't get any dirt or blood on his own clothes. Easily he lifted the boy and laid him in the bottom of the trunk. Within another sixty seconds, he'd bound the boy's hands and ankles with silver duct tape, then he covered Billy's mouth with the sticky stuff. Finally he placed two fingers on the kid's neck, feeling for a pulse, smiling when he caught the barest of beats.

He checked the road again, then threw the bike in on top of the boy and closed the trunk. At last he got back in the car and drove on to work, whistling all the way.

# SEVENTY

# ALEXANDRA MANDERLEY

They had spent more than an hour in the restaurant, lost in conversation, and both were surprised and disappointed when Carlo's watch alarm went off, alerting him that he had an appointment in fifteen minutes. They'd hurried back to his shop and now stood on his steps saying hurried goodbyes. "I never got my palm reading," Alex heard herself say. "Do I get a rain check?"

"Of course." He smiled hesitantly. "Would you like to have dinner with me tonight? I'll read it then."

"I'd have to check with Eric, of course." She shouldn't accept, but she couldn't help herself. "I don't think he'd mind. But there's one condition."

"What's that?"

"I'm buying this time."

"No. I'm cooking, but you can help wash the dishes, if you want. Do you like Italian?"

"Yes. Very much." Her voice cracked. "I love pasta," she added quickly.

"Good. Seven o'clock?"

"Seven's fine. That is, if it's all right with Eric, and no UFOs show up. I'll call you from camp within the hour and let you know."

"Good."

"Good-bye, Carlo," she said, extending her hand.

He took it, but instead of shaking it, held it in his own. He had the hands of a surgeon, strong and graceful. "Until tonight."

She thought he wanted to kiss her hand, but he hesitated, then squeezed lightly and let go. She smiled, walked down the steps, waving once, then strode away, refusing to allow herself to look back.

*I can't believe I'm doing this.* She drove the Bronco up the canyon, telling herself to call and cancel. Things might get out of control if she was alone with him. "No," she said aloud. "You're a grown woman, Manderley, and you won't let yourself get carried away. No clothing will come off!"

She turned onto the trail to the camp, slowing her speed to a crawl to avoid running off the cliff on one side or scraping the mountain walls on the other. She'd been celibate for years and that wasn't going to change, she told herself. No way was that going to change. Relationships just weren't worth the heartache they inevitably caused. An evening with Carlo would be fun, the conversation good, the food most likely excellent. And that's all it would be, no matter how much she wanted him. Even professional men—doctors, scientists—were inevitably intimidated by her and ended up resenting her devotion to her career. The double standard was dying a painfully slow, lingering death.

She pulled into the camp and parked. Eric opened her door. "Have a good time?"

"Wonderful. Um, would you mind if I left for a couple hours tonight? I'll be back before UFO hours."

"I already told you I don't mind, and I meant it. I have to work on my thesis, remember?" He smirked. "Got a hot date?"

"Well, sort of. Carlo's an interesting person. We share a lot of interests," she added, feeling stupid and embarrassed. "He wants to cook me dinner."

"That's great."

What she liked about Eric was that though he might tease her, he never went too far. "You're sure?"

"Positive." They walked into the shaded camp. "Are those yours?" Eric asked, pointing at a set of keys on the table.

"Lord, no! My God, look at that foot. Wait, I know who they belong to— Justin Martin!"

"Something funny's going on," Eric said. "I found these just after you left, and he showed up here an hour ago. He said he just stopped by to be neighborly, then he walked all over, out to the scope, around the rocks ... where I found the keys, then he said he had to go. And do you know what?"

"What?"

"He suddenly couldn't find his keys. I told him about these after he'd searched for a while, and he said they weren't his. About a split second later, he bent down and came up with a key in his hand. I thought he had it palmed when he bent down. Now I'm sure."

"Eric, Carlo told me he gave the boy a ride home last night. That his car was broken down on the main road near our turnoff. He must have been spying on us—"

"And lost his keys," Eric finished. "I asked him how he found us, and he said Carlo told him."

Alex shook her head. "I got the impression that Carlo doesn't care for Justin." She paused. "The boy must have followed me up here last night. Maybe I shouldn't leave you alone here if he's going to be skulking around."

"No, Alex, you go. He's just a kid. What's he going to do besides annoy me to death? Besides, it's you he's interested in."

Alex frowned. "Carlo agrees with you on that."

"Men know these things," Eric said with a subtle smile. "Trust us."

# SEVENTY-ONE

# MOSS BASKERVILLE

"Excuse me a minute, Colonel," Moss Baskerville said, hitting the button on the intercom. "Yes, Shirley?"

"Marie Lopez on line one, Chief. She says it's important."

"Thanks." Glancing at Dole, who had sat down but had yet to speak, he picked up the receiver. "Hi, Marie. What's up?"

"I was up in Rattlesnake Canyon a little while ago, and the two missing sheep are back."

"Alive?" he asked, aware that Dole was listening to his every word. *Goddamn bastard.*

"Dead, I think, but that's all I know. I was too far away to see if they were mutilated."

"I'll come by to check on things as soon as Al comes on duty. Somewhere around seven."

"I'll bet there's someone in your office, right?"

"It's a problem."

"I see. Well, don't bother coming by for now. I'm going back to the canyon, with my camera and some bags to get some samples for Alex."

"You sure that's a good idea?" he asked, watching Dole watch him. Chances were very good that Dole recognized Marie's name, he thought, since she was always up there in UFO country.

"I'll be fine, Moss. I'm just afraid the animals will disappear again if I wait. That tight-ass colonel will probably get wind of them and swoop down in his chopper."

"Interesting you should mention that." He smiled at Dole.

"What? The colonel?"

"Right."

"He's in your office?"

"Ever thought of entering law enforcement? You'd make a fine detective."

"Thanks. All the more reason for me to get back up there now."

"Sure you don't want me to check out your problem?"

"You'd need a CJ-five to get into the canyon, that or a horse. Your cruiser won't do. Do me a favor and have a nice long chat with that horse's ass, will you, Moss?"

"I'll try, but no guarantees."

He hung up. "So, what can I help you with, Colonel?"

Dole, ramrod-straight in his blue uniform, his heavy jowls darkened with imminent five-o'clock shadow, smiled or spasmed, Moss couldn't tell which. "Marie Lopez. She's the sheep rancher near Thunder Road."

"I'm surprised you concern yourself with civilians, Colonel."

"I heard she claimed some of her sheep were mutilated, some nonsense like that."

Moss smiled enigmatically. "You probably know more about that than I do."

Dole glared at him but said nothing.

"So, what is it that you and I have to discuss?" Moss asked as he checked his watch. "I have work to do."

"I've been informed that your town has been experiencing unexplained sightings in the sky."

"Like I said, Colonel, you'd know more about that than I would. In fact, I wouldn't be surprised to see *you* flying one of those saucers.

Maybe taking one for a test flight once in a while, keeping your hand in."

"The military has nothing to do with any alleged sightings, Chief Baskerville; let me make that perfectly clear."

Moss half expected Dole to make a victory sign, but he didn't. "Then what's your interest in them?"

"We have no interest. But you were overheard telling someone that you witnessed these alleged phenomena."

"Got spies, do you?"

Dole remained silent. "It's all over town, Chief."

"I'm sure it is. I wasn't the only one who saw them, after all." Moss thought briefly and realized that he'd probably admitted to a dozen people that he, too, had seen them. Most likely Dole or his flunkies heard him shooting the shit with Ray in the café yesterday.

"What's your point, Dole?" he asked bluntly.

"You saw nothing."

"That's untrue. And speaking of problems, I'm told some helicopters destroyed the camp of a friend of mine."

"Not to my knowledge." Dole leaned forward. "You're the chief of police in this town, and it won't do for you to tell Madelyn's citizens that you have seen these alleged UFOs. You will cease to do so immediately, and deny all knowledge of this conversation."

Cold rage filling him, Moss pushed back his chair and rose. "Or what?"

"Or you'll suffer the consequences."

"It'll cost me my job?" Moss asked sarcastically.

"Perhaps."

"Can't be done, son."

A short smile tightened Dole's features. "Yes it can. But your rumormongering might cost you even more. It might affect your loved ones."

Baskerville rose and stepped around the desk, then grabbed Dole's lapel. "Is that a threat?"

"A warning," Dole replied calmly. "Chief, you must do what's best for your country."

Nose to nose, Moss held the lapel. "A friend of mine is a close friend of the president's," he lied. "Maybe I ought to give him a call, have him speak to Bill about you."

Dole barked a gruff laugh as Moss let go of his jacket. "The president has no power in this matter, Chief." He walked to the door, then turned back to Baskerville, his stern gaze contradicting a bare trace of sadness in his voice. "Everything will be just fine as long as you follow my orders." With those words, he left.

"Jesus Christ." Moss flopped back in his chair. Several cops he knew had hinted at similar cover-ups, but he'd never believed any of it—America the free, that's what he'd always thought. America with the Constitution and freedom of speech. Live here and you could say anything you pleased.

"Goddamn it!" He punched the intercom. "Shirley, see what you can get me on Colonel Lawrence Dole, will you?"

"Sure, Chief. A fax is coming in for you. I'll bring it right in." A moment later Shirley arrived with several sheets of paper. "It's the info you requested on Jim-Bob Sinclair."

"Thanks," he murmured as Shirley left. He leaned back, put his feet on the desk, and scanned the information. He'd been meaning to get it for some time now, but it was his meeting with the man this morning that had galvanized him. There was no doubt about it, Sinclair had been impressive, charismatic, and apparently forthcoming, but as Moss scanned the report, it became evident that he had something up his sleeve: magic.

Born David King, he had changed his name to James Robert Sinclair when he started his ministry. As David King, he'd made his living as a magician. Prior to that, he'd been a theology student. There was no arrest record under either name.

Moss shook his head. The report was virtually useless. The comm buzzed. "Chief?"

He sat up. "Yes?"

"I can't get anything on Lawrence Dole. I've tried everything I know, but the files are locked."

Moss groaned. "Damn."

"I think it's some sort of military lock, but I wouldn't swear to it. Sorry, Chief."

"Not your fault. Thanks."

"Chief, I'm going home in a few minutes. Do you need anything before I leave?"

"No, that's it, Shirl. Have a nice night."

Setting the report on Sinclair aside, he leaned back and closed his eyes. He felt like everything was slipping away. He didn't know where the missing persons were, or who was behind the vandalism. After visiting Sinclair, he'd gone down to the alleged satanic cult, and found nothing but three nineteen-year-old losers squatting in an old abandoned shed. Not a devil symbol in sight. So, having written them off, he was back at square one. Maybe things would improve Monday when the new officer showed up to help out.

He sighed. Things were out of control, especially now with Dole's unbelievable threats. The man's granite-jawed dramatics would've almost been humorous if he had threatened only Baskerville. But he had to take him seriously because of the threats to Eve and Cassie. "Goddamn it," Moss muttered, wishing he'd listened more seriously to the other cops' UFO stories.

The comm buzzed. "Chief, got a call from a Denise Cole. She says her son is missing."

"Christ." For an instant the message was just one more pain in the ass, then his brain clicked in and he grabbed the phone.

A few minutes later, he set the phone down. The boy, Billy Cole, was supposed to be home at four-thirty, so he was little more than an hour late. Hardly much to get excited about, especially since the mother had panicked and failed to check all his friends' homes. He'd reassured the mother and asked her to start making calls while he went out and took a look around.

He rose and stretched. Normally he'd never go looking for a kid who was an hour late coming home, but things weren't very normal these days.

Entering the outer office, he said good-bye to Shirley and hello to Ken Landry, the night clerk. Quickly he briefed him on the latest events, then walked out to the cruiser.

There was at least an hour of daylight remaining as he left the station. With any luck, he'd bring Billy Cole to his mama before the boy's dinner was even cold.

In the distance, thunder boomed, and he saw a brief flash of lightning behind Olive Mesa. "Oh, hell, that's all I need."

## SEVENTY-TWO

# JUSTIN MARTIN

"Everything's locked up tight, Mr. Marquay," Justin told the old fart who was locked in the ticket booth tallying the day's take.

"Did some fine business today, son." Marquay made an effort to smile. "Madge'll be real pleased," he added, getting that glazed far-away look in his eyes again.

"See you tomorrow, Mr. Marquay."

Marquay nodded and Justin walked away from the mine ride, studiously controlling his urge to run. The boy in his trunk had been on his mind throughout the long afternoon, and he could hardly wait to see if he was still alive. He'd also had to figure out where to take the kid since he didn't dare use the mine again, even if the weather had cooled. He decided to keep him in the garden shed in his parents' backyard for a few days. *The tomatoes will never taste the same again.*

He let himself out the rear gate and trotted across the parking lot toward his car, which he'd parked far away, in an area that was nearly always deserted. Halfway there, he realized someone was leaning against the trunk. *Shit!* He slowed, squinting through the diminishing sunlight, unable to identify the fat fucker. Then the man turned and saw him. And waved. A beam of the setting sun reflected against his bald head. *Hannibal Caine, you fucking shithead!*

Justin waved and trotted across the lot. "Hi, Elder Caine!"

Caine stuck his hand out and shook Justin's vigorously. "I hear you passed our test with flying colors."

He leaned against the trunk again and Justin tried not to react. "Elder Blandings told you what I did with the goat?"

Caine nodded, eyes twinkling, his chubby cheeks pink above his salesman's smile. "Justin, I expect great things of you, though you do have to learn to follow orders." He chuckled. "But when I heard that you ran that goat right up a flagpole, well, I nearly bust my gut. You're going places, young man."

"Thanks." Right now Justin didn't give a rat's dick about getting his ass kissed by Hannibal Caine. "I'm sort of in a hurry, Elder Caine. Could we talk about this later?"

Caine's smile faded. "We have a mission tonight, Justin, and we'd like you to be part of it."

*I have a mission, too, Fat Ass.* "You should have let me know sooner. I'm really sorry, but I'm taking my parents to dinner for their anniversary, and my mom hasn't been feeling well lately, so I can't disappoint her."

"Commendable." The sleazy smile came back. "I understand completely and I think you're an unusually thoughtful young man. Why don't you come see me tomorrow morning? We have lots to do and little time to do it."

"I have to be at work tomorrow morning at ten."

Thunder boomed to the north, and Caine put his pudgy hand on Justin's shoulder. It was hard not to flinch.

"Do you know what that is, Justin? That's the first herald of the Horsemen. The world is at an end. It might be worth your while to skip work, son."

"I work for Hank Marquay, the man whose wife is missing, and I can't let him down. He's really depending on me right now." How dare this asshole suggest he skip out on a paying job to do his dirty work for free? "I could come by before work, though."

"Please do," Caine said, studying him carefully. "Come directly to my office. It will be well worth your while."

"I'll be there, sir." Justin moved to the driver's door, unlocked it, and slid into the seat. "See you tomorrow." *You fucking dickhead.*

Caine raised his hand, then walked away, and a moment later reappeared behind the wheel of a white minivan. "You cocksucker," Justin whispered, then pulled through the Madland lot to Old Madelyn Highway, to go home and stick the kid in the garden shed. *So much to do, so little time.*

# SEVENTY-THREE

# ELDO BLANDINGS

"You ready?" Eldo Blandings asked Apostle Mel Campbell.

"More than ready," Campbell growled. "Let's do it."

Blandings and Campbell were on foot, dressed in their desert cammies, and for Blandings, it was like old times. They'd been out here smoking and talking, watching and waiting, on the edge of Tom Abernathy's land for an hour now, hidden on a ridge dotted with Joshua trees. They were upwind of two dozen wild mustangs grazing only a few hundred feet south.

Originally Eldo had planned a solo trip to make that bastard Tom Abernathy pay for the humiliation he'd suffered at his hands yesterday in the park. But Mel Campbell went through worse today, and had come to Eldo privately to tell him he wanted revenge. Campbell was Eldo's best soldier, but he was also a hothead who had to be controlled, so Eldo had decided to include him in his own plans, rather than take the chance that Campbell would do something stupid, like going face-to-face. If he did, that would ruin all the other work the Committee had perpetrated because it would give away their identities.

At first, Campbell complained that Eldo's plan didn't go far enough: Instead of shooting a wild horse or two, he wanted to go right into Abernathy's stables and shoot his breeding stock. Eldo agreed that would be more satisfying, but maintained it couldn't be done, since Abernathy or his redskin ranch manager were always around. Campbell argued a little, then Eldo reminded him how quick the rancher could move. If Abernathy caught them, chances were they'd be shot down before they knew they'd been hit.

That insulted Campbell and he argued a little more, then Eldo reminded him who was in command, and that they'd do it his way.

Now Campbell lay on his belly, rifle up, tracking a chestnut mare. Eldo had a white one in his sights. "On three. One. Two. Three."

Both rifles blasted. The chestnut went down, but Eldo missed the white, and it stampeded away with the rest of the herd. "Damn!"

Two more shots rang out as Campbell kept blasting, cursing under his breath.

"That's enough, Campbell," Eldo ordered. "We don't want to draw attention to ourselves." A clap of thunder punctuated his words.

"It's not enough," Campbell growled. "Not enough to teach that bastard his lesson."

Eldo considered. "Perhaps you're right."

# SEVENTY-FOUR

# CARLO PELEGRINE

Carlo gave the simmering marinara sauce a quick stir with a wooden spoon, then returned to the cutting board to finish putting together a salad. He was so nervous that his hand shook as he picked up the paring knife and sliced through a large tomato. Having Alex to dinner was playing with fire, he knew that, and he'd picked up his phone to cancel several times this afternoon.

But he couldn't. He wanted to see her more than he'd ever wanted anything, and he promised himself that he would keep himself under control, refusing to even entertain the possibility that something would happen to ... mar the evening. *You have a gift for understatement, my friend.* He smiled bitterly and finished slicing the tomato, trying to keep his mind on the food, but unable to stop it from drifting back to the last killing.

It happened in his own neighborhood in Bensonhurst. He'd spent several hours after school playing basketball with Ted Furillo and some other guys at New Utrecht High, and he was dribbling the basketball as he walked home, enjoying the way the chill winter air felt in his lungs. Checking his watch, he realized that if he didn't step on it, he'd be late for dinner, so he tucked the ball under his arm and sprinted through the early evening darkness until he came to the shortcut: an alley separating two rows of brownstone apartment buildings, just off Thirteenth Avenue.

The alley was deserted except for trash cans and bins that made it barely wide enough to accommodate a car. Bare bulbs outside some of the buildings cast shadowy light down its length, and reflected the eyes of a rat crouching between two garbage cans. Carlo knew he'd make it home in time for dinner now, so he let the basketball bounce, once, twice, then started dribbling it down the alley, zigzagging back and forth, circling a lone garbage can, zigzagging some more.

"Hi, Carlo."

Halfway down the alley, he stopped dead in his tracks and looked around for the girl who had spoken. A moment later, she stepped out of the shadows.

"Sally?" he asked. She had been a couple years ahead of him in school until she dropped out two years ago. She had a reputation as an easy lay, and Carlo had heard she'd taken up with a gang in the last year or so. He wanted to sink into the asphalt, he was so embarrassed about her seeing him bounce the ball and goofing around, like a little middle school kid.

"Yeah." She smiled, a white flash between violet-red lips. "It's me. You still in school?"

"I'm a senior."

"Bet you get straight A's, don't you?" She snapped her gum and blew a pink bubble.

He shrugged, unwilling to be further embarrassed. "Uh, how are you?"

"I could use some money."

Carlo glanced around, wondering if he was about to be jumped, but nothing, no one, moved. "Out of work?"

She smiled and came farther out of the shadows. "I'm self employed."

He stared at her, taking in the stiletto heels, black nylons, red miniskirt, and the red and white striped tube top that barely covered her nipples. There was a tattoo of a rose on the swell of her left breast, and he couldn't stop staring at it.

"You like it?" she asked, stepping up to him.

He jerked his eyes up to her face, to the bleached hair and thick makeup that only accentuated her acne scars. "I, uh, just never saw a tattoo on a girl before."

"You want to touch it?"

His heart pounded and his fingers came up.

She laughed, stepping away. "You got money? You can touch it for five dollars." She blew another bubble, let it pop against her lips, then used her tongue to slowly, suggestively, pull the gum back in. "I bet you're a virgin, ain't you, Carlo? I'll blow a virgin for ten. Take his cherry for twenty. How 'bout it?"

The carefully buried memories of the two other whores tried to push to the surface. He fought them down and dug out his wallet, feeling almost like he was in a trance. His hormones refused to listen to the warning bells going off in his brain. He showed her a twenty. "Where?"

Smiling, she took his money and his hand, led him to a space behind two large Dumpsters, and pulled him down onto some dirty blankets. She peeled down her tube top, revealing her already sagging breasts.

A bare bulb cast enough light to let him examine the rose tattoo.

"Aren't you gonna unzip?" she asked, snapping her gum. She rucked up her skirt as he knelt above her. "I ain't wearing any underwear."

He made no reply, but watched his trembling fingers reach out to touch the tattoo. The hand, a separate entity, traced the outline of the rose, then the fingers trailed across her breasts. The other hand joined the first and they pushed themselves across her breasts, up to the shoulders, together to the neck. He saw them begin to squeeze, saw her eyes start to bug out, her tongue thrust from between her lips, the pink wad of the gum tumbling to the asphalt. For a few moments she made little choking sounds.

After her breathing stopped, he continued to squeeze her neck, or rather, his alien hands did. He hadn't remembered the other killings, but this time he witnessed every detail as if he were trapped in someone else's mind, a voyeur watching the crime. The hands let go of her and the right one pulled his jackknife from his pants pocket, opened it, then traced an oval around the rose on her breast.

Horrified, he watched as the knife blade worked under the skin and then his hand began carefully excising the tattoo.

It was half-done when he was released. Suddenly he could feel the knife in his hands, the flesh resisting the blade, feel her still warm skin. "No," he whispered, pulling the knife free. "No!"

By rote, he wiped the blade on her skirt and put it away. Numbly he backed up. He'd been able to forget the other two prostitutes only because he didn't remember what he had done. He'd known something was wrong, but he'd managed to shove it away. Until now, he had no proof that he was "the Peeler," as the newspapers had dubbed him.

The cold, detached part of him helped him remember to retrieve the basketball and continue down the alley toward home. It helped him eat dinner, make conversation, and finish out the school year. It stopped him from killing himself, and it helped him fake his own death instead.

He was a Jekyll and Hyde, part innocence and part pure evil, and it became his life task to keep the evil a prisoner within. Now, as he stirred the marinara sauce once more, he promised himself that if he even thought about laying a hand on Alex, he would take his rifle and blow his brains out. He would kill the monster.

# SEVENTY-FIVE

# TOM ABERNATHY

He'd planned on riding Belle down to the campground to tell a few tales tonight, but an hour after he'd taken his frustrations out on the trespassing Apostles, Marie had jumped back into his mind and stubbornly stayed there.

Belle paused at the end of the ranch road, waiting for Tom to signal the direction: down to the campground, or up to Marie's. He considered, and decided that Marie would probably do a lot of glaring and not much talking, even if he tried to apologize. "Guess we'll go tell stories, Belle."

They turned right on Old Madelyn Highway. It was getting dark fast tonight, no doubt because of the bank of clouds building behind the Madelyn Mountains. Thunder rolled more frequently now, and the lightning flashes were closer.

"We'll have to get back nice and early tonight, girl, or we might get ourselves drenched."

The horse nickered softly, then her ears went back as two rifle shots rent the air.

"Whoa." The shots came from the north, and Tom wheeled Belle around on the road, then waited, listening. A clap of thunder shook the valley, then two more shots rang out. Then nothing but silence.

"Maybe we'd better go see Marie after all." Tom flipped the reins and Belle took off at a near gallop. Lord, how that horse loved to run. There was no traffic on the highway, so he let her have her head, and within fifteen minutes, they arrived at the short road—a long driveway, really—that led to Marie's. Her modest ranch consisted of a small stable and barn, one corral, and a single-wide mobile home. As they turned up the dirt drive, Tom saw that the trailer was dark, though her pickup was in the driveway. Dorsey and Wild Bill started barking from somewhere around the stable.

Behind the trailer, he dismounted and led Belle to the watering trough inside the corral, leaving her happily drinking while he walked over to the stable. It was secured, but Marie had given him a copy of the padlock key, so he quickly took care of that. As he entered, he called out to the two dogs and the warning barks turned into ones of greeting. Letting himself inside, he petted the collies, then walked with them past the stalls. Marie's sheep, for the most part, were friendly: They were for wool, not meat, and nearly all the idiotic little critters came to see if he had something to eat.

At the far end of the stable, Rex's stall was empty, as he'd expected when he saw the truck and the lack of lights.

"So, boys, where'd your mistress get off to?" The dogs wagged and panted, but didn't tell him a thing.

Relocking the stable, he walked up the steps to the trailer's back door and tried it. Locked.

"Marie?" he called. "Marie? You home?"

Receiving no answer, he went down the steps and walked around to the little front porch, where he seated himself on a wooden glider. Marie wouldn't be long, he thought, since the sheep hadn't had their evening feed. He'd wait a few minutes.

Marie kept her place nice. She had honeysuckle growing up the crisscrossed redwood patio enclosure and a few pots of geraniums and brilliant orange poppies along the edges of the redbrick ground cover.

Rocking gently, Tom stared out at the Madelyn Mountains. Even this close, he could see the tops of the storm clouds rising up above the craggy peaks and plateau of Olive Mesa. Thunder drummed once more, and this time he could feel it vibrate against his feet. The storm seemed to be moving slow, but it could speed up and arrive in the next hour or two. Between the gunfire and the approaching storm, his hackles were up, and he shivered. "Marie," he said softly, "you're a confounded woman and I hope you come home soon."

# SEVENTY-SIX

# MARIE LOPEZ

Thunder boomed, and Marie Lopez nervously glanced up at the twilight sky. She'd gotten a late start back into the canyon because she'd decided she should stable her sheep instead of leaving them out where God-knew-what might happen to them. Then she had to drive into town for a roll of high-exposure film. Now, with the remaining sunlight exiled by the ring of mountains, it was nearly full dark in Rattlesnake Canyon, but at least there was enough moonlight to let her see the pale form of the nearest sheep.

Thunder clapped as she drew near, and Rex shied, giving a small distressed whinny.

"What's the matter, boy?" He was long over his fear of loud noises, never flinching even when she stood right next to him and fired her rifle, and this behavior seemed odd. Tom always said that your horse could hear and see a lot more than you, and only a fool didn't pay *attention—damn you, Abernathy!—* and he was right. She urged the horse forward, but he took two steps and stopped again. "Okay. We'll do it your way," she murmured, pulling her rifle free. Turning Rex, she scanned the canyon and the ridges but saw nothing unusual. "Come on," she told the horse, but again he wouldn't approach the dead sheep.

"Okay." She dismounted and walked up to the animal's corpse, then laid the rifle down and pulled a small flashlight from her jacket pocket. It was hard not to flinch. The ewe lay stiff-legged on its side, and the flesh was gone from the face and the upper portion of the throat, revealing gleaming bone. The tongue was removed, and lower, the abdomen had been dissected, though only a few drops of blood were visible. Instead, the strange blue gel dotted the wool, the viscera, and the ground.

Shaking her head sadly, wondering who or what would mutilate an animal like this, she picked up the rifle and walked back to Rex. She tried to lead him toward the sheep, but he stalled out after four paces. He'd balked with the mutilations as well, but at the time she assumed he smelled mountain lion. Turning, she stroked his muzzle, then opened a saddlebag and extracted her camera, a pair of latex gloves, a skinning knife, and the Ziploc bags, then returned to the corpse and positioned the flashlight's beam on it.

She took forty or fifty shots, then donned the gloves and kneeled, belatedly wishing she'd remembered to bring an old spoon or something so she wouldn't have to touch the gel, even through gloves. *Oh well.* Opening the bags, she tried not to cringe as she scooped a blob of gel with two fingers. It was ice-cold, even through the latex.

Next she used the knife to cut out a piece of flesh that contained a bloodless incision. She put that in another bag, then nervously decided that was enough and dropped the soiled gloves in the third bag, and her knife in the fourth, then packed it all in the saddlebags.

She looked at Rex. "I don't suppose you'd be willing to carry the sheep up to Alex, would you?"

He stamped his foot as if he understood her.

"I didn't think so." She swung into the saddle and began crossing the valley at a slow pace so Rex wouldn't trip. She urged him toward the other sheep—she just wanted to make sure it had met the same fate—but after a clap of thunder— closer now—she heard the distant roar of something in the sky. Helicopters.

"Come on, Rex," she urged, glancing up. The choppers hadn't come into view yet. The horse moved faster as she turned him in the direction of her campsite of two nights ago. They made the edge of the valley and quickly found the trail up to the huge overhang, with its camouflaging sage and mesquite bushes.

To get Rex beneath it, she had to dismount and bribe him with apples she'd brought along for that purpose. He was underneath, reasonably well hidden, by the time the roar reached the canyon.

Three helicopters, dark except for their running lights, appeared over the ridge. An instant later floodlights lit up the valley floor, playing over the dirt and rocks and Joshua trees.

"Good thing you're a black horse," Marie whispered when a light flashed near their hiding place.

A moment later, the dark choppers located what they wanted: the sheep. While one hovered above, the two other craft slowly descended, one landing on each side of the round valley. The blades kept whirring and Marie squinted to see the dark-clothed men, two from each vehicle, race to each sheep. Less than a minute later, both teams returned to the choppers carrying heavy bags between them— the sheep.

"We'll get out of here soon, Rex," she said as the men disappeared into the helicopters.

The choppers' blades picked up speed and they moved up into the air like giant locusts. One spotlight swept the ground again, and Marie was concerned when she saw that two men were still on the ground. The last chopper swooped and turned, then the men blended with the darkness.

Finally one of them turned on a flashlight. They were evidently searching the valley, and Lord, they might be down there all night. Marie reached up and scratched Rex behind the ears. "We might be here awhile after all."

# SEVENTY-SEVEN

# JUSTIN MARTIN

The stupid kid had gone and died on him, and Justin Martin wasn't what you'd call a happy camper as he drove out of New Madelyn and up Old Madelyn Highway.

Every Friday night dear old Mom and Dad drove into Barstow to catch the twilight matinee at the movies, and he'd counted on them being gone when he arrived home with his trunkful of goodies. But no, for the first time ever, they were running late, and he didn't realize it until his mother came out of the house just as he opened his trunk.

He was so wrapped up in his own business that she would have seen the kid if she hadn't alerted him by calling out, "Justin, honey, can you move your car out of the driveway so your father can pull the Buick out of the garage?"

He'd slammed the lid down, squashing the tip of his thumb. "Sure, Mom," he yelled, having a hell of a time sounding pleasant. But he did, and ten minutes later, the old farts were gone, and he'd backed the Mustang in the garage so that he could easily carry the kid and the bike through the back door and into the toolshed.

As soon as he was safely in the garage, door closed, he'd reopened the trunk, and realized that the kid was as dead as dead could be. In fact, he'd started to stiffen, and Justin had a bitch of a time trying to disentangle the boy's fingers from the bicycle spokes. Before he'd died, despite the taped wrists, he'd managed to latch on to one wheel.

Justin ended up breaking the fingers loose. They made an interesting *snap, crackle, pop* sound. Carefully he lifted the bike out, then opened the garage's back door. And that's when he found out that the neighbors were all outside. On one side of the chain link, Old Lady Quigley was out picking up dog shit with a paper towel and dropping it in a grocery sack. Her cocker spaniel stayed with her every step of the way, eagerly checking out each pile before she picked it up. He wondered if Quigley ever sniffed her fingers when she finished her shit-picking.

On the other side of the yard, the Egyptians—he'd never bothered to learn their names—were out. As usual, the old man was reclining in his chaise longue, beer in hand, barking orders to his kid and his ever silent wife to make the perfect yard more perfect, *now*. Finally, directly behind Justin's house, the Candy Asses were out in force. Dad was barbecuing, Mom was setting the picnic table, and the noisy little shit-kids were splashing around in the shallow end of their pool. None of the assholes were paying attention to the thunderclaps, and Justin didn't have time to waste waiting for the storm to arrive. "Shit," was all he said before he grabbed a shovel and returned to his car.

Now, as he turned on the dirt highway, his hands encased in gloves, the kid and its bike were still in his trunk. He'd thrown a short-handled shovel in, to boot. He had too much to do tonight to spend much time finding a good dumping spot. He needed to take some skin, bury the kid and the bike, see Christie if she was working, leave a gift for the Peeler, and if at all possible, do something about that key thief, Eric Watson. It was a tall order, especially since the storm was no more than an hour or two away.

That's when he spotted the Bronco turning in to the Madland lot.

He drove past, then pulled over. No one else was on the road, so he doused his headlights and hung a U-turn, then cruised back to the lot and parked across the road in the shadows of a road sign.

The Bronco parked under a sodium light, making it easy to confirm that it was Alex Manderley who exited the vehicle. A moment later, one of the small gates opened and Carlo Pelegrine came out. Alex handed him something, a bottle of wine maybe, and the two went through the gate. He heard Carlo relock it.

*He's gonna do her!* Excited, Justin briefly considered going to spy, but common sense won out and he decided he'd have to come back later, after he'd taken care of his own business.

# SEVENTY-EIGHT

# TOM ABERNATHY

It was full dark now, and there was no doubt about it, Tom was mightily worried about Marie Lopez.

In the stable the sheep bleated hungrily, and Tom rose from the glider, stretching and twisting. He left the porch just as thunder cracked in his ears and vibrated under his feet. As he trotted toward the stable, lightning, strobelike, briefly lit his path. He paused, sniffing the air, smelling the coming rain.

"Marie, where the heck are you?" he muttered, unlocking the stable and going inside to feed the flock and the dogs.

The job didn't take too long, and he soon returned to the open door and listened. He had thought he heard the whine of engines while he was doing the feed, and now he caught it again, faint but real, to the north. As he stared at the mountains, three helicopters rose above the ridge that hid Rattlesnake Canyon. Spotlights moved back and forth beneath them, and suddenly they clicked off and the choppers banked and flew away to the northeast.

*Marie's in that canyon.* The thought hit him with such jolting force that he immediately locked the stable, then went to the corral and freed Belle.

The crescent moon shone brightly to the southeast, and the going was easy at first: east on Thunder Road, then north up the trail into the Madelyns. When he reached the hills, he had to choose between the easy but slow, winding sheep path and the steep but direct hiking trail. After only a moment's hesitation, he decided there was enough moonlight and too little time before the storm to take the safer trail. He turned Belle and began the ascent, Tom fighting his impatience to let the horse decide the safest speed.

# SEVENTY-NINE

## CARLO PELEGRINE

Dinner had gone better than he ever expected, the food delicious and the conversation easy, and now Carlo and Alex sat on the sofa across from the fireplace, sharing a bottle of merlot and watching the flames lick and flicker around the logs. Carlo was especially pleased that, though he was fascinated by Alex's flawless skin, and had spent the evening so far in a nearly constant state of mild arousal, he felt little of the old, dangerous fire in his blood.

"Carlo, you're an incredible chef," Alex told him. "Where did you learn to cook like that?"

"I worked as a chef for a time before I came here."

Sipping her wine, she smiled at him. "Where did you grow up? What sort of child were you?"

A knot of anxiety formed in his stomach. Had he actually believed she wouldn't ask these questions? He knew better than that, and now, as he looked at her, he didn't want to lie, but he couldn't afford to tell the truth. "I was a quiet, nerdy kid," he said finally. "Nothing the least bit interesting. What about you?"

"Me?" She laughed. "The same. Quiet and shy. When I was a

little girl, all I wanted was a telescope and science fiction books, so all the other girls thought I was weird."

"What about the boys?"

"I was taller than all of them. And smarter. It was a deadly combination." She hesitated, her smile fading. "Then there was the racial problem. My dad was an African-American air force officer stationed in London when he met my mother, who's English, French, and Japanese. The combination wasn't good for my social life."

"You don't sound bitter."

"I'm not. My parents were—are—incredibly supportive, so no one ever quite convinced me that there was anything truly wrong with me—but I knew other people thought so." She sipped her wine. "I remember reading a science fiction story when I was about eleven or twelve. It took place in the future, and all the races were mixed so that everyone was a sort of tan color. I read that story over and over because the heroine was described as looking very much as I did. It made me feel proud instead of ashamed." She paused. "I loved science fiction stories about aliens, too. I always identified with them."

"I often feel like an alien myself," Carlo agreed, "although I don't quite understand racial tension," Carlo began. "My parents sent me to church—Catholic, naturally—but it never completely took. I'd think a lot about why we were here, and what God was. No one's answers ever satisfied me. I mean, can you imagine going and sitting around on a cloud playing a harp all day, or spending eternity shoveling hot coals for the devil?"

Alex laughed. "No, I can't. Those are human inventions. 'We can know what God is not, but we cannot know what He is.'"

"Saint Augustine," Carlo said, smiling. "More wine?" "Please." She held out her glass. "So what *do* you believe?"

"As I started delving into other philosophies, I became more and more sold on reincarnation—not the kind where you come back as an insect, but the kind that answers the big question, 'Why are we here?'

to my satisfaction." He took a deep breath. "Christianity bothered me because it made no mention of reincarnation, whereas it's an integral part of virtually all other religions. Then I found out that way back when, the Church removed a number of items from the Bible that they didn't want the common folk to know. Reincarnation was among them."

"Reincarnation takes power away from organized religion," Alex agreed. "It maintains that you're responsible for yourself, instead of groveling on your knees to a God defined by power-hungry humans who run a church that will forgive you if you turn over enough of your income and play by their rules."

An overwhelming surge of affection washed over Carlo, and without thinking, he edged closer to her. Their shoulders and thighs touched, and she made no move to pull away. "You sound like you buy reincarnation yourself," he said.

"If I buy anything." She set her glass down, leaning forward. "As a scientist, I'm naturally a skeptic, and I'm not willing to commit completely to anything I can't prove. Like the UFOs. I believe they exist, partly because of reports from unimpeachable sources, primarily because I've seen them. But I can't take the opinion of the majority of enthusiasts and say that I believe the phenomena are from another planet, because there's no way to know. Even if I saw the creatures or walked on a craft, I couldn't pronounce they were not of the earth because there's no proof. They might be other-dimensional. They might be angels, fairies, leprechauns, or all of them, for Pete's sake, or they might be a glitch in a Jungian cosmic consciousness."

She sat back and smiled. "I guess my point is that there's never been a time when I didn't live for information, and I've always felt that, for me at least, learning and growing is the primary purpose of life. How could we learn much of anything in just one go-round at this, in just one sort of body?"

"It's a strong argument. It explains the differences between people." He paused. "Their soul ages, if you will. I have several clients who come to me for advice, and it's frightening because they have utter faith in what I say. If they were into an organized religion, then they would be the ones who believed everything the church says, no questions asked."

"That kind of faith is silly," Alex said. "And frightening."

"I know."

"How do you handle such responsibility?" Alex asked, refilling their glasses. "It would scare me to death."

"It scares me at times. I try to convince them that the Golden Rule—endemic to every religion—is the one we should live by. And I try to keep their glasses half-full. Most of the searchers who come to me have half-empty ones."

"That's nice, really nice. Do you ever make mistakes?"

"With clients in general? I'm sure I make some, but I try my best not to. I never preach negatives."

"What about with your own life?" Alex asked. "I mean, if we're here to grow, that automatically means making mistakes. Do you have any regrets?"

He studied her dark fathomless eyes, knowing now that she wouldn't pry if he gave her some truth. "Three. And you?"

"One or two." She broke eye contact, obviously uneasy.

"Would you like me to read your palm now?"

"Yes, please," she said, her voice relieved.

Carlo put his glass aside and took the hand she proffered. His own hands trembled as they touched her skin, but she didn't seem to notice.

"A lovely hand, full of life," he murmured, lightly running two fingers across the heart line, the life line. "Full of love."

She looked at him. "Familial or romantic?"

"Both." It occurred to him that she might think he was handing her a line, so he pointed out to her the configurations of her palm that told him these things.

"I love my work," Alex said. "But I haven't had any romantic interests in many, many years, and I know there won't be any in the future. I wasn't cut out for it."

"It's the same with me."

"I gave up romance," Alex said softly, "because I always hurt those I loved."

Carlo's hand shook so badly that he had to let go of hers. He nodded, his throat too dry. "Me too," he whispered.

"How long has it been for you?"

She hesitated. "Ten years."

"Not so long," he replied softly. "It's been twenty for me." She tilted her head slightly as she gazed at him. "Truly?"

"Truly."

"I don't know why I accepted your invitation, Carlo. I shouldn't have."

"And I shouldn't have extended it," he whispered, "but I couldn't help it."

"Neither could I." She looked down at her hands. "All that reincarnation talk. Maybe we've known one another before. Been lovers ..." She laughed lightly, a false sound.

He barely heard her last words, they were so soft. All he knew was that he had to break the growing tension before it killed him. "I, ah, think I should clear the table," he announced as he rose. "I hate leaving dirty dishes in plain sight."

She smiled. "I'll help you."

"No, relax. This will only take a few minutes. Why don't you check out my bookcase."

"I can't resist an offer like that." Her smile was relaxed and she stood and crossed to the wall of books.

As he stacked the last dish in the sink, he knocked a paring knife off the kitchen counter and, without thinking, swooped his hand down to catch it before it hit the floor. "Gotcha," he whispered, then felt the sting as the blade bit into his fingertip. Dropping the knife in the sink, he turned the water on to wash the blood away, but he must have hit a small artery because the wound welled scarlet again and began dripping.

"Damn." He snagged a paper towel and wrapped it around the finger while he looked in the cupboard for his box of Band-Aids. He found it, opened it, and saw that it was empty. "Damn." There was another box in the bathroom, but he didn't want Alex to see what he'd done—he felt clumsy and stupid—so he wrapped the towel tighter and walked quickly through the living room, hoping she wouldn't notice.

But she turned, a book in hand, then saw the towel. "Did you hurt yourself?"

"It's nothing. Just a little cut. A Band-Aid will fix it right up."

She stepped closer to him, a fathomless look in her eyes. "Let me see," she whispered.

"It's nothing."

"I'm a doctor."

He grinned. "Of astrophysics."

She smiled back, her pupils huge now. "Picky, picky."

She gently took his hand in hers and led him back to the sofa. They sat, and she began unwrapping the finger slowly, so slowly.

She paused for several seconds when she got down to the bloodstain, then finished unwrapping the finger and set the towel aside. Blood oozed sluggishly from the cut as she studied it. She dabbed the blood away with the towel, then slowly lifted her head to meet his eyes. "I'll kiss it and make it better."

He couldn't read her, had no idea what to say except, "You don't have to do that."

"Yes, I do. I was thinking about what you said, that we're here to grow. There's more to life than books." Holding his hand in both of hers, she brought the wounded finger to her lips. And kissed it. Then she looked up at him, his blood dotting her lips, and finally he recognized in her a lust akin to his own. She parted her lips and the tip of her tongue appeared to cleanse the blood from them.

Carlo shuddered as her mouth closed around the tip of his

extended finger. He felt her tongue tickling his flesh, then she slipped the digit deeper and deeper into her warm mouth, until she made love to the entire finger. As she sucked, moving her soft lips up and down, swirling her tongue, Carlo lost track of everything but the sensations of her mouth and of her other hand, resting firmly against his erection.

He lifted his free hand to her shoulder, feeling, touching, then up to her neck. He nuzzled under her hair, kissing her skin, tasting it, as a connoisseur tastes wine, lost in the heady aroma and flavor.

His last victim hadn't been nearly so sweet.

"Oh, God," he cried, pulling away, his erection shriveling. "No! I can't!"

Alex let go of his finger and jerked away too. "I'm sorry. I'm so sorry. I shouldn't have—"

"I don't understand," he began, knowing he'd hurt her.

"I've always been afraid of my own passion. I've tried to kill it, but it never quite dies. Maybe it shouldn't."

"Why are you afraid of your passion?" Carlo asked gently.

She smiled bitterly. "I guess I'm a control freak and I can't stand losing control. I'd better go before I lose it again."

She started to rise, but he pulled her back down. "No. Alex, I've never desired anyone as I do you."

She wouldn't meet his eyes, but stared at her lap. "Sometimes my fantasies scare me," she said, her voice a whisper. "That's why I ended all my relationships. I wanted too much." She looked up at last. "And romance and career don't go together. I learned not to even think about relationships ... until I met you. Now I can't seem to get sex off my mind. Do you want me to leave?"

He took her hands in his, so overwhelmed that he could barely find his voice. "No. I don't want you to leave, Alexandra. When you say you're afraid of your passion, what is it exactly that scares you?"

"Hurting my partner."

"Physically?" he asked, surprised.

She smiled slightly. "Mentally and physically. What I did just now, for instance. Blood is dangerous. AIDS, infections. When I want something, I stop thinking. I just act."

"What you don't realize is that I understand. My reasons for abstinence aren't so different from yours."

"Tell me."

"I, well, when I was a child, I loved to spread glue on my hands, let it dry, then peel it off. I'd do the same thing when I got sunburned. I have a fetish for skin." *And by the way, I murdered three women.* "My passion is like yours. It takes me over. It's something—well, I just can't talk about it. Alex, you should leave now, and never come back."

"Do you want me to leave?" she asked quietly.

"No." He hesitated. "But it's dangerous for you to stay."

"Could you really be that bad?"

"Worse than I can tell you. I could lose control."

"So could I," Alex said. "Do you think ..."

"Think what?" he prompted.

"That self-control comes with age?"

"It's true that we're not teenagers anymore," he said slowly.

She blushed and studied her hands. "When I was nineteen, I got so carried away that I bit my boyfriend. He had to have stitches."

"Um, bit him where?" he asked carefully.

Her laughter broke the tension. "His arm! When I was twenty-three and in love, something like that happened again, so I gave up men. Even when I didn't lose control, relationships were hard. I don't mean to, but I seem to intimidate men. They all want to compete with my job for my attention."

Carlo took her hand. Her sins were nothing compared to his, yet she seemed to feel them so much. "I'm not intimidated," he said gently.

"Carlo?" Alex asked, taking his hand. "Do you have any candles?"

He nodded, puzzled.

She brought his cut finger to her lips and kissed it gently. "And matches?"

Trembling, he nodded again.

"Where?"

"In the linen closet, middle shelf on the left."

She rose and walked toward the hallway closet, then turned back to look at him. "I think you'll enjoy this," she told him. "Very much."

He didn't know whether her words thrilled or terrified him.

# EIGHTY

## TOM ABERNATHY

"Don't move, mister," Marie Lopez whispered fiercely. Tom heard her rifle cock very close to his head. "Don't shoot," he whispered. "We've got to stop meeting like this."

"Tom! Christ!" she hissed from the darkness beneath the rocky outcropping. "You scared the crap out of me."

"The feeling's mutual."

"Shhh! Come on. Get under here, quick! Belle too."

The thin moonlight caught her face briefly and he saw just how spooked she really was. He peered into the darkness of the cavelike overhang and realized that he could hear, but not see, Rex somewhere behind her. "I tethered Belle in that copse of Joshuas on the other side of the ridge," he told her as she took his arm and led him into the darkness. "The moon's too far gone to cast much light, and I sorta figured you might be here."

"You did?" she whispered in surprise.

"This is where you like to camp, isn't it?"

"You remembered that?"

"Course I did."

"That's sweet, cowboy." Her voice went kind of soft and nice. "I like that."

"I'm sorry I made you mad." The words came easily; he knew she was going to accept the apology since she'd given him back his nickname.

"Have you figured out why?" she whispered.

"Something to do with the story I told. But I wish you'd tell me exactly what so I don't go and say it again."

She sighed. "Later. What are you doing here?" "Looking for you. There's a storm coming, you know."

"I know. It's slowed down some."

That was true; the thunder was as loud as ever, but the storm seemed to have settled in for a rest just behind the Madelyns. "So what are you doing here?"

"Hiding. You see anybody on your way here?"

"Not a soul."

Quickly she told him about the sheep, the samples, and the helicopters. "They left two guys behind. They've been searching the valley floor. They're over there, I think." She pointed toward a fold in the mountains across from them as a flashlight beam shot out from behind one of the folds. "Until a little bit ago, they were way too close for comfort. I was just getting ready to sneak out of here when you showed up."

"Let's go before they get out in the open again."

"My sentiments exactly."

Thunder began to roll again, and as it did, Tom led the way out from under the shelter and up the trail. "Don't look back," he whispered. "And don't worry. They won't see us. Good thing you've got a black horse."

"Don't I know it." Behind her, Rex nickered softly.

Ten minutes brought them to the ridgetop, and in another minute, Tom was untying Belle while Marie squatted behind it and peered down into the valley.

"I think they saw us," she said softly. "They're walking across the valley, coming this way."

"Then let's get out of here. They'll never catch us, and I'm sure they don't know who we are."

"They're military," she reminded him. "They know."

"They can't do anything to us, Marie." He mounted Belle.

"They'll take my samples," she replied as she swung onto Rex.

Tom studied the sky. "No storm clouds yet. How about we ride over to Alex's camp and give them to her straightaway?"

She smiled at him. "You're one of the good guys, cowboy."

"I aim to please," he replied, his face heating up.

After the slow descent, the horses eagerly moved at a trot after reaching the sheep trail. They made good time, keeping to a narrow trail that led behind Dead Man's Hill toward Spirit Canyon.

The back trail ended and they moved onto Thunder Road for the rest of the trek into Spirit Canyon. "I think Belle'd fancy a little gallop," Tom said. The truth was, he fancied it too: The thunder and lightning were closer now, and those military types weighed heavily on his mind.

"Let's go-

The horses ran easily up the slightly moonlit road, not slowing until the ascent into the mountains. From there they moved at a moderate trot, and in a few minutes, turned down the narrow trail to Alex Manderley's camp.

"The Bronco's gone," Marie said as they approached the campsite.

One tent, lit from within, still stood, along with a chair and the card table, but everything else appeared ready for stowing.

"Alex?" Tom called.

A shadow crossed the tent and then a head stuck out. "Who's there?" called Eric Watson.

"Tom Abernathy and Marie Lopez," Tom replied as they rode up and dismounted. He grinned at Marie. "At least Eric's not pointing a gun at my head."

"I shoulda shot you, cowboy."

"I like a feisty woman."

"What are you two doing all the way up here?" Eric asked.

"Making a delivery," Marie said, handing him the samples and the roll of film, and explaining about the sheep and the military choppers.

"This is incredible," Eric raved, lighting a lantern on the card table and holding the bag of blue gel up to it. "Just incredible. I wish Alex were here. She's going to be in heaven over this!"

"Will she be back soon?" Tom asked.

"I don't know." Eric smiled. "She's having dinner with Carlo Pelegrine."

Tom and Marie exchanged surprised glances. "Well, I'll be doggoned," he said. "I didn't think Carlo'd ever spark to anyone."

"Alex is the same way," Eric supplied. "She never stops working. Until now."

"I think it's great," Marie said.

Tom nodded and turned to Eric. "You're planning to get out of the canyon before the storm gets going?"

"Yes. As soon as Alex gets back, we'll go into town."

"Good. We get some real gully washers around here. You wouldn't be safe up in the hills. One might wash down right on top of you."

"Does it flood here?"

"Not often, but it can, and those clouds look like they'll move in long enough to do the trick. There's nowhere for the water to go, so it just sits on top of the land. Nasty stuff."

"If you like," Marie offered, "I can drive back up here and you can throw your gear in my pickup and wait for Alex at my place."

"That's nice of you," Eric said, "but I'll wait here. Alex won't leave me to wash away, and there's always a chance of a UFO flying by."

"Well, you be careful," Marie told him.

Tom nodded. "Real careful. We'd best be on our way. Give Alex our regards."

"I will."

The ride back to Marie's was uneventfully pleasant, but the minute they trotted into the driveway, they saw that the stable doors hung open.

"Dear God!" Marie whispered, seeing the padlock that lay on the ground. It had been sliced through with bolt cutters.

"I locked the sheep in the stable!" Marie cried as they approached the open doors.

"I know," Tom said dully. "I went in and fed them, but I locked it up again, on my honor."

She glanced at him. "Thanks; I wouldn't doubt you, Tom. Some son of a bitch broke in. Dorsey?" she called. "Bill?"

In the distance, a dog barked in reply.

"God," she said, riding into the stable and flipping on the light. Red 666s were splattered all around, and the sheep's stalls were empty. She looked at Tom. "I gotta find them."

"I know."

They rode to the end of the stable and found the body of one of the collies. There was a horrible dent in its skull, and its flank was painted with the devil's symbol. Beside the corpse lay a two-by-four, matted with blood.

"Marie," Tom began.

"Don't," she whispered, eyes glistening. "Poor old Bill." Her lip trembled. "I have to get my flock rounded up, Tom. You go on home. Better check your own stables."

He shook his head. "Davy's there, and we're loaded with alarms. I'm not going anywhere." He rode to the wall where a battery-operated lantern hung, lifted it off its hook, and turned it on.

Marie pulled her flashlight from the saddlebag, and they rode out of the stable and into her pastureland, a handful of acreage sandwiched between a strip of land owned by the Apostles and Tom's property.

A dog was barking as Tom's eyes adjusted back to the dim light, and he saw the lone collie frantically trying to herd the sheep. Marie took off, Tom following, and in a few minutes they had the sheep back in the barn. "One's missing," Marie said, after a head count.

"Let's find it."

They saw nothing as they moved in larger and larger circles over her land, then Marie pointed. "What's that? Over there, on your side of the fence?"

Tom squinted. "Can't tell." He rode closer, then dismounted and leaned on the wooden fence. "It's one of the mustangs," he told Marie as she approached.

In an instant he'd climbed the fence and run to the animal, Marie right behind him. He squatted, holding the lantern up, cringing as he saw the slices in its belly, the missing ear, the blood. His eyes burned and he wiped them roughly.

Marie's hand came to rest on his shoulder. "That's not like the sheep, Tom. The sheep looked like somebody took a laser to them. This is human-done."

"Those damned Apostles." He rose, looking at Marie. "It's revenge, like as not. I had a little fun with them at the park today," he told her bitterly. "One tried to poke me with his umbrella, so I ran him down and roped him. The old coot in charge swore revenge."

Marie turned to him, putting her arms loosely around his waist. "I'm sorry, cowboy. I know how much you love those horses."

His hands came out to cup her shoulders and he pulled her close. He looked down at her, seeing the tip of her nose barely came to the middle of his breastbone, thought about losing her, as he'd lost the mustang. He couldn't bear the thought. "We'll call Moss after we find your sheep," he said roughly. "Come on."

He took her hand, the feeling of protectiveness amazing and over-whelming him all at once, and he held it until they reached the fence. They mounted the horses and rode on until they finally saw a white form lying on its back, legs pointed to heaven.

The lamb, very young, had been cut up the same as the horse, in a poor imitation of the other mutilations. Marie dismounted and examined the animal, then glanced back at Rex, took his reins, and led him closer. He allowed it. "Rex shied from the ones in the canyon. Wouldn't go near them," she said as she took a blanket rolled behind her saddle and wrapped the lamb in it. Tom helped her lift it up in front of the saddle horn. They rode back in silence.

While Marie found another padlock for the door, Tom took a shovel and dug a deep hole out back, a grave for Wild Bill. Marie returned and insisted on covering the collie herself.

"Ashes to ashes," she murmured, crossing herself. "Dust to dust. Come on inside, Tom. I'll make some coffee."

# EIGHTY-ONE

# JUSTIN MARTIN

Justin had pulled off Thunder Road and hid his car behind some rocks and mesquite about a quarter mile west of the fort. No one had noticed him or the Mustang, and he walked into the desert, then dug for two hours to make a deep enough grave to hold the kid and the bike.

Under cover of night, he carried the corpse to the grave and dropped it unceremoniously beside the hole before unwrapping it. In the dim light, he lifted the kid's pullover shirt and carefully cut an eight-inch square of flesh from his abdomen. After rolling it up like a parchment, he cut a piece of the plastic and wrapped the skin up in it, then rolled the body, facedown, into the grave.

He'd gone back for the bike, nearly falling into the grave when he tried to lower the bike into it noiselessly. Then he'd begun shoveling the sandy dirt back into the grave, but stopped briefly when he heard horses. He lay down on the ground and watched, saw the pale silver horse and the other, so black it was nearly invisible, pass quickly westward. The riders—Abemathy and a woman— didn't notice him, and he went back to work, finishing the job quickly. He tamped down the soil and looked up as lightning blazed in the sky. He had the feeling that the Voice that helped guide him was displeased with this waste, but at least the rain would remove the traces of his work. Exhausted, he picked up the roll of skin and returned to the car.

He backed out, lights off, then turned the car around, timing the move to a roll of thunder. His next stop was in Spirit Canyon to pick up his keys. After that, he had decided, he would return to town the back way so that it was less likely he'd be noticed.

He glanced at his watch as he turned down Old Madelyn. Good old Mom and Dad wouldn't be home yet, so he decided to stop off for a shower and a change of clothes before going to Alex's camp. That way, if he was seen, no one would wonder about his appearance.

EIGHTY-TWO

# ERIC WATSON

Eric Watson finished packing up the second tent and then stacked it with the rest of the gear under the overhang in case the rain began before Alex returned. Then all he'd have to do was fold up the card table and chair and pop it all in the back of the truck.

The wind had turned frigid and he hoped she'd be back soon. Pulling his windbreaker tightly around him, he sat down at the table and picked up one of the sample bags Marie and Tom had brought and held it up to the lantern. The clear blue material within might be anything from watery gelatin to a military invention to something from another world. He could hardly wait to get it to the lab and find out. The fact that the sheep had reappeared so mysteriously also fascinated him, and he suspected that the government might be involved in some way: Chances were the blue material was a red herring. Or blue herring, in this case. Whatever it was, it was a clue.

A single drop of rain splatted against the outer edge of the table just as he heard the roar of an approaching vehicle. It didn't sound like the Bronco and he rose, listening, but a thunderous rumble muffled the sound. Concerned that it might be Colonel Dole or one of his minions, Eric stashed the samples in the nearest duffel bag just as headlights flashed across the campsite.

Shielding his eyes, Eric walked out to meet the vehicle and saw that it was Justin Martin's black Mustang. He groaned, then decided that the teen was at least preferable to Dole. Thunder cracked and a flash of lightning tore the sky. A few more drops of rain stung his face.

"Hi, Justin," he said as the boy stepped out of the car. "What brings you up here so late?"

The youth grinned. "I found something I thought you and Dr. Manderley might be interested in."

"Really? What is it?"

"Well, Christie—that's my girlfriend—and I went hiking today around Olive Mesa, and we found this really strange piece of *something*. It's like metal, but not, and I can't tear or cut it, and I read in the paper about all the UFOs up here the other night, so I thought I should bring it to you." He paused, smiling winningly. "I know it's probably nothing, but ..."

"You never know," Eric said as he wiped several raindrops off his face. "Let's take a look."

"It's in the trunk." As he spoke, Justin reached behind the driver's seat and extracted a long black flashlight. "Come on back."

Eric trailed him around the car and waited while Justin opened the trunk. The boy stepped back. "Have a look at this."

Eric leaned over but saw nothing. "Turn on the flashlight, will you, Justin?"

"Sure thing."

Something hard cracked against the back of Eric's head. He reeled, grabbing the edges of the trunk, bright spots dancing before his eyes. Pain exploded in his head as another blow struck him. Then he was aware only of falling forward into a small dark place.

EIGHTY-THREE

# TOM ABERNATHY

F irst Tom had offered to stay at Marie's and keep a look out in
case the vandals came back, but she wouldn't hear of it. Then
he tried to convince her to accompany him back to his ranch and
sleep in the guest room, but she wouldn't leave her flock alone, and
frankly, he didn't blame her.

Now, as the first raindrops pattered off his Stetson, Tom rode
toward Old Madelyn Highway, and home. Lost in his thoughts—
about the cruel killing of his horse, the dog, and the lamb, not to
mention his feelings toward Marie—he didn't notice the nearly invisible car, its lights out, coming toward him on Thunder Road, until he
saw it turn south at the junction. Realizing it might belong to the
vandals, he strained to see it in the darkness, but it was impossible.

Grimly he continued on, thinking about the feeling he'd had a
few days ago, the feeling that something was going to happen. That
had certainly turned out to be true, but he'd never expected to get
involved. He was a man whose favorite trail was the one of least resistance. He'd never used his fists, and very rarely even got in any kind
of argument, let alone confrontation, depending on his way with
words to get him through life. He never thought he'd feel differently,

but this afternoon, when he'd bagged that damnable Apostle, he discovered an aggressive streak he hadn't even suspected he possessed. Tonight, seeing what had been done to Marie's place, and more, seeing his horse, he felt a rage unlike any he had ever experienced. And it was still growing. "Belle, I guess I'm ready to bust some ass."

The horse twitched her ears and snorted, as if she didn't believe him. Tom wasn't sure he did either, but the anger was undeniably real.

Just as Tom reached Old Madelyn Highway, a pair of headlights appeared out of Spirit Canyon. This vehicle was traveling at a good clip, and Tom wondered if it wasn't Alex and Eric coming out of the canyon for the night.

At the intersection, he halted and waited for the vehicle, deciding to be neighborly and invite the scientists to spend the night at his place. The headlights grew rapidly, their brightness making Belle fidget and snort.

"Just a minute, girl." Tom patted her neck as the vehicle came on, not slowing as it neared Old Madelyn. Belle whinnied nervously and backed up, then half reared as the vehicle turned, and Tom saw that it wasn't Alex and Eric, but that damned air force goon in his CJ-5. A grunt was driving and Dole glared at him from the passenger seat.

"You bottom-feeding belly-crawling lowlife son of a bitch," Tom called after the jeep. He nearly smiled to himself, bemused because his mouth seemed to have developed a mind of its own. Shaking his head, he stroked beaded raindrops from Belle's sleek silver neck. "Let's get home before the sky breaks open."

# EIGHTY-FOUR

# ALEXANDRA MANDERLEY

"Good night, Carlo." Alex stared into the man's eyes, barely aware of the rain that pattered around them as they stood beside her Bronco.

"I have no regrets," he murmured, as he took her hand and gently kissed it.

"That's exactly what I needed to hear," Alex said, her embarrassment lessening the slightest bit. "You really are a mindreader, Carlo." Caught in long- suppressed passions, Alex had virtually raped the man. In the beginning, at least. She had pandered to his professed skin fetish, dripping candle wax over her palm and asking him to peel it off. He tried to resist and she had been ready to go further, to dribble the hot wax on her abdomen or breasts to make him lose control. Thank heaven; the palm was enough. They left the fetish behind soon after, becoming caught up in lovemaking that had lasted far longer than either had realized. "No regrets," she murmured as she leaned forward to kiss him.

His hands found her hips and worked their way up her back as he met her kiss. The kiss began gently, with soft explorations, then the passion overtook them both once more and they held one another as if they were saying good-bye forever.

Breathless, Carlo finally pulled back. "You don't know what you do to me."

"The same thing you do to me."

He shook his head. "Alex. I have secrets. Things no one, *no one*, knows. Things that I can't talk about. You're playing with fire."

"We all have secrets."

"Not like mine."

She kissed him lightly. "I don't care if you're wanted for murder, Carlo." She saw him turn pale, even in the deceitful glow of the sodium lamp, but she pressed on. "I feel safe with you. More than that, Carlo, it's the first time in my life I've ever felt truly free. And accepted."

Holding her shoulders, he studied her. "You really mean that, don't you?"

"I always mean what I say."

"Alex, you make me feel the same way, but I have to warn you again. I'm not what I appear to be."

"I'll take my chances. Now, I'd better get going before Eric gets flooded out of the canyon."

"Be careful, Alexandra."

"I will."

As she pulled out of the parking lot, thunder shook the Bronco's windows and a ragged finger of lightning struck up on Thunder Road. Immediately a barrage of water hit so hard that the windshield wipers could barely keep up. It drove all thoughts of romance from her mind.

Doggedly she drove up Old Madelyn, telling herself the lightning had taller things to hit than her truck. It took a full ten minutes to make the junction, and as she turned toward Spirit Canyon she refused to think about the possibility of flash floods or landslides. She had to pick up Eric. He was depending on her.

Twenty minutes passed before she pulled onto the treacherous trail leading to the campsite. Blessedly, the pounding rain eased off, enabling the wipers to handle the steady downpour. She drove into the campsite and pulled up close to the overhang, relieved that Eric had packed up, guilty that he'd had to do it all alone.

"Eric?" she called, jumping out of the truck and running under the rocky shelter. "Eric? I'm here!" Behind the cooler and the equipment boxes, two duffels were still open, and she zipped them up quickly. "Eric!" she yelled, trying to be heard over the thunder and rain. All she could think of was her old partner, Jack Matthews, and how he had disappeared from their New Mexican campsite. How the hell could she have been so selfish? How could she leave Eric alone for so long?

*Don't panic yet!* Quickly she opened the back of the truck and began haphazardly throwing everything in, yelling for Eric until she was hoarse, her anxiety growing by the second.

*Someone gave him a ride!* The realization struck her like a bullet. *You idiot! You should have thought of that in the first place!* She'd forgotten to leave the cellular phone with him, so he couldn't let her know in advance, and if he'd left a note, it probably blew away already. She doubted he'd been gone long, and he must have assumed she'd pick up the gear, then meet him. *But where?*

By now, he might have phoned Carlo. Quickly she found his number and punched it into the phone. Just as quickly, she found out that Carlo hadn't heard from him.

She turned the truck around and began the hazardous journey back out of Spirit Canyon. Who would pick him up? Maybe that ever-present annoyance, Justin Martin? Moss Baskerville? Tom? Any number of people could have come by. *Dole?* The thought turned her stomach to ice because someone like Dole probably got Jack.

With the rain falling lightly, she made it back to Thunder Road in only fifteen minutes. By then she had calmed down and decided that Eric would likely try to meet her at Ray's Cafe. He was probably there now, wolfing down one of his beloved cheeseburgers while he waited for her.

Old Madelyn Highway was obviously built in a dry creek bed, and she silently thanked the powers that be for the invention of four-wheel drive as she sloshed and bounced down the road. At one point a monstrous pothole nearly took out her right front tire, but the wheel bounced free. Passing Madland, she saw that the gate, which normally kept traffic off Main Street, was wide open. Lights were on at some of the shops and a few vehicles were parked in front of them. She caught a glimpse of two people unloading sandbags near the gate by the arena, and it finally sunk in that this storm was a real hazard.

The rain picked up again just as the Bronco hit asphalt on the outskirts of New Madelyn. She turned the wipers up as high as they would go, but they did almost nothing. Water had already overflowed the gutters, but she didn't concern herself. The important thing was that she had made it to town safely.

Finally she pulled into Ray's Truck Stop and parked as close as she could— five rows back—to the restaurant. The place was teeming with truckers and other travelers waiting out the storm, and as she pushed open the café door, she saw that she wasn't the only one who looked like a drowned rat; nearly everyone in the restaurant was soaked to the skin. Except for the Apostles, no one in the desert ever carried umbrellas.

She counted three waitresses, plus Rosie Vine, rushing around trying to keep up with business. They didn't notice her, so she darted up the first aisle of tables, scanning for Eric. Then, crossing the short rear section where she and Eric had sat before, she came face-to-face with Lawrence Dole as he rose from his table.

"Colonel Dole," she said coolly.

He nodded, inspecting her with his grim little pig eyes. Then one corner of his mouth crooked up in a cross between a smile and a sneer. "Looking for unidentified flying objects, Miss Manderley?"

"That's *Doctor* Manderley, and I'm looking for my assistant, Eric Watson. Perhaps you've seen him?"

"Afraid not."

He started to step around her, but she blocked his path. "You're certain?" she asked.

"Absolutely."

She let him go past, then continued her circuit of the diner, finally coming to the counter seating. He was nowhere to be found.

"How're you doing, Alex?" Ray Vine, in his chef's whites, came out from behind the order window.

"Fine, Ray. But I'm looking for Eric."

"The tall boy with the red hair?"

She smiled. "That's him. Have you seen him tonight?"

"No, I haven't," he replied after thinking a moment. "Have you checked the tavern?"

"No, but Eric doesn't drink."

"What's he driving?"

"Nothing. I think someone picked him up while I was away from camp."

Ray crossed his arms. "Hmmm. We've got flash flood warnings, so Moss might've sent someone after him. Check at the police station, and if they don't know, talk to Tom. He knows everything." Ray chuckled. "And if he doesn't, he'll make it up."

Rosie Vine bustled up and snapped the order slip onto a clip by the order window. "Ray, I need six cheeseburger platters! Hi, Alex," she added, turning to go back into battle.

"Rosie," Ray called. "Ask the waitresses if they've seen a tall, carrot-topped young man here tonight, will you?"

She nodded and disappeared, then breathlessly returned about a minute later. "No one like that's been in here."

"Thanks," Alex said as she headed for the door.

"No problem. You be careful out there."

"I will."

The rain wasn't so bad as she pulled from the lot and drove up the street to police headquarters. There, the clerk tried to raise Moss Baskerville on the radio, but the storm was playing hell with the radios, and the best he could do was take her report and promise to get back to her.

While she was running back to the Bronco, the rain stopped and a slice of moon appeared from behind glowing clouds. Heartened, she decided to follow Ray Vine's advice and go see Tom Abernathy.

# EIGHTY-FIVE

# TOM ABERNATHY

Tom Abernathy stood back to let the soggy scientist into his house. "Doc, what are you doing out in this weather?"

"Looking for Eric." Alex looked down at the puddles forming around her shoes on the terra-cotta tile. "I'm sorry."

"No problem. Wait right there." He disappeared, then returned almost instantly with a towel. Gratefully she began drying her hair.

"I saw Eric a couple hours ago," Tom told her. "Marie and I rode up to your camp and left some samples with him." He told her about the sheep and Marie's near run-in with the military types.

"They got him, those bastards got him."

"What?"

She explained briefly, then studied Tom. "I ran into Dole at Ray's a few minutes ago, but he claimed he hadn't seen Eric."

"Well, I'd guess he was lying. When I was riding home from Marie's, two vehicles came along. The second was Dole's and he nearly ran Belle off the road."

"What about the first one?"

"I don't know if it came out of the canyon or not. It had its lights out and it was a car, but that's all I can tell you." He paused. "You think Dole took the samples?"

"I'll have to go through the bags, but if they're gone, I'm sure he did," Alex told him.

"Think he took Eric too?"

"I wouldn't be surprised. Damn it, this is all my fault. I shouldn't have left him alone." She paused. "It's not raining now. I'm going up to the canyon to take one more look around."

"It's too dangerous to go up there, Alex. You've never seen a flash flood in the desert, have you?"

"I can't leave him up there, Tom." She smiled. "I'll be fine. In and out just like that."

"Well, I guess I can't stop you, but I wish I could. Did you check the motels in town?"

"No, not yet."

"Come on, we'll do that first." He took her to the kitchen phone and let her do the calling. Finally she put the receiver down. "Eric hasn't checked in anywhere. Thanks for your help, Tom. I'd better go before it starts raining again."

Reluctantly he led her to the door and opened it. It was blacker than pitch out there, except where the moon glowed dimly behind a cloud, and the air felt heavy with water. "Be careful," he told her, "then come on back here if you like."

"Thanks, Tom. We will if we can't get a motel room."

He watched her drive away. First Marie wouldn't accept his help, and now Alex wouldn't listen to his advice. An ornerier pair of females had never lived. He glanced northward, hoping Marie was safe from Dole and from the rain, then put a tape of *The Searchers* in his VCR. But even John Wayne couldn't quite get his mind off his troubles.

# EIGHTY-SIX

# JUSTIN MARTIN

Even if that nerdface Eric Watson hadn't been quite dead when Justin buried him in a shallow depression under a half dozen shovelfuls of damp dirt, he surely was by now—if not from suffocation, then by drowning.

Killing Eric had been a spur-of-the-moment thing and, in retrospect, probably unnecessary. Justin smiled to himself as he hauled another sandbag out of Marquay's storage shed next to the mine ride and threw it in the wheelbarrow. He had only one regret: It was too bad he had to dump another perfectly good body. But tonight there just wasn't any time, and now that he had his rabbit's- foot key chain back, he was more interested in what Carlo and Alex Manderley were doing than in slicing up the nerdman.

But when Justin had returned to Madland, the gates were open and the shopkeepers were sandbagging. At first he was annoyed, then he realized the activity gave him more freedom to move around without drawing attention to himself.

Passing by Main Street, he turned in to the parking lot instead and found Manderley's truck was already gone. *Shit!* He pulled around to Main, then drove toward the mine, where, sure enough,

Old Man Marquay was lugging the heavy sandbags out, huffing and puffing like he was going to rupture the veins sticking out on his neck and temples. Seeing Justin, he proclaimed him a wonderful boy. Justin gave him a line of shit about how he wished he'd been here sooner, and the old fart lapped it up. Before the last big downpour began, Marquay had gone gratefully home, leaving Justin to finish the work by himself, which was exactly what he wanted.

He shoved the last bag in place, then locked the shed and returned to the Mustang. As he opened the door he saw that nearly everyone had gone now, and the few remaining were finishing up.

He slid into the driver's seat and pulled the door closed, then extracted his gift to the Peeler from its hiding place beneath the seat. Quickly he penned a note and attached it to the square of skin with a silver safety pin, then folded it all and slipped it into his jacket pocket.

He climbed from the car and walked down to Main Street to the Sorcerer's Apprentice. The shop was dark except for a faint glow emanating from somewhere in the rear. Casually he stepped onto Pelegrine's porch and padded softly to the front door.

*What to do, what to do, what to do?* He had no way to attach the skin to the door, so he finally draped it over the doorknob for the Peeler to find in the morning. After that, he walked purposefully back to his car and drove away.

# EIGHTY-SEVEN

# ALEXANDRA MANDERLEY

As Alex turned onto Thunder Road, she noticed a strange circular opening had appeared in the thick clouds, allowing her to see the stars beyond. She'd never seen anything quite like it, and by the time she entered Spirit Canyon, it had doubled in size. Though she wanted to watch it, she forced herself to keep her eyes on the winding, muddy road.

Expecting the rain to begin again, she traveled as quickly as she dared, and as she rounded a hairpin curve near the turnoff, her instrument panel flickered twice, then went out. "Damn," she whispered, tapping it with her fingertips. A second passed and the truck began shaking.

Above, the clouds had taken on an eerie greenish glow. Abruptly the headlights went out and the engine died.

"What the hell's going on?" she whispered, trying vainly to restart the engine. Realizing the Bronco wasn't going anywhere, she opened the door and stepped out to study the sky.

"My God," she breathed. The huge UFO hovered in the now enormous circle of open sky, so low, it nearly scraped the mountain-tops. Head tilted back, she held her breath and took in the dark craft, the size of a football field, at least. Except for three concentric ovals of blue and green lights, she could see no details: It seemed to be a void, a black hole in space.

Alex's brain clicked in and she quickly climbed in the Bronco and pulled out the Minicam bag, unzipping it as fast as she could. She brought the camera up as she swung out of the car, but its charge light flickered and went out. "Damn!" She turned to get the thirty-five-millimeter camera, but before she could grab it, the truck began to vibrate and she looked back up just as the blue-green lights on the UFO winked twice. Then the craft, or whatever it was, began to rise slowly, straight into the sky. When it was perhaps a thousand feet up, it remained stationary for a moment, then whisked away to the west at an impossible speed. In a split second it disappeared. "What are you?" she whispered. "Who are you?"

The headlights and dash lights flickered to life as the clouds around the circular hole began to swirl closed. Alex started the engine, drove cautiously to the turnoff, and parked at the side of the road. The earth was too waterlogged now to risk driving the trail.

Rain began falling lightly as she got out of the truck, and as she pulled on her trench coat, cursing because she had forgotten to buy an umbrella in town, the cellular phone rang. She grabbed it. "Eric?"

"This is Moss Baskerville. My clerk told me you were looking for me. Sorry it took so long. We're having one hell of a busy night. Your assistant disappeared?"

"Yes." Quickly she recounted the night's events.

"Where are you now?"

"In Spirit Canyon, just outside the camp." As she spoke, the rain fell harder.

"Christ." Baskerville paused. "Did you see that UFO a while ago?"

"yet."

"The whole town blacked out while it was visible." Baskerville's voice crackled with static. "Cars, buildings, streetlights, everything. I thought we were having an earthquake until I looked up and saw that damned thing glowing in the clouds. Now we've got several wrecks to deal with on top of everything else. You're not stuck, I hope?"

"No. I'm fine. I'm just going to walk to the campsite and take one more look for Eric."

"No," he ordered sternly. "It's not safe. Like as not, you'll get covered in a landslide. There's no ground cover holding those hills together, and we have slides nearly every time it rains. Best thing you can do is get out of there now. And I mean *pronto!*"

As he spoke, the rain poured suddenly, as if a plug had been pulled in the sky. Alex climbed back into the truck and shut the door. "Moss, there's one other thing. We received some samples from a sheep mutilation. Eric did, that is. Tom Abernathy delivered them and later he saw Colonel Dole racing out of the canyon. I have a feeling Eric's disappearance and Dole's visit are tied together. Can you find out?"

There was a long silence. "I can try. Where are you going to be if I need to reach you?"

"I'm not sure." She had to yell to be heard over the rain pounding on the Bronco. "But you can reach me at this number anytime."

"Okay. It looks like I'll be out all night, so I'll ask around and keep an ear open. If he doesn't show up by morning, I think we might be able to get a search-and-rescue team up to take a look. Now, you get out of that canyon."

"Don't worry," she replied, and broke the connection.

She turned the headlights on and angled the truck so that they illuminated the trail. Suddenly she heard a rumble and, ten feet ahead, a part of the hill gave way, slipping down onto the trail in a huge mound of reddish earth. "Okay, Moss, I'm out of here." Remembering the near river that Old Madelyn had become during the first deluge, she didn't turn around, but headed down the back way.

The rain fell harder, the noise of it reaching an almost unbearable crescendo as it beat on the Bronco's roof, turning the dangerous drive down into a hair-raising one. At one point, another landslide blocked the road just behind her.

Her shoulders and neck were painfully stiff by the time she made it out of the canyon and onto the graded dirt road. If anything, it was more badly flooded than Old Madelyn Highway, the water level rising too quickly for comfort. At last she reached pavement and the fork leading to Madland. The road continuing on to New Madelyn was submerged beneath rapid-flowing muddy water, but Ghost Town Road, leading toward the park, didn't look too bad.

Gritting her teeth, she turned and began bouncing along over dirt and rocks that had washed onto the asphalt. It finally brought her to Madland's parking lot, and she pulled all the way through to check on the state of the highway. It was a river. Possibly she could get through. Possibly she'd get stuck, or worse, swept off the road.

She looked back at the Madland buildings and spotted a light on in what she thought was Carlo's upstairs apartment. Picking up the phone, she punched in his number. He answered on the third ring, sounding very surprised to hear from her. But after she told him her problem, he promptly invited her to stay the night, and told her to pull around front because the gates were open. She thanked him and hung up.

Before pulling out, she turned on the interior lights and went through the luggage, but found no sign of the samples. "Damned government," she whispered. If she had lost Eric the same way she lost Jack, she'd never forgive herself. God only knew what the military might do to him. *Or whatever is in those UFOs.*

Navigating the twenty feet up the river of Old Madelyn was difficult, and she almost went off the road before she finally found the wide gates and drove through. She crawled along Main Street, noting the sandbags lining the south side of the street, knowing her brakes were soaked and barely working. Finally she arrived at Carlo's.

She grabbed her phone, bag, and a small nylon bag that held her personal items, then ran for the door. The porch and downstairs were dark; Carlo hadn't come downstairs yet, and guiltily she wondered if she had gotten him out of bed. She knocked, then tried the doorknob.

She felt something cold and slimy under her fingers and pulled back, a startled cry escaping her lips. Whatever was on the knob fell with a wet plopping sound to the wooden porch. Involuntarily she stepped back. At least it didn't feel like another dead animal.

At that moment, the porch light came on and she saw what she had touched. It was a small heap of red and white matter, with a note pinned to it.

Carlo started to open the door. "Wait," she called, bending to pick up the object. "There's something on your porch. Let me get it."

She pinched her fingers around the edge of the object and picked it up, nose wrinkling. The note read, "I know who you are. I know what you do. I want you to show me." She stepped back, stomach curdling as she held the object closer to the light. *Skin!* With a strangled moan, she let the flesh drop.

Carlo pushed the door open, almost knocking it into her forehead. "What's wrong?"

She looked at him, then down at her feet.

"What?" he whispered, squatting down.

"I think it's skin," Alex managed.

He looked up, his face dead white.

"There's a note under there somewhere."

Using a pen, he turned the flesh over and uncovered the note. If it was possible, he turned even paler. "Where was it?"

"On the doorknob," she said, her stomach turning over. "Is it ... Is it skin?"

He nodded. "Someone has a very sick sense of humor. You didn't see anyone out when you pulled up, did you?"

She shook her head. "Carlo, I have to wash my hands." She was also afraid that she was going to throw up.

He rose and moved out of the doorway. "Go ahead. I'll take care of this."

"What are you going to do? Call Moss Baskerville?"

"For now, I'm going to get it off my porch." He paused. "Look, you're soaked through. Go on upstairs and take a shower. There's a robe and towels in the bathroom. Bring your clothes down after and we'll wash and dry them."

"Thank you, Carlo." Refusing to think about the flesh or even Eric, for fear her tired brain would short-circuit, she wiped her feet and walked inside.

# EIGHTY-EIGHT

# JAMES ROBERT SINCLAIR

The sky opened and the light shone down upon him.

James Robert Sinclair waited, kneeling, hands clasped, head bowed in prayer. All around, the storm pounded Olive Mesa, but no rain fell upon him, on his white robe, his bare feet, or his hair, loose and whipping in the wind.

*The time is at hand. Arise, my son.*

The words resounded in his brain, thundered in his ears, and Sinclair rose slowly, head still bowed, hands still clasped.

"What do you wish of me, Father?"

*The Horsemen shall ride, and they shall herald the end of the world, just as you have prophesied. The Living Savior, the New Christ, is returned to the world. He is here and He shall lead the people unto heaven.*

"He is *here?*" he cried joyously. "How shall I know Him, Father?"

*Look!*

Slowly Sinclair opened his eyes and raised his head. White light, blindingly beautiful and brilliant, surrounded him, and he raised his hand to his eyes to shield them.

*Look, and you shall know your true nature, my son.*

Sinclair pulled his trembling hand from his eyes. A dark silhouette, only a distant pinpoint, appeared within the light. The figure slowly walked toward him, and Sinclair involuntarily stepped back.

*Do not fear, my son, but look upon the face of the Living Savior and you shall know Him.*

Trembling, quaking on his feet, Sinclair stood his ground and forced himself to gaze upon the approaching figure, upon the Dark Angel, upon the Son of God. Now he could see the hair that flowed over the Son's shoulders, the beard. From a distance he was the classical Christ of Christian mythology. The eyes were dark and unfathomable, and Sinclair averted his gaze, knowing judgment was at hand.

*Look! And know your destiny, my son, for you are the Chosen One.*

He looked. The Christ was a dozen feet away, ten, six, and He held out His hands, showing the scars of crucifixion. Sinclair flinched, his own hands burning with pain, his feet, too. But he did not look away.

The Christ was four feet away, and his dark brown eyes held nothing but love and compassion. Three feet, and a gentle smile graced his face. Two feet, and He halted. Again He lifted His arms.

*Take my hands.*

This was a new voice, new and yet familiar. This was the voice of Christ, and Sinclair knew it well. Slowly he brought his own hands up and saw that they bled. Though he did not look, he knew his feet were bleeding as well.

The Son of God took his hands in His own and blood dripped between their fingers.

*The Lamb has returned.* The first voice, God's voice, nearly deafened him. *Do you understand now, my Son?*

Sinclair stared into the face of the Living Savior, knowing it, yet a stranger to it as well. He said nothing.

The Christ's gentle smile returned, then He spoke aloud. "I am your mirror. I am your soul. I am the Lamb."

The pain disappeared from Sinclair's feet and hands, and the

Christ turned his palms upwards. The blood was gone, but each palm held a freshly healed scar of crucifixion.

Sinclair looked back into Christ's eyes. "Tell me."

"I am you." The Christ put His hands on Sinclair's shoulders, then enfolded him in His arms. Suffused with love and a peace he had never before known, Sinclair received the Christ into his body.

# EIGHTY-NINE

## CARLO PELEGRINE

*I* *know who you are. I know what you do. I want you to show me.* The words in the note had been indelibly imprinted in Carlo's mind.

He couldn't tolerate the idea of having the human flesh in his house, so while Alex took her shower, he had wrapped the skin and the note pinned to it in foil, then pulled on his rain poncho and went out the back door and tossed it in the trash bin.

Now, sitting alone at the table in his reading room, he considered the note as, upstairs, the shower continued to run. *I know who you are. I know what you do. I want you to show me.* He had been found out: That much was clear. That someone had committed a murder to impress him was all too clear. *Perhaps more than one. The disappearances ...* He sighed *and rubbed his* temples.

Upstairs, the water turned off. Alex would be down shortly, and she'd be asking questions he couldn't answer. "What am I going to do?" he whispered.

Suddenly someone hammered on the front door, filling Carlo with dark terror. Panicked, he rose, nearly knocking his chair over in his haste. There was nothing he could do but answer the door.

He took a deep breath and reluctantly moved through the shop and switched on the porch light as the knocking continued. Steeling himself, he grasped the knob and opened the door.

Justin Martin gave him a varsity grin. "You're the Peeler." He paused, then the grin widened. "I hope you liked your gifts."

"I don't know what you're talking about." Carlo was surprised by the strength in his voice, which belied the shock numbing his body. "You shouldn't be out in this weather, Justin. It's dangerous."

The youth pulled a paperback book out of his jacket, opened it, and thrust it at Carlo. The page showed the old newspaper photo of him and Vic. Carlo chuckled, trying to hide his trembling hands. "This is a picture of a kid named Charles Pilgrim. What's your point?"

"It's you," Justin said, the smile broadening. "Carlo Pelegrine is Italian for Charles Pilgrim. And you can't deny that, can you?"

"Where did that piece of skin come from, Justin?"

"You're the Peeler, aren't you?" the boy persisted, his impossibly blue eyes lit with cold fire. "Admit it."

"You're wrong, Justin. And even if it were me, the caption identified them as witnesses, nothing more."

"The Voice told me I was right, Carlo. I suspected and it said I was right!"

Carlo studied him, mildly relieved. "Hearing voices isn't normal, Justin. Perhaps you should see a psychia—"

"No!" the boy spat angrily. "Don't pull that shit on me. It's the Voice, the same one you heard before you chose a victim."

"I've never heard voices, Justin, and I'm not this Pilgrim person. Now, where did that skin come from?"

"I called information and got Victor Pilgrim's phone number in Brooklyn, New York."

A knot twisted up in Carlo's stomach.

"Actually, there were five Victors. The third one I tried was your brother." The youth's blue eyes glittered, the anger gone as quickly as it had come. "I told him I was an old friend, trying to track you down.

He said you died in Europe the summer before you were to begin college. I said I wanted to visit your grave, and he said that there isn't one. Your body was cremated overseas."

"Justin, you're imagining things."

"Victor gave me your parents' phone number." He smiled. "Your mother died last year. Did you know that?"

Refusing the tears that tried to flood his eyes, Carlo did his best to appear impassive. "I'm going to have to phone the police if you don't leave."

"Don't force me to share your secret with them, Mr. Pilgrim."

"There are no secrets to share."

"Do you think I'm stupid?" Justin's smile disappeared and his eyes darkened with barely concealed rage. "The Peeler left fingerprints. They're a matter of public record. I got a copy and checked them against yours. You're the Peeler."

Was he bluffing? Carlo honestly had no idea.

"Carlo. Charles. Or is it Charlie or Chuck?"

"It's Mr. Pelegrine."

"I don't want to have to turn you in." Justin's eyes were too bright, his cheeks too flushed. "I want you to teach me your art."

There was no art. He had killed and he had cut some skin and the press had built a mythology around "the Peeler," one that grew until most people thought the killer had totally skinned his victims.

"Well? Will you teach me?"

Chances were, it was all a bluff, but Carlo feared otherwise. For now, he decided to play along. "You want to be my apprentice," he said sternly, trapping the youth in his unwavering gaze. "Answer me."

Justin's expression turned to utter, deranged adoration. "Yes."

Carlo frowned. "Your work is very sloppy. The skinned rabbit came from you as well as the human flesh?"

Eagerly Justin nodded. "I know it's sloppy. I practice and practice, but I need instruction. From a master."

"You practiced on what? Animals?"

"Sure. Since I was a little kid." He grinned again. "Old Lady Quigley thinks all her cocker spaniels run away."

If Justin knew how that woman cried over her dogs, he would only laugh, but the admission made Carlo sick at heart. He hid it. "But the skin you left tonight was human."

Justin nodded. "It's my best work. Did you like it?"

The youth desperately wanted his approval. Curling his lip, Carlo sneered, "It's atrocious. I don't believe you could ever learn."

"Yes I can!" This, urgently.

"How much practice have you had with human skin?"

"Not a whole lot. Yet."

"You're responsible for the missing people?" Carlo held Justin's gaze. "Are they dead?"

The boy's look of cunning returned. "Alex Manderley is here. Did you do her already?"

"No." Carlo put his hands in his pockets to hide their trembling. "Who did you kill, Justin?"

"I'll tell you what you want to know after you let me watch you do her. *Peel* her. When are you going to do it?"

"I don't know."

"Tonight," Justin ordered.

"No. Not tonight."

"Then tomorrow. I'll come back tomorrow night and watch you peel her." He grinned that horrifying all-American grin. "If you won't do it tomorrow, you'll never do it." His eyes narrowed. "Maybe you've gone soft. Do it tomorrow or I'll tell Baskerville."

"He'll never believe you."

"Do you want to play chicken, Charlie?" He chuckled. "I'll fax your fingerprints to the FBI."

"Carlo?" Alex called from the top of the stairs.

"I'll be right up," he called, praying she wouldn't descend. He turned to Justin, knowing there was no more time for cat and mouse. Drawing himself to full height, he spoke imperiously. "You be here tomorrow night."

"Hi, Dr. Manderley!" Justin called, his voice utterly charming.

Alex had come downstairs, wearing Carlo's short white terry cloth robe and carrying her wet clothes. She stopped three steps from the floor, startled. "Hello, Justin. Have you seen Eric?"

*No!* Carlo's mind reeled. Did the skin belong to Eric Watson?

"No, I haven't, Dr. Manderley."

"You weren't in the canyon tonight?"

"Of course not!" He looked taken aback. "There are flash flood warnings posted."

"Someone picked him up, Justin. Rescued him, I believe. I was hoping it was you."

"Sorry. I wish I had. I'll keep my eyes open, though."

"Thanks."

"The washer and dryer are in the utility room just beyond the reading room," Carlo told her. "I'll be back to help you in a moment."

Alex gave him a puzzled look, then disappeared behind the dark green curtains that led to the reading room.

Carlo turned to Justin. "Whose skin did you leave here? Is it Eric's?"

Justin smiled, slow and syrupy. "Heck no."

"You haven't seen Eric?"

"Scout's honor." The boy saluted, and Carlo's stomach turned over. "I'll be back tomorrow afternoon."

"Evening," Carlo told him. "There are things I need. Certain tools to do a proper job."

Justin lapped it up. "Can I help you peel her?"

"Your work is an embarrassment," Carlo hissed. "Sloppy. I doubt that you're worthy." He paused, studying the boy's eager puppy-dog face. "I'll have to think about it. Now, get out of here. I have work to do."

Justin's teeth flashed white. "I'll bet you do." He turned and walked out, disappeared into the rain. Carlo shut and locked the door, then leaned against the wall, eyes closed, rubbing his forehead.

"Carlo? What's wrong?"

Alex stood in the doorway of the reading room, holding one curtain back.

"Nothing," he said, going to her. "Let me help you with the washer."

"I figured it out. Tell me what's going on."

He stared into her huge brown eyes, then took her hand and led her back into the reading room. "Sit down."

As she did, the robe's lapel folded outward, revealing a swell of breast. Carlo averted his eyes as he seated himself across from her. "Alex, that boy is dangerous. To you in particular. Never be alone with him."

"What's going on?"

Carlo put his hands together and twined his fingers on the table. He stared at them, unable to look Alex in the eye. "You remember that I told you I have three regrets?"

"Yes."

"And that I'm dangerous?" "Yes, but—"

"I never would have made love to you if I hadn't wanted you so badly. Alex, there's a reason I've been celibate for twenty years. Something happened ..."

"Whatever it was, twenty years is a long time. You were little more than a child."

"Seventeen. Old enough."

"You were a rapist?" she asked, eyes wide. He laughed bitterly. "No. Worse."

"Tell me." She leaned across the table and put her hands over his.

"Alex, you'll hate me. By making love to you, I put your life in grave danger." He hesitated. "And by making love to you, I learned that whatever beast was within me is gone now." Finally he looked into her eyes. His own were full, tears brimming at the edges. "But I gambled with your life, and there's no excuse for that. I used to black out when I became too excited. It happened three times. Each time ..." *Dear God, I'm telling her!* The realization was too much and he pulled his hands away. "Justin knows. I don't know how, but he knows."

Alex stared at him. "Tell me."

"I promised myself three things: that I'd remain celibate the rest of my life, that I would never again harm another living creature for *any* reason, and that I would help everyone I could. In atonement. Now I've broken one of the promises."

"You've helped me, Carlo, by breaking that promise. You showed me I could live again." She smiled gently. "Besides, I didn't give you a chance to refuse. Now, please tell me what you did."

He smiled sadly. His world was crumbling around him and there wasn't a thing he could do about it. Except kill Justin. But he couldn't do that either: He wouldn't break another vow.

"You killed someone, didn't you?"

Her words, spoken in a near whisper, struck cold into his heart, and he couldn't reply for a long time. Finally he spoke. "Have you ever heard of the Peeler?"

Alex gasped. "You're not ..." She paused, shaking her head. "The skin fetish ... The Peeler skinned his victims. Justin brought you skin." Her face bleached white in the dim light.

"There's little truth to the stories that are told now. Not that that excuses anything. I took far less skin than Justin brought here." He paused, staring uncomfortably at a point beyond Alex. "I don't remember much about the first two times. The third time, I was aware, although I felt like a spectator, watching while someone else used my hands to strangle the girl. I regained control just as he began to cut a tattoo from her breast."

"Carlo," she whispered. "No."

"I graduated from high school, went to Europe, and let my family think I'd died in an accident. I knew I was sort of a Dr. Jekyll and Mr. Hyde, and I never let Hyde out again. Never even risked it until I met you."

Alex stared at him. "And no one has ever figured out who you were."

"No. Not until now. He could be bluffing, but I can't take the chance. He said voices told him. He's dangerous and I have to do something. He admitted to killing animals. I'm sure he's killing people as well."

"People?" Alex's eyes widened.

"He didn't say so outright, but I know he did. Madge Marquay and the others who disappeared are his victims, I'm certain."

"Do you think he has Eric?"

"I don't know."

"We should call the police." As soon as the words were out, she stopped and stared at him. "That endangers you."

"I deserve to be behind bars."

"From what you've said, you suffered some sort of temporary insanity. And you've certainly served your time, far better than you would have in prison." She paused.

"Eric," Carlo began.

"I doubt Justin did anything with Eric," she interrupted. "I think Dole's responsible."

Carlo felt his mouth open, but at first, no words came out. "How can you accept me so easily?"

"I'm in the business of accepting," she said, all business. "But," she added, studying him, "I'll have to think about it. Meanwhile, what should we do?"

"I'll call Tom Abernathy. He's got a four-wheel-drive pickup truck with oversized tires. I'm sure he can get up here and take you back to his place tonight."

"I'm not going anywhere," she said firmly. "Carlo, we have to handle this ourselves. We have to handle Justin ourselves, whatever it takes. We'll talk about it in the morning." Taking his hand, she led him upstairs. Wonderingly, he followed.

# NINETY

## ERIC WATSON

Coughing up rainwater, Eric Watson returned to consciousness. His head throbbed painfully, and for a moment he couldn't remember anything: where he was, what had happened, or even who he was. His right leg was ablaze with agonizing pain. There was dirt in his mouth, and he spat it out, then tried to raise his hand to push wet hair from his eyes, but met resistance; the arm was stuck in sucking mud. panicky, he tried the other arm, but found it similarly trapped. After two hard pulls, his left arm came free. He could feel grit and sand all over his hand, under his shirtsleeve, so he held it out and let the rain wash it. It took only seconds. Calmer, he pulled his other hand free.

*Justin!* Suddenly it came back to him. The kid had hit him over the head, and the next thing he vaguely recalled was being dragged from a dark place—*the car trunk!*—then rolled down the side of a hill. His leg had snapped then. He remembered the horrifying sound and feel of bone crunching.

After that, he was barely conscious, but he had heard the steady sound of a shovel digging into the earth. Each time a mound of wet dirt was thrown over him, he thought he was going to suffocate.

Then there was nothing, not until now. The rain had saved him, he realized, by washing the dirt off his face. His head lay slightly higher than his feet, and he was lucky the kid hadn't thought to turn him around, because he'd be dead now. Slowly he sat up, the mud sucking at him as he moved. He looked around, but it was too dark, too rainy, to see, so he began scooping his hands into the mud covering his hips and legs, helping the rain do its job. After only a few moments, dizziness overtook him again, and he had to rest.

## NINETY-ONE
# JAMES ROBERT SINCLAIR
### SATURDAY

James Robert Sinclair awakened and lay in his bed for a long moment, looking about the room with wonder. And then the dream came back to him. The dream of Christ. The feelings of peace and love, of overwhelming calm, still filled him.

Naked, he rose from the bed, saw his white robe, stained red with mud, in a puddle on the floor. *This was no dream!* He looked at his palms and saw the new red scars, peered at his feet and saw those scars as well.

He walked across the room to the dresser mirror and leaned forward, and gazed into the eyes of the New Christ.

# NINETY-TWO

# ELDO BLANDINGS

"Campbell, you take the back door with Ferguson. Clayman and I will take the front. Deitz, you keep watch." Eldo Blandings consulted his watch. "Move in at oh four hundred."

He finished speaking and the Special Projects Committee moved into position. This kidnapping was the first offensive action of many they would undertake today. He had chosen the shepherdess partly because she had repeatedly sent the church's missionaries away, with no grace whatsoever, and primarily because she lived in isolation so nearby. Capturing her would be relatively simple, and a good trial run for what was to come.

Mel Campbell and Lorraine Ferguson disappeared around the back of the trailer, and Marie Lopez's remaining dog went into a frenzy of barks and yelps as it scratched at the barn door. He wished they'd killed it last night when they had the chance. The rain had slowed to a drizzle for the moment, allowing him to hear the sheep bleating in response to the dog.

"Five," he whispered, gazing at his watch. "Four. Three. Two. One!"

Clayman and Deitz bashed in the flimsy mobile home door,

almost tripping on one another in their eagerness. He followed them into the trailer, hearing Campbell and Ferguson enter the rear door.

A rifle blasted so close, he felt the wind of the bullet.

"Hold it right there, both of you. Hands up. Now, turn around." Marie Lopez, dressed in black sweats, hair tousled from sleep, didn't look sleepy at all as she leveled the rifle. "What the hell are you supposed to be?" she asked, taking in their cammies. "Survivalists?"

"We're Apostles," Eldo said proudly.

"Scum suckers," Marie spat. "Get over there into that corner by the door. That's right." Keeping the rifle trained on them, she reached for the phone.

Suddenly Lorraine Ferguson appeared in the doorway behind Lopez. The six- foot, two-hundred-pound Amazon leaped suddenly into the air and came crashing down on the tiny shepherdess, who struggled like a wildcat, twisting around to face Ferguson. She spat in the Apostle's face and Lorraine's grip loosened momentarily. Lopez clawed at her eyes, but Ferguson's fist came down, punching Marie Lopez in the temple, stunning her.

"You fucking bitch," Ferguson growled, wiping saliva from her face. "You're gonna pay for that, you goddamn stinking bitch!"

Marie's arms came up weakly, then dropped, the blow having done its job. A moment later, Ferguson and Campbell had her bound and gagged.

NINETY-THREE

# HANNIBAL CAINE

Hannibal Caine gasped when Jim-Bob Sinclair walked into his office looking for all the world like Jesus H. Christ Himself. He'd finally donned a robe, as he'd ordered his followers to do, and his hair flowed loosely around his shoulders. That, combined with his customary beard, was a shock: Hannibal had never thought the handsome prophet looked anything like someone who was supposed to be humble.

"Hannibal," Sinclair said in a calm, reassuring voice, "I have come to tell you what I know."

Caine had thought Sinclair had a charming smile and charismatic eyes ever since they'd first met, but with this change in dress and hair, the man looked downright beatific. Frighteningly so.

"James," he invited, "please sit down."

Sinclair nodded, and as he sat, Caine was shocked to see that the man was barefoot.

"Groups of Apostles will be out today, spreading the word," Caine said.

"I want no violence," Sinclair responded. "Give the word, but there must be absolutely no violence."

"James, may I ask a question?"

"Anything you like." There was that disconcerting smile again.

"Until a short time ago, you wanted us to use weapons, even take prisoners. You said it was the first phase of the final battle, and that the second would take place after the Horsemen ride. You had us learn to handle the weapons. Why the change?"

"I was filled with greed and grandiosity then, my dear friend. I had forsaken God for my own glory. I sinned, but now I am repentant, and God has seen fit to use me as His vessel."

"I don't understand, James."

"I am the Lamb of God, Hannibal." Sinclair turned his palms upward on the desk, revealing shiny red stigmata. He touched his breast. "The Living Savior is here, in me." So saying, Sinclair rose. "Have the Apostles preach today. Until supper, I will be in retreat, and after the sermon I shall return to my room to pray until tomorrow morning at six. I'm putting you in charge until then. Good luck, Hannibal. I love you." With that, he left the office.

Not believing his good fortune, Caine was euphoric for several minutes before reality set in. "Crazy as a loon," he murmured. "Stark staring mad." Madness made it all the easier. Sinclair's retreat would keep him out of the way while Hannibal and Eldo Blandings oversaw the invasion—he smiled—not the conversion, of Madelyn.

During the night, Caine had planned the final service, from the abduction of sinners to poison-laced wine for those high up in the church. The plan was complete from every angle, except one: The wild card was Sinclair himself, and while his self-imposed retreat greatly eased the problem, underestimating the Prophet, insane or not, could be a grave error.

When Sinclair was normal—greedy and selfish—these plans would not have been necessary. Sinclair would have left and given Caine the reins of the church. But it was time for action: Caine no longer had any doubt that Sinclair was canceling Armageddon and sticking around. He intended Sinclair, along with Eldo, to take the blame for the violence and the deaths of the upper echelon of Apostles, for the atrocities committed by the Special Projects Committee, and for the abductions. The only problem was keeping Sinclair under control. Perhaps something in the dispensary or in their store of illegally acquired drugs might do the trick. Caine smiled to himself. A dash of Valium, a pinch of Thorazine.

There was a knock on the door. "Come," he called.

Eldo Blandings, a little soggy, his toupee askew, but as happy as Hannibal had ever seen him, entered. "We got the shepherdess." Behind him, Mel Campbell, Corky Deitz, and Steve Clayman all came in and shut the door.

Hannibal nodded. "Where is she?"

"The choir room. She's tied up and locked in. Lorraine Ferguson's on guard detail."

"Very good, Hannibal. What's next?"

Blandings grinned, an expression that made him look like a demon. "We go after the other prisoners."

"Very good."

Blandings nodded. "We'd best be on our way."

"You kids have fun," Hannibal called softly as the four marched out of his office.

# NINETY-FOUR

# ERIC WATSON

Eric Watson opened his eyes on a drizzly gray dawn. HIS leg tortured him, but he was alive, and very grateful for that. Craning his neck, he saw a huge boulder just behind his head, and realized that it had deflected most of the water and kept him from drowning.

Low dark rain clouds were massed in the sky, but what fell now was light, almost refreshing. Eric knew he should be freezing, but not burning up, and he knew he needed help before the fever grew fiercer.

He sat up, stiff and sore, a mass of contusions and bruises, and looked down at his body. He lay in a low depression in the ground, the shallowest of graves. Twenty feet below, water filled the narrow valley between the hills.

He saw that the depression surrounding his body held two or three inches of water. A deformed bulge pushed against his pant leg, halfway to his shin. The material wasn't torn, although there was a bloodstain on it: The skin had broken—hence the fever—but blessedly not enough to let him bleed to death.

He turned his head, wincing as the knot on the back of his skull protested the movement. Far ahead, a hundred feet or more, Eric thought he would find the road.

Scanning left and right, he saw nothing he could brace his leg with: just muddy dirt and rocks. He was going to have to drag himself to the top. He grunted, rolling over, his leg screaming in agony, and put one arm out, and then the other, dragging himself around the boulder, his clawed hands sinking into the mud, pulling it away, instead of pulling him up.

After twenty minutes, he'd moved a total of six feet, but at least he was resting on top of the boulder instead of beneath it.

The rain had ceased and there was enough daylight now to return color to his vision. Hearing raucous cawing, he looked up in time to see a dozen large black crows fly overhead.

And then everything fell silent. Not a drip of water, not a whisper of wind. Everything waited, and Eric did as well.

Then it began.

The deep rumbling was not quite a sound, the vibration not quite movement. A whip-crack followed and the boulder bucked underneath him as the ground moved in one sharp jolt. To his left, a patch of water-sodden earth broke free, crashing down into the water below.

Silence again, and Eric clung to the rock, waiting. Another sharp jolt hit twenty seconds later and his boulder seemed to settle deeper into the muddy earth. But it didn't slide. "Thank you, Lord," Eric whispered as he watched a layer of the sodden mountainside to his left slip down into the water below.

# NINETY-FIVE

# TOM ABERNATHY

Tom Abernathy lowered the brim of his hat and pulled his slicker closed. "I shouldn't be too long," he told Davy Styles as he swung onto Belle's saddle.

"Going to check on Marie?"

"Yep. Tried to call her, but the phones are out. I want to make sure she didn't float away last night or get knocked off her foundations this morning. After I make sure she's okay, I'm going to check on the mustangs."

He rode out into the light but steady rain, feeling just a little guilty about leaving Davy with all the morning chores. But he was more worried than guilty.

"Come on, girl, we'll go cross-country instead of taking the road." Old Madelyn Highway was always a mess when it rained, and going across the ranch land would probably be easier, faster, and if another deluge hit, far safer. Whole pickup trucks had washed off Old Madelyn in lesser storms than this.

Belle, a surefooted animal, seemed to enjoy picking her way across the land, and when Tom glanced toward the highway, he was very glad he'd chosen this way: Several groups of white-robed figures, clustered under their umbrellas, were walking toward town, no doubt under the impression that they could walk on water. "What do you think they're up to, Belle? No good, I'll wager."

They kept moving, Belle stepping carefully around rodent holes. Tom wished he'd been able to connect with Moss Baskerville last night to tell him about the new vandalism and mutilations, but both he and Al Gonzales were out on calls. Ken Landry took the report and promised to give it to Moss first thing, but Tom hadn't heard a peep. He'd tried him again this morning, but the quake had taken out the phones and the electricity. The early morning temblor hadn't felt like much at Tom's reinforced home, but it sure had played hell with the utilities.

Finally Marie's outbuildings became visible, gray on gray. Reaching the stable, Tom found that the barn was still padlocked. Inside, Dorsey barked and the sheep bleated. Alarmed, he rode up to the mobile home.

The back door hung open.

*Dear God.* "Marie!" he yelled as he dismounted and wrapped Belle's reins over the stair railing. "Marie! You in there?"

He climbed the stairs and saw that the door had been forced. "Marie!" he yelled, running inside. "Marie!"

The kitchen looked normal, but when he entered the living room, he saw that the front door hung broken on its hinges. A chair was knocked over, as was one end table. Quickly he checked the bedroom and bathroom, but Marie was nowhere to be found. He moved through the trailer again, noticing muddy footprints too big to be Marie's, several sets of them, then he found a torn bit of tan material on the front-door hinge. But that was all.

Tom walked out front, looking for tracks that might tell him the direction her attackers had come from, but that was a futile effort; the rain had washed everything away, even on the front porch, which was under a couple inches of water.

After shutting the doors as best he could, he mounted Belle, trying not to worry, and wondering about the best course of action.

Notifying the police was his first priority, and he decided the quickest way to do that was to stop at Cassie's on the chance Moss might have gone home for a little shut-eye.

Though his watch claimed only fifteen minutes had passed, it seemed like it took hours to reach Cassie's house. Leaving Belle partially sheltered under the porch, he mounted the steps and knocked, surprised and heartened to see the vandalized door had already been repainted.

"Mommy!" he heard Eve call. "Somebody's at the door. I'll get it!"

"No!" Cassie yelled. "Don't touch that door." Her voice became louder as she approached the door. "Who's there?"

"Tom Abernathy," he said.

"Tom." She opened the door and practically dragged him inside the dark house.

"What's wrong, Cass? You look spooked."

She smiled self-deprecatingly. "Worked myself into a lather, I guess. Before the phones went down, I kept getting hang-up calls, and I think there was someone prowling around last night. Is your electricity out, too?"

"Sure is. Where's Moss?"

"He came by and looked around, but didn't find anything. That was last night. I thought everything was all right this morning until I looked out and saw all those Apostles walking down the road, toward town. They give me the ever-loving creeps."

Tom nodded. "Have you seen Marie?"

"No, why?" she asked, her concern instantly evident. "Somebody broke into her place. She's gone."

"Dear Lord," Cassie whispered. "You better go find Moss."

"I will, as soon as I drop off Belle and get my truck." He peered out the window. "The rain's stopped for the moment. Why don't you and Eve come down and stay at the ranch for a while? The Apostles won't bother you there."

"Thanks, but they haven't bothered us yet."

"They're responsible for the graffiti."

"They're cowards. They only attack when no one's around. If I leave, they'll mess up my paint again."

"I'd feel better if you'd come."

"Like I said, I don't want them messing up my paint again."

"Do you expect to see Moss any time soon?"

"I hope so."

"Then have him drop you off at my place. That way, your car will still be here and they won't know you're gone."

"Can't argue with logic like that." Cassie smiled and laid her hand on his arm. "You'd better get going, and for Christ's sake, be careful. Those Apostles are all over the place." A grin erased the worry from her features. "And I'll bet they'd love to get their hands on you after that little roping exhibition."

"They're probably just going to put in a full day of annoying people," Tom said with a wry smile. "The Apocalypse isn't until tomorrow. Then God'll save 'em the trouble."

"That's not funny, Tom. And if you're not worried, where do you get off worrying about me?"

He held up his hands and shrugged helplessly.

"Men." Cassie shook her head in mock irritation. "Go on, get out of here before you really stick your foot in it. And, Tom?"

"Yes, ma'am?" "Be careful."

"I will if you will."

"Deal," she said and shooed him out the door.

"But don't you take any chances, Cassie," he admonished. "I'll see you later."

"Good luck," she called as he headed out the door.

# NINETY-SIX

# MOSS BASKERVILLE

"**W**ell, you're a tough one to track down," Tom Abernathy said. Moss Baskerville looked up wearily from his coffee cup, glad that Ray had a generator to keep things running during the power outage. He'd have passed out without his morning coffee.

He'd been on the move all night, and as he waited for the waitress to bring him his breakfast, it was good to see a friendly face. Only Abernathy didn't look all that friendly this morning. "It's been one of those nights, Tom. Have a seat."

"Don't mind if I do."

Immediately the little blonde waitress named Christie swooped down on them, trying to smile but obviously still hurting over the death of Rick Spelman. She refilled Moss's cup, then turned to Tom. "Coffee?"

"Yes, please."

"Breakfast?"

"The special, over easy, sausage, well done."

Moss waited until Christie was gone. "Tom, you don't look too happy."

"I came to report a missing person."

"You mean Eric Watson?"

He shook his head. "No. Marie's gone. Her place has been broken into, and there are signs of a struggle." He dug a piece of tan cloth out of his pocket. "Found this on the door."

Moss took the cloth. "You should've left this where you found it. It might be evidence."

Tom looked pained. "I know that, Chief, but with the flooding and the earthquake, I didn't figure anybody was going to get out there soon."

"Unfortunately, you're all too right." He turned the scrap of cloth in his fingers. "This could've come from a pair of pants, a heavy shirt, most anything. You got yourself any theories?"

"I guess I do." Tom stopped talking to stare at the door. "Well, if it isn't one of my suspects now. No, don't look. It's Colonel Dole, and he's headed this way."

Dole passed their table without looking at them and sat down in the next booth, his back to Tom.

"You think he kidnapped Marie?" Moss asked quietly. He couldn't tell for sure, but he thought Dole was probably eavesdropping. After his threats yesterday, Moss didn't want the man to overhear anything.

"Maybe. But the Apostles are at the top of my list." Tom sipped his coffee, then briefly told him about last night's other problems, which definitely pointed a finger at the cult.

In a way, it was a relief, because Baskerville's first thought was that Marie had met the same fate—whatever it was—as Madge Marquay. Of course, there was always the chance the Apostles were behind it all, but at gut level, he didn't believe that was true.

"Another peculiar thing," Tom was saying. "Marie said last night's mutilations were nothing like the previous ones and—"

"You have any earthquake damage this morning?" Moss interrupted, as Dole cocked his head attentively.

Tom hesitated, then caught on. He nodded. "Not much. A couple flowerpots fell, and a picture came off the wall. You?"

"I don't know. With the phones out, I haven't been able to talk to Cassie. I've got to get by there soon and make sure everything's okay. Also, if I don't catch a nap soon, I'll be creating accidents instead of taking reports on them."

"I saw Cassie a little bit ago. She was fine, but nervous as a cat." Tom waited while Christie placed their breakfast platters in front of them. "I invited her down to the ranch, but she wouldn't go."

"Is the flooding getting worse up there?"

"No, she's fine so far, but she doesn't want to leave the house. She's afraid those damned Apostles will do more damage. They're all over the place. I spotted several groups of them walking toward town in their robes. Guess they finally have a use for their umbrellas." He buttered his toast.

"They're *walking* in this weather?"

Tom grimaced, nodding. "Guess it makes 'em feel all sorta warm and martyrish inside. They're gonna have a heckuva laundry load." He forked hash browns into his mouth. "Did she tell you about the phone calls?"

Startled, Moss looked up from his plate. "What phone calls?"

"Before the lines went down, she had a series of hangups."

"She thought she heard a prowler last night, and I got by to check on that, but there was no sign of one. She didn't mention the phone."

"She knows you're busy. Probably didn't want to worry you."

"Damned independent woman," Moss grumbled.

"Tell me about it."

"I wish I could call in some backup, but we're pretty much cut off from everything right now between the phones being down, even long distance—the microwave tower in Barstow got skewed—and everybody being busy taking care of their own." He paused. "The point is, Tom, I promised Alex a search for her assistant, but I can't deliver—the rain's got the rescue people too busy. They've got more problems than we do, over Barstow way. The quake did some real damage there. I'm not too worried about those Apostles—all they'll do is irritate people—but I've got three fresh disappearances now, and very little help."

"Hold it. Three? There's Marie, Eric, and ... ?"

"Little boy name of Billy Cole didn't come home yesterday."

"Christ."

"Plus, we've got the usual traffic problems. There's hardly a Californian born who can drive in the rain. It's like they forget how."

"About the mutilations," Tom said, tipping his head slightly toward Dole. "Maybe we should talk to one of my favorite suspects since he's sitting there eavesdropping on us."

Moss saw Dole's stiff shoulders go stiffer. "Don't worry about the mutilations, Tom," he said uneasily. "They just don't matter right now."

"The hell they don't." Tom spoke softly, but Moss had never heard so much veiled anger in the man's voice before. "They're tied into Marie's vanishing, just like those missing samples are tied into Eric's."

"Tom—"

But Tom wasn't listening. Instead, he stood up and walked two steps, and turned to face Dole. "Mister," he began, his voice surface-friendly, "last night you took some little plastic bags full of blue stuff from a camp in Spirit Canyon. You evidently also kidnapped the young man at the camp, and then maybe you also took off with Marie Lopez. Looked to me like she got dragged out of her bed."

Dole's eyebrow came up. "Samples?"

"Don't bullshit a bullshitter, Colonel."

Dole stood up, probably aiming to intimidate Tom, but it didn't work. Tom had half a foot on him. Dole looked at Moss. "Chief Baskerville, this man is harassing me."

Baskerville stood up. "Did you stop by Alexandra Manderley's camp last night?"

"Certainly not."

"I saw you come out of the canyon," Tom said sourly.

"I travel through the canyon regularly. That means nothing."

"What about Marie Lopez?" Moss asked.

"I don't know the woman. I suggest you bumpkins look elsewhere for your explanations. The U.S. government doesn't kidnap people. Any good American knows that." Dole glared a warning at Baskerville, then turned on his heel and strode out of the diner.

"Tom, what'd you have to go and do that for?" Moss asked.

"Why'd you shush me every time I talked about the mutilations?"

Moss didn't answer. "I gotta go see Cassie." He paused. "Tom, how about letting me deputize you?"

"You know I don't get involved in that sort of folderol."

"You're going out to look for Marie, aren't you?"

"Of course."

"If you've got a badge on, you can ask more questions. Look, Tom, I need help. I'll be useless soon if I don't catch a nap, plus Al's been on duty longer than I have, and he and I are it. I need someone out looking for those people, and you're about the only person I trust with a job like that." He paused. "With *real* bullets in his gun."

"What about Ray, or Carlo, or even Father Mike?"

"Mike's busy setting up a shelter in case things get worse, you can see how busy Ray is, and Carlo just isn't the type to walk up to people and question them."

Tom nodded. "Okay, but just for today."

Moss smiled, feeling the first ounce of relief he'd had for twenty-four hours. "Come on, let's get over to the office. I'll swear you in and find you a badge."

# NINETY-SEVEN

# ERIC WATSON

A t least he wasn't thirsty. Eric Watson still lay on the boulder imbedded in the mountainside, his broken leg throbbing worse than ever. Below, the waterline in the canyon had risen within fifteen feet of his perch. The boulder had, thankfully, remained stationary, though several more landslides had occurred since full daylight. If the rain stayed away, he might be safe.

Above, he'd heard no traffic, nothing except rain falling down, and he knew his luck was running thin. Now, at least, the rain was letting up, and he knew Alex would be looking for him. All he could do now was lie there and wait, and try to stay awake so that he could start yelling the minute he heard a car.

*And what if it's Justin Martin?* Aloud he said, "Then I'm dead."

# NINETY-EIGHT

# TOM ABERNATHY

"Okay," Tom said, pinning on the badge as he sat in Moss Baskerville's murky office. "Why'd you clam up when I asked you about the mutilations?"

"Dole threatened me. Sat right here in that same chair you're in and said I was interfering in military business—in government business, for Christ's sake—and told me to butt out if I didn't want anything to happen to Cassie and Eve."

Tom saw real anger in Moss's eyes. The chief wasn't the type to back off easily or put up with threats. "Are you sure he's for real?"

"I tried to check him out yesterday," Moss explained. "Or rather, Shirley did, but it turns out his files are all sealed. Top secret stuff. That woman's a computer genius—she can get into anything—but she couldn't crack his files. She was lucky to get past the data that claimed he didn't exist."

"So he may not be a regular military type?"

"Maybe he's not military at all," Moss said. "But he's something very, very secret."

"CIA for instance?"

Moss nodded. "That or worse, I expect. The thing is, I know

some police officers who've had the same kind of threats made after they reported UFOs or tried to investigate mutilations. One continued talking about it, and his wife and kids went up in a freak fire. They couldn't even prove arson. Tom, I just want to keep a low profile. I'll be damned if Dole's going to tell me how to do my job, but I can't risk Cassie or Eve until I know enough to make it safe. Besides, looking for the missing people is far more important right now."

"Yes." Tom leaned forward, elbows on Moss's desk. He studied the chief. "See why I thought maybe that son of a bitch is behind the disappearances of Marie and Eric?"

"You better hope he isn't. The bastard's a brick wall."

"How about a little police brutality?"

Baskerville eyed him. "I do believe you mean that."

"Maybe I do."

"What's gotten into you, Tom? You've always been the big peacemaker around here. I didn't think it was even possible to piss you off."

"It takes a lot, Moss. A hell of a lot."

"It's Marie, isn't it?"

Tom hesitated. "It's Marie, the others, my horse, her animals. Hell, we're losing our town."

"You want to go with me out to the Apostles' compound and have a look around? I think we might find some answers there."

"You think they'll let us in? Without a warrant?"

"Sinclair told me I was welcome." Moss leaned forward. "Funny thing about him. I thought he'd be the asshole of the century, but he seemed like a nice guy. Sincere."

Tom laughed bitterly. "You're pulling my leg." "You're the leg-puller in this town, Abernathy."

"Well then, Sinclair's a bigger one." Tom shook his head. "That's how he makes his living. Don't be taken in by all that charisma, Moss."

"You want to see for yourself?"

"That I do. Have you checked this guy out, or is he top secret, like Dole?"

"Checked him, but there wasn't much to learn. No arrest record. He went to divinity school, then quit to become a magician."

"Well, that sorta fits, doesn't it?" Tom stood up. "A magician and a minister in one package. That's a little scary."

Moss shook his head. "It is, at that." He rose. "Let's go." Tom nodded. "I want to check Marie's on the way."

Following Moss's cruiser out of town, Tom saw little clusters of Apostles walking up and down the streets pressing flyers into people's hands.

Only a few spatters of raindrops fell as they drove up muddy Old Madelyn. They turned west on Thunder Road, and by the time they pulled into Marie's driveway, their windshields were dry. While Moss checked the trailer for clues, Tom fed the animals, carefully relocking the stable before joining Moss.

"Find anything?"

Baskerville shook his head. "You're right about a struggle and a break-in. There was more than one of them, or they wouldn't have broken both front and back doors. Probably stormed the place."

Tom left his pickup in Marie's driveway and climbed into Moss's passenger seat. "You think that makes it more likely to be the Apostles?"

"You got me." Moss pulled out of the driveway. "At least it makes it less likely that she's been taken by Madge's attacker."

"Well, that's something." Tom held his hands clasped tightly in his lap, afraid they'd shake if he didn't. He never should have let Marie talk him into leaving her alone.

"Back in the diner," Tom began, "I started to tell you that these mutilations were different than the ones in the hills."

Moss glanced at him. "How so?"

"Marie said those were clean and bloodless. These were crude, lots of blood."

"Christ. Copycat mutilations. That's all we need. Damn, look at that."

The gates to the compound were closed and two Apostles stood guard. Moss rolled down his windows as one of them, a young woman, approached.

"Can I help you?"

"I hope so. I'd like to see Mr. Sinclair, please."

She looked troubled. "He's in retreat and can't be disturbed."

"I need to see him, ma'am. It's an emergency."

"Well, I'll try." She walked back inside the gate, locked it behind her, then climbed in a little golf-cart-type contraption and drove through the parking lot, disappearing behind the church.

Five minutes passed. Ten. Fifteen. Just as Tom was running out of any kind of patience, the cart reappeared, carrying a passenger.

"That's not Sinclair," Moss grunted as the cart approached. "He's tall and thin, with a beard."

This guy was a bald dumpling man in a gray suit, the only unrobed Apostle in sight. Moss and Tom got out of the cruiser and walked up to the gate as the man approached, a jack-o'-lantern grin carved on his face.

"Chief Baskerville, it's a pleasure to meet you," he said from behind the chain link, making no move to unlock the gate. "I'm Elder Apostle Caine. What can I do for you?"

"We'd like to see James Sinclair," Baskerville told him.

"I'm afraid he's meditating right now. I'm in command today. How can I help you?"

Tom disliked the butterball in gray from the moment he laid eyes on him. He looked like the kind of man who would sell his own mother a bad insurance policy, the kind that would ask about your health and after you tell him you're dying of cancer, clap you on the back and say, "That's just great, Tom! Great! Now, let me tell you about this bridge I can sell you, cheap!"

"We'd like to come in and have a look around, Mr. Caine," Baskerville was saying.

"I'm afraid that's not possible right now. You can come back for the Prophet's sermon tomorrow night, if you like. Perhaps he can talk to you afterward."

"Mr. Caine, yesterday your boss invited me to talk to whomever and go wherever I wanted in the compound. Why aren't you following his orders?"

Tom could see the cunning beneath Caine's helpless smile. "The Prophet told me nothing about inviting you here."

"Then call him," Tom said.

"I can't do that. He's incommunicado."

"You're telling us that he's here but you can't disturb him?" Baskerville asked testily.

"I *won't* disturb him, sir. For anyone."

"What do you know about the disappearance of Eric Watson from a camp in Spirit Canyon last night?"

"Nothing. I've never heard of the man."

Tom thought he was telling the truth, but you could never be sure with sidewinders like him.

Moss cleared his throat and asked patiently, "What do you know about the disappearance of Marie Lopez?"

"Nothing. Nothing at all. Who's she?"

"You're lying," Tom said, stepping forward. "You're lying, you dirty, low-down—"

Baskerville firmly grabbed Tom's arm as the Apostle scurried back from the fence. "Tom, hold it." He glared at Caine. "You're forcing me to get a search warrant. It would be much easier if you just let us take a look around. Or speak to your boss."

"Easier for you," Caine said. "For both of us. Be sure of that."

Caine didn't reply, but turned and seated himself in the cart. "Let's go," he ordered.

"Son of a bitch," Moss muttered as they returned to the cruiser.

"He's lying," Tom said, trying to keep the rage he felt from seeping into his voice.

Baskerville drove towards Marie's. "I don't think he knows where Watson is."

"No, me either. But he sure as hell knows something about

Marie." He looked toward the mountains. "Maybe they dumped her up there."

Baskerville pulled up behind Tom's truck. "Maybe. You going to take a look?"

"I'd like to. What about that search warrant?"

Moss shook his head. "Sky's clearing up. I can send Shirley, and get my night clerk to take over for her. He can use the overtime. Why don't you find Alex Manderley and make sure she hasn't heard from Eric yet, then get your search party together to look for him and Marie. And the kid, too, if he's in the Madelyns."

Tom nodded. "Okay. But when that warrant comes back, I'd like to go with you. Unless I find Marie first."

"Check with me in the late afternoon. It's going to take a while on a Saturday, especially with the mess in Barstow. I'm going to go by Cassie's and catch a half-hour nap. Then I'll drop her and Eve at your place, if you don't mind. There're just too many of those sheet-wearing buffoons running around." He smiled slightly. "If some of those Apostles come to her door, she's likely to do something to 'em. She's got a temper," he added fondly.

"That she does," Tom agreed, opening his truck door. "See you later."

# NINETY-NINE

# MARIE LOPEZ

Somebody was operating a jackhammer in Marie Lopez's head, but she resisted the urge to moan. Vaguely she recalled waking earlier, and when she'd made a sound, some woman with a harsh voice had stuck a chloroformed rag over her face.

Without raising her head, Marie opened her eyes. She was tied to a straight wooden chair, and in the dim light she saw that nylon rope secured her wrists in her lap, and her ankles below. More of the narrow rope bit painfully into her waist, forcing her back hard against the slats of the chair. For a long moment she listened as she stared at the oak floor.

Silence. Slowly she lifted her head. What little light there was came from an underpowered fluorescent fixture overhead. No one appeared to be in the room. The walls were white, and the room was bare except for a long coatrack that held white satin gowns with blue trim. *Choir robes!* She was in a choir room, but it sure as hell wasn't in the Catholic church.

*What in hell would the Apostles want with me?* Not that it mattered now. What did matter was getting loose. She looked at the ropes around her wrists and smiled to herself. The idiots had tied them over the thick cloth of her black sweatshirt.

Patiently she began to work at freeing herself.

# ALEXANDRA MANDERLEY

"I think the rain's stopped for now," Alex Manderley said as she gazed at the Madelyns from Carlo Pelegrine's upstairs window. Dark clouds still draped the sky and shrouded the tops of the mountains, but a few ragged patches of blue had appeared. "It's time I get out there and start searching for Eric."

"You're not thinking of driving into the canyon yet?" Carlo stood behind her, his hands resting gently on her shoulders. "It's not safe."

She turned to face him. "I know, but I at least need to drive down to the police station and see about the rescue party." She paused. "I should have been down there hours ago."

"It's not your fault the electricity went out and the alarm clock didn't go off." As he spoke, the overhead light blazed to life.

Despite her worries, she'd fallen into a deep sleep the minute she'd crawled into bed last night, and except for a few groggy moments during the earthquake, she didn't wake up until long after the sun came up. Carlo had tried to insist she take his bed while he slept on the couch, but despite his confessions, she felt safe with him and insisted they share the bed. When she finally woke up this morning they had been spooned together, his arms protectively around her, and she lay there far too long, relishing the warmth of him, the sound and feel of his soft breath against the back of her neck. It was the first time in her life she'd ever actually slept with another human being, and she loved it. Now she felt guilty for indulging herself while Eric was lost.

"At least have a little breakfast," he said. "It's going to be a long day. You'll need it."

How could this gentle man ever hurt anyone? Looking at him filled her stomach with butterflies again. It wasn't that she didn't believe his story—she did—but she also knew that whatever he was now, he was no killer. The killer was dead and gone, and she realized that she loved what remained. She took his hands. "A quick bite would be good, but let me do it."

One corner of his mouth crooked up. "Eric said you can't boil water. Is that true?"

"I can boil water," she said.

"Can you make an omelet?" The smile broadened.

"Well ... I can operate a toaster."

"Okay, you're in charge of toast. Why don't you see if the phone's working, then go downstairs and get your clothes out of the dryer while I start the omelets?" He paused. "Did you hear that?"

"What?" She turned.

"Horses. Look." He had turned and was pointing out the window.

Tom Abernathy, unmistakable on his silver mare, was leading a saddled chestnut horse. Behind him were five more riders in slickers and western hats. A moment later, they heard the downstairs bell ring. "Excuse me," Carlo said, and headed for the stairs.

Alex pulled his terry robe tighter around herself, then followed, remaining out of sight in the shadows of the stairs.

"Tom, hello," Carlo said after he opened the door. "You're wearing a badge," he added in a startled tone.

"Moss is hard up for help. He twisted my arm."

"What's going on?"

"I thought maybe Alex was here?" He nodded at her truck.

Alex stepped into view, mildly amused by the surprise on Tom's face when he saw her attire. "I'm here."

"We're riding up into the hills to look for Eric and Marie."

"Marie?" Carlo asked.

"She's missing too."

Alex heard the pain in his voice as he explained what had happened. "Tom, I'm sorry."

"We'll find them," he said stolidly. "You mentioned that you ride. I brought along my gentlest mare in case you want to come along."

"Yes, absolutely." She looked at Carlo.

"I can manage a nice flat trail," he said. "But otherwise, I'm hopeless. Tom knows."

The cowboy nodded. "Gospel truth. You have any earthquake damage?"

"Just the mess you see here." He gestured at some packs of incense, books, and cards scattered on the floor. "Nothing serious."

"I'm going to get dressed. I'll be out in a minute." Alex went into the laundry room and quickly slipped into her clothes and shoes, then returned. "I'm ready."

Carlo handed her a rain poncho and a cowboy hat. She slipped the poncho over her head, then put on the hat. It fit perfectly. "I can't quite picture you in this," she told him.

"I'm afraid I don't wear it much."

"City boy," Tom chided. "Let's go."

"The keys to the Bronco are on your dresser," Alex told Carlo after they walked out onto the porch. "If you need to go somewhere, use it, please."

"Thanks. I doubt we'll do any business today, but I'll probably stick around here anyway. Clean up the place, see if anyone else needs help." He glanced at Tom. "When do you think you'll be back?"

"Barring heavy rain, after we find them. I'll be back by this afternoon either way. Moss is sending someone for a search warrant to get into the Apostles' compound, and he should have it by then."

Surprised, Alex asked, "The Apostles? Why would they take Eric?"

"Don't rightly know, but they're prime suspects in Marie's disappearance."

Alex turned and kissed Carlo lightly on the lips. "I'll see you later?"

"Count on it."

## CASSIE HALLOWAY

"You sure you don't want to nap another hour?" Cassie asked, handing Moss his gun belt.

He took the belt and kissed her. "I'd love to, Cass, but it'll have to wait. You want me to drop you and Eve off at Tom's?"

"You said he's out with the search party."

"He is, but Davy's there to let you in."

Although she knew that going to Tom's was probably the smart thing to do, she hated deserting her little house. "The rain's slacked off, and not a single Apostle has come to the door. Do you really think it's necessary?"

"I'd sure feel better knowing you were there, Cass. Until the phones are working again, you couldn't call for help if you did need it." He folded her in his arms. "You and Marie are the only people living so far from town. Marie's missing and you've been vandalized. That's why I want you to go. Besides, you know how much Eve loves it at Tom's."

"You're right. We'll go, but I'll take my car."

"I thought—"

"It's easy to repaint the house, not so easy to repaint the car."

"Good." He kissed her nose. "Love you."

"Love you too. Take care of yourself, babe."

She stood at the door and watched him drive away before entering Eve's tiny bedroom. "We're going to Tom's as soon as I finish the dishes. Pick out some toys to take along, and get your jacket, boots, and raincoat."

"Goody!" Eve trilled. Immediately she began digging in her toy box.

In the kitchen, Cassie began washing the lunch dishes. As she put away the last glass, Eve came in, carrying her favorite rag doll. "Is that all you're going to take, sweetheart?"

"Huh-uh. The rest's by the front door."

"The rest? Did you bring everything in your toy box?"

Eve giggled. "No, Mommy. Only my ball, and my Candyland, and my Barbie and her clothes, and my horse models, and three coloring books—"

"And your crayons," Cassie finished. "That's fine, sweetie. Why don't you color a picture for a few minutes while I finish up and change my clothes."

"Okay!" Eve dashed from the room.

Drying her hands, Cassie stared out the kitchen window. Outside, rain was just beginning to fall again. She sighed. She had hoped that it had stopped for good; her house wasn't far enough from Old Madelyn Road to be safe if things got really bad.

Hearing the low roar of an engine as a vehicle pulled up the side of the house, she smiled. "Moss, you old worrywart." He'd probably come back to see her safely to Tom's place.

"Mommy!" Eve called, running into the kitchen. "Somebody's here."

"Not Daddy?"

"Huh-uh. It's a bunch of people dressed like ghosts."

She laughed. "Ghosts?"

"Uh-huh."

Cassie dropped the towel on the counter as someone began

pounding on the front door. She went into the living room and peeked out the window overlooking the driveway. "It's those damned Apostles," she hissed, seeing a white-clad figure sitting in the driver's seat of a muddy white van.

"Open up, whore!" a man yelled. The hammering on the door increased.

She ran to the phone and snagged it up. Still no dial tone. "Damn! Evie, Eve, come here, baby."

The little girl, eyes wide, still holding her rag doll, ran to her, and Cassie scooped her into her arms as the Apostles began breaking the front door down. "Don't cry, baby," Cassie soothed. "Be brave for Mommy."

Frantically she glanced around as the door began to crack. There was nowhere to hide—they had to run.

"Whore! We know you're in there!"

Wood cracked sickeningly as Cassie opened the back door and carried Eve out into the rain. She started running across the dooryard, hearing shouts and heavy footsteps behind her.

Then she was tackled from behind.

She fell in the mud, rolling to protect her daughter, then someone was trying to yank Eve from her arms. The girl clung to her neck, screaming and sobbing in her ear.

"Let go, whore!" A man in white yanked on her wrist. "Let go!"

Another kicked her in the ribs, once, twice, a third time, so hard that it knocked the breath out of her. The man at her wrist began prying her fingers away. He got one up and yanked it back until she felt the bone snap.

"No!" she screamed, trying to wrap herself around Eve and roll over to protect her.

"Listen, Evie," she whispered urgently, "when I say 'Go,' you run as fast as you can. Go to Tom's house, or Madland, just don't let them catch you. When I say 'Go,' remember."

They grabbed her hair, pulled it, yanking her head back, while other hands turned her onto her back. Vaguely she saw horrible distorted faces with bright mad eyes as they wrenched her daughter from her. Cassie felt no pain, only fury, as her arm was twisted behind her and she was yanked to her feet.

There were a dozen of them circling her, both men and women, poking her with their umbrellas. One man held Eve by her arms as she struggled to get to her mother. In vain Cassie kicked backwards at the man holding her.

"Stop struggling, whore." An old man with icy eyes and a hawk nose stepped forward. He was wearing military fatigues, no robe. "You can't escape us."

He turned, looking around the circle of zealous faces. "This is the Whore of Babylon. Look upon the evil!" He came nose to nose with her and she balled her free hand into a fist as he reached out and tore her shirt open. "Look upon the whore, covered with the devil's calling card. Six six six. This is the devil's bride."

Cassie's fist shot out so fast that the old bastard barely saw it coming. She socked him in the gut, but not hard enough. She cried out in pain as the one holding her wrenched her arm up.

The old man caught his breath. "Whore, you dare to touch an Elder Apostle! You dare to touch a man of God!"

"You're no man of God," Cassie spat. "You're a tiny little freak. You're a stupid fanatic and you can go to hell!"

"Campbell," the old man said calmly. "Show her the way."

A broad-shouldered man stepped forward, a perverted smile plastered across his face. He raised his huge, meaty fist and drove it into Cassie's gut. She fell.

"Mommy!" Eve screamed as she broke free, running to her mother.

"Go!" She could barely breathe, but she screamed the word as she dragged herself to her knees and launched herself at the old man, clinging to his leg, biting it through the filthy camouflage fatigues. Eve hesitated only a fraction of a second, then ran for all she was worth. One of the men gave chase, but tripped on his muddy robe. Eve zigzagged, eluding another and another.

Then Campbell tried to pull Cassie off the old man, but she held on harder, biting until she felt the flesh give and she tasted blood. He screamed, and Cassie kicked and flailed. Pulling herself free of the man's leg, she screamed, "Go! Go! Go!" then sank her teeth back into the old man's flesh.

They tried to pull her off their leader, yanking one of her arms back, but before they could get the other, she made a grab for the old man's crotch.

*Bull's-eye!* The man screamed as she dug her fingers into his scrotum.

"Stop her!" he screamed in a voice an octave higher than he'd used before. "Stop her!"

As they fell upon her, she couldn't see Eve anywhere. *Please, God, let her live. Please let her live.*

# JUSTIN MARTIN

Justin pulled into the nearly empty parking lot behind Madland and parked near Carlo's shop, right next to Alex Manderley's Bronco, thinking that the fortune-teller must have pulled it around back after she left. He knew from asking around that Alex had ridden off with Tom Assholenathy and a bunch of the stuntmen to look for Eric Nerdface. *Good fucking luck!*

Justin hadn't bothered keeping his appointment with Hannibal Caine because that was small potatoes compared to what he and the Peeler were going to do. Last night he'd heard the Voice again when the town was blacked out, and it told him that what he planned was far more important than what the Apostles were doing.

He trotted along the walkway to the main entrance and onto the Main Street sidewalk, keeping under the awnings as a steady sprinkle began again. Though Madland was open, it was virtually empty, and many of the shopkeepers hadn't bothered to open. When he had showed up for work this morning in the pouring rain, it had been a cinch to talk Old Man Marquay into taking the day off. He promised to open up if the sun came out, and that meant he now had the day free.

Carlo's shop was closed, but the shop lights were on. He knocked on the door, and Carlo opened up. He wore a green butcher's apron and held a broom and dustpan. His pleasant expression curdled when he saw Justin. "What do you want?"

"I want to talk to you."

Carlo blocked the doorway for a long moment, then finally stood aside and gestured him inside, locking the door after him. "This way," he ordered, and led him into his reading room. "Sit down."

Justin had never been in here before, and he looked around, impressed with the rich, dark colors, the candlesticks and stacks of cards, the Tiffany lamp in the corner. He sat at the table and reached for the crystal ball.

"Don't touch that."

Justin hesitated, then withdrew his hand.

Carlo folded his arms and leaned against a rolltop desk. "What do you need to talk about?"

"Tonight. What we're, I mean you're, going to do to Alex Manderley."

"Peel her," the man said slowly. "What else is there to discuss?"

"You're going to do it?"

"Yes."

"And you're going to teach me?" he added hopefully.

"You may watch. Whether you can learn or not is a question that remains unanswered."

The doorbell rang, and Carlo stood. "Come back tonight at midnight. You may go now."

Justin rose, in awe. The man was a king, a leader among men, with a voice so commanding that Manderley would probably peel her own skin from her bones if he asked. Even Jim-Bob Sinclair couldn't match it. "Midnight," he repeated, following Carlo back to the door.

"Hello, Carlo," Old Lady Quigley said as he opened the door. "Might I get a reading today?" She paused, spying Justin's smiling face.

"Certainly," Carlo replied, his voice entirely different now, soft and respectful. "Justin was just leaving, weren't you, Justin?"

"Yes, sir. Have a nice day, Mrs. Quigley." He trotted toward his car.

Inside, he turned on the radio. "This is Diane Rice with the desert headlines. Flash flood warnings are in effect for the next twelve hours or until further notice. In Barstow, several homes have been heavily damaged by the storm. An earthquake measuring four point four on the Richter scale hit the high desert early this morning, causing only minor damage and spotty power outages and telephone problems. No injuries have been reported, but Cal Tech seismologists say that it was not, as previously thought, an aftershock of the 1992 Landers quake. Now back to Charlie Ray and the smooth sounds of Sheena Easton—"

Justin slipped his Doors cassette into the player and thought about the Peeler. He wanted to impress the man tonight, more than he'd ever wanted anything. He wanted the Peeler to allow him to wield the knife under his watchful eye, he wanted to make him proud. He wondered if he should bring him another offering. Yes, maybe he should. *Something that will really impress him. Something he'll appreciate.*

"Come on, Christie, light my fire," he sang as he headed for New Madelyn.

## ONE HUNDRED THREE

## EVE HALLOWAY

When her mother yelled, "Go," Eve had run as fast as she could, straight to her favorite hiding place—up the little apple tree in the front yard and onto the front porch roof. She'd quickly crawled into the narrow space where the house's eaves overhung the porch roof, and there she'd remained, watching as the bad people hunted for her.

When they drove away, she crawled out and ran to the backyard, then into the house. Her mother was gone. Eve had tried to call Daddy after that, but the phone wouldn't work, so she'd decided to do as her mother said, and go to Tom's.

Leaving the house, she found that it was raining again, harder every minute. She'd never walked to his house before, but she thought she knew how to get to it if she stayed on the road.

But there was too much water on the highway to walk on it, and she fell down twice as the rain began pouring. Once, she was almost swept away, but she finally made it to the roadside, and though she didn't even know which side of the street she was on, she started walking. It was raining so hard now that she couldn't even tell where the mountains were to make sure she was going in the right direction.

She walked forever, more and more worried about her mother. Those ghost people were hurting her, making her scream, and all Eve wanted to do was find Tom and make him take her to her daddy. He'd find her and put the bad people in jail.

More time passed and she couldn't find Tom's, or Madland or anything. As panic welled up in her, she heard an engine somewhere behind her. Eve whirled, saw headlights coming at her, not from the road but right across the desert. Startled, she halted, staring as the lights came closer and closer. She couldn't move.

Suddenly a horn honked and the vehicle jerked to a halt, just a foot from her.

"What the hell?" cried a man's voice. She could hardly hear him because of the rain. Realizing it might be one of the ghost men, she turned and ran blindly into the storm.

"Hey! Stop!"

She ran faster, then her foot caught in a rabbit hole and she fell on her face in the mud. Crying, she struggled to rise, but suddenly hands lifted her up from behind.

"No!" She screamed the word, struggling and scratching at the hands, but they wouldn't let go. "No! No!"

"I'm not going to hurt you!" the stranger said in her ear. "No!" She kicked frantically.

The man lowered her to her feet and turned her to face him. "What's wrong, honey? What are you doing out here all by yourself?"

As he knelt before her, she looked at him for the first time, calming as she took in the blue uniform under an open trench coat. "Are you a policeman?" she asked hopefully.

The man hesitated, then took a soggy handkerchief from his pocket and wiped the mud from her face. "I'm a kind of policeman," he told her.

"Are you my daddy's new cop?"

"No, honey. Can you tell me your name?"

"What's yours?" she countered, on guard.

"Colonel—that is, Officer Dole."

"I'm Eve Halloway and bad men took my mommy." Tears sprang to her eyes. "Ghost men, and they punched her. They hurt her." The tears flowed down her cheeks. "They took her away." Throwing her arms around Officer Dole's neck, she let herself collapse against him. "Get my daddy! Please get my daddy!"

The officer carried her to his green jeep and settled her in the passenger seat, buckled her in. "Who are the ghost men, Eve?"

She hiccuped and tried to stop sobbing. "They had white sheets like ghosts."

"Apostles."

She nodded. "Except one was dressed like a soldier." "Like me?" he asked, sounding surprised.

"Huh-uh. Like GI Joe."

"I see. Your mama will be all right, don't worry." He turned the key and the engine roared to life, but the jeep wouldn't go. He tried again, then turned off the ignition.

"The wheels are stuck," he told her as he climbed out and walked to the rear of the vehicle. "I've got a shovel back here. We'll be on our way in a jiffy."

Hearing shoveling sounds over the rain, Eve let herself out of the jeep and came around to watch Officer Dole. All around, the desert was a gray, rainy blur, then she thought she saw something move. Squinting harder, she was sure there were several people coming toward her. "Officer Dole!" She tugged his pant leg and he looked at her, eyebrows raised.

"The ghost men are coming." She pointed.

Pulling a gun like her father's from a holster under his arm, he stared at the approaching figures. "Eve," he said as he pulled a dark green blanket from the back of the jeep, "I want you to get on the floor of the backseat and wrap this around you, your head, too, then stay very still and quiet until I tell you it's okay to come out. Do you understand?"

Lower lip trembling, she nodded and let him lift her into the jeep. He began tucking the soggy blanket around her. "Be brave."

"Then we can get my daddy?"

"Yes." He pulled the blanket over her. "Don't move."

Nothing happened for a moment, then she heard the horrible voice of the old man dressed like a soldier. "Got a problem?" Trembling, terrified, she listened.

"Stuck in the mud," Officer Dole replied gruffly. "What are you doing out here?" asked the bad old man.

"Military business. I might ask the same of you."

"God's business, sir. Have you been saved?"

There was a long pause. "You people move along," Dole ordered. "I've got work to do."

"He's a sinner!" rasped a woman's voice.

"Do you repent your sins?" called another man.

"Okay, folks." That was Officer Dole. "I'm armed and prepared to shoot if you don't move along. You're interfering with government business."

"Stone him!" cried the old man. "Kill the sinner."

First something hit the side of the jeep, then a shot rang out, and another. A woman screamed. Something else clanged against the jeep, then a hailstorm of muted thumps, and she heard Officer Dole groan in pain. The bad people were all around, very near, and someone yelled, "Shoot him!"

"No!" cried the old man. "Put him in his vehicle. We'll free it, then clamp the accelerator down." She heard a seat belt click. "It'll look like he crashed."

Suddenly the jeep rocked as they threw Officer Dole into the driver's seat in front of her. Eve held her breath as the seat jiggled against her. *Please don't let them find me!* She repeated the prayer over and over, listening to Dole's faint grunts and groans.

"Okay, Campbell, you other men, push!" ordered the old man.

The jeep rocked back and forth, and under the blanket, Eve clung tenaciously to the bar that ran beneath the rear seats. Suddenly the vehicle jolted forward and the rocking ceased.

"This is for the Prophet!" the old man cackled, as she heard the engine roar to life. "Hand me that stone there. No, the big one." Eve jumped as the rock was dropped into the jeep. Abruptly the engine roared loudly, like at the start of a race.

"Is it in gear?" someone asked.

"Yes," spat the old man. "Get back. I'm releasing the parking brake ... *Now!*"

The vehicle lurched forward, engine thundering over the sounds of the storm. Eve held on as the jeep moved faster and faster, rocking and bumping across the desert floor. Suddenly one side jolted down lower than the other and then they were rolling over and over. The blanket flew free, but Eve hung on, hands clenched around the seat bar, legs drawn up, feet braced.

It seemed to roll forever, then there was a sick crunching sound and the jeep abruptly came to a halt on its side, then rocked back onto its wheels. The engine died and Eve waited a long moment, listening to the hiss of steam and soft squeaks and groans.

She let go of the bar and tried to open the low door, but it was stuck, so she scrambled over the side, sore and bruised but unhurt. Glancing around, she saw no sign of the bad men.

"Officer Dole?" she asked, seeing the slumped figure in the front seat.

He answered with a moan. Hesitantly she stepped to the driver's door and tried to look at him, but his head was against the steering wheel. Bracing herself, she pushed his head and shoulders back against the seat. Blood seeped from his mouth and one ear, only to be washed away by the rain. His face was lumpy and scratched and there was a huge welt rising on his forehead where it had hit the steering wheel.

"Officer Dole?"

His eyes opened slowly, and he tried to reach a hand out to her, but it was all twisted and funny-looking, and with an agonized grunt, he let it flop into his lap. "Eve," he rasped through cut, swollen lips. "You're okay?"

She nodded. "Can we go?"

"Not me." He paused, breathing heavily. Blood oozed from his nose. "You have to go, Eve. It's not safe for you to stay."

"Alone?" she asked, lip trembling.

"You're a brave girl," he managed. "You can do it. We're close to the park. You can get help there. Okay?"

She stared at him, at his broken body, cringing as she saw one leg was bent unnaturally forward at the knee. "Okay."

"Go slowly, try to keep near bushes and rocks where you can hide, and watch out for the Apostles. Hide if you see them. Do you understand?"

Fear growing, she stared at him.

His eyes blazed suddenly. "Eve, you have to do this to help your mother. She's depending on you! You must be brave!" The last words trailed off and Dole's eyes closed briefly.

"Officer Dole?" she asked, touching his sleeve. The eyes fluttered open.

"I don't want to leave you."

"It's okay."

"Are you dying?"

He looked at her a long time, even though his eyelids kept trying to close. "Not if I can help it," he whispered at last.

She nodded, and turned to go.

"Eve?" he rasped.

She turned back. "Yes?"

"Tell your father—" He coughed, spraying blood-flecked foam. "Tell your father I'm not—I'm not the bad guy."

"Okay," she said as his chin dropped onto his chest.

She watched him a long moment, then began walking in the rain, unable to see more than ten feet in front of her, praying that she was going in the right direction.

# ONE HUNDRED FOUR
## MARIE LOPEZ

Marie loosened the rope that tied her to the chair and sighed with relief. While she was working on the bindings, the Amazon Apostle had come in twice, and both times Marie had passed inspection. Now, finally, she was free.

For at least an hour, she'd been hearing the echo of voices in the church. A man—it didn't sound like Sinclair—spoke in muted but thunderous tones, and sometimes there was singing. Marie hoped the service or whatever it was continued long enough for her to escape this place.

Just as she started to rise, she heard a key in the lock. The woman was back and there was no time to do anything but put her hands and feet together and slump over in the chair. She hoped the woman wouldn't notice the ropes she'd kicked behind the chair.

"Okay, bitch, I know you're awake." The woman's harsh voice drowned out the sermonizing, and Marie kept her head down as the woman crossed the room.

"Wake up, whore!" The woman grabbed Marie by the hair and yanked her head back. "Wake up!"

Enraged, Marie managed to keep her eyes closed, her face expressionless.

Suddenly the woman slapped her across the cheek, and that was it.

Marie exploded out of the chair. The startled Apostle let go of her hair, and before she could fight, Marie was on her, bowling her over, fighting like a cat fending off a bulldog.

The woman was built like a small tank, all steroidal muscle and sinew. Marie scratched and bit, her entire body in constant motion so that the square-jawed Amazon couldn't get a good hold on her. She pulled her arm back, made a fist, and brought it down, smashing the Amazon's nose.

The woman howled as Marie leaped away and sprinted to the door. As she yanked it open, the woman was already rising, blood streaming down her face.

Marie ran down the hall to a short flight of stairs, which dead-ended into two doors. The first one she tried was locked. The second wasn't, and seeing the Amazon come into the hall, she jerked it open and ran in.

Suddenly she was in the church, on the rostrum, a dozen faces staring at her. A round, bald man at the podium turned toward her and she ran straight at him, right into his arms. He stared at her in surprise, his hands closing on her shoulders.

"Please!" she cried. "Help me!" Simultaneously she slammed her knee into his groin. He gasped, letting go, and she raced toward an open door on the far side of the rostrum.

"Stop her!" screamed the Amazon.

Before she could reach the door, two robed figures moved to block the exit. Marie feinted, left, then right. The church was nearly empty, and if she could get past these people, she could get out the doors at the back of the church. But the small congregation got to its feet, blocking her way, as the Amazon yelled again. She turned, saw another door on the other side of the rostrum, and sprinted toward it.

"Get her!" cried the bald man.

Out of the corner of her eye, she saw the Amazon barrel across the rostrum. Marie kept running, but the woman suddenly tackled her, toppling her to the floor.

"Got you, you little whore!"

Hands closed around her neck, pressing into her flesh. Marie, trapped under two hundred pounds, kicked, turning blindly to claw at the woman's face. Spots danced before her eyes.

"Don't harm her!" the bald man ordered as more hands grabbed her hands and ankles. "Bring her to me!"

Someone pried the Amazon's hands from her neck, then two men pulled her to her feet and dragged her up to the pulpit. The bald man, his round face beet-colored, had his hands protectively over his groin. He smiled sickly at her. "Too bad you're an unrepentant heathen. You'd make an excellent warrior for the Living Savior."

"Go to hell." Marie spat at his face. The men tightened their grips.

"Yes, it's too bad," the man repeated.

Behind him, a woman moaned. Marie looked up and gasped. On either side of the huge rostrum were two crosses, perhaps eight feet tall. The right was empty, but there was a body tied to the left. Cassie Halloway, her shirt torn away to reveal her tattoos, stared at her through swollen eyes. Blood dripped from a cut on her cheek. She moaned again.

"Cassie!" Marie screamed.

"Elder Caine!" The beaky old man in wet camouflage fatigues who'd been at her house entered through a side door, followed by several others wearing sodden robes. He trotted up to Caine, and spoke so softly that Marie barely made out his words. "The child is still missing."

"Damn," Caine whispered, then looked out at the faces surrounding him. "Okay, we know the crosses will support the weight, so Campbell and Deitz, take the tattooed whore down and lock her up. Make sure she doesn't die. The rest of you, go find your squad leaders and get back to work."

The old man in cammies drew a pistol and aimed it at Marie. "You two may wait outside," he told the Apostles holding her.

Caine waited until the church was empty to speak again. "You've searched everywhere for the child?"

"Everywhere we can without drawing attention to ourselves. She ran out into the desert and we lost sight of her. She could be anywhere. If she gets to the park, she'll report us, and we can't take that chance."

Caine shook his head. "I can't believe a dozen people could lose a little girl, Elder Blandings."

"Neither can I," Blandings growled.

*"You* were in charge, Eldo. *You* are responsible."

The old man looked at his hands. "We'll continue to try to locate her."

"Do that." Caine glanced at Cassie as the Amazon and another Apostle undid her bonds. "Find the girl and get us an alternate. She's in bad shape, and that's your fault as well, Eldo. If she dies, we need another."

Blandings nodded at Marie. "What about her?"

"She'll do nicely. Try to show the same restraint on your next choice."

Marie aimed a gob of saliva at Caine's face. "What the hell are you talking about, you crazy bastard?" she demanded.

"Please, no spitting, young woman. You'll find out soon enough."

"Hannibal," Blandings said. "I have someone else in mind."

Caine raised an eyebrow. "Who?"

"The man who humiliated me. Tom Abernathy."

"He was here with Baskerville this morning," Caine told him. "Looking for her." He nodded toward Marie.

*Thank God they know I'm gone!* Marie was filled with renewed hope.

"Does that matter?" the old man asked.

"Yes," Caine said firmly. "They're coming back with a search warrant."

"What does Prophet Sinclair say? Will he let them in?"

"No, Eldo. This is a church, a sanctuary, and we've doubled the guards. No one will enter unless we let them. The point, however, is that Abernathy is too big a risk."

"He humiliated me," Blandings growled. "He did the same to Campbell. He deserves to die."

"And he will, when the Horsemen ride. Be patient, Eldo. Satisfy yourself with someone else."

Eldo Blandings was looking at Caine, not Marie, and the gun barrel lowered slightly. Marie took a slow deep breath as the Apostles continued to argue. The barrel dropped another fraction of an inch, wavered.

Marie kicked suddenly, her foot connecting with the pistol. It flew from the old man's hand and slid across the floor, Marie leaping after it. She ran, barely slowing as she swooped down and snatched it up.

"Guards!" Caine yelled.

Marie pivoted and ran toward the far door as two more Apostles entered.

"Get her!" Caine yelled. "Beat her, but don't kill her."

Marie didn't wait to give them a chance. She was out the door in a flash, sprinting outside, knowing she'd never get over the twenty-foot-tall chain-link fence, let alone the razor wire topping it.

The area was nearly deserted and she ran between the church and the next building, then turned down a narrow central walkway to the second building. She came to a door and tried it. Locked. The next one was, too, but not the third.

She heard the Apostles' running footsteps, still far behind her, as she slipped into the darkness beyond the threshold.

# JUSTIN MARTIN

"Happy birthday, Christie." Justin handed a pink envelope to Christie Fox when she brought him his Coke.

"My birthday's in two weeks, but thanks." She set the serving tray down on Justin's table and opened the card. He'd chosen it carefully. It was sweet but harmless, a stupid card featuring Charlie Brown and Lucy, and sure enough, it made her smile. "Thanks, Justin, that's sweet."

"I have a surprise for you too. A present. But I have to take you somewhere to give it to you."

"I still have another half hour to work." She glanced around the café. "And I don't know if I feel much like going anywhere, Justin. I really miss Rick."

Her eyes teared up, so Justin patted her hand. "Christie, I know your birthday's not for two weeks yet. I just wanted to cheer you up a little."

"Where would we have to go?" she asked quietly.

"That's a surprise."

"I don't want any surprises, Justin. Let's just forget it."

"Okay, I'll tell. We're only going to Madland."

She looked out the window at the pouring rain. "How are you going to get there? By raft?"

"The back way is no problem."

"Let's wait until a nicer day."

He smiled. "We can't wait. You have an appointment."

"An appointment?" Her interest had been piqued, though she tried to hide it. "In Madland? For what?"

"Do you really want me to tell you?"

"I hate surprises."

"I got you a half-hour palm reading at the Sorcerer's Apprentice."

Her eyes lit up, just like he knew they would. He'd heard her, and lots of other girls, comment on Carlo Pelegrine's dark good looks. They all wanted to fuck him. If they only knew ... Justin smiled to himself.

"Really, Justin?" she asked, excited now. "Really?"

"I sure did. In one hour."

She squeezed his hand, the first sign of affection she'd ever shown him. "That's really thoughtful, Justin. It's just what I need right now. Can you hang around? I'll be done in half an hour."

"I'm not going anywhere without you," he said.

*Charles Pilgrim, you're going to love this present!* He sipped his Coke and imagined the reaction Carlo would have when he brought the girl to him.

# CARLO PELEGRINE

A lex had said she'd see him later, but she hadn't specified where, and Carlo's anxiety increased as the afternoon wore on. Flooding had been imminent for the last hour, and there was no way Tom would let her stay up in the hills in that kind of danger.

Idly he picked up the Bronco keys she'd left for him, turned them in his fingers. He'd used them to move the truck into the lot once the park opened, but now it occurred to him that she perhaps meant for him to pick her up at Tom's, since she'd be returning his horse.

"Of course," he told himself as he pulled on his trench coat and pocketed the keys.

Fifteen minutes later, after navigating the short but treacherous stretch of Old Madelyn Highway separating Madland from Tom's, he turned off on the ranch road and spent another ten minutes driving up to the house. He let himself in the gate and knocked, but no one answered.

Davy wasn't in his cottage either, so Carlo hurried across the open area to the stables, and walked along until he heard a man's soft voice and a horse's soft nicker. He opened the top half of the outer stable door, and Davy Styles, grooming his black and white pinto, looked up warily, then smiled. A rifle lay on a bench nearby within easy reach. "Carlo, what are you doing here?"

"I thought the search party might be back."

"Not yet, but it shouldn't be long, not in this rain. It's dangerous up there."

"I know."

"You want to go in the house and wait?"

"No," Carlo said. "Frankly, I'm too nervous to sit still." He hesitated. "Could you use some help?"

Davy looked him up and down, and laughed. "You're serious?"

"I am."

"Come on in."

A moment later, Carlo hung his coat over the inner stable door and picked up his first currycomb.

Grooming the horse turned out to be surprisingly pleasant. There was comfort in touching the huge, solid animal, but as he worked, he worried about Justin Martin. Alex, who was full of surprises, had said they'd take care of him, and now he wondered what she meant by that. Someone who would accept a murderer as a lover might also accept murder, and he had promised he would never kill again, no matter what the circumstance. He couldn't break that promise.

"Carlo?"

He whirled, and the pinto snorted.

"You're sure jumpy," Davy told him.

"Sorry."

"It's okay. Ranger's had enough brushing." He patted the gelding's muzzle affectionately. "He's spoiled rotten. Come on," he said, opening the stall door. "I'll introduce you to Diamond Lil. You'll like her."

Carlo nodded and followed him and was soon so enchanted by the beautiful white mare that he actually forgot to worry for a little while.

# JUSTIN MARTIN

W hen Justin pulled into the Madland parking lot, Christie Fox at his side, the first thing he noticed was that Alex Manderley's Bronco was gone. She must have come back from her trip to the mountains and taken off. He hoped she'd be back soon, but for now he had Christie.

Happily, no one saw them as he led her through the back gate, then walked her down the service road behind the shops. She was all tits and ass, and she didn't even wonder why they were going the back way, she just thought it was a big adventure.

Finally they arrived behind Carlo's shop. He led her past his storage shed and right up to the back door. He knocked. And knocked again. But no one answered.

"Justin? I thought you said—"

"He's probably upstairs and can't hear us. You wait right there. I'll go up and get him."

"But how?"

"Just watch. And wait."

Justin let himself into the storage room and turned on the light. There, he found Carlo's motorcycle, some cans of paint, tools, and, finally, a telescoping ladder hung sideways on one wall. Quickly he removed it and carried it outside.

"Justin, are you going to break in?"

He gave her a shit-eater. "Carlo told me to. He said he can't hear anything upstairs and that if he didn't answer, to come in the window and get him."

"That's weird," Christie whined.

*Shut up, you stupid cunt!* Smiling, Justin shrugged and positioned the ladder beneath the second-floor window he'd pointed out. *If that thing's locked, I'm going to take that bitch in the shed, bend her over his fucking motorcycle, and cut her open with his garden shears!*

Fortunately for Christie, the window wasn't locked. He pushed it up, then turned and waved. "Be right back. Stay put."

"Okay." He climbed in, then turned and saw her down there putting on lipstick to impress the Peeler. She'd do better to impress *him*, but she'd figure that out soon enough.

Justin looked around the room he'd entered. It was the bedroom, very neat, the bed made, the dresser gleaming. Quickly he pulled the bedspread and blankets down and bent, sniffing the sheets. His cock twitched at the scent of pussy. Alex Manderley's pussy.

Reminding himself that he had younger snatch waiting for him downstairs, he left the bedroom and checked the rest of the apartment. Carlo wasn't here, and a slow anger began burning inside him. Had he taken Alex somewhere so that he could do her by himself? The more he thought about it, the more he suspected it might be true.

By the time he reached the first floor, he was sure Carlo was trying to cheat him. "Fuck you," he whispered. "You'll be sorry."

He walked into the reading room, pausing at the small rolltop desk in the corner. Curious, he lifted the cover, and it rolled smoothly back. A small basket containing three oranges rested on the desktop, and in a cubby just above, something glittered. Slowly Justin drew it out.

It was a knife with a four-inch blade that was honed to razor sharpness. Justin turned it in his hand, then wrapped his fingers around the slim silver handle. It fit perfectly in his hand, and he felt the power of it surge through him. Was this the knife that the Peeler had used to skin his victims? No wonder he had done such perfect work. No wonder, with a knife like this.

"Justin!" Christie hammered on the back door, startling him.

"Bitch," he whispered. He closed the desk, then brought the knife to his lips and kissed it.

"What took you so long?" Christie whined as he opened the door and she flitted in.

Justin didn't answer. Instead, he raised the knife.

# ONE HUNDRED EIGHT

## HANNIBAL CAINE

Because he didn't want to draw attention to himself, when Hannibal Caine left the compound to check up on the doings of his flock, he dressed casually in a maroon turtleneck, windbreaker, and chinos. He hadn't intended to leave the compound today at all, but since that idiot Blandings had screwed up so much already, he decided it would be prudent to conduct a clandestine inspection.

When he had pulled into the Madland parking lot, he'd been surprised and very interested to see young Justin Martin escorting a blonde teenager through a back gate. Staying low in his car in the near-empty lot, Hannibal watched as the boy disappeared behind one of the buildings and, a few moments later, reappeared climbing in an upstairs window of the same building.

Hannibal strolled across the lot to the small gate and found that Justin had left it unlocked. He slipped through and shut it behind him, then strolled casually toward the building, arriving just as the back door opened and the young blonde disappeared inside.

He walked around to the front of the building, found it was the fortune-telling shop, and that it was closed. *Curiouser and curiouser.*

Returning to the rear of the building, Caine waited for twenty minutes, but there was no sign of Justin or the girl.

Checking his watch, he knew he had other things to do, so he approached the back door and knocked. There was no reply, so he tried the knob, found it unlocked. He walked in.

He found himself in a small utility room, with a white washer and dryer, shelves of cleaners, and a deep sink, where a splotch of crimson caught his eye.

*Blood. Fresh blood.*

There wasn't much, but it turned his stomach, and he nearly bolted outside, then caught himself. There was a closed door leading to another room, and trembling, he pushed it open. A blood-speckled crystal ball rested in the middle of a small round table in the middle of the windowless room. As he stared at it, a drop of blood spatted against it, and Hannibal glanced up, saw the awful, bleeding thing above him. He didn't even know what it was.

"Elder Caine," Justin Martin said as he entered the room from behind dark green drapes. He held a bloody knife in one hand. "What are you doing here?" He stepped closer.

"I came to talk to you, son," he said, hoping his voice wouldn't betray his fear and disgust.

"You did?" Justin gave him a vulpine smile and raised the knife.

"Yes. We missed you this morning."

"I was busy."

"Yes. But we need you."

The boy's face opened up slightly. "Need me?" He chuckled. "What the hell for?"

"I can see you're the right man for the job."

"What job?"

Hannibal was winging it, but doing a good job, he thought. "We need someone to capture—alive—a person to use on our cross for tomorrow's services."

The teen's eyes glittered. "You're going to crucify somebody?"

"You bet. Two people, in fact. We've captured one already, but we need another. And we need someone with your cunning to do the job." Wondering why he didn't bother telling the boy about the shepherdess, he spread his hands. "I'm afraid Elder Blandings just isn't the man for the job. He keeps making mistakes."

"You want me in charge?" The boy was beaming now.

"Yes, Justin."

"Are you going to kill the people on the crosses?"

"No. We expect the world to end, remember?" Caine smiled. "I suppose God will kill them. Of course, you might be the hand of God in this case. If you'd like."

"I can have both of them after?" Justin grinned broadly, and added, "Assuming the world doesn't end."

"Absolutely. We'll give you a safe place to do ... whatever it is you want to do with them, all the privacy you want."

"Who've you got already?"

"The tattooed whore."

"Cool. I'm going to skin her."

Caine smiled sickly. "All right."

"Can I choose the other one?"

"Of course, young man. I expect you to use your discretion."

"Alex Manderley."

"Who's that?"

"A UFO researcher. I was gonna do her anyway." He snickered. "I was practicing when you walked in."

"She sounds perfect. Can you bring her to us tonight?" Caine watched the wheels turn in Justin's head.

"And I get to do whatever I want with her after?"

Caine plastered on his salesman's grin. "Absolutely!"

"How do I know I can trust you?" Justin asked, his eyes narrowing again.

"Easy, son. I've told you we kidnapped the tattooed woman. If I told on you, you'd tell on me."

Justin hesitated, then nodded. "Okay. I'll be there tonight, but you'd better keep your word."

"Don't worry."

"You go now. I have work to do." He grinned to himself, his eyes bright and glittering. "Man, this'll really impress him." So saying, Justin turned and walked through the drapes without looking back.

Hannibal let himself out the back door, careful to wipe his prints from the knob. He'd gotten out of that rather neatly, he thought, and getting rid of Justin once he appeared at the compound would be simple.

# ALEXANDRA MANDERLEY

After leaving Madland, the six-person search party had split into three pairs, Tom Abernathy and Henry Running Deer taking the treacherous Spirit Canyon, and Shorty Sykes and Red Fitch, the Olive Mesa area. Alex had accompanied Mad Dog Steinberg into Rattlesnake Canyon, and despite several deluges, they stayed on their search.

She and Mad Dog, who told her he acquired his nickname because he could look crazier than Jack Nicholson when he wanted, sat on their mounts and looked down into the meadow where Marie had had her close encounter. The valley floor was covered with muddy water. There was no telling how deep it was and they hadn't gone down, searching instead with binoculars from the relative safety of the ridge trail. They found no sign of Eric, Marie, or the missing boy.

"We've got to get out of here, Alex." Mad Dog stared up at the clouded sky, and rain ran off the back of his Stetson. "Storm's getting worse. It's really going to break loose soon."

"Are you certain?"

"Hell no, but we're risking our luck." He tapped his watch. "The other parties will be heading back about now. Who knows? Maybe Tom and Henry will have Eric with them."

"You're right." Even as she spoke, the rain fell harder.

It took nearly half an hour to reach Thunder Road, and when they did, they found Shorty and Red waiting for them.

"We're empty-handed," Shorty called. "There's nothing around the mesa."

"Us too," Mad Dog commiserated, then pointed toward Spirit Canyon. "Look!" A lone rider on a dark horse appeared as the rain momentarily let up. "It's Henry," Mad Dog said. "He's got something slung across his saddle. Let's go!"

The five met just east of the rain-filled Old Madelyn Trail, and as they neared, Alex's stomach knotted. Whatever was thrown over his saddle was wrapped in black, and might very well be a body.

"Henry!" Shorty asked. "Where's Tom?"

"He's still in the canyon, the darn fool."

"What's that?" Alex forced herself to ask.

Henry looked at her, his dark eyes unreadable. "A body. We found it before we got into the canyon, but figured it'd be best to stash it and go ahead with the search. We think it was buried and the rain washed it up. Tom asked me to fetch it back now, in case of flooding."

"For God's sake, Henry," Mad Dog said. "Quit the dramatics and tell us who it is." He gave Alex a sympathetic smile.

"It's the missing kid, we think. Matches the description the chief gave us. You want to see?"

"No, we don't wanna see."

"Do you?" Henry asked Alex.

"A lady don't wanna see a dead body," Red Fitch put in, then spat a wad of tobacco.

"She's a doctor," Henry explained impassively. "This body's weird. Some skin's gone."

"I'm not that kind of doctor," Alex said, her mind reeling. "But what do you mean, some skin is gone?"

"Big square of it on the stomach is cut out. You okay?"

"Fine," she managed. "I'm fine."

Thunder clapped and lightning flashed behind them over Rattlesnake Canyon. "Let's get out of here," Mad Dog said, "before all hell breaks loose."

# TOM ABERNATHY

Tom Abernathy had a hunch, and that's why he'd stayed in Spirit Canyon despite the danger of flooding and mountain slides. He didn't know what the hunch was about exactly, but it was strong, and he couldn't leave.

He'd spent most of his time checking the treacherous area near the campsite, but he had found nothing. Now he sat on Belle, letting the rain wash over him, his eyes closed, just letting his mind wander toward the hunch.

After they found the boy, he'd had a bad feeling that whoever had done that killing had also attacked Eric, maybe even Marie, but even now, he couldn't give up. Not as long as the hunch remained strong.

Finally he opened his eyes and, without thinking about what he was doing, rode farther into the canyon, turning off on a short trail that led to another primitive campsite.

He rode to the edge of the steep cliff and peered over from a safe distance, seeing only water filling a narrow gorge formed by this and three other hills. Thunder clapped and Belle whinnied.

"You oughta be used to that noise by now, girl," he soothed.

She whinnied again, and then he thought he heard something

else. Listening hard, he waited, watching the horse's ears. They cocked as he heard the sound again. It sounded like a human voice. "Belle, I think you're on to something." He jumped down too quickly and slipped in the mud, barely managed to keep on his feet. "Stay," he told Belle, and moved closer to the cliff's edge.

Below, barely in view, was a man's lower leg. "Eric!" Tom called at the top of his lungs. "Eric Watson!"

"Help!"

The voice was weak, but the leg moved. Tom lay down flat on his belly and looked over the edge. Eric was pulling himself up, but even from here, Tom could see that his other leg was broken. "Stay put!" he ordered. "Wait for the rope."

Without waiting for a reply, he went to Belle and took his lariat from the saddle. Quickly he fashioned a slipknot, then secured the other end to the saddle horn. Returning to the cliff edge, he squatted. "Here it comes!" he called, lowering the end of the rope. "Grab it!"

It only took a few tries before Watson caught the rope. Quickly he slipped it around his waist, then twisted it through his hands. "Ready!" he cried.

Tom mounted Belle and slowly, slowly, she backed up, continuing until the boy was up and over the edge of the cliff.

Tom trotted back to the young man and helped him free himself from the rope, then propped him up. "I was about to give up on you. Good thing Belle found you."

"Your horse found me?"

Tom nodded. "You gotta listen to your horse. They sense things you wouldn't even know existed. Like your whereabouts, for instance. Listen, Eric, have you seen anything of Marie? She's missing too."

Eric's eyes closed for a moment, then reopened, slightly unfocused. "Sorry. What did you say ...?" His words trailed off, and his eyes closed again. Concerned, Tom felt his pulse—weak and rapid, but there nonetheless. "Eric?"

He didn't answer.

"Best you sleep through the ride anyway," he said, picking him up. "Otherwise you'd hate my innards for how much I'm gonna make that busted leg hurt."

By the time he got the unconscious boy on the horse, then himself, Tom was exhausted. "We're going home, Belle," he said. "But we're going the back way so we can get Eric to Doc Hartman's a little sooner." They rode out of the campsite and Tom tugged the reins, indicating direction, then let the horse have her head for the long, slow ride.

# MOSS BASKERVILLE

"Any sign of Shirley yet?" Moss Baskerville let go of the button on the two-way handset and static crackled out the radio.

"No, Chief."

*Goddamned storm.* He had barely heard Ken Landry's words for all the interference. He and Al Gonzales had been running themselves ragged between idiot tourists getting stuck in the mud, car accidents, and looking for missing people.

Between downpours, Moss had ventured up Old Madelyn to Tom's, but Davy informed him that no one was back from the search yet. Nor had Cassie and Eve shown up at the ranch as planned. Alarmed, Baskerville had left for Cassie's, sighing with relief when he turned in to the driveway and saw her yellow Honda. He shook his head; he should have known she wouldn't leave her house. She was hardheaded that way.

Now he climbed out of the mud-caked cruiser and walked to the front door, getting ready to try to cajole her into going to the ranch, but he stopped cold when he saw the broken door hanging ajar. *Shit!* Drawing his gun, he plastered himself against the wall next to the doorway. Slowly he edged over the threshold, into the house. "Cass?"

Silence. His foot hit something and he looked down, saw Eve's toys in a jumbled pile. *They* were *getting ready to go, but something happened. Dear God, that was probably hours ago!*

He quickly checked the other rooms, coming last to the kitchen. The back door was open. Across the threshold lay Evie's favorite rag doll. "No," he whispered, picking it up. It was wet and smudged with dirt from someone's shoe. "Dear God, no."

## ONE HUNDRED TWELVE
# MARIE LOPEZ

Marie had hidden in the darkened room until her eyes adjusted, then she began to explore. According to every rumor she'd ever heard about the compound, it was honeycombed with tunnels. She hoped to find one that would lead her out.

To that end, she'd begun exploring the building, her bare feet making no sound. The place was a maze of dimly lit corridors and stairwells, and she'd long since lost her sense of direction when she came down a flight of stairs into a windowless corridor. Gun ready, she took the dimly lit right-hand hallway, keeping close to the wall, her gun ready.

She'd seen no one so far, and she guessed most of them were out doing a little last-minute raping and pillaging in the name of God. Grimacing, she rounded a comer into another corridor and there saw another descending staircase. She waited in a shadowed doorway, and as she was about to sprint across the hall to the stairs, she heard footsteps. Pressing herself into the shadows, she watched as a single white-robed, hooded figure passed by and turned down the stairwell.

She followed. The stairwell, barely lit at the head, led down into near-total darkness. As the Apostle neared the bottom of the stairs,

Marie silently moved closer, holding the gun by its barrel. The robed figure reached the bottom step and reached a hand around the corner. Just as light bloomed in the room, Marie bashed the gun butt into the back of his head.

Without a sound, he crumpled to the floor.

Quickly she stepped around the body, taking the feet and dragging it out of sight. Glancing around, she saw that she was in a Sunday school room, with felt boards and blackboards and tiny chairs.

Marie bent and turned the Apostle over, smiling as she recognized the bullish Amazon who'd given her so much grief.

Quickly she stripped the robe off the woman and slipped it over her head. It was far too long for her, but she found some string in a desk drawer and cinched it in. The woman wore blue tennis shoes, and Marie took those, too, surprised when they actually fit. Beneath the robe, the woman wore cammies, and Marie struck gold when she went through the pockets and found a key ring and an odd- looking credit card. She took them both, then pulled the woman into a storage closet and locked the door.

"Hello?" called a young man's voice. "Anybody here?"

She didn't answer until she heard him coming down the stairs. Quickly she pulled the hood over her hair, then greeted him with a smile. "Hi. What are you doing here?"

Taking the offensive worked. Embarrassed, he waved a credit card like the one she'd taken from the Amazon. "Elder Blandings asked me to bring him some boxes of clips."

"Oh," she said authoritatively. "That's fine. Go ahead."

The blond youth crossed the room. Holding her breath, Marie watched, her gun ready within the robe's wide sleeve in case he opened the closet where she'd stashed the Amazon. She exhaled as he passed it by and instead opened what looked like a broom closet. Holding the card out, he stepped inside. She heard a soft sliding noise. Then he was gone.

Marie went to the teacher's desk at the other end of the room and opened a drawer. There was a sheaf of papers covered with childish writing, so she pulled that out, along with a red pencil, and sat down to wait. As soon as she heard him return, she looked up from the papers and smiled. The man was carrying boxes of clips as well as an AK-47.

"Loaded for bear," she said, still smiling.

He paused, a flirtatious look in his eyes. "We've got a big mission in a little while."

"A bloody one?" she asked, batting her eyelashes.

"Could be. I've been a member for five years, but I just moved here two weeks ago. My name's Fred. What's yours?"

"Wilma." The word popped out unbidden, so she smiled coyly to cover. "You're cute, Wilma." He winked to show he got the joke. "We could use another hand on the mission. Would you like to go along? Maybe afterward, we could get together for coffee, and, well, you know, tomorrow's the end of the world and all ..."

Marie bit her tongue and made herself smile. "Maybe." *What a line!* She studied the automatic weapon. "Who are you going after?" She hoped her voice sounded casual.

He shook his head. "I don't know, but we're supposed to bring one back alive."

*You're going to be sorry you ever talked to me.* She put the pencil eraser to her lips and studied Fred. "Who are you going to shoot, then?"

He shrugged. "Maybe nobody. Elder Blandings wants us to be ready for anything. He was a lieutenant in the Viet Nam, and he's a really tough old bird."

"When are you going?"

"Half an hour. We're meeting out in the parking lot. By the white van."

"Well, maybe I'll come along." She smiled. If she didn't find a passage out, she could leave with the group. "I could use some fresh air."

"Great!"

A moment later, he was gone. Quickly Marie pulled out the credit card key and crossed to the broom closet. Inside, at eye level, was a slot, and she pushed the card through it. A green light flashed on, then the back of the closet slid away to reveal another stairwell, lit from below.

It was an armory filled with more weapons and ammunition than she had ever seen in one place before. Thank God the sweats she wore had big pockets in the top and two smaller ones in the pants. She went around the room, taking half a dozen grenades, smoke bombs, clips for the pistol, a revolver and ammo belts, and finally, an M-16 and extra magazines. "Rambo, eat your heart out," she whispered, as she grimly hid everything except the M-16 under her robe.

The weapons weighed her down, but she figured that having them would be well worth it. Satisfied that everything was secure, she examined the room, hoping to find a hidden door into a tunnel. No such luck. With a sigh, she climbed the stairs and closed the broom closet, then walked confidently up to the main corridor. The few people she passed didn't give her a second glance. She thought about trying to find Cassie, but she had no idea where to look, and her friend would never be able to get out with her. No, it would be smarter to get out and call the cavalry.

After fifteen minutes of wandering, she found her way outside. Relieved to see that the rain had let up again, she walked briskly up to the knot of Apostles gathered near a white van. She was happy to see there were at least two dozen of them, since that would allow her more anonymity.

Fred saw her and waved. She joined him, keeping her hood low over her forehead. A few raindrops fell, and Fred and a few others raised their hoods as well. "So what are we waiting for?" she asked finally.

"Elder Blandings and Lorraine Ferguson," Fred said. "Here comes Blandings."

The old coot stomped up, an automatic rifle in his hands, his toupee askew. "Where's Ferguson?" he barked.

No one knew.

"Well, we can't wait all day. Let's march, double time!"

# ALEXANDRA MANDERLEY

S itting in Tess's saddle, Alex watched the stuntmen ride briskly down Old Madelyn Highway. At last she was alone with her thoughts arid worries.

The deluge they'd expected had lasted less than a minute. Despite intermittent thunder and lightning, the sky seemed to have run out of rain, and since there were no Apostles in sight, she had told Shorty, Henry, Mad Dog, and Red to go back without her. They hesitated, all four of them glancing at the plastic- wrapped body on Henry's saddle, then at one another. Finally Mad Dog cautioned her to keep heading in the general direction of her destination—Tom's ranch—then tipped his hat and rode off with the others.

After the riders disappeared, she urged Tess across Thunder Road and down onto the desert floor, then dismounted and led the chestnut mare along, weaving slowly among the mesquite and Joshua trees, letting the horse nibble at clumps of hardy spring grasses.

Alex felt as if her head might explode as she thought about Carlo. Here she was, falling for a confessed killer, promising to help him destroy an enemy, even though she had nothing but Carlo's word that Justin Martin was a murderer. Was she being foolish? At the intellectual level, she knew this was true, but her instincts said otherwise, and through long, hard lessons, she had learned that her instincts knew best.

She patted Tess's muzzle, then put her foot in the stirrup and swung into the saddle. Eric was still her primary concern, and as she continued across the prairie, guilt began to weigh her down. She should never have left him alone at the camp, not after the way her old partner, Jack Matthews, had disappeared. *You knew better than to leave Eric alone, but you did it anyway. Could you have acted any more selfishly?*

Bitter tears of self-loathing rolled down her cheeks and she drove them away by thinking about how much she'd like to wrap her hands around Dole's neck and squeeze the truth out of him.

Beneath her, Tess chuffed and stopped moving, her ears flicking back. "What's wrong?" Alex turned her head and scanned toward Old Madelyn Highway, but saw no movement. Behind her, Thunder Road remained equally deserted. The horse snorted, and Alex glanced left. The day was rain-colored drab, the desert foliage half-hidden in low mist, but something didn't look quite right. "Come on, Tess." She urged the reluctant horse eastward, toward something that at first appeared to be a large, oddly shaped boulder. The horse protested again, but kept moving as Alex squinted at the object.

"Dear God," she whispered as it suddenly came into focus. It was a vehicle, a green jeep, smashed up against a stand of Joshua trees. Dole's CJ-5, or one like it.

Dismounting, she tethered Tess to a mesquite bush, then walked determinedly toward the wreck, her steps faltering when she recognized Dole's license plate, catching her breath when she saw the body slumped forward over the steering wheel, its arm dangling loosely at its side.

"Colonel?" she called, still ten feet away.

"Help."

The voice was a mere croak, but it galvanized Alex. She ran to the jeep, then grimly studied the way the steering column had shot forward to press into Dole's chest, trapping him against the seat. The misshapen swellings on his face and head looked critical. "You're pinned," she said, her emotions a confusion of pity and hatred. "I'll have to get help."

The military man stared up at her with bleary bloodshot eyes. "No," he whispered. "There's no time. It's over."

"You don't know that—"

The eyes glared through the pain. "I know I'm dying, Dr. Manderley. I knew that when the girl left. Did she send you?"

"What girl?"

Dole coughed, and thick blood bubbled between his lips. "Little girl," he managed at last. "Eve."

"Eve Halloway?" Alex asked, instantly suspicious. "What did you do with her?"

"I rescued her, Doctor." His eyes closed briefly, and when he reopened them, they were full of pain but not malice. "Sinclair's people kidnapped her mother, and she was on the run. I was taking her back to town when they attacked. They stoned me, Dr. Manderley. Stoned me. Isn't that something?"

"What happened to Eve?"

"She was fine, a good little soldier. Obeyed my orders. She hid until it was over. I sent her toward town, told her to keep off the road, to hide. You haven't seen her?" His eyes opened wider, worry behind the pain.

"I've been up in the canyon, Colonel, not in town. I hope she made it. It was raining too hard to see well."

"She should've sent help by now if she made it," Dole grunted. More blood bubbled, this time from his nose.

"I'll alert the police," Alex promised. "Someone will be here soon."

"Dr. Manderley," Dole growled. "I'm dead already. Why were you in the canyon during the storm?"

"We were searching for my assistant, Eric Watson. He disappeared," she added, anger boiling away her sympathy for Dole. "He disappeared. Why don't you tell me what you did with him? And with the samples?"

Dole studied her. "Looking for a deathbed confession, Doctor?"

"What have you got to lose?"

"I did retrieve the samples last night. But your assistant wasn't present. I found them in the second duffel I checked. Right on top."

That jibed with the two open bags Alex had found. "Are you telling the truth? Eric wasn't there?"

"On the honor of the United States, he was not there."

Visions of Oliver North danced through Alex's head, but she pushed them away.

"Doctor, we're not enemies, no matter what you think."

"Then you'll answer my other questions?"

"If I can."

Alex pulled a handkerchief from her pocket and wiped away the blood dripping into Dole's eye. "Jack Matthews," she said, watching Dole's eyes. "And don't tell me you don't know the name."

He studied her. "He was your partner. He disappeared in New Mexico during a close encounter."

Alex nodded. "What did you do with him?"

"Nothing."

"I don't believe you."

"It's the truth." Dole's breath rattled through his lungs. "We let you assume we were responsible for the disappearance, but we had nothing to do with it. Jack Matthews was abducted by ..." His words trailed off, then he finished dryly, "A flying saucer."

"Why would the military take the blame?"

"First rule of espionage, Doctor. Always pretend to know everything. We couldn't let other countries think we weren't in control." His laugh was a painful bark. "We couldn't even let *you* think we had no control." He hesitated. "I'm not proud of some of the things I've done in the name of God and our country, Doctor. Threats. Blackmail. Assassinations. All to keep our secrets—and our ignorance—to ourselves." His eyes closed.

"Colonel?"

Eyelids fluttering open, he gazed at her. "Yes?"

"Is the military flying any UFOs?"

"A few, or so I've heard. I know the ones we've seen here aren't terrestrial in origin, nor were those in New Mexico. Doctor, you must understand something." He paused, catching his breath, and one ice-cold hand reached out and gripped hers. "I'm nothing but a glorified grunt. I follow orders. The people in charge of UFO research aren't part of the regular military. I take orders from them."

"They're not military?"

"I don't really know what they are. The president doesn't know. Congress doesn't know. We refer to them as the Secret Government. Whoever they are, they're dangerous. They do anything they want, and if you cross them, you're dead. They would eliminate me for telling you this much, and they'll eliminate you if you open your mouth. Do you understand?"

Overwhelmed, Alex whispered, "Yes."

"They didn't take Jack Matthews," Dole continued, choking as blood flowed freely, filling Alex's nose with its metallic smell. "I know that, because they're still looking for him."

"They think he's alive?"

Dole nodded almost imperceptibly. "If he is, they want him to talk to them, and only them. After that, he'll be eliminated."

"Do you know where he might be?"

"Peru. He was spotted in Peru."

Blood gushed suddenly from his mouth, spraying Alex, but she barely noticed. "Are you sure this Secret Government didn't take Eric?"

"Yes. They would've taken ... the samples." The eyes shut and his breathing stuttered. Alex started to pull her hand free, but the grip instantly strengthened. Dole's eyes opened. "I'm not the enemy, Doctor." His gaze drifted from her to the sky. "*They* are."

And with a quiet sigh, he was gone.

# ONE HUNDRED FOURTEEN
## EVE HALLOWAY

Some time after the rain ended, Eve Halloway finally poked her head out from her rocky shelter. She'd never found Madland or Tom's house, though she'd tried and tried. Finally, when the rain was pounding down so hard that she was sure she would drown, she practically stumbled on the huge mountain of boulders.

Though she could barely see it, she knew where she was: Dead Man's Hill. Her parents had brought her here to climb and picnic dozens of times. Relieved, she found her way to her favorite path. Slipping and sliding, she climbed the rounded stones, stopping halfway up at the Cave, which wasn't a real cave, but a jumble of monstrous rocks forming a small, dry grotto. There, she curled up and waited for the rain to die down enough for her to walk down Old Madelyn. Exhausted and bruised, lulled by the storm, she had fallen asleep.

She had come suddenly awake and panicked, almost hitting her head on the top of the cave as she jumped to her feet. Then it came back to her, all of it, her mother, Officer Dole, the bad men. Now, as she peered out, she saw a vehicle way down on Old Madelyn. It was slowly coming this way. She'd be saved! Glancing toward the Apostles' church, she gasped at the sight of at least twenty white-robed figures marching down Thunder Road, coming her way. Instantly she squatted down, out of sight, and began reciting the only prayer she knew by heart.

"Now I lay me down to sleep, I pray the Lord my soul to keep." She peeped out, saw the Apostles moving closer, the vehicle—it was a light blue van, she could tell now—drawing near. "I pray the Lord my soul to keep, I pray the Lord my soul to keep." She watched, repeating the words over and over, a litany against her terror.

# MARIE LOPEZ

Marie Lopez and two dozen Apostles marched down Thunder Road. She was careful to stay out of Blandings' line of vision —he would certainly recognize her. Others might, too, so she kept her cowl up and her head low, walking at the rear of the group, the annoyingly horny bastard Fred right beside her. Fortunately, Blandings had ordered silence, so Fred had to content himself with leering grins.

When they passed her ranch, it was all she could do not to bolt, but she knew she had to wait. Now they were nearing the Old Madelyn junction, and she hoped she could disappear behind a rock, a bush, something, anything, soon. Then she'd get to town as fast as she could.

A pale blue van approached, and an instant later, Marie recognized it as Janet Wister's. She'd seen it many times because Janet and her Space Friends group frequently parked along Thunder Road. They would unload their chaise longues and folding chairs, their binoculars and signal lights, and spend many evenings UFO-watching by the rocks. Now that the sky was clearing, that's probably what they were up to now.

"Halt! Weapons ready!" Eldo Blandings commanded in his wavery old man's voice. "Block the road! Move it! Double time!"

*Dear God, help them!* Marie waited as the pack of Apostles strung out across Thunder Road, and exhaled with relief when Janet's van didn't turn toward the compound. Instead, it turned right, Space Friends gawking at them from the windows, and proceeded another fifty feet to Dead Man's Hill. There, it pulled into a hard-packed turnout and parked.

"Follow me!" Blandings ordered. "Weapons ready." He started marching, almost goose-stepping, passing Old Madelyn, heading for the rocks, the group of gun-toting Apostles right behind him. Marie moved along with them, her hidden weaponry weighing her down, her mind reeling as she realized she was about to participate in a kidnapping.

The doors of the van opened and people piled out. Marie recognized Janet and several of the others. She counted ten Space Friends and they all stood watching as the Apostles hustled into the turnout.

Despite the clearing sky, thunder boomed overhead.

"Fan out," Blandings ordered, and immediately the group formed a large half circle around the Space Friends. He turned to them. "In the name of God and the Living Savior, do you repent your sins?"

Janet Wister put her hands on her hips. "What are you? Rabid Jehovah's Witnesses?"

"We are the Chosen," Blandings boomed. "We are the Apostles! Join us or die, for the time of reckoning is at hand."

A long-haired man standing by Janet laughed. "And people think *we're* a bunch of nuts!"

Blandings, hood back, face red with anger, turned to his Apostles. "These are unrepentant sinners! They work for Satan!" He turned back to the Space Friends and pointed at Janet. "Take her alive. Kill the rest of these devil worshipers."

"Hey," Janet Wister yelled. "This is a free country—"

A hulking Apostle named Clayman opened fire, then others

followed suit. The long-haired man screamed and whirled as a bullet took him in the chest. The others began to scatter, running for cover, Janet heading behind Dead Man's Hill. Beside Marie, Fred raised his AK-47 and glanced her way. "Let's kill us some sinners!"

She lifted the M-16 and fired at nothing. She had to do something, but what? If she turned her weapon on the Apostles, they'd cut her down instantly. She couldn't reach the grenades, and in horror she watched as Apostles fired and the Space Friends danced spastically in the rain of bullets. Beside her, Fred chuckled as he took out a tall, well-groomed man. After he went down, Fred kept shooting and laughing as the body convulsed under the bullets.

"Charge!" Eldo Blandings cried, and the Apostles ran forward. Fred leaped in front of Marie, going after a thin man as he sprinted away. He fired, and so did Marie. Fred's head burst in an explosion of blood, brains, and bone. The thin man glanced back and Marie raised her weapon to scare him away. It worked, but a moment later he was cut down by someone else's bullets.

In three minutes it was all over, the ground strewn with bodies. Nine out of ten Space Friends were down. One man moved slightly, and the hulking Apostle Clayman put a bullet through his brain at close range. "This is for the Living Savior," he intoned.

All at once the fine hairs on Marie's body stood on end and she could feel the hair on her scalp trying to prickle up as well. The air filled with an energy that hummed all around her. Just as she looked up, a blinding bolt of lightning crackled down from above.

It struck Clayman's shoulder, and Marie's brain slipped into slow motion as she heard the sizzle, saw the arm of his robe smoke and darken. The bolt passed out his extended fingers into the ground, and with the white robe flying, he looked like a medieval wizard casting a spell.

Thunder shook the earth as Clayman fell. Blandings knelt beside him. "He's alive. Put him in the van!" As two Apostles moved to follow orders, Blandings turned to the others. "Deploy and find the woman. I want her alive."

"It's a sign," a woman breathed, staring at the sky.

Blandings glared at her. "It sure as hell is. Apostle Clayman fired before I gave the order." Vulturelike, he peered at the rest of the group. "The rest of you remember that!" He turned slightly, mouth open to say something more, then stopped, spotting Fred's blood-soaked body.

Marie melted into the group as he approached. "What happened?" he asked, glaring. "Who shot him?"

No one replied. Blandings glared some more, then barked, "We'll deal with this later. Find the woman!"

The Apostles broke and scattered around Dead Man's Hill, and Marie saw her chance. She went straight to the rear of the rocks and glanced around, making sure no one was looking. Then she started to climb, the weapons clanging around her. She'd spent her childhood climbing this little mountain, and her feet and hands remembered where to go, what to do.

Just six feet up, she ducked into a hidey-hole and watched as Janet Wister appeared below. She nearly called out to her, but the swarm of Apostles appeared too fast. They surrounded the woman. Then her screams reverberated off the rocks.

"Don't kill her!"

Marie was glad to hear Eldo Blandings's order to cease beating her, and she waited as they dragged Janet to her feet and pulled her away. Marie peered up. Dead Man's Hill had seen many shoot-outs in its heyday, but she doubted that any were as cold-blooded as this. She stripped off the robe and began climbing, making her way slowly around to the old cave where she and her friends used to play gunfighters. She would wait there until the Apostles left.

Some of the Apostles were dragging bodies out of sight behind the rocks, leaving red trails behind them, as Marie neared the cave. She hunkered down, watching as two others tossed Janet Wister through the rear door of the van and slammed it shut. "Listen up!" Blandings barked. "We have done God's will, and one of our own has fallen. We will fight twice as hard in his name!"

He went on and on, a little peacock strutting his stuff, and all the Apostles' eyes were on their leader. Marie moved through the last open area before the cave, then awkwardly hoisted herself over a boulder into the cave, a robbers' roost where silver thieves a century ago had fended off the law.

The last thing she expected was to see a child rolled up in a ball, cowering in the darkness. "Hey," she called softly.

The girl looked up and screamed at the top of her lungs.

*Shit!* "Eve, it's okay! It's Marie, remember?"

Eve's mouth clamped shut, then she exploded out of the back of the fortress and into Marie's arms. Meanwhile, the Apostles were shouting.

"Stay here!" Marie ordered, then climbed back out and peered down.

"Up there!" one of the bastards called, and instantly an automatic rifle coughed. Marie ducked, shards of stone shrapnel pelting her back.

"Hold your fire!" yelled Blandings. "I want her alive!"

"Shit!" At least he didn't know she was armed. *But he will soon!* Marie grabbed one of the grenades from her belt and pulled the pin. "One, two, three," she whispered, then rose up and lobbed it straight into a group of Apostles huddled at the foot of the rocks.

She didn't watch the explosion, but ducked and grabbed a second pineapple, yanked the pin with her teeth, and stood, this time throwing it into another group, well away from the van. She didn't want to hurt Janet.

As the second grenade exploded, she lowered herself behind the rocks, but not before she caught sight of the human wreckage the first grenade had created. "God forgive me," she whispered.

"Retreat!" Blandings yelled. Marie looked out, saw him and a few others climbing into the van. The engine choked, then caught, carrying the remaining Apostles toward the compound at breakneck speed. They were scared shitless. Her smile faded as she saw the dead and heard the moaning of the wounded. The Apostles would come back for them soon, and they'd be armed to the teeth.

"Come on, Evie," Marie said, turning. The girl was all over her and Marie held her, stroking her hair. "We have to go, Evie. Can you climb down?"

"The ghost men got my mama! We have to get her back!" "We will, Evie. We'll tell your daddy."

As she spoke, Marie watched the van grow smaller and smaller until it was just a speck pulling up at the compound gates.

"Okay, Eve, we'll go this way." She pointed to the western side of the rocks, where there were no bodies. "My house isn't far. We'll get Rex and ride to town."

The rocks rumbled beneath them as an earthquake began to roll. Marie clung on to Eve, glad they hadn't started down already. Unlike the earlier jolt, this sounded like distant thunder and felt like she was on a boat riding gentle waves. She counted to ten before it stopped, then counted another sixty seconds of stillness. "Okay, Evie, let's go."

# JAMES ROBERT SINCLAIR

J ames Robert Sinclair sat on his bed, legs crossed, hands clasped. He had spent the day in prayer and meditation, preparing himself for the trial to come.

In those hours he had begun to understand what was happening in a way that had eluded him until now, and the revelation awed and frightened him at first. Now he still felt the awe, but with acceptance came tranquillity, and a sense of sadness, intermingled with joy.

He felt the earth roll gently beneath him, and he knew this was a sign from God, a sign of something greater on its way.

## ONE HUNDRED SEVENTEEN
# ALEXANDRA MANDERLEY

M adland was open and a few tourists – a very few -- strolled the forlorn, muddy streets as Alex rode Tess toward the Sorcerer's Apprentice. Hopefully the phones were back in order now, but if they weren't and Carlo hadn't already driven her Bronco down to Tom's, she'd ask him to go into town and alert the police about Dole's accident while she took the horse back to the ranch.

As she approached Carlo's, she wasn't surprised that the Bronco was gone, because if he was there, he'd have moved it around to the parking lot. Dismounting, she led Tess between Carlo's building and the next, tethered her to the back-stairs railing, then walked to the access road and peered at the parking lot. Only a dozen vehicles were parked there, none of them a red Bronco.

She returned to the mare, then heard a creaking sound. The back door wasn't latched. It creaked again, touched by the damp breeze. Curious, she walked up the stairs and pushed the door open a few inches.

"Carlo?" she called. "It's Alex. Are you here?"

There was no reply. A knot of alarm formed in the pit of her stomach. Carlo, she already knew, was very exacting in his habits. He'd never forget to lock a door. *Unless something's happened.*

"Carlo?" She stepped inside the little back room containing his washer and dryer and turned on the light. Everything. looked right, except that the door leading into the reading room hung ajar. As she approached it, she detected a faint but familiar odor beneath the fragrances of incense and perfumed oils. She sniffed again and the hairs on her arms and neck prickled up.

Nervously she pushed the door open a little more and reached around the comer, feeling for the light switch. There were two, and she tried the first. The ceiling fan whirred to life, its motor humming loudly in the confines of the small room. She flicked the second and the light came on. Swallowing, she stepped inside.

Drops of moisture hit her face and she looked up.

At first she didn't comprehend what she saw. She stared at the thick golden ropes attached to the fan blades, then at the hunk of red —meat?—at the lower end. "What the—?" *It can't be.* Then a droplet splashed her hand and she stared at it in horror—*blood!* The thing rotating lazily on the fan was a scalp attached to long blond hair.

Faint, Alex staggered between the green curtains and sat down on the bottom step of the staircase to the apartment. "Carlo," she whispered. "Dear God, Carlo."

Emotions rushed through her, fear for Carlo, fear *of* Carlo, a flurry of feelings that gave her no answers. Finally she stood and, willing herself to stop trembling, peered around the shop, saw nothing unusual. She hesitated, wondering whether or not she should go upstairs. *What if Justin's up there? What if Carlo's up there? What if he's hurt? What if he's not?*

Refusing the thought, she started up the shadowy stairwell and arrived at the top to find the door to his apartment wide open. "Carlo?" she called. *He's not here, Alex. The Bronco's gone, remember?* But maybe someone else took it, hurt him and stole it. Wasn't that possible? *Anything's possible.*

She shivered and stepped inside.

Without the masking fragrance of incense and oil, the metallic smell of blood was much stronger here. Nothing was out of place in the living room, or so she thought until she looked down and saw bloody footprints on the pale carpet. Stifling a gasp, she forced herself to examine them. They probably belonged to a man, but that's all she could tell. *If you're smart, you'll get out of here now.*

But she couldn't turn back now—she'd never forgive her own cowardice. Steeling herself, she entered the bedroom. The bedclothes had been torn back— she and Carlo had made the bed together this morning. Also, the bedroom window was wide open, letting cold damp wind blow into the room. She crossed to it, looked down, and saw the ladder below. She felt unbridled relief to know absolutely that someone had broken in. *Justin! It has to be!*

She tiptoed into the bathroom, found reddish soap scum ringing the sink and streaks of blood on the sky blue towels.

Only the kitchen remained now. Hesitantly she walked back through the living room, into the dining room, then peered through the wide kitchen entrance.

The counter, its white tiles spotless this morning, was covered with raw meat. In horror Alex stared at it from the edge of the dining room, her mind slowly deciphering what she saw: a body, covered in blood. The skin, what she could see of it, was piled in the sink.

Nausea hit abruptly, starting in the pit of her stomach and moving upwards so quickly that she barely made it to the bathroom. After, hugging the toilet bowl, trying to catch her breath, she had only two thoughts: Either Justin Martin was a cold-blooded psychopath—or Carlo Pelegrine was. She hadn't doubted Carlo when he'd told her Justin had delivered the square of skin last night. But could she be wrong? she wondered. Justin gave her the creeps, while Carlo excited her. Seduced by the man's charm, could she have been fooled because she disliked one man and was falling in love with the other?

He'd been so understanding, so gentle and loving, and so obviously regretful for what had happened in his past. *But sociopaths are consummate actors. They're neighbors, husbands, boyfriends, and those who love them are the last to suspect.*

Tears threatened, and she refused them fiercely. Alex Manderley never gave in to weakness. *Never.* She rose, flushed the toilet, then turned on the bathtub faucet and kneeled, rinsing her mouth, then letting the water run over her face and arms, washing the blood droplets away. She turned the faucet off, knowing she was fouling the crime scene, not caring.

She had to find Carlo, had to talk to him. She had to find out the truth, whatever it was, and then, if he convinced her of his innocence, she would help him take care of Justin, as she had promised. If Justin was responsible for the horror in the kitchen, she would do whatever it took to stop him. *And if Carlo is?*

Eyes forward, she walked out of the apartment, down the stairs, through the reading room, and out the back door.

The horse whinnied as she approached. *Maybe she smells the blood.* "It's okay, Tess," she said, petting her muzzle, then untethering her. "It's okay, girl."

The mare stamped her foot, head nodding back, a flash of white showing in her eye. Alex took the rein firmly, murmuring her name. Behind her, she heard the sound of a foot scuffing wet cement, but before she could turn, a white cloth reeking of chloroform was clamped over her nose and mouth. The world began to fade, and as it did, strange hands caught her beneath her arms and she heard Tess galloping away.

# TOM ABERNATHY

Tom Abernathy walked out of Doc Hartman's small clinic feeling more than a little relief. Eric Watson was running a fever, and the leg had a nasty break, but Hartman had assured him the young man would be fine.

Moss Baskerville drove up, and he strolled over to the cruiser. "Eric's okay," he told the chief. "Any word on Marie?"

Moss shook his head. "No, not yet. Henry brought the boy's body in." He paused. "Cassie and Eve are missing, Tom."

"They're not at the ranch?"

"House was broken into." Baskerville's eyes were dark and indecipherable. "Goddamned religious nuts." He paused, then asked gruffly, "Eric tell you anything?"

"No. He passed out a few minutes after I found him. The doc thinks he'll come around before too long, though. You get that search warrant?"

"No. Shirley never showed up. I just went by her place, and she and Larry have their hands full sandbagging. They live up by Rhyolite Wash, and their whole street's threatened."

"You want to go to the compound and try to get in again?" Tom asked.

"You bet your ass I do." His face reddened with barely contained fury. "Goddamned Apostles and their goddamned Apocalypse. First the graffiti, now the people." He took a deep breath. "Tom, we're not going to get inside before they open up to the public for their big morning service, and I'm afraid that by then, it'll be too late. We've got to get that warrant, and hope it gets us inside today. If it doesn't, well then, we'll explore other options. You willing to make the drive to Barstow?"

It was something to do to keep his mind off Marie. "Be glad to."

## ONE HUNDRED NINETEEN
## HANNIBAL CAINE

"Very good, Justin," Hannibal Caine said, looking at the unconscious body of Alexandra Manderley on a rear church pew. The boy had performed beyond his expectations and looked inordinately pleased with himself.

"I get her tomorrow; that's the deal."

"Correct."

"She's all mine," he persisted.

"Yes. If you're worried, why don't you spend the night here? Attend our morning services."

"Yeah, well, I guess. But I've gotta go home first." He stared at Caine with those disturbing blue eyes. "Clear it with my parents, you know?"

Caine nodded, smiling cherubically. "Of course, of course. I'll leave word with the guards that you may come and go as you please." He didn't want the young killer to leave, but he didn't want to hold him against his will, and thought it was a sure bet Justin would be back, especially if he gave him the freedom he demanded.

"What are you going to do with her now?"

"We'll lock her up. Don't worry, she's not going anywhere."

The boy grinned, then turned on his heel and trotted out of the church.

Troubled, Caine watched him for a moment, then turned to two hulking Apostles he'd appointed as his personal guards. "Put her in the room with the tattooed whore. Tell the guards to check on them every hour. And do it in pairs," he added, remembering how easily the shepherdess had escaped. "Make sure the door is secure."

He watched the men lift the woman off the wooden bench and position her between them, her arms over their shoulders. "Take the back stairs and don't draw attention to yourselves."

He walked to the front of the church and stood in the side doorway, staring at the Fellowship House, where tonight's dinner would take place. About half the Apostles were still out on their day's missionary work, and the compound seemed nearly deserted at the moment. Hannibal was taking extra precautions because few of these people were aware of the activities of the Special Projects Committee. Tomorrow, the women on the crosses would be an awe-inspiring, mystical sight for them, but today, the more Apostles who witnessed preparations, the more who would have to be marked for death. He didn't care to diminish his flock any more than necessary.

He was about to go out the door and return to his office when he heard Eldo Blandings call his name.

"Yes, Eldo?"

Half a dozen blood-stained, muddy Apostles stood behind the wild-eyed old man, two of them dragging a forlorn-looking woman between them.

"We've had casualties, Hannibal. We have to go back for the wounded with reinforcements."

"Back where?"

"Dead Man's Hill." Blandings paused. "I have disturbing news, Hannibal. About the shepherdess. Somehow she infiltrated our group, then escaped, heavily armed, up Dead Man's Hill, and we think the child is with her. She killed a dozen of us, at least."

"That was very incompetent of you, Elder Blandings," Caine

said, his voice soft and controlled. "Get back out there immediately and recapture them both. Is that clear?"

"That was my intention."

"Who's this?" Hannibal stared at the woman as he walked forward.

"She's the replacement you requested, Hannibal."

"She's in worse shape than the tattooed whore. I told you to be careful." He shook his head. "I'll be surprised if this one lasts the night. Shoddy work, Eldo. You know better."

Blandings's face blazed with humiliation, his eyes with icy anger. "We'll procure another."

"No. Confine yourself to cleaning up your messes. Young Justin has brought us a fine specimen. I'm very impressed with his work," he added, enjoying twisting the knife into Eldo's back.

"Put her with the others," he told the guards who had just returned from taking Justin's trophy away. He turned back to Eldo. "Don't let me down again, Elder Blandings. More importantly, don't let the Prophet down."

# PART FOUR
# APOCALYPSE

... Then they shall seek a vision of the prophet ...
  —Ezekiel 7:26

And I will show wonders in the heavens and in the earth The sun shall be
  turned into darkness, and the moon into blood ...
  —Joel 2:30, 31

... I beheld Satan as lightning fall from heaven.
  —Luke 10:18

Perhaps the truths about alien contact, like those of the metaphysical kind, are the truths of masks.
  —Jacques Vallee, *Revelations*

# TOM ABERNATHY

Back at the ranch, Tom hadn't even gone in the house. He'd put Belle's reins in Davy's hands, then climbed in his blue Ford pickup and headed down to Interstate 15, intent on getting to Barstow and returning with the warrant as soon as possible.

Though Tom doubted it would get them inside the compound, it was worth a try. He also had every intention of asking the Barstow police if they could spare a few hands; he doubted that Moss would mind, but since cops could be awfully territorial, he had decided not to mention it beforehand.

Raggedy swatches of blue had appeared to the south, and as the lowering sun came out from behind a cloud, he pulled the visor down to shield his eyes. He passed a double semitruck, its open trailers loaded with oranges, and as he swung around it, he was glad to see that there was little traffic ahead of him.

His watch beeped five o'clock as he passed the sign announcing that Barstow lay just ten miles ahead. Halfway there.

*Something's on the wind.* With the thought, his skin rose in gooseflesh, and as he continued driving, he felt as though some internal compass were spinning out of control. A second passed. Two.

The world cracked with thunder unlike anything he had ever heard, like a thousand rifle shots combined with the savage roll of timpani. A flash of brilliant light blinded him momentarily, and the truck started to fishtail on the rain- slicked road.

Tom regained control, cursing himself for his slow reflexes, for his unaccountable fear. The primitive within screamed at him to turn around and race home, but he told it to shut the hell up and he clenched the steering wheel, knuckles white.

This all in the space of a heartbeat. Then something went wrong with the truck, a blowout, he thought, or he'd dropped an engine bolt. He hung on to the wheel, slowing, trying to keep the vehicle under control until he could pull over.

He caught a glimpse of the semi in the rearview mirror, saw oranges tumbling out of its open trailers, rolling across the freeway like billiard balls.

The earth was shaking, not his truck, and that realization calmed him. Long seconds passed, and more. Silently he began to count, knowing that every shaker felt like it lasted forever while you rode it out, waiting to see if it was the Big One.

*Fifty-nine. Sixty.* He'd never counted past twenty seconds before and his alarm returned, growing in tandem with the unending force of the temblor.

Suddenly the truck jumped, landed, jumped again, a bucking bronco. Up ahead, a black Camry skittered across three lanes of high-way, onto the shoulder, crashing against the chain-link fencing. Behind him, one of the semi's trailers jackknifed and overturned.

*Maybe this is the Big One.* He gave up counting but decided to keep driving, even though most everyone else had given up. As a longtime Californian, he had ceased to believe that the fabled Big One was anything but a good tale. Sure, there were quakes, and damage here and there, sometimes major like the Landers quake or the Northridge shaker in '94, but the Big One, the one that kept on going and going and going until everything came loose or turned the

Mojave into beachfront property, well, he just didn't believe in it. *Maybe you should reconsider.*

He watched the asphalt road roll like low breakers on the sea and he surfed them doggedly, hanging on to the wheel, refusing to let anything, not even Mother Nature, keep him from his task.

He wasn't too worried about his ranch. His stables were built the same way as his house, with springs and reinforcements in the foundation and walls, and glass that would bend long before it would break. He also knew that Davy would calm the animals. He prayed that Marie, Cassie, and Eve were safe.

"Whoa!" he yelled as the truck bounced sideways. It came down on the passenger side wheels and he thought that he was going over, but miraculously the truck fell back on all fours. And kept going, creaking and groaning with every buck of the earth.

He was coming up fast on the Cuhilla Wash Bridge, and he slammed on the brakes as the pavement on the bridge pushed up in a mountain before him. The low pillars holding the road above the wash suddenly broke free, exploding out sideways like broken teeth. Tom let off the brake and prayed no one was behind him as he turned the steering wheel hard left. Brakes locking, the truck skidded. He corrected the wheel and abruptly the Ford stalled out sideways in the number three lane.

*Delirium tremens.* The earth rattled beneath him, and he stayed with the truck, riding it out. Finally it began winding down, the ground shivering with little shakes and tremors. *Death throes.*

Sitting there facing the wrong way on the freeway, Tom stared out at the scattering of cars, trucks, and oranges. Some of the vehicles were still moving, others beginning to move again. Tom opened the door and got out, his legs still insisting the ground was moving, his eyes telling him otherwise. He walked to the broken bridge. It looked like a drawbridge, raised and open in the center, and there was no way to cross it—the damage was done on both sides of the highway. In the distance, a billboard hung sideways, and a few cars dotted the road. The sun, low in the sky, cast beautiful colors on the silvery clouds around it. It was a particularly magnificent sunset.

Then he heard a sizzling sound, an electric crackling buzz. On the shoulder, directly opposite his truck, a towering utility pole was cracking like a matchstick, the lines swaying drunkenly. "Christ Almighty!" He jumped in the truck and turned the key. It didn't start. The pole cracked and tilted more as Tom tried again. No luck. "Lord, if you're there, I could use a hand!"

The engine caught. Stomping the accelerator, he tore out of the way just before the pole crashed down right where he'd been parked.

Slowly he drove the wrong way along the buckled median strip until he found a break in the oleander bushes that separated the two sides of the interstate. He pulled across it, then began the ten-mile trip back to Madelyn.

# JAMES ROBERT SINCLAIR

C hairs had tipped over and small objects flew to his bedroom floor, but Sinclair had barely noticed. This earthquake was far more than broken glass and toppled furniture; it was the unmistakable herald of Armageddon, the thunder of horses' hooves as the Four descended to earth. It filled him with sadness and joy as he went forth, to minister to his people.

He found only minor damage to the compound: broken windows, fallen paintings and furniture, broken dishes in the cafeteria. There was much to clean up, but he had built this place to withstand earthquakes, and it had protected his people well. The electricity had been out for less than a minute before the compound's emergency generators kicked in, giving them light once more. The cross would burn brightly tonight in an otherwise lightless land, a beacon to the faithful, a promise of hope for mankind.

His people stared at him, and he smiled and soothed, knowing they had never before seen him as he appeared now: barefoot, in robes, his hair loose over his shoulders.

He was glad that they seemed to find comfort in his appearance as he made his way to the infirmary. The twenty-bed clinic was two-thirds full, most of the patients suffering cuts that needed stitching, some with broken bones. Then he saw Senior Apostle Steve Clayman, hooked to an IV, his left arm swathed in bandages.

"What happened to you?" Sinclair asked as he sat in the chair by the bed.

Clayman stared at him, then opened his cracked lips. "Struck by lightning during the mission."

"The mission?" Sinclair asked. "While you were witnessing in Madelyn?"

"No. When we did the UFO freaks." Clayman tried to smile. "I killed one for you—"

"Prophet Sinclair! I didn't expect to see you here!" Hannibal Caine bustled up. "Don't try to talk, Steve. Doctor's orders."

Sinclair rose and motioned Caine to follow him outside. "What's he talking about, 'UFO freaks'? Who was killed?"

"I don't know the details, James," Caine said in a conspiratorial tone. "But I believe that Eldo may be interpreting your orders as carte blanche to behave in a more aggressive manner than you intended." He laid his hand on Sinclair's wrist. "I was just trying to find out what happened myself."

"I know Eldo has his problems, but I believe in his ability to follow my orders." He studied Hannibal, and for the first time, saw something he didn't like. It had always been there, a calculating look behind the smiling blue eyes, but it had never registered before. Perhaps because he didn't want to see it. *He's the one.*

"Are you intending to speak to Eldo?" There was the slightest hint of worry in Caine's voice. "Perhaps you'd like me to do it for you?"

"No, that won't be necessary." The words filled him with infinite sadness. "It is the way of things. The signs are progressing as God told me they would, and whatever happened today is part of the cycle. Tomorrow the world ends, and Clayman's being struck by lightning is just another portent of what is to come. Others will fall as well." He paused, watching Hannibal's cheerful mask fade slightly.

"Is the radio station broadcasting yet?" Sinclair asked after a long pause.

"Not presently, but we have a crew on their way up to the tower. There are no stations on the air at present, James."

"Good. Perhaps the earthquake has ensured that we will have a large audience tonight."

"Including many of our resident Apostles," Caine said. "About half were out on missionary work when the earthquake struck. I doubt if many will be able to return."

"That's unfortunate. I hope they're all well." Sinclair hesitated. "Keep watch for them. I'll see you in the private dining room at six-thirty." He turned and started to walk away.

"Prophet?"

Sinclair turned. "Yes, Hannibal?"

"About tomorrow's open services."

Sinclair waited.

"The earthquake did some damage, and Davis in the business office says we can't open to the public until an inspection is completed. We may have to be content with a closed service. We can broadcast, of course."

"That would be a shame, Hannibal. Perhaps we can hold an open-air meeting instead. Work on that, will you?"

Hannibal looked supremely pained. "Yes, Prophet. Are you returning to your chambers now?"

"Soon. Why?"

"Just in case." Caine smiled, waved, and walked off in the opposite direction.

"Eve? Where are you?"

Marie's mobile home had fallen off its foundations and lay in a crumpled heap on its side. She'd left the little girl inside while she was out saddling Rex for the ride into town. Thankfully, she'd left the stable doors wide open, and when the shaking began, she was able to lead the horse out without problems. An instant later, half the building was gone. Sheep were still running out of the destruction, thanks to Dorsey, who was herding for all he was worth.

Marie stared at the wreck that had been her home. "Eve?" she yelled. "Eve? Answer me!" She turned off the propane tank. "Eve! Where are you?"

"Marie!"

The voice was small but strong, and Marie waded into the wreckage. "Eve. Where are you?"

"Under the table."

"Keep talking so I can find you."

Climbing through the debris, she followed Eve's voice until she finally spied the top of her dinette table, tilted sideways against the wall. "Eve?"

The child's face appeared, then she crawled out from behind the table, and Marie lifted her out of the mess and carried her outside.

"Wait here. I'll be right back." She went back into the wreckage and soon reemerged with her Remington rifle. Despite all the fancy weaponry she'd stowed in the barn to pack on the horse, the Remington was her favorite, and the only material possession she really cared about. She brought it out, then walked behind the trailer, peering around it into the after- . noon sun. Down the road she could see the compound, the guards at the gates, and if she could see them, they would see her.

"Eve," she told the little girl. "I'm going back in to find us something to eat. We have to wait a little while before it's safe to leave."

# MOSS BASKERVILLE

"Wipe your face, Moss," Ray Vine said, handing Baskerville a dish towel. "Won't do for the chief of police to go around bleeding on people."

"Thanks." The cut on his forehead wasn't bad, but it bled like a son of a bitch. He wiped the blood away, then pressed the towel firmly against it and stared at Ray's Cafe. He, Ray, and Rosie, along with a group of other shell-shocked people, stood outside the diner. Across the parking lot, trailer rigs had been tossed about like Tinkertoys, and cars had bounced and crashed into one another. The café itself was a disaster. Ray had extinguished two kitchen fires and turned the gas off. Now the biggest immediate problems were the broken glass and fallen light fixtures and ceiling fans.

"Won't be shut down more than a week," Ray said, reading Moss's mind.

Moss nodded. "I wonder where the quake was centered."

"Good question."

The electricity, in addition to the phones, was out now, and none of the radio stations were on the air, not even the fifty-thousand-watt station that broadcast from Los Angeles. The thought that L.A. might be completely knocked out was almost too much for him. After dark, when the strong stations in Colorado and Nevada began coming in, he'd know more, but right now there was only uncertainty. Even the police band gave nothing but static. "Looks like we're on our own, Ray."

"It sure does." Ray shook his massive head, surveying the damage.

"I'm going to need some help," Moss announced. Action was not only called for, it was the best cure for worry.

"I can't leave my property, Moss. I'm sorry, but I'm dead-on for looters."

"Didn't expect you to. But you're a deputy as of now, just the same." He smiled grimly. "That'll make it easier for you to protect your place. You got a piece?"

"Thirty-eight semiautomatic."

"Carry it. Now, listen. It's going to be dark soon and people will come here from town, just like they always do. Pick out someplace to set up a campground in your parking lot, will you?"

"I can do that. Look there." Ray pointed at a blue pickup coming across the center divider on I-15. It cut across the westbound lanes of the highway.

"It's Tom." The eastbound Madelyn exit was an underpass, and Abernathy was obviously taking no chances. Moss watched as he turned down the westbound off-ramp, disappeared for a moment, then came around the bend and into the lot, weaving between cars. The cowboy pulled up and hopped out.

"Couldn't get through," Tom said, wiping sweat from his brow with his kerchief. "Almost bit the bullet a couple times. It's bad out there, and we're cut off. The interstate's out of commission ten miles up the road."

"Things look bad here, too." Moss shook his head. "I was just about to tell Ray that we need to organize groups to go into town and check every house for wounded and to make sure the gas is off. We're making Ray's lot command central." He smiled bitterly. "That's the most official-sounding thing I've ever heard leave my lips."

"I'll organize a group to go into Madland," Tom told him.

"Great. Ray, I'll send Ken Landry over with maps, and you two can figure out who to send where in town."

"Okay."

Tom glanced at his watch, obviously eager to get to his ranch. "Moss, did you go back to the compound yet?"

"Just left there, right before the quake. They had guards posted on all sides, and they're packing some serious weapons. A warrant wouldn't have done us a bit of good," he added grimly.

"We'll just have to get in tomorrow morning." Tom shook his head. "Damn."

"Afraid not," Moss answered. "They also had a sign posted on the gate announcing that the compound would be closed due to earthquake damage."

"Earthquake damage?" Tom repeated. "*before* the quake? I guess old Jim-Bob really *is* a prophet."

"I assume it referred to the earlier quakes," Moss said dryly. "Not that I believe it for a minute."

"Might be true now," Ray murmured, staring at the wreckage of his coffee shop.

"Might be," Moss agreed. "In any case, we're not going to see backup any time soon."

Tom took off his hat and ran his fingers through his hair. "We're going to have to get in there one way or another."

"What the hell are those psychos guarding, anyway?" Ray asked.

"My guess is that they're afraid we're going to come in and get Marie, Cassie, and Eve back," Moss told him.

"It's got something to do with their big Apocalypse tomorrow," Tom explained. "And I'm guessing that means we have just until tomorrow morning to get them out of there safe and sound."

Moss studied him. "I hope so. In the meantime, I'm declaring martial law. Needs to be done, plus it gives us more leeway in dealing with the Apostles, or whoever else is causing us trouble." He patted his gun.

"You thinking of Dole?" Tom asked.

Moss nodded. "If you see that bastard, bring him to the station. Maybe we'll get some answers out of him." He looked at Ray. "I'll be by every little while. I hope." He turned back to Tom. "After you get done checking Madland, we need to meet up. Bring your sorry ass back down here and we'll figure out how to get into that compound."

Tom climbed back in his truck. "I'll do that."

## ONE HUNDRED TWENTY-FOUR
# JUSTIN MARTIN

Justin sat in the Mustang and fondled Carlo's knife. After he'd left the compound, he'd gone home to clean up, but then the quake struck and his mother went into hysterics, clinging to him and sobbing about the shattered this and the broken that. Her histrionics were so disgusting that he'd been ready to bash her brains in, just to shut her up. He would have, too, if dear old Dad hadn't shown up. Relieved of his mother, Justin quickly dressed in black for tonight's meeting with Carlo and went out to kill a couple hours.

He was parked in Madland's lot, way back at the rear where he wouldn't be noticed, but where he could keep an eye on the road. He wanted to know when Carlo returned. If he returned. Justin wanted to tell him where Alex, sweet Alex, was and to invite the Peeler to accompany him to the compound, where there would be one big difference: Justin would be in charge, not Carlo.

When he'd first arrived, he'd immediately checked Carlo's place to make sure the fortune-teller wasn't inside. Though he couldn't get upstairs because most of it was now downstairs, the little reading room was virtually untouched by the quake. Christie's scalp still hung from the ceiling fan, and that probably meant that Carlo hadn't been here.

After that, he'd checked on the mine ride and was pleased as hell to find that it was impassable. He thought it unlikely that the lower level where the bodies were buried would ever be accessible again. Smirking, he gazed up at the twilight sky. Everything was going as promised. He was invincible.

After checking the mine, he'd looked around a little more, telling the stunt people and others whom he ran into that he was searching for injured persons. They thanked him and left him alone, too involved in moving the animals and assessing their own damage to waste his time with idiot questions.

Finally he had returned to the Mustang. He'd been sitting there about twenty minutes now, listening to the Doors and thinking about tomorrow, about the things he'd do to Alex while the Peeler watched and instructed.

Killing Christie had been easy, skinning her, hard work, and it was a damned shame she was too hard to find in the wreckage, because he thought he'd done a fine job, by far his best. He wanted Carlo to see—it might help convince him of Justin's natural abilities.

Hearing the roar of engines, he looked up and saw a set of head-lights coming up the highway. He turned off the tape and waited. It was a full-size blue pickup truck, and Justin slid low in the seat watching as it pulled into the parking lot.

As soon as the driver climbed out of the cab, Justin recognized that rich hayseed, Tom Abernathy. His passenger stepped out. It was Carlo Pelegrine.

"Bingo," he whispered.

Justin waited until the pair disappeared into the park's main entrance, then exited the car and let himself in the far end. Quietly he moved down the service road, climbing over wreckage, skirting glass and metal, until he arrived at the Sorcerer's Apprentice's back entrance. He figured Carlo would show up sooner or later, so he let himself into the little reading room and sat there, stroking the knife and contemplating Christie's magnificent mane of blond hair.

# CARLO PELEGRINE

"What a mess," Tom Abernathy said as he and Carlo walked through the Madland gates.

Carlo nodded, playing his flashlight over the broken buildings. Alex had never shown up at the ranch, and he was becoming very anxious. "I want to talk to the stuntmen first."

"Sure thing." They headed for the stables behind the arena, but as they approached, they saw no one around. Tom cupped his hands around his mouth. "Anybody here?"

"Just us chickens." Shorty Sykes, carrying a bright lantern, appeared from the shadowed recesses of the stable area.

"When did you last see Alex?" Carlo asked, too abruptly. Sykes raised his eyebrows. "Why? Didn't she get back?" "No," Tom said. "You split up?"

"It wasn't raining, and she's a good rider, so we didn't think much about it when she said she wanted to meander along and do some thinking. Then she was headed for the ranch." He looked at Carlo. "She said she was looking to hook up with you there."

"Where did you split up?"

"Just south of Thunder Road. Henry had that boy's body on his horse and I figured it was bothering her, that was why she hung back. I'm sorry—"

"It's not your fault," Carlo said. "Did you pass anyone else on the road after you left her?"

"Not a soul." He glanced back at the stable as timbers settled, then another flashlight bobbed out of the darkness beyond.

"Heard you found Eric Watson," Mad Dog called as he approached.

"Sure did," Tom said.

"We're happy to hear it," Mad Dog told him. "Listen, we've got the animals together. Would it be all right if we herd them all down to your ranch?"

"Wouldn't have it any other way. Any of them hurt?"

"We lost a few chickens, and some have scrapes and cuts, but otherwise, they're fine. How about you?"

"We fared just fine. The damage is minimal. One of you boys needs to go down to Ray's and check in for all of you—we're trying to get a head count." Tom paused. "After that, if anybody asks, they can camp in Ray's lot. You folks can stay at my place."

"Much obliged," Mad Dog called as he turned and headed back toward the stables.

Tom pulled a wrench from his back pocket. "We're going in to check for gas leaks and wounded before it gets any darker."

Shorty nodded. "A few people are already doing that. They started in the middle and are working their way out from there. Well, I better get back to work."

Carlo watched Shorty disappear. "Tom, why don't you take Tumbleweed, and I'll take Main? We'll work until we run into the others."

Tom looked surprised. "Well, sure, that sounds fine. Shut off the gas, mark buildings where you can see there are wounded or fatalities, but don't go inside. It's too dark to do a thorough search tonight."

Carlo nodded, then as Tom headed toward Tumbleweed, where Cassie's theater was located, he turned back toward Main Street.

Playing his light over the buildings as he made his way to the Sorcerer's Apprentice, he cringed at the sight of the lopsided structures, at
the window glass, placards, and broken boards and plaster littering
the sidewalk and street.

At last he stepped up onto the wooden sidewalk fronting his
shop. His green tablecloth was on the ground, along with a few
candles, crystal balls, and a scattering of tarot cards. The sight
numbed him.

Grimly he moved to the door and inserted his key. It unlocked
easily, but he had to put his shoulder to it and shove repeatedly to get
the door unstuck.

It opened so suddenly that he stumbled inside and nearly fell on
the broken glass. Shining the flashlight through the room, he saw that
the glass display cases had shattered and his antique cash register lay
on the floor halfway across the room, nearly hidden under mounds of
fallen books.

He heard a noise beyond the green drapes and, startled, turned.
"Alex?"

No reply, only the uneasy sound of timber cracking somewhere
above. Glancing up, he saw the ceiling fan swaying, half-ripped from
its moorings. Quickly he stepped out from under it. Tom was right:
He shouldn't be in here, but he had to make sure that Alex wasn't
trapped here.

Another sound, like a chair scraping, floated in from beyond the
drapes. Carlo stepped toward the curtains and began to push them
aside, pausing to kneel and pick up his favorite deck of tarot cards
from among the others on the floor. He slipped the pack in his pocket.

His crystal ball rolled slowly toward him, coming to rest against
the toes of his shoes. Without thinking, he scooped it into his hand.

"Heads up, Charlie!"

Carlo looked up into Justin Martin's smiling face. The boy sat on
a wooden chair in the midst of chaos. "Kind of a mess in here, huh?
Real pain in the ass!"

"What are you doing here?" Carlo asked.

"I was checking for victims. I found one."

"Did you?"

"Yes." He looked up. "She met with a nasty accident."

Filled with dread, Carlo followed his gaze, gasping as he saw the scalp dangling by long blond hair from the skewed ceiling fixture.

Justin rose, slowly pulling a shining blade from inside his jacket.

"My knife," Carlo began.

"*The* knife. You use it to peel your victims."

"I use it to peel oranges, Justin." Everything, especially his thoughts, had been moving in slow motion, but his mind suddenly shifted into gear. "Where's Alex?" he demanded. "What have you done with her?"

The boy waved the knife menacingly. "Nothing. She's safe." An oily smile slid across his face. "She's with friends."

Carlo stepped closer. "Tell me where she is."

Another sickening smile. "In the hands of God."

"You son of a bitch," Carlo exploded, throwing the crystal ball. Justin sidestepped neatly, and the orb crashed into the wall behind him. Carlo leaped at Justin, tackling him, barely noticing the pain that abruptly sliced into his side. He wrestled, pinning Justin down and forcing his hand open. He tore the knife away, brought it up, and slowly lowered it until the tip rested just beneath Justin's chin. "Did you kill her?" he managed through clenched teeth. "Did you?"

"No," Justin whispered, his eyes bright, pupils dilated. "Are you going to kill me?"

He wanted to, wanted to sink the knife to the hilt in Justin's throat, then yank it back and forth and watch the life drain out of him. He wanted to feel the hot blood gush over his hands, to slice that insane smile off his face.

*You're no different from him!* The thought slammed him. The knife wavered, drew a single drop of blood. Justin smiled. "Do it," he whispered. "The ultimate thrill."

"Where is she?" Carlo growled.

"I gave her to the Apostles. I get to have her after they're through with her." He smirked, despite the knife. "That way, I don't have to share her with you. But you can help *me* if you want."

Carlo's hand trembled, ready to plunge the blade. He knew doing so would break his vow not to hurt others, would mean that his life had meant nothing, but he didn't care anymore. He could feel blood drizzling over his rib cage from the fiery wound in his left side. It was the only thing that seemed real. *Alex is real!* She was the reason he wouldn't commit murder; if he killed Justin in cold blood, he knew he would eventually be compelled to end his own life. He could never have a life with Alex, and he suddenly knew that he wanted that more than anything.

Hand trembling, he slowly, so slowly, pulled the knife away from Justin's neck.

"Chicken?" the youth goaded.

"You're not worth it," Carlo hissed. He threw the knife across the room, then, feeling Justin's muscles tense, ready to fight, he made a fist and knocked him cold with a blow to the temple.

It was oddly unsatisfying. Carlo rose, standing over the body. He had to bring the boy to justice, but he couldn't let it jeopardize Alex's life or his own by simply turning him in. His mind reeled and he finally shut off all thoughts but those concerning Alex. He had to get into the compound and rescue her. No doubt the others were imprisoned there as well.

He knew what he had to do, what his purpose was. He grabbed the knife and stuck it in his belt, then left the building, the pain in his side a dull ache, blood oozing sluggishly, sticking his shirt to the wound.

Outdoors, he quickly checked the other buildings on Main Street, impatient to be on his way. It was a miracle that no fires had broken out in Madland, Carlo thought as he walked along behind the buildings and turned off the gas at each one. Even though the buildings didn't look too bad from the outside, peering into windows revealed the same kind of damage his had sustained. In places, the wooden sidewalks were impassable because of fallen awnings and broken posts and windows, and some of the structures that at first looked sound had slipped off their foundations.

He ran across a half dozen shopkeepers and told them all to go down to Ray's. Amazingly, he found no wounded: It was fortunate that the day had been too stormy for the park to be full of tourists.

When he met up with some of the stunt people at the end of the street, he asked them to tell Tom he'd meet him back at the ranch later. Then he trotted to his storage shed and carefully extracted his motorcycle from the rubble. Opening the ditty bag behind the seat, he pulled out a wool muffler, took off his leather jacket, and lifted his shirt, cringing as he pulled it away from the gash.

The wound was two inches long, painful and bloody, but not deep—the blade had been deflected by a rib, and it gaped open, needing stitches. Gingerly he pressed the edges together, then tied the muffler tightly around his midsection, hoping that would stop the bleeding. He put his black jacket back on and zipped it up. Grimacing with pain, he climbed onto the Harley and turned the key, listening to the engine's soothing, powerful thrum.

There was no point in going to the Apostles' front gate. He knew the stories about the tunnels beneath the compound—one of the books he carried in his shop went into them in great detail, though he suspected it was all fabrication. But finding one was his best bet, at least if the quake hadn't collapsed them. *But where?*

He recalled Alex's story about the UFOs she and Eric had chased on Olive Mesa, about the clothing she had found there. *Sinclair sees them as angels.* That's what she'd said. It would be reasonable that a passage led between the compound and the mountain just north of it, if Sinclair spent time there, left his clothes there.

Carlo revved the engine, then rode off, headed for Olive Mesa.

As he slowed to turn onto Thunder Road, he saw the brilliant cross gleaming on the church, the only light in the endless night.

## ONE HUNDRED TWENTY-SIX
# TOM ABERNATHY

W hen Tom arrived at the Langtry Theater, he found it virtually intact, except for one of the double front doors, which hung crazily from one hinge. He mounted the steps to try to position the door back in its frame and at least make it appear closed and locked, and that's when he had a crazy idea, one that might get him and a few others into the Apostles' compound.

Shining his light inside, he saw that the walls and ceilings appeared stable, so he walked in and found his way backstage, stepping around broken chandeliers and toppled sets. In the costume room, he filled two boxes with clothing and props from the Halloween show, then carried them across Madland and out to his truck. He placed his booty in the bed, then turned and started back into the park, nearly running smack into Justin Martin, his face pale except for a purpling welt on the side of his head.

"You all right, son?"

The boy's customary smile was gone, replaced by a sullen glare that made the hairs on the back of Tom's neck get ticklish.

"You all right?" he repeated.

The Martin boy's lip curled up in a mock smile, and without

answering, he pushed past Tom. A moment later, a car door slammed, an engine gunned, and the teen's black Mustang peeled out across the lot. Tom whistled, low. *Something strange is going on there.*

"Tom!"

He turned at the sound of Henry Running Deer's voice. "Hey, Henry."

"Who was that?"

"Damn fool kid. How're we doing?"

"The animals should be arriving at your place any minute now, and all the buildings have been checked." Henry shook his head. "Man, we were lucky. No serious injuries in the park. No deaths; at least we don't think so."

"That's good news," Tom said as he and Henry began walking down the access road behind Main Street. "Anybody still inside?"

"We're standing two-man guard all night. Shorty and I are up first. That is, when he gets back from your place."

"Good planning," Tom said, his mind mostly on Marie. He wanted to get back to the ranch and give his half-baked plan some thought. "Have you seen Carlo anywhere? He came in with me."

"Oh, yeah. He left a message for you, said to tell you he'll meet you at the ranch later. He took off on his motorcycle. I think you just missed him."

"Where'd he go?"

Henry shook his head. "He didn't say."

They stood behind the Sorcerer's Apprentice, and Tom glanced at the back door. "Well, I guess there's no point to looking in there for him."

"Did you hear that?" Henry cocked his head at the sound of gunfire.

"Come on," Tom whispered. Hunkering into the shadows, he led the way up the side of Carlo's building. As they approached the sidewalk, an engine roared and a vehicle's bright headlights splashed against the broken buildings. Another round fired, closer now. Quickly he and Henry backed into the shadows.

A few seconds passed and the vehicle came into view. It was a white van, and it pulled to a stop two doors down in the middle of the street. White-robed, hooded figures piled out of it, two carrying automatic weapons, six more holding long sticks that Tom mistook momentarily for baseball bats.

He heard the slosh of liquid, caught the sharp tang of gasoline in the air, then one of the sticks flared with fire, followed by another and another. The Apostles fanned out on the street, singing a hymn that sounded vaguely like "Onward Christian Soldiers."

"Tom!"

Henry's whisper just about made Tom jump out of his boots. "What?"

"I'm going to get the fire department. You staying here or what?"

Tom stared at the figures, listened to their singing voices, heartsick as he watched the candy store across the street catch fire. "When I settle with the insurance company, you're a witness, Henry. This fire's no act of God."

Henry nodded. "Let's go!"

He followed Henry into the parking lot. The stuntman hopped in his Four-Runner and was speeding out of the lot before Tom even turned his key. Maybe, he thought, Madland wouldn't go up since the wooden buildings were rain-soaked. *Maybe, but I doubt it.*

And as he pulled out of the parking lot, he saw flames dancing in his rearview mirror.

# ONE HUNDRED TWENTY-SEVEN
## MARIE LOPEZ

Marie and Eve had been ready to leave an hour earlier, but just as she was about to set Eve on Rex's back, a van full of Apostles came down the road and turned on Old Madelyn. It wasn't long before she heard gunshots, then smelled smoke. Numb, she and Eve listened to distant sirens and watched the flames consume the park. The van soon returned, but she still couldn't leave because the Apostles were watching the fire too. She didn't dare make a run for it, not with the weapons they were carrying; they would cut her, Eve, and Rex down instantly.

Now Madland was dark, the Apostles invisible. Leaving Dorsey to mind the sheep, Marie lifted Eve onto Rex, then climbed up herself. "Here we go," she whispered, as they set off cross-country toward Tom's place.

## ONE HUNDRED TWENTY-EIGHT
# ALEXANDRA MANDERLEY

She awoke in darkness, her head aching, her body stiff from lying on the cold, hard floor. The only sound was breathing; her own and someone else's.

"Hello?" Alex whispered, getting to her feet. There was no reply, only a catch in the soft, ragged breaths. She massaged the numbness out of one arm, then pressed her fingers against her throbbing forehead, a chemical stink still in her nostrils.

"Who's there?" She waited. "Please, who's there? I won't hurt you."

"Alex?" an uncertain voice asked.

"Cassie? Is that you?"

"Yes."

"Where are we?"

"In the compound," Cassie managed, her voice tinged with pain. "They're going to crucify us."

"What?"

"Tomorrow."

Alex felt along the walls for a light switch. "Are you sure?"

"Yes. Alex, have you seen Eve?"

"No, but don't worry. Moss is looking for her." Her fingers found the switch and flipped it. Light bloomed overhead, making her squint.

Cassie was propped in a corner, bruised and battered, her gaze not on Alex but on the opposite corner. "Dear God," she whispered. "It's Janet Wister, from the diner."

Alex saw a plump, middle-aged woman lying on her back, her clothing torn and muddy, her face mottled blue and purple. "The UFO waitress?" she asked, crossing to the woman and kneeling beside her. Two dark bullet holes, one in the shoulder, another in her abdomen, had stopped bleeding. Blood had jelled over the wounds.

"Yes, that's her." Cassie watched, her eyes wide. "Is she ... ?"

Alex felt Janet's neck for a pulse. Finding none, she nodded.

"I thought so. I heard her breathing for a little while, then she just stopped. Just like that."

Alex crossed to Cassie, concerned about the dazed tone, the shock in her voice. Only when she squatted beside her did she see the extent of the other woman's injuries.

"Alex," Cassie said, staring at the corpse. "That's why you're here."

"What?"

"You're her replacement. There are two crosses in the church. They tied me to one for a little while, to try it out, I guess, but tomorrow they're going to use nails." Tears washed over her bruised cheeks. "I'm sure they are. Marie was here," she added without pausing for breath. "I saw her twice. Once as a prisoner and later in a robe. Did she get out?"

"I hope so." Cassie was near delirium, and Alex did her best to soothe her. "Moss will be here soon. He's coming for you. He knows you're here."

"It won't do him any good. They're all armed."

More tears flowed as Alex removed her denim jacket and draped it over Cassie's bare shoulders.

"We're getting out of here, don't worry. Can you walk?"

Cassie shook her head. "My ankle's wrenched or maybe broken."

Alex looked at the dark swollen leg and knew there was no way Cassie would be walking out of here. Forcing a smile, she rose and crossed to the door, tried it unsuccessfully.

"The guards might hear you," Cassie whispered. "Don't rattle the knob."

Alex nodded, and studied the dead bolt above the knob. Drawing a bobby pin from her hair, she set to work.

"Do you know what you're doing?" Cassie asked.

"Haven't a clue, but it's all we've got."

# JAMES ROBERT SINCLAIR

He had broken bread and drunk wine with his most trusted Apostles. Sinclair had enjoyed their company, even that of his Judas, and as he made his way toward the church to deliver his final pre-Apocalyptic sermon, he knew that everything was in order, even those things that he dreaded. The course was set.

"James?"

He stopped walking and turned to survey Hannibal Caine. "Yes?"

"After the sermon, I wonder if I might have a word with you in private."

*And so it begins.* Sinclair smiled gently. "Yes, of course. Where?"

"In the steeple tower, perhaps? It's a beautiful night. It would be pleasant to look out at the stars one final time."

"Very well," Sinclair said, feeling the faint, fleeting edge of sorrow. "Very well."

## ONE HUNDRED THIRTY

# TOM ABERNATHY

There was a horse and rider leading a second horse on the ranch road, and as Tom pulled closer, the rider turned and stared at his lights, then trotted south about twenty yards.

"Who the hell is that?" Tom murmured as he pulled up parallel with the rider. He stopped, idling the truck in the road, and rolled down his windows. "You're on private property! Identify yourself!" He squinted into the darkness, unable to see more than vague shadows.

"Cowboy! It *is* you!"

Marie galloped toward him, and he could hardly get the door open fast enough, almost tripping on his own boots as he got out. When she was ten feet away, he saw that she had a child riding in front of her. *It can't be!* But it was. "Eve! You two are a sight for sore eyes!"

Marie swung off Rex and lifted the child down to the ground. "Is my mommy here?" she asked as Tom scooped her up.

"Not yet, honey." Holding the girl in one arm, he grabbed Marie around the waist and buried his face in her hair. "I was afraid I'd never see you again. I was about out of my mind."

She looked up at him, eyes shining. "Thanks, Tom. I like knowing that."

Reluctantly he let go of her, peering at the riderless horse. "Tess?"

"She was grazing in your north field. I found her on my way down here. She throw a rider?"

"I don't know. Alex Manderley rode her out this morning and never came back."

"Good Lord."

"It's the Apostles, isn't it?"

Marie nodded, then reached up and put her finger to his lips, glancing meaningfully at Eve.

Another set of headlights appeared on Tom's road. Tensing, he placed Eve in his truck, then walked out to meet the vehicle. Behind him, he heard Marie cock her rifle. His own hand resting on his holstered revolver, he waited.

"I think it's got a light bar on top," Marie announced.

"Yep." Tom sighed in relief. "It's Moss."

The chief pulled up and Tom walked to the window. "Marie and Eve just showed up."

"Thank God. What happened to them?"

"Don't know yet. Let's get to the house."

"AND THAT'S HOW WE GOT AWAY," MARIE TOLD TOM, MOSS, AND Davy Styles fifteen minutes later as they sat in flickering lantern light in Tom's den.

Moss stroked his sleeping daughter's hair and she unconsciously snuggled harder against his chest. "So you think Cass is safe until the eclipse?"

Marie nodded. "Probably. And I think that's where Alex is too. They probably took her to replace me." She paused. "Where's Carlo?"

"You got me," Tom replied. "He's supposed to be back here later; that's all I know."

"Damn fool's probably trying to rescue Alex by himself," Moss said. "Maybe I'd better try to get in again."

"Fool's errand," Marie told him. "They'd shoot you down before you could say boo. That's what they did to Janet Wister and her friends."

Moss nodded. "Dole's dead too. Looked like an accident, but I don't think so."

"Colonel Dole?" Tom asked in surprise.

"Car wreck on the desert above Madland."

"Daddy?" Eve interrupted sleepily. "Is he an officer? He said he was."

"You talked to him?"

"After the bad people took Mommy, I got lost and he found me. He was gonna bring me to you, then the bad people got him, too." She paused. "Daddy, he said to tell you he wasn't a bad man."

"Evie," Moss said gently. "Did you see who took Mommy?"

"That icky old man with the big nose that we saw at Madland. He had soldier clothes on." She closed her eyes and snuggled against his chest, thumb corked in her mouth.

Marie glanced at the others. "When's the morning serve-ice? We can get in then, if we can't before."

Moss shook his head. "Nope." He told her about the sign posted on the compound gate.

"Damn." Marie pushed a lock of hair from her face. "Then we have to get them out before the service. The sooner the better."

"You didn't find any of those fabled secret passages, did you, Marie?" Tom asked, rubbing his chin.

"No, but I'm sure they exist. The place is a regular honeycomb, hidden doors all over the place. I did find a room full of weapons—the illegal kind," she added, glancing at Moss. "And they're already using them."

"Did you ever get a look at Sinclair?" Moss asked:

She shook her head. "No. I almost think he doesn't know what Caine and Blandings are up to. It's just a hunch, though."

"Can I put Eve down in the other room?" the chief asked Tom. "She needs to sleep, and I don't want to chance her having more nightmares than she's already stuck with."

"I'll take her," Davy said. Taking a lantern, he carried the child from the room.

Baskerville leaned forward. "Here's how it is. Martial law's in effect. We've got a nine-o'clock curfew, and we have some of the townsfolk patrolling the streets. In the morning they'll start searching for wounded and the dead in earnest. The town's pretty much a wreck. I'd say fifty percent of the houses are still livable, half the businesses are all right." He hesitated, then fixed his gaze on Tom. "I'm sorry about Madland. Did you see who torched it?"

The hollow spot in Tom's gut returned. There had been nothing he or anyone else could do except stand back and watch it burn. "White van full of Apostles. Didn't see any faces."

Moss shook his head as Davy returned. "I'd love to get my hands on those goddamned murdering bastards. Here's the problem: We're cut off. The only radio station back on the air is that strong one in Los Angeles, and it says we had a seven point one, centered around the Cajon Pass. That's a good piece south of us, so I guess everything from Riverside County up to Kern County has been affected. Palmdale and Lancaster are messes, and from what the newsman said, nothing's left in Victorville, and San Bernardino and Barstow are almost as bad."

"So we got off easy?" Marie asked.

"Appears so. Our big problem now is that whatever we do, we're on our own, probably for some time to come. I'm not going to be able to call in backup from other cities, even when the phones start working again. National Guard's busy where they really got hit. So what I want to know is this, folks: Now that they're not opening the compound up in the morning, how are we going to get into that compound and effect a rescue?"

"Well, I had me a little idea," Tom drawled. "It's kinda crazy, but it might work. Davy, there're two boxes in the truck bed. Would you mind fetching them?"

"No problem." The ranch manager left the room.

"So what's in the boxes, cowboy?" Marie was sitting right next to him, and he loved feeling the warmth of her against his shoulder and thigh. Casually he put his arm back, resting it on the couch behind her. He felt like a thirteen-year-old, but that was all right: As soon as he told them what he had in mind, he'd be feeling more like a ten-year-old.

"Spill the beans, Abernathy," Moss asked.

"Well, it's a way to get into the gates."

"Spit it out, Tom," Marie said.

"It'll put at least four of us in a whole lotta danger, and I don't know if it'll work."

"Look who I found," Davy said as he entered and set down a large carton marked "Langtry Theater" in front of Tom. Behind him, also carrying a box, was Father Mike Corey. He placed it beside the first carton.

"Tom, I was hoping you could spare some kerosene for the campground," said the young priest.

"Sure. But can you sit a minute, Mike? I'd like your input on my plan."

First he brought Corey up-to-date on the kidnappings by the Apostles, then he reluctantly reclaimed his arm and bent forward, fiddling absently with a drift of black fabric topping one crate. "I was checking the theater, and I decided to go inside because it seemed to me there were a bunch of people working on the scenery today. It wasn't hard to get in—it withstood the quake relatively well. I went poking around, but nobody was there. In back, all the racks of costumes had fallen over, and one item in particular caught my eye."

"What the hell are you talking about?" Moss asked impatiently. "Don't tell a good story, just give me the facts."

"Calm down," Tom drawled. "We can't do anything until

tomorrow anyway. Not if you want to go with this. I saw this." Lifting the black material, he pulled out a fancy rubber skull mask.

"I don't get it," Marie said.

"Well, then, does this give you a clue?" He pulled out a dull copper helmet.

"You stole a prop from *Camelot?*" Moss asked dryly.

"Tom, would you happen to have a crown in there?" Father Mike asked, beginning to smile. "Or maybe a bow and arrow?"

He grinned. "Everything but a set of balances. One of us will have to raid the drugstore for that."

"Did you get a scythe?"

"Halloween props. Most of the robes came from there. There's makeup and a couple portable microphones. Even got some smoke bombs."

"Me too," Marie said. "But what's all this for?"

"A little self-fulfilling prophecy, I guess. Father Mike, you tell them. You sure as heck know all about this stuff."

The priest smiled. "Who are the Apostles expecting tomorrow?"

"Who will they throw open their gates for?" Tom added.

"The Four Horsemen of the Apocalypse," Marie said, wonder in her voice. "That's brilliant, Tom."

"You really think those people will buy it? What kind of person honestly takes that stuff literally?" Moss asked, examining the mask.

"The Apostles do," Davy said. "Even if their leaders don't, the followers have bought into it, and they're going to open the gates when they see the Horsemen. I'd bet my life on it."

"We're betting a lot of lives on it," Tom said solemnly. "Davy, see if Sinclair's station is up and running. I'm sure it is. He's not going to miss out on a captive audience, and the radio tower's in easy reach. He probably had that thing fixed within an hour after the quake."

Davy tuned in, and sure enough, there it was. The choir was singing part of the *Hallelujah* Chorus.

"I'll be damned," Moss said.

The music ended, and Sinclair's voice filled the room, more passionate than usual. "My friends, tomorrow the Horsemen ride. God has told me this and more. The Living Savior is among you, ready to forgive you in the name of God. The Lamb of God is manifest and He has no will of his own, only God's will. And God's will shall be done, my friends. No one may stop it, not you, nor I. Tomorrow, as the sun disappears and day turns into night, the Horsemen shall ride down from heaven and across Thunder Road, to the place of the Chosen Apostles. Be here at nine A.M., friends and neighbors, that you, too, shall find salvation. Our final Communion begins at eleven-thirty."

"Sounds like Sinclair doesn't know about that sign saying they're closed to the public," Tom said, glancing Moss's way.

"Interesting," Moss said. "Do you really think this plan of yours will work, Tom?"

"I don't know, but I think it's the best we've got. We do it just like Sinclair says, except we come out of Spirit Canyon instead of Heaven. We ride, they open the gates, we ride right into that church of theirs and take back our own. By the time they figure out what's going on, we're out of there." He paused, then added, "If we're lucky."

"I wonder if Sinclair plans to do in his congregation," Mike said. "That's very common historically, in this sort of situation."

"Jim Jones," Marie said. "David Koresh."

"Could be," Moss grunted. "There's no way to know."

"We're likely to end up dead if we try this," Tom said, "so this has got to be a volunteer thing. I'll supply the horses, and dress as Death. Belle's a pale horse, just like in the Bible."

"Who rides the black horse?" Marie asked.

"Father. Mike?" Tom asked. "I'm not sure which is which, beyond the pale rider."

Marie smiled at him. "Tom got his biblical training from Clint Eastwood."

"And I'm proud of it."

"Besides the pale rider, there are Famine, who rides a black horse, War, on a red horse, and Pestilence, on a white horse."

"Rex and I'll take Famine, then," Marie said.

"Marie," Tom began. "I can't have you risking your life—"

"You're risking yours, cowboy, and you're not doing it without me. Besides, I know the place."

"I haven't been on a horse in twenty years," Moss said, "but I'll do one."

"No offense," Tom said, "but I think it'd be better if you and Al are waiting in the wings to snag the head honchos if you can. You can create a diversion while we're leaving, if necessary, too."

"I'll do it," Davy announced.

"You're sure?"

"Absolutely."

"Thanks, I'll accept your offer."

"I'll go too," Father Mike offered.

"Can you ride?"

"No, not really."

"This might call for some fancy horse work," Tom explained. "It'd be best if you tended to the community. But I sure do appreciate the offer."

Mike looked relieved.

"We'll worry about getting the last rider later," Tom said. "Mad Dog or Henry will be up for it. I'll supply the right color horses. Tess is a bloodstone chestnut; she can be War. And I've got a great white filly, Diamond Lil, for Pestilence."

"So let's start strategizing," Marie said.

"I'm due to make another pass through town," Moss said.

Father Mike rose. "And I should get back to Ray's."

"Come on," Davy offered. "We'll get the kerosene."

Tom looked at Marie. "I guess it's just you and me, partner."

She smiled softly, but didn't reply.

Walking Moss out to his car, Tom stared at the chief. "We'll get Cass back, Moss. That's a promise."

The chief looked old and tired as he halfheartedly attempted a smile. "You always were a great storyteller, Tom. Now you're proposing to act one out. Hope you can do that as well."

"Believe me, so do I." Tom looked toward the compound. The cross was glowing dimly. "Generators," he said.

"Yeah," Moss replied. "Hey, get a look at the moon."

Tom turned and stared, his neck prickling up as he saw the color of the disk. Except for an infinitesimal crescent of brilliant white, the moon was a dark, dusky red. He knew it was due to the changing weather and dust in the atmosphere from the quake, but it gave him the creeps.

"Blood on the moon," Moss murmured.

"One of the signs of the Apocalypse, if I remember my Sunday schooling correctly," Tom said, ice in his gut. *What if it's true?* He couldn't believe he was even considering such a thing.

"You a religious man, Tom?"

"Not church religious. I go sit in the hills by myself to commune with, well, God, nature, whatever it is that's behind everything."

"I'm an old Presbyterian, I suppose, and, Tom, this is starting to get under my skin. I know Sinclair's a nutcase, but I wish you could've met the guy. I wish I had your take on him."

"You will tomorrow. You don't think he's legit, do you?"

"No, but something's going on here that I don't understand, and if you tell anybody that, I'll skin you alive."

"Don't worry," Tom said slowly. "I feel it, too, but I'm inclined to believe it has more to do with natural things than supernatural." He paused. "For instance, today's quake. My skin went up all cold and clammy seconds before it hit. I can't explain it, but I know it probably has to do with magnetics or air pressure, something someone like Alex could explain."

"You make a good point. With all the minerals and magnetic ores around here, it's a wonder we're not all crazy already."

"Still," Tom said wryly, "It'd be a real predicament if we started riding down Thunder Road and the real Horsemen came up behind us."

"Wouldn't that be a kick in the ass?" Moss's chuckle was genuine. "And if you pull this off, I'm sure that's how you'll tell the tale." He clapped Tom on the shoulder. "Thanks. You don't have to do this."

"Yeah, I do. I've been living my life so easy for so many years, never getting into arguments, never declaring for a woman, just sort of watching everything from the edges. I guess it's time for a change."

Moss nodded, then solemnly shook his hand. "I'll be back later. You and Marie take care, now, hear?"

"Sure will."

## CARLO PELEGRINE

C arlo rode the Harley as far as he could up Olive Mesa before giving up and hiding the bike among a trailside crop of boulders. Hampered by the pain in his side and a dying flashlight, it took him nearly an hour to climb to the top of the mesa.

Normally, when there was even a crescent moon over the high desert, a flashlight was unnecessary, but tonight things were decidedly abnormal. A chill wind had partially cleared the overcast sky. High thin cirrus clouds framed the moon and dust lifted into the atmosphere by the earthquake, had turned the moon a muddy red, the color of old blood. The color of death.

The first thing he did after gaining the plateau was examine it for openings, walking in concentric circles until the flashlight gave out near the center of the mesa. He found nothing.

Now, exhausted, disheartened, his wound a persistent, throbbing ache, he sat down cross-legged to rest, but the sight of the dying embers in Madland and the enduring smell of smoke on the wind did anything but soothe him.

Carlo shivered and pulled his jacket closer around him. What had seemed like a brilliant plan—finding an entrance to the compound here—had been an exercise in foolishness. He shoved his hand in his pocket and found the pack of tarot cards he'd rescued earlier. Drawing them out, he opened the box, let the cards fall into his hand. Even in darkness he recognized their smooth familiar feel, the warmth of the energy imbued in them through hundreds of readings. They gave comfort, and without thinking, he fanned through them, his fingers searching the invisible surfaces until he found one that felt right. He drew it out and placed it on the ground, then repeated the process twice more.

A triad of cards, visible only as pale shadows against the darkness. The lower two represented the past and future, the topmost his significator, his part in the puzzle. Squinting, wishing he could make out the cards, he suddenly understood the desperation of many of his clients. They had given up on reality, on making their own destinies without guidance.

Sinclair's followers were much the same as his clients, as were, to varying degrees, the devout of most religions. People seemed to need reassurance, they needed a father figure to take care of them, to remind them to behave and to confess their secrets to; to reassure them that everything would be all right in the end. To assure them of their fate. And thus assured, they carried it out.

He turned his head and gazed down at the Madelyn valley. Down by the interstate, a glow was visible from Ray's Cafe. The only other lights tonight gleamed in the Apostles' compound, a mile away, but appearing much closer in the clear desert air. Dim yellow lights dotted the compound, and the cross on the steeple shone brilliant white. As he looked at it, it blinked out, leaving an afterimage burning behind his eyelids. *God has left the building,* he thought with bitter amusement.

God had left him long ago. After each murder, he had prayed to God for guidance, for help, but had received no answer, and he slowly learned that the only help could come from that little part of God within him. When John Lennon upset the world by saying, "We are all God," Carlo had found enlightenment in the phrase. It explained fate. If enough people believed something would happen, it was likely to, in some form. God, the God who lived within all creatures, was a great power, made good or evil by the thoughts and actions of people. Prophecies came to pass because the believers made it so.

The light in the steeple blinked out. Tomorrow, the Apostles believed, was the end of the world, and the flooding, the fire, the earthquake, even the red moon, bore the earmarks of biblical prophecy. Though intellectually Carlo could not see those things as anything but coincidence, at the core of his being, he couldn't help but wonder if the power of a group of human minds hadn't helped create them. Or perhaps, as Alex maintained, the UFOs somehow influenced human action, history, and myth. She said they'd been interpreted as angels, as devils. As God.

Then perhaps fate did exist in a way, but that didn't mean it couldn't be altered. Were the cards merely symbols to awaken the mind to possibilities, or were they, as his clients believed, harbingers of something more? Perhaps it wasn't so idiotic to throw them. In frustration, he turned back to the three invisible cards.

And saw them. Clearly.

His significator was Death. It might be literal, or it could mean metamorphosis, a phoenix rising from the ashes. Or both.

Below Death, to the left, was the Tower, representing the past. The Tower signified destruction. *Of Madland. Of the town. Of the world.* It could also mean something more personal: the destruction of his existing beliefs. *Enlightenment comes in the flash of lightning that hits the tower.*

The Moon was the future. A mysterious and ominous card, showing the moon illuminating a path leading out of murky water, a treacherous road guarded by dogs, bounded by towers, leading finally to open country. This card spoke of supernatural guidance, and the faith to follow the light out of darkness.

*The light.*

Slowly he looked up.

"What are you?" He whispered the words to the glowing ball of bluish light hovering fifty feet above him, but like God, it didn't answer. He rose, staring in awe at the globe, and as he did, it began to move slowly north. He followed it, staying just out of its glow, to the edge of the mesa, where it descended to perhaps twenty-five feet, bathing him in its cold light. Electricity filled the air, tugged at his hair. Carlo lowered his gaze to a mound of boulders to his right. Bathed in eerie blue light, they looked unnatural, a ten-foot-wide patch of stones, a rock garden, arranged with purpose. *To hide something?*

*That's your imagination.* Even as he entertained the thought, he put one foot on a low stone and began to climb, feeling the hum of electricity around him as the globe neared. He stepped onto the tallest rock—all of five feet—and looked down at a four-foot-wide space of bare ground in the middle of the mound. Suddenly there was a sliding sound and the earth slid away, revealing perfect darkness below.

Carlo looked up at the globe, and as he did, it began a slow ascent. He thought of the cards, considered the nature of fate, then he climbed down to the opening. There was barely room to stand, so he lowered himself into a sitting position, his legs dangling into the black pit. One foot touched something solid. *A step!* Carefully he moved his other foot onto it and eased himself down, one step, two. *Does this qualify as guidance by a supernatural being?* He looked up once more, but the globe was gone.

He didn't know the answer, and he didn't care as he descended fifty spiraling steps into complete darkness, because this meant he was going to get into the compound and find Alex. *And Sinclair.* He didn't know why this seemed important, but he knew it was.

Sensing he'd entered a larger space, he walked around it, hands extended, feeling its perimeters, until one hand touched something large and metallic—a jeep of some sort.

He kept moving and soon came to an opening less than five feet in diameter. Fresh cool air wafted from its depths, and he knew this was what he had been searching for.

# HANNIBAL CAINE

"Hello, Hannibal."

Caine whirled as Jim-Bob entered the steeple observation area, walking so quietly around the catwalk surrounding the open shaft that he hadn't heard a thing.

"Hello, James," he said, recovering himself. *This is it!* He had brought up two glasses of red wine, one doctored with sleeping pills, the other for himself, and he'd been staring out at the crimson moon as he waited for Sinclair to show up. "Here," he said, turning to take one glass from a small silver tray. "A toast."

Sinclair took the glass and studied him with kind, sad eyes that gave Hannibal the creeps. He had never seen him like this before the last day or two. The man's natural charisma had changed, grown stronger, quieter, and for an instant, Caine had an urge to knock against the wine, to spill it. *No. Not after all you've worked for. Don't be a coward!*

Although Sinclair seemed as healthy as ever, there had always been an exuberance to him, nervous energy that flowed around him like sparks. Now the man's calmness was very nearly overwhelming. *He really believes he's the damned Living Savior,* Caine reminded himself. *He's completely mad.* There was no other explanation for the oddness of his behavior.

"What shall we toast?" Sinclair asked.

"The end of the world?"

"No, Hannibal. The beginning of a new life."

They touched glasses. His unnerving gaze never wavering, Sinclair slowly drained his glass. "What did you want to talk about?"

The pills would kick in very soon; all Hannibal had to do was bullshit for a few minutes. "About tomorrow morning. What music would you like the choir to perform?"

A gentle smile creased Sinclair's face. His features had taken on a gaunt look in the last few days, and now, with the wavy golden brown hair, the beard, and his white robe, he looked more than ever like a Jesus on black velvet. All he needed, thought Caine, was a crown of thorns. And he'd have one soon. "Hannibal, you didn't ask me to meet you here to talk about music. Please be honest with me. Tell me why." His eyes unfocused for an instant, then he regained control.

"James, I don't understand."

"Have courage and tell me why you drugged the wine."

Shocked, Caine stared at him. "What are you talking about?"

"I knew it was drugged before I drank it, Hannibal. God told me this was to be. He told me other things as well." Sinclair leaned against the wall, then began to slide gracefully to the floor, finally coming to rest in a sitting position, propped against the wall. He stared up at Caine. "You are forgiven, Hannibal," he whispered. "You were chosen to be the Judas this time." He smiled again and his eyes closed. With painful slowness, the Prophet's body collapsed completely.

Caine stared at him, shocked. The insane often seemed to have superhuman powers of observation, and Sinclair was an artist to begin with. A magician. *Don't worry about it now.*

He opened a small control panel in the wall and switched off the lights on the cross on the steeple, then, after finishing his wine, he punched another button. A sphincter opened above them, and slowly the cross descended, the cable in the middle of the steeple disappearing below.

When it was entirely in the room, Caine switched off the elevator mechanism, halting the cross's descent into the church. Swallowing hard, he opened a small storage area built into the wall and withdrew the spikes and mallet. He brought out a coil of rope as well, then stood, staring at Sinclair's supine body, at the mallet and spikes, at Sinclair again. *Get this over with, Hannibal, and you're home free.* But he had no taste for blood. He never had.

He began his work, not thinking about what was to come. First he stripped Sinclair and used cloth from the white robe to wrap around the man's pelvis in the biblical manner. The next thing he had to do was tie Sinclair in place on the cross.

It took an hour, and Caine was sweating by the time he was finished. He stared at the body, its positioning so perfect that it might be a statue. Perhaps the spikes weren't necessary. This was authentic enough.

"I'm sorry," he whispered as tears rolled unheeded over his plump cheeks. *You are forgiven, Hannibal. You were chosen to be the Judas this time.* Caine shook his head. *The ravings of a madman.* He let himself sink to the floor in front of the man on the cross. Beside him, on one side, the hammer and nails waited. On the other side, a crown of thorns. He wasn't even sure that he had the stomach to put that over Sinclair's head. He put his head in his hands, lost in thought.

"Elder Caine!"

Shocked, he looked up to see Justin Martin, dressed in black from the tips of his Reeboks to his turtleneck collar. The boy grinned down at him, then glanced at Sinclair's body. "Whatcha doing?"

"How did you find me?" Caine demanded, scrambling to his feet as panic shot through him. "How did you get in here?"

Justin shrugged, his blue eyes bright. "The Voice in the sky."

"What is that?"

"The Prophet calls it the Voice of God."

"What does this voice tell you to do?" Caine stared at the boy, at a loss.

The barest sneer crossed Justin's features. "It doesn't tell me to *do* anything. Nobody orders me around." He paused, studying Caine as if he were brain- damaged. "It just tells me things. Like how to find you. How's Alex?"

"She's fine. The deal stands." Caine was at a loss as he stared at the boy. Could he and Sinclair possibly both be under the same influence? It didn't seem possible. One was insufferably peaceful and pacifistic, the other—

"Satan's own," said Sinclair, impossibly.

Startled, Caine looked up, saw Jim-Bob unconscious, hanging from the cross. He glanced at Justin, thought he caught a fleeting look of surprise instantly masked beneath the boy's arrogance. *You only imagined he spoke. If you're not careful, you'll catch their disease.*

"Something wrong, Elder Caine?" Justin sounded like Eddie Haskell on "Leave it to Beaver."

"No."

"Do you need some help?" Justin asked, looking down at the mallet and spikes.

"What?"

"Help. Do you want me to help you with that?"

"You're serious?"

"I'm great with a hammer and nails."

It was such an easy way out of a delicate situation that Caine couldn't believe his ears. "What do you think you're supposed to do with them, Justin?"

The youth chuckled. "Drive 'em home," he said, bending and picking up the mallet and one spike. He approached the low guardrail around the shaft and studied Sinclair. "We should do the hands first. Can you lower him a little?"

Numbly Caine pushed a button and slowly brought the cross down so that Sinclair's left hand was even with Justin. He could see the strange red scars on the palms that had appeared a day before, and he shivered, reminding himself that this was nothing other-worldly. Jim-Bob Sinclair was a magician; he knew how to make things appear to be what they were not.

Justin held a spike up to Sinclair's palm. "X marks the spot." Holding the iron spike in place, he brought the mallet back. Caine looked away as he struck.

"Want to hand me another spike?" Justin asked as he walked around to the other hand.

Hand shaking, he gave one to the boy, who pounded it through Sinclair's hand into the smooth wood with the skill of a carpenter.

"Raise him up and I'll do the feet."

Caine did so, his eyes on Justin. The youth's eyes glittered with a mad light, one even more unnerving than the expression he some-times saw in Eldo Blandings's eyes. Justin Martin was a sadist who put old Eldo to shame.

Caine heard the crunch of bone as the third spike drove through Sinclair's feet, heard Justin's heavy breathing and a soft, pleasurable laugh. If he had this to do all over again, would he have gone this route? *You were chosen to be the Judas this time.* Yes, he thought, he probably would.

"All done," Justin said. "Oh, we forgot the crown. Lower him again, please, Elder Caine."

Dully Caine did so.

Justin picked up the sharp thorny crown and examined it, then thrust it toward

Caine. "You should do this."

He stared at it, not wanting to touch it. *You have to or he'll know you're a coward.* Caine forced himself to take the crown, then approach Sinclair. He'd avoided looking at him, but now he did, seeing the blood dripping from the hands, seeing the smooth uncon-scious features of the Prophet. *Of the Living Christ.* No, that was foolish. Steeling himself, he bent over the railing and pressed the crown onto Sinclair's head.

Despite the sleeping pills, Sinclair moaned and tears ran silently down his face. Abruptly his eyes fluttered open, which was impossible, given the amount of drug he'd ingested. "You are forgiven, Hannibal," he whispered, then the eyes shut once more.

"Let's go," Caine said quickly. Obediently Justin led the way down the circular stairs. At the bottom Caine locked the door and checked it twice. He turned to Justin. "This is our secret."

Justin's eyes shone. "Of course. Elder Caine?"

"Yes?"

"Do you want me to do Cassie Halloway and Alex, too? I wouldn't mind."

"I know you wouldn't, and if we decide to do them the same way, then you'll be the one we ask."

"Okay."

"Good. Perhaps Elder Blandings can find you something enjoyable to do. Thank you for your help."

Justin grinned and disappeared out the church doors. *Satan's own. Ridiculous.* Hannibal Caine sat heavily in a front pew. He thought he had given Sinclair enough sleeping pills to put him in a deep coma and, eventually, kill him. *Very little time has passed,* he thought, reassuring himself that a bit more time was all that was necessary, and turned his mind to other things.

In the morning he would begin the service, and bring the cross down into the church. By then, Sinclair would be comatose, and what would be left would be the miraculous sight of Jesus on the cross. The two women were merely window dressing, and a good way to hide his real plans.

It was too bad that so many of the Apostles had been out on missionary work and hadn't made it back after the earthquake: They would miss the spectacle. But even with half the congregation attending, he would conduct a magnificent Communion, and declare that Christ had returned to give the world a second chance so that the Horsemen would not ride.

And then Hannibal would inherit the ministry and all the benefits, monetary and otherwise, that went with being top dog. Everything was in place; Eldo would be blamed for the murders, as well as the kidnappings and vandalistic acts. Now he would have company, Caine decided, in the form of young Justin Martin.

They both would take the fall for the poisoned wine—amaretto, actually, to cover the taste of the cyanide—that would remove certain members of the Apostles, those who were especially loyal to Sinclair and knew some of his secrets.

He smiled. Eldo and Sinclair went insane, leaving Hannibal Caine to carry the ball. *You were chosen to be the Judas this time.* The words were a bare echo in his mind as he stood on the church threshold and breathed in the chilly night air. Not bad, he told himself, for a plan conceived only two days ago.

He still had to attend to the Communion preparations: to choose a special carafe for the poisoned amaretto, and to get Eldo's prints on it and the cyanide container.

Obtaining the poison had been as simple as visiting the armory and unlocking the heavy metal cabinets that held illegal substances of all sorts. He would have preferred to use arsenic, which provided a less violent death, but lacked the speed and certainty—not to mention the dramatics—of cyanide. *At least it won't be as bad as watching the spikes being driven into Sinclair. At least there won't be blood.*

Looking at his watch, he decided to check on the state of the prisoners before getting down to work.

# CASSIE HALLOWAY

Cassie's broken fingers were swollen purple sausages and her ankle didn't look much better, but her entire body hurt so much that these things were almost minor in comparison. She glanced up, saw Janet Wister's body in the comer, looked quickly back at her hands, but that only made her imagine nails being driven into them.

She fixed her gaze on Alex Manderley. Cassie had no idea how long the scientist had been stubbornly working at the dead bolt with her bobby pin, but it had become obvious that lock-picking didn't number among her talents. At first Cassie had been sure that the guards would hear, or at least notice the light beneath the door, but no one had come.

"Damn," Alex said, turning to show Cassie the mangled pin. "This isn't working."

She silenced at the sound of approaching footsteps. Putting her finger to her lips, she moved to the hinged side of the door.

"Guard?" a man called. Cassie recognized the voice of the fat bald man, Caine. He rapped on the door. "Guard? Are you in there?"

Cassie heard mumbled cursing, then a key slipped into the lock.

Alex pressed herself against the wall, the bobby pin clutched in her fingers.

The lock clicked, then the doorknob began to turn. Terrified, Cassie watched it, watched Alex, wondering if she was going to still be alive in five minutes.

The door swung silently inward a few inches, then the barrel of a gun appeared, and above it, a man's blue eye. "Guard?" he asked. Receiving no answer, he pushed the door open farther and stuck his head inside, peering around cautiously. "Damn you, Eldo," he muttered, seeing Janet Wister's corpse. He turned his gaze on Cassie, his face an expressionless mask. Then his eyes widened, darting around the room. "Where's—"

Alex sprang, slamming the door against his skull. Caine yelped, staggering, one hand grasping at the doorframe. "Guard!" he squealed.

Mercilessly Alex shoved on the door while Caine's face turned redder and redder. She glanced back at Cassie, her face a desperate question.

"Run, get help!" Cassie cried, telling her what she needed to hear.

Alex nodded, and suddenly Caine's hand was on hers, trying to pry her fingers from the knob, his face bulldogging through the door as he gave up pulling and started pushing. Instead of fighting, Alex yanked the door inward and Caine stumbled into the room, immediately turning, hands going for her throat, face livid, foam at the corner of his mouth. Alex backed up only one step before racing forward, her arms up, blocking his hands. She grabbed his shoulders and brought her knee up, connecting solidly with his groin.

The Apostle screamed and fell back, cursing. Alex stepped around him and glanced out the door, then glanced at Cassie again. "I'll be back," she breathed.

And then she was gone, unaware of Caine's feeble grab at her ankle.

Cradling his crotch, Caine got to his knees, then shakily stood up.

Tears of pain streamed down his cheeks and his eyes were bright with fury as he staggered toward Cassie. She pressed back against the wall, expecting him to lash out, to kick or hit her. But he stopped short and turned toward Janet's body, stared at it for a long moment. "Damn you, Eldo," he whispered. Then, without looking back, he strode out of the room, locking the door behind him. Faintly she heard him yelling for the guards.

# ALEXANDRA MANDERLEY

R acing out of the room, Alex had run out into a long, bleak, and blessedly deserted hallway, knowing only that she had to get out and get help for Cassie.

She didn't try any of the closed doors until she turned a comer, then the two she tried were locked. Glancing behind her, expecting Hannibal Caine to appear at any moment, she moved on and, in ten paces, was rewarded with a narrow stairwell leading down into darkness. A chain bearing a placard reading "Private" was strung across it.

Squatting down, she slipped under the barrier and, hand lightly on the railing, descended two stories, finally coming to another corridor. Dimly lit, it led in two directions. She hesitated briefly, then chose the right-hand path.

There were no doorways for twenty feet, then she came to another hall, one that was nearly lightless. She stepped into it and, trailing her fingers along the wall, continued on, alert to every sound. The passage turned once, twice, and she wondered if she'd ever find her way out, whether by locating a robe to disguise herself as Cassie said Marie had done, or by locating one of those tunnels she'd heard

about at Tom's the other night. A night that seemed a very long
time ago.

She paused, hearing the echo of voices and running footsteps.
*The guards are looking for me!* Panicked, she started trotting, trying
the few doors she passed. All locked.

The footsteps were closer now, but she had no idea if they were
ten yards or a thousand yards away, not in this echo-filled tomb. She
ran, only noticing a dark, chained-off hallway as she passed it. Turning, she hesitated as she heard the footfalls again. Close, very close. *If
I can hear them, they can hear me.* Crouching, she crawled under the
chain.

"You hear that?"

"Come on!"

Men's voices, very close. She ran into the darkness, suddenly tripping, tumbling down a short flight of stairs. Picking herself up, she
found herself at a dead end. *This has to lead somewhere!* Frantically
she felt for a doorknob, found it. Behind her, the voices approached.
*Dear God, let it be unlocked!*

Beneath her fingers, the knob turned by itself. Dumbly she let go
as the door opened, revealing warm yellow light and a white-robed
figure.

"Down here!" came one of the male voices.

Blindly she brought her fist back to punch the Apostle before her.
As her arm pistoned forward, the figure caught her fist in his hand
and yanked her inside, slamming the door behind them. Frantically
she tried to twist out of his grip.

"Alex!"

Startled, she looked up, straight into the man's eyes.

"Carlo!" she whispered, and fell into his arms.

His hands pushed into her hair, holding her to him, and the
sound of his voice whispering her name was the sweetest sound she'd
ever heard. Then there were three sharp raps on the door.

"Prophet Sinclair?" called one of the men.

Carlo stared at her, then turned to face the door. "Yes?" he said, in a clipped, deep voice.

"Sorry to disturb you, sir." The man paused, and they heard soft murmuring outside the door.

"Yes?" Carlo called impatiently.

"Um, Elder Caine sent us to see if you need anything."

"No. Good night."

"Good night, sir."

Alex put her ear to the door, listening until she could no longer hear the voices, then turned to Carlo. "What are you doing here?"

"Looking for you." He took her hand and led her across the simple but elegant bedroom.

"How?"

He pointed at a smooth wall paneled in oak, except for a black, door-sized opening propped open with a straight-backed chair. "One of your UFOs was kind enough to point out a secret passage."

She felt her jaw drop. "You're joking."

"No joke." He paused. "Mine is not to reason why."

She studied him, afraid to ask the next question. "Eric?" she asked finally.

"Tom found him. He'll be fine."

"Thank heaven," she whispered, relief flooding her. "What about Marie?"

"I don't know. Have you seen Cassie and Eve?"

"Cassie. She's hurt. We have to get help."

"Where is she?"

"This place is a maze," Alex told him. "Is there something to write on around here? I should try to reconstruct the route I took before I completely forget."

They found a pad and pen in a small writing desk and she quickly tried to sketch a schematic of the way she came. "I don't think I've drawn this right. Maybe we should go and get help, some weapons."

"Come over here." He led her to the opening in the wall panels.

Reaching inside, he flipped a switch and a dim light came on, revealing a tunnel extending into darkness. "Look," he said, pointing at an electric cart waiting just inside. "This will take you to Olive Mesa. At the end of the tunnel, take the stairs upward. You'll be on the north side of the plateau. Go across to the trail on the south side— the one you used before. Can you find it?"

"Yes, of course. But, Carlo—"

"Near the bottom of the mesa, you'll find my bike hidden behind some rocks. It should be in plain sight from your angle. Can you ride?"

She nodded. "You're not staying here by yourself, are you?"

He looked deeply into her eyes. "I have to. As long as the Apostles are wearing their robes, I'll blend right in." He paused. "I can't explain, but it's something I have to do. I don't know what it is yet, but I have to be here."

She stared at him, saw the determination in his eyes, and nodded her acceptance.

"Go to Tom's, and if I'm not back by dawn, send the cavalry." He said the last with false levity. "Don't worry. I'll be back. But if I'm not, you'll know what to do."

"How can you be so sure?"

"There are wheels in motion already. You'll know."

"You're talking like a fortune-teller," she chided, trying to hide the fear she felt.

"I'm sorry." He smiled tightly. "There's no time to explain now, even if I thought I could." He sat down in the cart, started it, and pulled it into the path. He turned on its headlights, then rose, gesturing her to take his place.

She did. "Carlo?"

"Yes?"

"Be careful. I don't want to lose you."

He bent and kissed her, his lips warm and soft against hers. "I love you," he whispered.

"I love you," she murmured, meaning every word. They kissed again. "Be careful."

"You too," he said.

She pulled into the darkness, heading toward freedom.

## ONE HUNDRED THIRTY-FIVE
# HANNIBAL CAINE

Standing in his apartment, Hannibal Caine popped four Excedrin into his mouth and washed them down with brandy. "Eldo," he began, turning to face Blandings, "where's the shepherdess?"

Eldo, a robe thrown over his fatigues, his toupee crooked, met his eyes. "We were unable to locate her or the child, Hannibal."

Caine started to shake his head in disgust, but the throbbing pain immediately made him stop. "There's no excuse for the incompetence you and your committee have displayed. Why weren't guards posted outside the prisoners' room?"

Eldo's eyes blazed. "Number one, I wasn't here to supervise. Number two, I'm told you only ordered them to check on the prisoners once an hour."

"Um-hmm," Caine said, barely controlling his own temper. "Don't you think they should at least know enough to tie up the prisoners?"

"They do what they're ordered to do," Blandings said grimly. "But I'll speak to them."

"Speak to them about their indiscriminate use of force, too. The prisoner— Wister, I believe is her name—died."

"And the tattooed whore?"

"Stable. You were lucky there, Eldo. Very lucky."

"If that's all—"

"That's not all. The other prisoner, Manderley, has escaped. She's somewhere in the compound. Organize whatever's left of your committee and organize a real search. Keep it quiet. When you find her, tie her up, but *do not* damage her. Is that clear?"

Glaring sullenly, Blandings nodded.

"One more thing. The gates are to remain locked. Instruct the guards that no one may leave or enter without the express permission of Prophet Sinclair, to be obtained through me while he is in retreat."

"Some of our members caught in the quake today may show up tonight. Are they included in this?" Blandings asked, his voice a sneer.

"Have them all checked for ID." Caine paused. "If anyone shows up for the services in the morning, tell the guards to politely deny entry due to earthquake damage. And, Eldo, make sure the guards are armed, but tell them no aggression. There's to be no shooting unless someone actually breaks through the gate, and then only if they are threatened with weapons. Otherwise, use less drastic measures."

"I suppose you expect them to check with you before they let the Four Horsemen enter?" Eldo asked snidely.

Caine studied him, finally deciding he was serious. Eldo took the Horsemen as literally as most of the Apostles seemed to, and that was something Caine couldn't comprehend. However, he was quite willing to accept it. "Eldo, *if— when* the Horsemen show up, welcome them, by all means."

Stonily Blandings nodded, then turned on his heel and walked out, leaving the apartment door hanging open behind him. Caine shut the door, then refilled his brandy snifter before returning to his kitchen, where he went to work measuring twenty portions of cyanide and amaretto into a silver carafe.

*You are the Judas this time.* Sinclair's words haunted him as the clock chimed midnight.

## ONE HUNDRED THIRTY-SIX

# CARLO PELEGRINE

### SUNDAY

He carried no weapon as he wandered the compound. Carlo had expected the place to be teeming with Apostles preparing for the last day of the world, but the compound was surprisingly quiet. Of course, it was now nearing three in the morning, but even at midnight there were few of the faithful out and about. He'd passed several pairs of armed Apostles who were obviously searching—for Alex, he assumed.

Things had seemed so clear on the mesa, but now, standing in the shadows of the church, he floundered. After Alex had left, he'd decided his best course of action would be to find Cassie and somehow spirit her down to Sinclair's quarters, retrieve the electric cart and take her out of the compound, alert Moss, then return to do whatever it was he was supposed to do.

But hours had passed and he'd seen no sign of her. There was little time left. *For what?*

To find Sinclair. Though he had nothing to say to the man, he knew he had to see him. *Why?* He thought of the future card—the Moon—with its murky, mysterious meanings, and the ball of light that led him here, and realized that he was fated to be a cog in the machine. *You don't believe in fate, remember? Find Cassie and get out of here!*

But the imperative only grew stronger when he tried to fight it. "Apostle, come here a moment."

Swallowing panic, Carlo turned to face a round bald man in a shirt and tie who matched Alex's description of Hannibal Caine. Behind him, a side door into the church yawned open. Carlo had been so wrapped up in his thoughts, he hadn't even heard the door open, and that wasn't good.

Caine pulled the church door closed, then approached. "What's your name, Apostle?"

"John Smith," Carlo replied quickly.

"You're new here, aren't you?" The man eyed him narrowly. Carlo could see bags under his eyes and dark swellings on his cheeks. Now he was certain this was Caine.

"Yes, I am, Apostle Caine."

Caine smiled. "Elder Caine. You work in the cafeteria, don't you?"

"Yes, I do," he replied without hesitation.

It was the right answer. Caine smiled. "Yes, I thought I recognized you. What are you doing out here?"

"I couldn't sleep."

"Excited about tomorrow?"

Carlo nodded.

"Apostle Smith, I'm exhausted. Perhaps you can help me."

"I'd be glad to."

"Follow me."

Caine led him to the next building. Inside, they passed a multitude of numbered doors that Carlo assumed led to dorm rooms. Further on, the doors were farther apart, and Caine went directly to the last door and inserted a key in the lock.

Carlo followed him into a spacious modern apartment, through the living room into a dining area. Caine crossed to a glass and iron table that held an intricate silver carafe and a large cardboard box. He pulled a small bronze key from his jacket pocket and handed it to Carlo. "I want you to take the box into the church. You'll see a long table set up in front of the rostrum. There are some pitchers on it." He picked up the box and handed it to Carlo. There were paper cups, napkins, and a plastic bag filled with small round biscuits resembling Communion wafers inside it. "Set these things out on the table and ditch the box beneath it. Just leave the key on the pulpit for me, and make sure you close the door as you leave. Is that clear?"

"Yes," Carlo said, smiling into Caine's bloodshot eyes.

"Don't dawdle, Apostle." Caine led him back to the door and opened it. "Do this errand correctly and you won't be forgotten."

"Thank you, Elder Caine," Carlo said, and walked briskly out the door.

As he returned to the church, Carlo wondered why the man had trusted him. Perhaps it was simply for the same reason he was successful at fortune-telling: Most people trusted him. He had that kind of face. Or maybe it was part of whatever brought him here. *You're reading too much into this.*

He let himself into the church. Faintly lit, it was starkly beautiful, with two large crosses on the wall to either side of the austere rostrum. The pews were simple golden oak, the central and side aisles carpeted in pale blue. The white walls were studded with tall arched windows, modern stained glass depicting the Apostles' starburst crosses. The place looked like a normal church, not the den of cultists who kidnapped and murdered. Shaking his head, Carlo set out the Communion paraphernalia, then bent to put the box under the table. There he discovered several gallon jugs of cheap red wine. Kneeling, he examined them and found the screw-top lids untampered-with. He was surprised. If Sinclair was going to pull a mass suicide, he hadn't poisoned the wine yet.

Carlo stepped onto the rostrum, started to place the key on the lectern, then pocketed it instead. He walked to the rear and studied the crosses, no doubt the ones meant for Cassie and Alex. They were wooden, bleached oak, the horizontal and vertical wood heavy four-by-fours, the X-shaped starbursts behind them half that. There was a gently convex twelve-foot span between them, and approaching it, Carlo spotted an almost invisible white cable in its center. He looked up.

Fifteen feet above was a circular opening lined with spotlights, off now, and beyond that, only darkness. A thrill of excitement coursed through him. He had to get into the tower.

Accepting the urgent need without question, he trotted down the rostrum steps and followed a curved walkway behind it to a flight of carpeted stairs. He took them two at a time, found himself in a choir loft left of the rostrum, could see a matching one directly across it. At the far end of the loft, he found another flight of stairs and took those, coming up short at a closed door. This had to be the entrance.

It was locked. There was no dead bolt, just a keyed knob, similar to the one outside.

He jiggled the knob to no avail, then remembering Caine's key, pulled it from his pocket. *What the hell, it might work.* After all, this was a church, not a bank. He inserted it in the lock. It fit tightly and wouldn't turn. Then he tried lifting the knob, wiggling the key at the same time. Suddenly the key broke off in the lock. "Damn," he whispered, his hand still on the knob. Frustrated, he twisted it, and the door opened. He stared at it in amazement for several seconds, then walked inside, shutting the door behind him. He found a light switch on the wall, flipped it, and saw a narrow spiral staircase built between the outer wall and the inner one that the main cross traveled in.

He climbed the stairs, his stomach full of butterflies. At last he saw a ceiling above him with an opening for the stairs. Swallowing, he took the last few steps.

It reminded him of a lighthouse. The tall, darkened room was lined with windows that let enough light in for him to see a low handrail around the bare outline of the twelve-foot cross that had disappeared from the top of the steeple. Carlo shivered and reached out to find a light switch.

"No, lights, Charles. They'll be seen."

Carlo couldn't move, couldn't find his voice.

"Come here, Charles."

The soft voice, tinged with pain, broke his paralysis. He took slow steps around the catwalk, stopping when he faced the cross. Raising his eyes, he made out the figure of a crucified man. As his eyes adjusted to the dim light, he could make out the nearly naked man's long hair and beard, see the oversized nails in his hands and feet. "Dear God," he whispered, almost feeling the man's pain. He glanced at a small control panel on the railing. "I'll get you down."

"No, that is not to be. Sit down, Charles."

"Why do you call me that?"

"It's your name."

"How do you know?" Carlo lowered himself to the floor, sat cross-legged, peering up in fascination at the man's shadowy face.

"God knows all."

"You're telling me you're God?"

"I am the son of God."

"You're Sinclair."

"I am that, but I am also the son of God." Even in darkness, his eyes bored into Carlo's. "Just as you are the son of God. We are all His children."

"But God told you my name?"

"He speaks to me, yes."

The man seemed to be a lunatic, but Carlo couldn't quite dismiss his ravings as delusions brought on by psychosis or pain. As Moss had mentioned, there was something about him, something defying definition, that went far beyond simple charisma. How could this man be nothing but a money-grubbing evangelist and give off such peace, such love, even after being stripped and nailed to a cross?

"He spoke to you as well. He guided you here."

"Something pointed the way."

Despite the dim light, Carlo saw Sinclair's gentle smile. "You've lost your faith."

"I used to pray. I needed help." He paused. "I prayed for self control."

"And you have it now, don't you? It doesn't matter what you call Him, God exists. Some believe He is an external force, but He is internal. He is your conscience. He is love."

Shakily Carlo got to his feet. "It doesn't undo the past." "You are truly repentant for the murders."

In shock, Carlo backed against the wall. "How?"

Again the gentle smile. "It has been given to me to know these things. You are acutely aware of your past. In atonement, you have spent your life giving help to others. You are forgiven."

Tears streamed freely down Carlo's cheeks. "I can't forgive myself."

"I know," Sinclair said softly. "But consider the joy you have given others. Ask yourself why you were guided here this night."

He wiped the tears away. "I am here to rescue my friends."

"And?"

"To see you. But I don't know why."

"It will become clear. Charles, there is great evil in the world. There are people here who have exorcised the divine spark within them, people who have no love, no empathy. They are not quite human. There is one among us now. He has already caused great pain, and he will continue to do so until he is stopped."

"Hannibal Caine?"

"No. His plans must be altered, but the one I am speaking of is pure evil, not merely greedy and misguided."

"Justin."

"Yes." Sinclair's voice was softer now, weaker, and Carlo had to strain to hear him.

"I'll turn him over to the police."

"No. This goes beyond earthly law. He is empty, devoid of the things which make us human. If you were a devout Catholic, I would tell you he is a demon, the son of Lucifer. He has killed his own soul, his spark. You are prepared to give your own life, and so you must deal with him. If you don't, he will kill many more tomorrow." His voice trailed off in a pain-filled sigh, his eyes closing.

"Let me get you down."

The eyes fluttered open. "No. It is my destiny to bring new hope, as it is yours to destroy the evil present here."

"You're telling me to kill Justin Martin? But I vowed never to kill again."

"Listen to your soul and you will know what to do." Sinclair's eyes closed and his body shivered, then became still. Carlo watched him, was relieved to see that he was still breathing. He turned away to gaze out the windows facing Olive Mesa, wondering what would happen tomorrow, wondering if he would ever see Alex again, and if he would ever see another sunset.

CARLO HAD SPENT THE REST OF THE NIGHT HIDDEN IN THE ONLY place he could find: under the long Communion table. Its underside was completely hidden by a floor-length white tablecloth, and if anyone happened to look beneath it, he hoped that his white robe would make him invisible.

About dawn, the church's side door opened, and carefully parting two edges of the cloth at a table corner, Carlo watched Hannibal Caine, carrying the large silver carafe he'd seen last night, strut into the church, followed by two guards supporting Cassie Halloway between them. Apparently unconscious, she was dressed only in a small white toga, and it was everything he could do not to jump out as the guards stood on stepladders and tied her to the left-hand cross. He didn't know how he could have stood it if they had driven spikes through her hands. Thank God they hadn't.

While they worked, Caine set the silver carafe on the table, then picked up the bottles of wine and poured them into the empty pitchers. From the sound of things, by the time the guards finished tying Cassie, Hannibal Caine had laid out a table to make Miss Manners proud. The Elder dismissed the guards, then disappeared upstairs for a few minutes, no doubt checking on Sinclair.

As he returned to the rostrum, the side door opened again. "Elder Caine?" said Justin Martin in his treacly voice. "You wanted to see me?"

"Yes, Justin," Caine said as Justin came into view. The boy, like Caine, wasn't wearing a robe. "I have some disturbing news, and I think you're just the person to help handle the situation."

"What?" Justin asked suspiciously.

"I'm afraid Alex Manderley has escaped."

Silence, then Justin exploded. "Escaped? How could you let her escape? After all the trouble I went to! You promised I'd get her. You promised!" That last, the voice of a petulant child.

*You bastard!* In his hiding place, Carlo clenched his hands so hard that his nails drew blood. *You filthy bastard! I'll see you in your grave!*

"Listen to me!" Caine ordered as Justin continued to rant. "Be quiet and listen!"

"What are you going to do about it?" Justin growled after a pause.

"She's in the compound, Justin. There's no way she can escape, and chances are, we'll find her soon. She can't hide forever. You'll still have her, don't worry about that." Caine paused. "Meanwhile, would you like to punish the person responsible for the escape?"

"You better believe it. I'll skin him alive."

Carlo wondered if Hannibal Caine had any idea that Justin meant that literally.

"I have something else in mind. If we don't find Miss Manderley in time for the services, we'll need a substitute. I want you to go to Elder Blandings's apartment and tell him I need to speak with him here, immediately. When you get him in here, shut the door and knock him out."

"How?"

"I've brought some chloroform and a rag. Whatever you do, don't mark him or kill him. Remember, Justin, he needs to suffer for his sins." Caine checked his watch. "It's six o'clock now. I'll return at six-thirty, and I expect to find him unconscious. Then you and I will prepare him and put him on the cross."

"Nail him," Justin said firmly.

"That would detract from the main show, don't you think?"

Justin considered, then spoke in a sly tone. "I watched you last night, Elder Caine. You don't like blood, do you? It bothers you. That's why you don't want to spike him." He nodded toward Cassie. "Or her."

"It's not your place to question, Justin. Will you do it?"

"On one condition."

"And that is?"

"Whether you find Alex or not, I want her, too." He pointed at Cassie's limp body.

"For?"

"For whatever I want. Aren't you going to kill her after the service anyway?"

"No, of course not."

"You lie. Give her to me and I'll do Blandings."

"I suppose that's reasonable."

The two moved onto the rostrum, still talking, then Justin left. A moment later, Caine followed. As soon as the door shut, Carlo climbed out from under the table and approached Cassie.

"Cassie?" he asked, his voice echoing through the vast room. "Cassie, it's Carlo!"

Her chest rose and fell softly, but she didn't respond. He tried for another minute, then, wary of the time, returned to his hiding place. He hoped that what Sinclair had told him last night was true: that when the time came, he would know what to do. Right now he didn't have a clue.

## ONE HUNDRED THIRTY-SEVEN
# MOSS BASKERVILLE

The morning had dawned red in the east, with blue sky above and black clouds hanging low over the mountains far to the south. At first light, Moss Baskerville had toured New Madelyn, cringing at the sight of houses with their roofs fallen in and homes tipped and twisted on their foundations. The volunteer fire department had put out three small fires during the night, and that damage, at least, was minimal.

The park hadn't been so lucky. Main Street had burned to the ground, and most of the remaining buildings would have to be bulldozed, even though they were untouched by flames. The rides were a shambles; Ferris wheel seats were tossed everywhere, and the wheel itself had fallen on its side. The octopus ride's arms had cracked and broken like twigs, and carousel horses faced one another or hung sideways on their poles. The Haunted Mine Ride had fallen in on itself, and that was one attraction that couldn't possibly be rebuilt.

So far, six fatalities had been discovered in the Madelyns, New and Old, and thirty-six more people were still missing.

After Alex Manderley had shown up at Tom's sometime after

midnight, Moss had driven up to the compound, but it was heavily guarded, just as it was at dawn, when he returned. Knowing Cassie was alive was a great relief; knowing she was there terrified Moss. Between those times, they had discussed going in through the tunnel, but Alex discouraged it, citing the maze of buildings and the presence of armed Apostles, and the difficulty of getting out again safely. Hopefully Carlo would appear with good news soon. Unfortunately, he had to agree with her. They would only enter through the tunnel if Tom's plan didn't work.

Alex seemed to think it would. When Tom told Alex his plan, she declared him brilliant, talking about the power of belief and the element of surprise, just as Father Mike had. She volunteered to ride —insisted on it—and Tom finally agreed.

Moss kept busy the rest of the night, cruising the mangled streets, watching for looters, stopping at Ray's for coffee and at Tom's for hope. Cassie was on his mind constantly, and rest was out of the question.

It was now ten in the morning, and Moss was following Tom's truck across Ghost Town Road to the far side of Spirit Canyon. Tom was hauling his four-stall horse trailer, and from the moment they met up this morning, he had a determined look that Moss had never before seen on that easygoing man. Perhaps he meant it last night when he said it was time for a change. Moss figured his near loss of Marie had a lot to do with that.

Tom pulled to a halt near the end of the buckled asphalt in an area camouflaged by a small grove of Joshua trees. Moss parked just ahead of the trailer, parallel to the truck bed, where Mad Dog, Alex, and Davy were riding, along with those damned costumes. He turned off the ignition and got out.

"You're sure you all want to do this?" he asked as Tom and Marie got out of the truck.

"We're doing it, Chief," Marie told him. "And if we don't get in, we'll go straight up the mesa to the tunnel."

"Too bad we can't call in the FBI." As soon as the words were out of his mouth, Moss regretted them. "Forget I said that," he muttered.

Mad Dog tried to talk Alex into letting him go in her place, but she wasn't having any of it, arguing that if necessary, she had the best chance of finding the tunnel from Sinclair's room again.

Giving up, Mad Dog went to unload the horses while the others began putting on their costumes. Moss, feeling unnecessary, stood back and watched the show. "You're about the most ridiculous-looking bunch of critters I've ever seen," he said in a kindly tone. In truth, the costumes were terrific. "You people have to forgive me. This isn't normal police procedure," he added as Marie pulled a box of makeup from the cab and handed it to Alex. She and Davy carried it to the far side of the truck and went to work.

"I guess I'm lucky I don't have to put that stuff on my face," Tom said, looking at his mask. He wore a black cowled robe with wide sleeves. He'd blushed and refused the black leotard Marie tried to get him to wear beneath it, opting instead for black boots, Levi's, and shirt. He'd told her that if he had those tights on and lost the robe, he'd have to shoot himself because he'd be too humiliated to live. They'd fitted the skull mask with the portable microphone and polished up the long-handled scythe he would carry. In addition to that, he had his revolver and his ever-present lariat. Like the other riders, he also had smoke bombs, grenades, and some fireworks Moss had scared up in the police station's vault. All had little bags of dry ice attached to their shoes. They would tear the plastic off the bags before they got to the compound, and hopefully the ice would add a nice ethereal touch as it vaporized into white smoke. These things, along with the automatic weapons Marie had taken from the compound, were hooked to the saddles and would be hidden by their flowing robes.

Moss had found a set of balances in town, and Marie set them on the hood of the trunk. She, too, wore a black cowled robe, with a gray leotard beneath and thin gray gloves on her hands. Instead of makeup or a mask, she had opted for a gray nylon stocking. Now she pulled her hair back and rolled the stocking down over her head. It was a creepy faceless look, and she disappeared behind the truck with Alex and Davy, then reappeared a moment later with dark gray shadows brushed on at mouth, cheekbones, and eyes, making her Famine a horrifying creature.

"Well, what do you think?" Alex stepped out from behind the truck, Davy trailing self-consciously behind her. Alex, who would ride as War, wore a black robe trimmed in red. Her gloves were black, and gold piping crisscrossed her breast. She had stuffed her hair up under the coppery knight's helmet and made up her face with a bronze-red base, using highlighter the color of dried blood to accentuate her high cheekbones and eyes. She was by far the most frightening- looking one. The sword hanging from her hip wasn't the stage prop Tom had brought in last night, but one Moss had borrowed from Ray Vine, who liked to collect such things. This double-sided antique was his pride and joy, and he had insisted she use it. He claimed it had been lucky to all who wielded it, and Moss hoped it would be for Alex as well.

"So let's get a look at you, Davy." Tom pulled on a pair of black gloves, then crossed his arms. "We're waiting."

Alex took his arm and tugged him forward. "He's gorgeous. Come on, show yourself."

He stepped out, and Moss was stunned. He was the horseman Pestilence, but he looked like a king in his white, gold-trimmed robes and his silver crown. He, like Alex, had traded his stage bow and arrow for the real thing, in his case a crossbow found in the back of one of Tom's closets last night. He wore a light coating of some sort of makeup that made his skin glow with pale luminescence, and Alex had sprayed his eyebrows and hair a silvery white. His dark eyes glowered beneath the makeup. "I feel ridiculous."

"You're not getting any sympathy from me." Marie laughed and patted his shoulder. "I never knew you had the face of a monarch," she added, then turned and looked at Tom, who had donned the heavy skull mask and pulled up his cowl. "And you're just an old hunk of a skeleton."

Tom bowed slightly. "You're not bad for a starving stocking-head."

"Okay, okay, you people have to take this seriously." Crossing his arms, Moss stared at the group, knowing their jokes were born of nervousness. He'd seen cops act the same way. The best remedy for their incipient hysteria was gruffness. "This isn't Halloween, so quit clowning around. You're all carrying more weaponry than my men even dream of."

"Moss," Tom drawled, "don't get your bowels in an uproar. We know what we're doing." The note of hilarity was gone from his voice. "It's just looking at each other that makes us want to laugh."

"That's what worries me," Moss said. "What if those Apostles laugh at you right before they kill you?"

"No," Alex said, all seriousness now. "It won't happen. The Apostles are expecting this. They've had it pounded into them. And there's the eclipse. That guarantees success."

"Why so?"

"Instinct, pure and simple. We're still prey to that same emotion that our cave-dwelling ancestors were when they saw the sun swallowed up in the daytime. For most people, it's mild—an eclipse is exciting because it's a safe thrill, like a roller coaster. For the Apostles, who have, for all intents and purposes, been brainwashed, it will be far more frightening."

"I hope you're right," Moss said.

"Me too." Alex's smile looked fierce because of the makeup.

"Okay. Al and I will be parked at Marie's as you enter the compound," Moss said. "We'll try to get through the gates after you're inside."

Tom nodded. "We'll see you later, Chief."

"Good luck!"

The four mounted their horses, and Moss had to admit they were an eerie sight as they moved up the canyon road. "I hope to hell this works," he called to Mad Dog, then turned around and started back down the road. Behind him, Mad Dog turned the truck and trailer and followed slowly.

"Lord, if you're listening," Baskerville said aloud, "please give us a break."

# HANNIBAL CAINE

The church was lit with candlelight and Hannibal Caine stood on the rostrum, enjoying the eyes upon him. Behind him, the tattooed whore and Eldo Blandings, clad only in a loincloth, hung from the crosses on each side of the church.

"Ladies and gentlemen," he began. "A miracle happened here last night, and that is why I am here, speaking for our beloved Prophet."

He signaled the choir to sing, and as they did, he looked out over his flock. Though only half were in attendance, they were a sight to behold in their white robes, their eyes bright with wonder as they stared up at him and the two sinners on the crosses. They were at a fever pitch this morning, far beyond questioning anything that happened now. As far as they were concerned, this was the end of the world, and everything that happened now, miraculous. Jim-Bob Sinclair had done his job well. The Senior Apostles and the committee members, along with those who had unknowingly helped him accomplish his task, were seated in the front two rows, and even they were filled with wonder. Hannibal detected no questioning looks among them, except for Justin Martin, who smirked at him from his seat on the central aisle. At least he was now wearing a robe, just as Caine was.

Justin didn't worry him, because the youth was interested only in whatever it was he wanted to do to the whore—Caine didn't want to know what—after the service.

The choir finished their song and the silence was perfect. Caine adjusted the pulpit's microphone. "The Savior has come," he thundered. "He has come *before* the Horsemen, and do you know why? Because He wants to give us a second chance. Last night the Lord came to our Prophet and told him that if one man would be willing to let the Spirit come inside him, and would give his life as His son incarnate, then the world might be given a reprieve."

A hushed murmur filled the church. The doors at the rear were wide open and the day had dimmed slightly. The eclipse was beginning.

"And do you know what our humble Prophet did? He offered his own body to God to save us all. You all saw Prophet Sinclair last evening as he spoke to you from this very pulpit. But do you realize that you witnessed him in his transformation, in his magnificence? Can you doubt you were in the presence of holiness?"

Again the murmur, softer now, filled with awe. They were buying the goods. They were nothing but children in white robes, all the same except that some wore bits of gold on their sleeves to signify rank.

"Last night our Prophet, filled with the spirit of Christ, disappeared into the desert. And now he is back, *miraculously* back."

He raised his arms and the main cross began its descent from the tower.

Sinclair as Christ was truly an inspiring vision, one leg bent over the other, just so, head tilted down, the crown of thorns placed exactly as it was in the most famous Crucifixion paintings. The silence was perfect; the entire congregation held its breath.

Suddenly Eldo Blandings, on the right-hand cross, cried, "You killed him! You killed the Prophet!"

Startled, Caine glanced at him, saw the bleary eyes glaring at him. He had personally reapplied chloroform only moments before the service began. This shouldn't have happened, but then Eldo had always been full of surprises. Mind racing, Caine decided to denounce Blandings as a murderer, but before he could turn back to the flock, a real miracle happened. Sinclair, who should have been deep in a coma, raised his head and spoke.

"I am the Lamb of God," he whispered in a voice that echoed throughout the church. "As it is written, so shall it be." He gazed at the congregation. "God bless and forgive you all." His head drooped and he fell silent.

"You are witnessing a miracle, my friends," Caine thundered. "A true miracle. Remember this day. The Prophet has asked me to watch over his flock as we begin the world anew. We must not waste this precious gift the Prophet and God have given us." He turned toward Sinclair. "God's Son has entered this man's body to show his unquestioning love. He has given His life so that we may live."

The sky darkened as the service continued, interspersed with hymns and prayers. Finally, when the sky was deep twilight, Caine began the Communion service. He came off the rostrum and stood behind the Communion table overseeing as ushers took bowls of wafers to pass along each row. After that, they returned to the table and poured wine from the pitchers into paper cups, then placed them on trays and began distributing them, beginning two rows back, as Caine had instructed. Just before the last usher took his tray, Caine took one of the untainted cups for himself, then began pouring cups from the silver urn for the first two rows, knowing no one would question that the ranking members should be given special treatment. *Very special.* Smiling to himself, he placed the cups on a silver tray and carried it to the first row, handing it over with a flourish.

After pausing to retrieve his own cup and wafer, he returned to the rostrum and raised his cup. There was darkness outside, and stars.

And then there were shouts from the guards outside, and the sound of the gates being rolled open.

"The Horsemen are coming! The Horsemen!"

"Quickly!" Caine yelled. "Finish Communion or you will not be saved." With that, he popped the wafer and tossed back the wine, so that the flock would follow his example. But few did. In the front rows, he saw half a dozen drink, but the rest turned instead to peer at the doors at the back of the church. Then, as one, the entire congregation rose, hearing the sound of hoofbeats thundering out of the darkness.

Caine stayed at the pulpit. Behind him, the whore moaned, and then Sinclair's voice could be heard over the clattering of hooves.

"I forgive you, my Judas," he said softly. Then he cried out for all to hear, "The Horsemen come, just as I told you."

ONE HUNDRED THIRTY-NINE

# TOM ABERNATHY

They rode through the darkness and Tom felt a strange deep fear as the sunlight disappeared and unreality set in. Ahead, the compound loomed and he heard the shouts as he led the other riders down Thunder Road. The gates rolled open and some of the white-robed figures ran toward the church, shouting that the Horsemen had arrived. Others remained at the gates, and Tom heard them shut behind them. That took care of the backup. Maybe.

He rode Belle right into the church, and found it filled with a sea of white- gowned Apostles, standing and staring with wide eyes. Many fell to their knees as he started down the center aisle, the dry ice attached to his boots wafting foggy mist around Belle's flanks. Behind him, Alex remained in the doorway while Marie and Rex moved to the left aisle and Davy rode Lil to the right, keeping pace with him and Belle. Dry ice smoked around them.

The church was lit dimly, but the rostrum was clearly visible, lit from behind and above with golden light. Hannibal Caine stood unmoving at the pulpit, a paper cup in his hand. Behind him were not two but three crosses, all bearing bodies, the central one a lifelike effigy of Jesus. Cassie was tied up on Marie's side, and an old man—

Eldo Blandings, he realized—on Davy's. Tom glanced around, hoping to see Carlo, but there was no sign of him.

There was utter silence as they approached the rostrum. Tom rode to the first row and signaled Belle to halt. As she did, he turned on the microphone and spoke in the New England tones of his boyhood. "We are here to receive our sacrifices."

He nodded at Davy and Marie and they rode forward, right up onto the rostrum, each to one of the outer crosses, to cut down the prisoners.

Suddenly Belle shied as the Apostle standing next to him on the left moved. Tom turned his head and found himself staring into the barrel of an AK-47, the weapon half-hidden in the billowy robe sleeve. His gaze moved upward, into the cold blue eyes of Justin Martin. The boy smiled, edging around Belle to stand before the Communion table. His eyes darted back and forth and he opened his mouth to speak, but suddenly a pair of hands appeared from beneath the tablecloth. Tom barely stopped a gasp as he recognized the onyx ring on one of the long, tapered fingers. *Carlo!*

The hands closed on Justin's ankles and yanked. As the youth went down, Tom signaled Belle to rear and whinny, covering the action, he hoped, as Justin disappeared under the table. As Belle came down, he heard the distinct sound of a fist connecting with its target. There was a barely discernible grunt, then silence.

Praying for it to continue, he looked left and right, relieved to see that the incident seemed to have gone unnoticed. Half a dozen Apostles on either side of him were lying unconscious, or choking, clutching at their throats. One convulsed. All eyes were on him or the poisoned Apostles.

Tom urged Belle around the table and up to the rostrum steps. He stared at Caine. "You are not the Prophet," he intoned, thinking he probably sounded more like Darth Vader than the Pale Rider. Dry-ice smoke curled around him, tickling his nose. He gave Belle the signal to rear back on her hind legs and whinny again.

"These sacrifices are not for you," Hannibal Caine said as Marie and Davy cut the ropes. "They are for God."

"We are His messengers, fool!" Tom was surprised by the fury in his voice. He raised his scythe. "Who are you that you dare speak to a Horseman?"

Suddenly the effigy of Jesus on the cross lifted its head and spoke in a voice that carried through the entire church. "He is Hannibal Caine. He is Judas Iscariot."

Immediately Tom rode onto the rostrum, up to the Christ figure. To his left and right, Davy and Marie were easing Cassie and Blandings across their saddles.

"You are Sinclair?" he asked, horrified to see that spikes were driven through the man's hands and feet.

"Yes. And the Son, as Hannibal said."

Tom switched off the mike. "Did Caine do this to you?"

"He is my Judas."

"Tell your congregation, Sinclair. They'll save you."

The smile was beatific. "Hannibal was chosen, just as I was. I am one with the Lamb, as he is with Judas."

"I'll get you out of here," Tom said softly, "very soon."

Again the soft smile. The man seemed to glow with a light of his own, and Tom understood why he so confounded Moss Baskerville. "I am already saved, you see. I fulfill the prophecy, as does Hannibal. As do you."

For a second, Tom was sure that this man, in his delirium, knew his identity. But that was impossible. They'd never even met, and his own mother wouldn't know him in this costume. He noticed that Marie and Davy were no longer on the rostrum, then heard the horses' hooves as they made their way back up the aisle, following the plan to the letter, whereas Tom had been ad-libbing ever since Justin disappeared under the table. He figured he'd better stop before he got them all killed.

"Apostles!" Sinclair's voice boomed in Tom's ears. "Hear me now and remember. The Horsemen have taken their due, and I have taken your sins upon myself. The world will not end this day. Go, Horseman, and tell my Father I am on my way!"

Suddenly the cross Sinclair was nailed to began to rise.

"What the hell?" Caine cried, forgetting his microphone. "Get that thing back down here now!"

"I can't. It's moving by itself!" yelled a bespectacled young Apostle standing at a console below the choir loft. "I didn't touch anything! It just started moving!"

The cross disappeared into a light-lined opening in the ceiling. Sinclair had given him his chance to get out, and now Tom turned Belle to face the congregation and saw that the other riders were waiting at the rear entrance. He pulled a smoke bomb from his saddle and threw it hard toward the rostrum. It exploded in a miasma of colors, but Tom didn't wait around to watch. He spurred Belle and she took off down the center aisle at lightning speed.

He joined the others and they rode toward the compound gates. Tom pulled his revolver and pointed it at a surprised guard. "Open it!"

Behind him, an engine revved and an old black Mustang streaked out of the lot. Almost instantly, another engine roared and a white Cadillac pulled up. The window hummed down and Carlo Pelegrine peered out at Tom. "Alex?" he asked.

"On Tess."

Carlo glanced back at her, then looked at Tom. "If I don't come back, tell her I love her." The window started to roll up.

"Hold it," Tom hissed. "What the hell are you doing?"

"Duel," he said. "Justin chose the weapons." He patted the steering wheel, then the window went up and he drove out of the lot and a hundred yards down the road, where he idled as the Mustang's taillights dwindled toward Spirit Canyon.

ONE HUNDRED FORTY

# CARLO PELEGRINE

Under the communion table, Carlo had punched Justin in the jaw, then kicked away his gun. Then he was on top of him, twisting his arm behind him with one hand and holding his knife to the boy's throat with the other.

And while Tom played Horseman, he and Justin struck a deal in tight urgent whispers. A fight to the death, just the two of them, Carlo told him, a fight to see who was the better man. As Carlo expected, it was the kind of power trip the youth could not resist.

"You challenged me," he whispered. "I pick the weapons."

Carlo was surprised when he chose cars, not knives. "A game of chicken?" he asked.

"It's no game," Justin replied. "On Thunder Road. You start here, I start at Spirit Canyon. I'll flash my lights twice and then we drive." The tone of his voice told him that he had no intention of ditching the duel. Neither did Carlo.

When the smoke bomb went off and chaos broke out, Carlo shoved the youth out from under the table and they ran out of the side door of the church and into the parking lot. Justin had jumped in his Mustang and was out the newly opened gate just as Carlo had lucked out and found the keys in the white Cadillac.

Now in darkness, he sat awaiting his death, heart pounding, as two police cruisers pulled out from behind the ruins of Marie's place and drove slowly up. The first stopped beside him, and he rolled down the window. "Hello, Moss."

"Is Cassie okay?"

Carlo nodded. "But you'd better get in there. Things are dicey."

Moss nodded. "Don't worry, I'm not going to ask what you're doing."

"Thanks."

As the second cruiser passed him, Justin's headlights flashed once, twice. Leaving the window down, Carlo swallowed and gripped the steering wheel, then punched the accelerator. The Cadillac roared with power and he let off the brake, the wheels digging into the earth, spitting gravel.

He drove, watching Justin's headlights approaching, knowing that, no matter what, he was not going to swerve. Sinclair had said this was to be a battle between Good and Evil, and Carlo believed that, and knew that if Good was to die, it would take Evil with him.

He roared past Marie's place, watching the oncoming headlights grow larger and larger.

Suddenly the lights flicked out. Carlo's foot eased off the gas pedal briefly, then grimly, he increased his speed. An instant passed and he caught the sight of the approaching car in his own headlights. At that moment Justin began flashing his brights at him, off and on, off and on. Carlo squinted and grimly accelerated, holding the wheels straight, the car locked on its target.

*Five,* he counted as the Mustang neared. *Four.* Justin flashed his lights once more, then left the brights on, headed dead at him. *Three.* He could see the youth's grin through the windshield. *Two.* Caught in a time warp, he watched Justin's grin fade, his eyes widen, saw him start to turn his wheel in syrupy slow motion.

*One!* The world exploded in grinding metal and shattered glass and something flew out at him, suffocating him as the Caddy spun out of control, off the road, bouncing backward and down, finally coming to a halt half in a drainage ditch.

The air bag deflated and Carlo sat, dazed, for a long moment, then carefully moved each arm and leg, found that the only real pain he felt was still from the wound in his side.

The car door wouldn't open and he could see that trying the passenger side would be useless: The entire right side was crushed. Shakily he pushed himself out the open window, down onto the ground. After a brief rest, he rose and climbed out of the drainage ditch, his legs weightless and rubbery, barely obeying him.

Justin's car was a smoking heap of mangled metal resting on its roof, twenty feet farther onto the desert floor. Carlo walked to it unsteadily, smelled the gasoline in the air. He squatted down by the window and came face-to-face with Justin Martin. The boy was alive, staring at him as rivulets of blood streamed into his eyes from the cuts on his face. A chunk of glass was stuck in his cheek, and Carlo reached over and pulled it out.

Somehow the boy's hand came up and grabbed his wrist as a twisted scarlet grin creased his face. "Good driving," he said. "Get me out of here."

*If you were a devout Catholic, I would tell you he is a demon, the son of Lucifer.* Carlo stared into the cruel, soulless eyes and recognized the evil that Sinclair had spoken of.

"Get me out of here!" the boy rasped angrily.

Carlo twisted out of his grip and stood back, his eyes on the gasoline dripping from a broken fuel line. *You will know what you have to do when the time comes.* Sinclair was right: He did know.

Grimly he pulled the robe off himself, then dug in his jacket pocket and brought out a pack of matches.

Justin's eyes widened. "What do you think you're doing, you fucking asshole?" he squawked.

*He has already caused great pain, and he will continue to do so until he is stopped.* Barely aware of the hot tears coursing down his cheeks, Carlo threw the white robe on the ground near the fuel leak, sopping up gas, then stretched the sodden cloth out as far as it would go. All the while Justin cursed and demanded his help.

Carlo stood back and opened the matchbook, tore one free. "Get me the fuck out of here, you motherfucker! Now!"

Carlo struck the match. "Good-bye, Justin," he whispered, and put it to the cloth.

He turned and ran, throwing himself in the ditch just before the explosion. He waited, then looked up, saw the fire, the billowing smoke. For an instant he saw Justin's burning arm reaching out the window, then it was consumed by flames.

Carlo climbed out of the ditch, onto Thunder Road, knowing that he had done the right thing. He looked up at the compound a mile away and began to run.

# ONE HUNDRED FORTY-ONE
## TOM ABERNATHY

As the police cars slowly drove past Carlo, Tom heard a loud *pop* and a bullet ripped into his arm. Shocked, he nearly toppled from Belle, but quickly regained his balance and turned to see Hannibal Caine running at him, waving a pistol. Instantly Tom took aim and shot the gun from the man's hand.

Caine yelped, shaking his hand, then clamped it protectively under his other arm. Behind him, Apostles were streaming from the church. Caine turned to face them. "He is not Death," he yelled at the top of his lungs. "Does Death bleed?"

Beside him, Davy had pushed Eldo Blandings off his saddle and had drawn his gun. Alex, also flanking him, had done the same. Glancing back, he saw that Marie had her weapon trained on the guard at the gate, who was reluctantly opening up again to let Moss and Al inside.

Tom turned back to Caine, readying his lariat, then paused, looking up at the steeple. The cross bearing James Sinclair pushed slowly upward until it was in its customary position on top of the steeple. The brilliant white lights flashed on. The shell-shocked Apostles all turned to look at it.

Tom pulled the mask off and dropped it on the ground, then pushed the hood back. "The way I see it, mister, you're a cold-blooded murderer," he told Caine. Around them, robed figures were gathering, listening, dazed looks on their faces as they divided their attention between him and the figure on the cross. Behind him, he heard the gates open and Moss's voice saying, "Cassie, oh God, Cassie," and Cassie saying, "Moss," real soft. Things were going on back there, the wounded being loaded into the cruiser, but that was none of Tom's concern. This man was his only business at the moment. Marie, stocking mask discarded, hair blowing in the wind, was beside him on Rex, staring down at Hannibal Caine as well. Somewhere, something exploded, but Tom paid no attention.

"Caine, you got on my bad side when you killed this lady's sheep and dog. You made it worse by killing one of my mustangs. You defaced Mike Corey's church and the homes of my friends. And then you kidnapped people, and after that, you shot them down in cold blood."

"I didn't do any of those things," Caine said. "My hands are clean. Eldo Blandings was behind those acts of violence. I tried to stop him."

"My ass." Tom glanced at Marie. "I'm getting real sick of people who don't take responsibility for what they do. What about you?"

"Damned sick, Tom. You got a hole in your arm that he put there, and that makes me want to tie his tongue to his tonsils and use him to ream out my septic tank."

"Better'n he deserves. I was thinking more along the lines of a little public humiliation."

"Works for me," Marie told him, eyeing the bald Apostle.

Tom turned to Caine and raised his lariat. "Now, I'm a sporting man," he said, "so I'm gonna give you a head start." Caine didn't move, so Tom nudged Belle and she lunged toward the man. Caine turned and ran. Tom waited a moment, then took off, letting Belle cut Caine out of the herd of Apostles, then going after him and bringing him down midstride. Tom jumped off the horse and started to hog-tie

Caine, but his damned left arm wasn't cooperating. Marie rode up and jumped down. "Want some help?"

"You bet."

She finished the tie, then looped the rope over her saddle horn and let Rex drag the squirming Apostle over to Al Gonzales, who promptly shoved him in the back of his squad car.

Marie pulled off her robe and tossed it on Caine, then walked back to Tom and crooked her finger at him, evidently wanting to say something in private. He bent down, and that's when she kissed him, square on the lips.

"Alex!"

"Carlo!"

Tom and Marie turned to see Alex dismount and run to meet the fortune-teller as he walked through the gates. The two fell into each other's arms, inspiring Tom to go for seconds himself.

Then something happened. The hairs stood up on his arms and neck, even some on his head. "What the hell?"

"I've felt this before," Marie began. "Come on!" She grabbed his hand, and they led their horses back to Alex and Carlo. "You know what's happening?" she asked Alex.

Alex nodded. "It's coming."

"Another quake?" What he felt now wasn't like the feeling he'd had in the truck yesterday.

"No." Alex pointed at the sky. "Look. There it is."

Silence fell over the compound as the huge UFO and its two dancing satellites rose over Olive Mesa. The balls of blue-green light whizzed at impossible angles, racing out over the compound, circling Sinclair on the cross above the steeple. The monstrous object, dark except for a few blue and green lights, moved toward them in a stately manner. As Tom watched, barely able to believe his eyes, he felt tugging on his arm, and glanced down. Marie was tying cloth around the wound.

"You were bleeding all over the place, cowboy," she said gruffly.

Normally he would have answered in kind, but this time he didn't joke. "Thanks," he murmured, and put his arm around her.

Behind Sinclair, a slice of sun appeared, haloing his body. The UFO moved silently closer, and Tom could see that Sinclair was watching it.

Finally it was directly overhead, blotting out the sun, blotting out the stars, erasing Sinclair's silhouette. The thing was at least the size of a football field.

Suddenly a burst of light from the center of the craft nearly blinded him. Tom put his hands to his eyes for an instant, then looked again. The craft had risen, and again the sun could be seen.

And James Sinclair was gone, the cross empty.

"I'll be damned," Tom murmured.

"They did it," Alex said. "The angels, the aliens, whatever you want to call them. They've written a new chapter for the Bible. Or perhaps it will merely be added to our folklore."

"Sinclair claimed he talked to God," Carlo said softly.

"Look at them," Alex said as the ship rose higher. "They shape our lives and we don't even know it. They shape our myths."

"Maybe they are God," Carlo said. "Maybe they are," she agreed.

Standing there, his arm around Marie, Tom felt the hairs on his neck rise again as a chilly wind swept over them. He thought he heard the sound of hoofbeats in it, imagined he saw shadowy horses and riders galloping away down Thunder Road. But it was still too dark to be sure.

# EPILOGUE
## OCTOBER

On the highest ridge above Rattlesnake Canyon, Tom and Marie sat on their horses and looked down at the park. The fort was the only original building still standing, and Cassie's theater, one street of shops, the arena, and stables had already been rebuilt and another row of shops framed.

Already the tourists were returning, filling up the campground and the stunt- show bleachers. Tom thanked his lucky stars he'd carried earthquake insurance on all the property he owned there. Between that and his own good luck with money, he'd been able to subsidize the rebuilding of the entire place. A bigger, better Old Madelyn Park would be complete by this time next year. It would not stay a ghost town for long.

When they'd bulldozed the mine ride, they'd found some of the missing bodies, and there had been the bones in Carlo's old place as well. The murderer, Justin Martin, had been killed in a crash that Moss had never bothered to investigate.

Someday Justin would probably become part of the Madland mythology, just like Olive Carmichael, the ghostly hitchhiker. But not for a long time. The wounds had to heal.

The Apostles' compound was a modern-day ghost. Empty now, under investigation, with Caine and Blandings and several others imprisoned, it still drew pilgrims who stood outside the gates and stared at it wonderingly, wanting to know if the Savior had really died again. That question wasn't pondered much by the residents of Madelyn, but sometimes when Tom took a midnight ride, he stared up at the black velvet sky and wondered who the visitors had been, wondered about Sinclair, maybe because some of Alex Manderley's stories had stuck stubbornly in his head. They'd even begun to insinuate themselves into his own campfire tales.

After the eclipse, Alex and Carlo had stayed at the ranch for a few days, then one night Carlo took him aside and quietly told him he was leaving for good with Alex. Just last week, he finally sent a postcard from Peru, where Alex was working and he was studying: He had become passionately interested in UFOs from a metaphysical rather than analytical point of view. The card had a postscript saying that Eric had received his doctorate and was working at APRA. Tom was happy for Carlo, but amazed: He never thought the fortune-teller would hook up with anyone. But then, he never thought a lot of things would happen.

Six weeks after Madland's destruction, Cassie and Moss had finally married in the courtyard where Father Mike's chapel was now being rebuilt. Eve was the flower girl, and he and Marie served as best man and maid of honor. Inspired, Tom had proposed to her that same night, and a month later, they'd eloped, slipping away to Lake Tahoe, telling no one but Davy.

"What're you thinking about, cowboy?"

He looked at Marie and drawled, "Oh, about that time you about twisted Franklin Hank's wiener off."

She punched him lightly. "Tell me the truth."

"Thinking about how nice the park's gonna be. How nice it is that Carlo finally got himself a girl. How nice it is that I did. Come on down here."

Dismounting, he waited for her to do the same, then took her hand and led her to a shady spot. They sat down on the ground, resting comfortably back against the boulders providing the shade. She leaned against him, took his hand again, and fiddled with the ring on his finger.

"You trying to take that back?" He looked at her from under the brim of his hat.

"Just making sure it's on real tight." Marie slid down so that she was in his arms, her face shaded by his Stetson. He took her hand and rubbed his fingers over the gold band, then dipped his head down to kiss her.

Before he got there, he lost his hat. He snagged it and put it back on his head. "Guess I'll have to try that again," he said, going in for the kiss.

"That's what I like about you, cowboy. You never give up." She reached for him, pushing her fingers into his hair as their lips met. His hat went flying again, but this time he didn't even notice.

# AUTHOR'S NOTE

While **Thunder Road** is pure fiction, inspiration for Madelyn can be found in some real places. Throughout the west, you'll find historic ghost towns, restored gold rush towns and wild west parks open to the public. Three locales made special impressions on me. One, Old Tucson Studios in Arizona, is a movie-set town turned amusement park. Another is Bodie, a once-notorious ghost town that has been kept in near-perfect condition near Mammoth in California. The third, and most important, is Calico Ghost Town, a real silver boom town that is part historical site and part amusement park. Located in the Mojave desert on the highway between Los Angeles and Las Vegas, it's only a few miles from fictional Madelyn and provides visitors with history lessons, tours, stunt shows, and evening ghost tours of the best kind—no special effects, just stories and, sometimes, a glimpse of something inexplicable. The area around Calico is also known as a place where you might see strange lights in the sky on dark, still nights.

**Thunder Road** is not so much about aliens and other anomalies as it is about people's varying views of such things. Much of my inspiration comes from the work of Dr. Jacques Vallee, who has written many books about ufology, folklore, and perceptions. Dr. Vallee sees a strong correlation between modern UFO phenomena and older folkloric stories, pointing out that the shape of our myth changes with the times. Thus, in the age of technology, earthly elementals are often converted into unearthly ones. The books quoted within **Thunder Road,** *Dimensions, Confrontations,* and *Revelations,* along with his many other works, may be found in libraries or online.

# ABOUT THE AUTHOR

Tamara Thorne's first novel was published in 1991, and since then she has written many more, including international bestsellers *Haunted, Bad Things, Moonfall, Eternity* and *The Sorority*. A lifelong lover of ghost stories, she is currently working on several collaborations with Alistair Cross as well as a new solo novel, Old Wives' Tales, that kicks off a series starring Sheriff Zach Tully from *Eternity*. Learn more about her at TamaraThorne.com

In collaboration, Thorne and Cross are finishing several new novels, including the next volume of their popular gothic series, *The Ravencrest Saga: Shadowland,* and their new thriller, *Spite House*. Their first novel, *The Cliffhouse Haunting,* was an immediate bestseller. Their thriller, *Mother,* has been optioned for film.

In addition to writing, Alistair and Tamara currently host *Thorne & Cross: Carnival Macabre,* where listeners can discover all manner of demented delights, unearth terrifying treasures, and explore the dark side of the arts. You can even pick up pointers from experts in writing, editing, and publishing.

From 2014-2020, Alistair and Tamara hosted the radio show, Thorne & Cross: Haunted Nights LIVE!, which has featured such guests as Charlaine Harris of the *Southern Vampire Mysteries* and basis of the HBO series *True Blood,* Jeff Lindsay, the man behind *Dexter,* Jay Bonansinga of *The Walking Dead* series, Laurell K. Hamilton of the *Anita Blake* novels, Peter Atkins, screenwriter of *HELLRAISER* 2, 3, and 4, worldwide bestseller V.C. Andrews, and New York Times best sellers Preston & Child, Christopher Rice, and Christopher Moore.

For book deals, updates, specials, exclusives, and upcoming guests on Thorne & Cross: Carnival Macabre. join our newsletter by visiting TamaraThorne.com

# ALSO BY TAMARA THORNE

## BRIMSTONE

### Family Secrets

The Brimstone Grand Hotel, owned by reclusive former movie star, Delilah Devine, looms high on Hospital Hill, harboring long-buried family secrets that whisper of unimaginable horrors. Horrors that will echo down through generations.

### Twisted History

When Delilah's granddaughter, Holly Tremayne, who has seen ghosts for most of her eleven years, first comes to live in the Brimstone Grand in the summer of 1968, she's delighted by its majestic western beauty - and its chilling history. But as she settles in, making friends and enemies alike, the nightmares begin.

### Terror in the Night

Within the walls of the Brimstone Grand, the past has come back to life, and Holly and Delilah are faced with an ancient familial evil that rages just below the old hotel's serene facade. An evil that won't rest until it possesses Holly - body, mind, and soul.

## HAUNTED

### Murders and Madness

Its violent, sordid past is what draws bestselling author David Masters to the infamous Victorian mansion called Baudey House. Its shrouded history of madness and murder is just the inspiration he needs to write his ultimate masterpiece of horror. But what waits for David and his sixteen-year-old daughter, Amber, at Baudey House, is more terrifying than any legend...

### Seduction

First comes the sultry hint of jasmine...followed by the foul stench of decay. It is the dead, seducing the living, in an age-old ritual of perverted desire and unholy blood lust. For David and Amber, an unspeakable possession has begun...

## CANDLE BAY

Shrouded in fog on a hillside high above an isolated California coastal town, The Candle Bay Hotel and Spa has been restored to its former glory after decades of neglect. Thanks to its new owners, the Darlings, the opulent inn is once again filled with prosperous guests. But its seemingly all-American hosts hide a chilling, age-old family secret.

Lured to the picturesque spot, assistant concierge Amanda Pearce is mesmerized by her surroundings--and her seductive new boss, Stephen Darling. But her employers' eccentric ways and suspicious blood splatters in the hotel fill her with trepidation. Little does Amanda know that not only are the Darlings vampires, but that a murderous vampire vendetta is about to begin--and she will be caught in the middle. For as the feud unfolds and her feelings for Stephen deepen, Amanda must face the greatest decision of her life: to die, or join the forever undead.

## ETERNITY

### Welcome to Eternity

### A little bit of Hell on Earth ...

When Zach Tully leaves Los Angeles to take over as sheriff of Eternity, a tiny mountain town in northern California, he's expecting to find peace and quiet in his own private Mayberry. But he's in for a surprise. Curmudgeonly Mayor Abbott is a ringer for long-missing writer Ambrose Bierce. There are two Elvises in town, a shirtless Jim Morrison, and a woman who has more than a passing resemblance to Amelia Earhart. And that's only the beginning.

Eternity is the sort of charming spot tourists flock to every summer and leave every fall when the heavy snows render it an isolated ghost town.

Tourists and New Agers all talk about the strange energy coming from Eternity's greatest attraction: a mountain called Icehouse, replete with legends of Bigfoot, UFOs, Ascended Masters, and more. But the locals talk about something else.

The seemingly quiet town is plagued by strange deaths, grisly murders, and unspeakable mutilations, all the work of a serial killer the locals insist is Jack the Ripper. And they want Zach Tully to stop him.

Now, as the tourists leave and the first snow starts to fall, terror grips Eternity as an undying evil begins its hunt once again ...

## MOONFALL

Moonfall, the picturesque town nestled in the mountains of southern California, is a quaint hamlet of antique stores, cider mills, and pie shops, and Apple Heaven, run by the dedicated nuns of St. Gertrude's Home for Girls, is the most popular destination of all. As autumn fills the air, the townspeople prepare for the Halloween Haunt, Moonfall's most popular tourist attraction. Even a series of unsolved deaths over the years hasn't dimmed Moonfall's enthusiasm for the holiday.

Now, orphan Sara Hawthorne returns to teach in the hallowed halls of St. Gertrude's where, twelve years before, her best friend died a horrible death. In Sara's old room, distant voices echo in the dark and the tormented cries of children shatter the moon-kissed night.

But that's just the beginning. For Sara Hawthorne is about to uncover St. Gertrude's hellish secret...a secret she may well carry with her to the grave.

## BAD THINGS

The Piper clan emigrated from Scotland and founded the town of Santo Verde, California. The Gothic Victorian estate built there has housed the family for generations, and has also become home to an ancient evil forever linked to the Piper name. . .

As a boy, Rick Piper discovered he had "the sight." It was supposed to be a family myth, but Rick could see the greenjacks--the tiny mischievous demons who taunted him throughout his childhood--and who stole the soul of his twin brother Robin one Halloween night.

Now a widower with two children of his own, Rick has returned home to build a new life. He wants to believe the greenjacks don't exist, that they were a figment of his own childish fears and the vicious torment he suffered at the hands of his brother. But he can still see and hear them, and they haven't forgotten that Rick escaped them so long ago. And this time, they don't just want Rick. This time they want his children ...

## THE FORGOTTEN

### The Past ...

Will Banning survived a childhood so rough, his mind has blocked it out almost entirely--especially the horrific day his brother Michael died, a memory that flickers on the edge of his consciousness as if from a dream.

### Isn't Gone ...

Now, as a successful psychologist, Will helps others dispel the fears the past can conjure. But he has no explanation for the increasingly bizarre paranoia affecting the inhabitants of Caledonia, California, many of whom claim to see terrifying visions and hear ominous voices. . .voices that tell them to do unspeakable things ...

### It's Deadly

As madness and murderous impulses grip the coastal town, Will is compelled to confront his greatest fear and unlock the terrifying secret of his own past in a place where evil isn't just a memory. . .it's alive and waiting to strike ...

## THUNDER ROAD

The California desert town of Madelyn boasts all sorts of attractions for visitors. Join the audience at the El Dorado Ranch for a Wild West show. Take a ride through the haunted mine at Madland Amusement Park. Scan the horizon for UFOs. Find religion with the Prophet's Apostles--and be prepared for the coming apocalypse.

Because the apocalypse has arrived in Madelyn. People are disappearing. Strange shapes and lights dart across the night sky. And a young man embraces a violent destiny--inspired by a serial killer whose reign of terror was buried years ago.

But each of these events is merely setting the stage for the final confrontation. A horror of catastrophic proportions is slouching toward Madelyn in the form of four horsemen--and they're picking up speed.

## THE SORORITY

They are the envy of every young woman--and the fantasy of every young man. An elite sisterhood of Greenbriar University's best and brightest, their members are the most powerful girls on campus--and the most feared ...

### Eve

She's the perfect pledge. A sweet, innocent, golden-haired cheerleader, Eve has so much to gain by joining Gamma Eta Pi--almost anything she desires. But only a select few can enter the sorority's inner circle--or submit to its code of blood, sacrifice, and sexual magic. Is Eve willing to pay the price?

### Merilynn

Ever since childhood, Merilynn has had a sixth sense about things to come. She's blessed with uncanny powers of perception--and cursed with unspeakable visions of unholy terror. Things that corrupt the souls of women, and crush the hearts of men. Things that can drive a girl to murder, suicide, or worse ...

### Samantha

Journalism major Sam Penrose is tough, tenacious--and too curious for her own good. She's determined to unearth the truth about the sorority. But the only way to expose this twisted sisterhood is from within ...

## BOOKS by Tamara Thorne and Alistair Cross

### THE GHOSTS OF RAVENCREST

#### Book 1 in The Ravencrest Saga

#### Darkness Never Dies ...

Ravencrest Manor has always been part of the family. The ancestral home of the Mannings, Ravencrest's walls have been witness to generations of unimaginable scandal, horror, and depravity. Imported stone by stone from England to northern California in the early 1800s, the manor now houses widower Eric Manning, his children, and his staff. Ravencrest stands alone, holding its memories and ghosts close to its dark heart, casting long, black shadows across its grand lawns, through the surrounding forests, and over the picturesque town of Devilswood, below.

#### Dare to Cross the Threshold ...

Ravencrest Manor is the most beautiful thing new governess, Belinda Moorland, has ever seen, but as she learns more about its tangled past of romance and terror, she realizes that beauty has a dark side. Ravencrest is built on secrets, and its inhabitants seem to be keeping plenty of their own - from the handsome English butler, Grant Phister, to the power-mad administrator, Mrs. Heller, to Eric Manning himself, who watches her with dark, fathomless eyes. But Belinda soon realizes that the living who dwell in Ravencrest have nothing on the other inhabitants - the ones who walk the darkened halls by night ... the ones who enter her dreams ... the ones who are watching ... and waiting ...

#### Welcome to Ravencrest ...

Who is the man digging in the garden beyond Belinda's bedroom window? Who - or what - is watching her from the vents? From ghostly screams and the clutching bony fingers of death in the indoor pool, to the trio of gliding nuns in the east wing who come at Belinda with black blazing eyes, to the beckoning little girl in the red dress who died more than two centuries ago, Belinda is thrust into a world of waking nightmares where there is no distinction between the living and the dead, and there are no limits to the horrors that await. Witchcraft is afoot at Ravencrest and as unspeakable terrors begin to unfold, Belinda realizes that her beautiful new home is a keeper of tragedy, a collector of souls. And it wants to add her to its collection ...

## THE WITCHES OF RAVENCREST

### Book 2 in The Ravencrest Saga

### Dark and Unnatural Powers

In a remote part of California just above the coastal town of Devilswood, Ravencrest Manor, imported stone-by-stone from England more than two centuries ago, looms tall and terrifying, gathering its dark and unnatural powers, and drawing those it wants as its own.

### Murder Lurks in the Shadows

Governess Belinda Moorland has settled into life at Ravencrest and, as summer gives way to autumn, romance is in the air. She and multi-millionaire Eric Manning are falling in love ... but powerful forces will stop at nothing to keep them apart. And as the annual Harvest Ball is set to begin, evil abounds at Ravencrest. Murder lurks in the shadows, evil spirits freely roam the halls, a phantom baby cries, signaling a death in the mansion, and in the notoriously haunted east wing, three blood-soaked nuns, Sisters Faith, Hope, and Charity, tend to the demented needs of a maid gone mad.

### Vengeful Spirits

Ravencrest has come to life. In the gardens below, granite statues dance by moonlight, and a scarecrow goes on a killing rampage, collecting a gruesome assortment of body parts from unwilling donors ... But Belinda's greatest danger is the vengeful spirit of Rebecca Dane. Once the mistress of Ravencrest, Rebecca Dane has a centuries-old axe to grind with the powerful witch, Cordelia Heller - and Belinda becomes her weapon of choice.

## EXORCISM

## Book 3 in The Ravencrest Saga

### The Jazz Age

In the 1920s, Henry Manning ruled Ravencrest with an iron fist. He held debauched parties that would have inspired Jay Gatsby himself. From the Manning fortune to a beautiful wife, the silent film star known as the White Violet, Henry had it all ... including a loyal cult that worshipped the demon Forneus.

### Deal with the Devil

Violet lost her life putting a stop to the demented perversions that Henry and his demonic familiar visited upon Ravencrest ... but now that evil has returned.

### The Soulless Child

In the night, an innocent maid is seduced by a demon lover. A child is born, but it is not of this earth. Father Antonio DeVargas is summoned as ghostly parties light up the old poolhouse and phantom screams rip open the night. Meanwhile, the White Violet wanders the halls of Ravencrest warning the inhabitants of death and disaster to come.

And the current master of Ravencrest, Eric Manning, is decidedly not himself.

## MORE BY THORNE & CROSS

## DARLING GIRLS

### Fang Meets Fang ...

The vampires of Candle Bay and Crimson Cove come together for the Biting Man Festival in Eternity, California, to celebrate a centuries-old tradition that quickly turns murderous as they're faced with old enemies, uncontrolled bloodlust, and the unpredictable antics of a self-proclaimed vampire slayer who is hellbent on destroying them all.

# MOTHER

### A Girl's Worst Nightmare is Her Mother ...

Priscilla Martin. She's the diva of Morning Glory Circle and a driving force in the quaint California town of Snapdragon. Overseer of garage sales and neighborhood Christmas decorations, she is widely admired. But few people know the real woman behind the perfectly coiffed hair and Opium perfume.

### Family is Forever. And Ever and Ever ...

No one escapes Prissy's watchful eye. No one that is, except her son, who committed suicide many years ago, and her daughter, Claire, who left home more than a decade past and hasn't spoken to her since. But now, Priscilla's daughter and son-in-law have fallen on hard times. Expecting their first child, the couple is forced to move back ... And Prissy is there to welcome them home with open arms ... and to reclaim her broken family.

### The Past Isn't Always as Bad as You Remember.

### Sometimes it's Worse ...

Claire has terrible memories of her mother, but now it seems Priscilla has mended her ways. When a cache of vile family secrets is uncovered, Claire struggles to determine fact from fiction, and her husband, Jason, begins to wonder who the monster really is. Lives are in danger - and Claire and Jason must face a horrifying truth ... a truth that may destroy them ... and will forever change their definition of "Mother."

## THE CLIFFHOUSE HAUNTING

### When the Blue Lady Walks...

Since 1887, Cliffhouse Lodge has been famous for its luxurious accommodations, fine dining ... and its ghosts. Overlooking Blue Lady Lake, nestled among tall pines, Cliffhouse has just been renovated by its owners, Teddy and Adam Bellamy, and their daughter, Sara.

Cliffhouse has not always been a place of rest and respite, though. Over the years it has served many vices, from rum-running to prostitution - and although the cat houses have been replaced by a miniature golf course and carousel, Cliffhouse retains its dark history; darkest during the Roaring Twenties, when a serial killer called the Bodice Ripper terrorized the town, and a phantom, the Blue Lady, was said to walk when murder was imminent.

### Death Walks With Her...

Now, there's a new killer on the loose, and the Blue Lady sightings have returned. The Bellamys are losing maids, and guests are being tormented by disembodied whispers, wet phantom footprints, and the blood-chilling shrieks of mad laughter that echo through the halls of Cliffhouse in the dead of night.

The little mountain town of Cliffside is the perfect hunting ground for a serial killer... and the Blue Lady. Police Chief Jackson Ballou has bodies piling up, and between the murders and the mysteries, he can hardly pursue his romance with Polly Owen. And Sara Bellamy may lose her true love before they even have their first kiss.